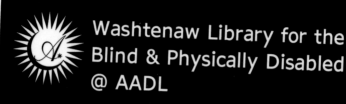

Washtenaw Library for the Blind & Physically Disabled @ AADL

If you are only able to read large print, you may qualify for WLBPD @ AADL services, including receiving audio and large print books by mail at no charge.

For more information:

Email • wlbpd@aadl.org

Phone • (734) 327-4224

Website • wlbpd.aadl.org

A Stillness of Chimes

Center Point
Large Print

**This Large Print Book carries the
Seal of Approval of N.A.V.H.**

A Stillness of Chimes

Meg Moseley

CENTER POINT LARGE PRINT
THORNDIKE, MAINE

This Center Point Large Print edition is published in the year 2014 by arrangement with WaterBrook Press, an imprint of the Crown Publishing Group, a division of Random House LLC, New York.

Scripture quotations and paraphrases are taken from the King James Version.

The characters and events in this book are fictional, and any resemblance to actual persons or events is coincidental.

The text of this Large Print edition is unabridged. In other aspects, this book may vary from the original edition. Printed in the United States of America on permanent paper. Set in 16-point Times New Roman type.

ISBN: 978-1-62899-026-3

Library of Congress Cataloging-in-Publication Data

Moseley, Meg.
A stillness of chimes / Meg Moseley. —
  Center Point large print edition.
pages cm
ISBN 978-1-62899-026-3 (library binding : alk. paper)
1. Fathers and daughters—Fiction. 2. Fathers and sons—Fiction.
  3. Family secrets—Fiction. 4. First loves—Fiction.
  5. Georgia—Fiction. 6. Large type books. I. Title.
PS3613.O77876S85 2014
813'.6—dc23
                                                    2013045139

To our wounded warriors and their loved ones.
You have my unending respect and gratitude.

WoundedWarriorProject.org

*Love is not love which alters
when it alteration finds.*
William Shakespeare, Sonnet 116

❧ One ❧

Eighteen years ago

Laura Gantt didn't believe in ghosts, but sometimes she wondered if living across from a graveyard had warped her. Part Irish, all southern, descended from moonshiners and holy rollers, she'd always believed in things she couldn't see. Her dad said it was just the old whisperings in their blood.

All morning, she'd heard soft, sure warnings. Some kind of trouble was on its way. The whisperings hinted it would come for Sean.

She and her friends, plus one tagalong kid sister, had been picking blackberries for an hour in the brambles that lined the railroad tracks. Trees choked with kudzu vines loomed above them like green monsters.

A few feet away, Cassie Bright and her little sister worked side by side, their blond hair damp with sweat. Sean Halloran was bent over the brambles farther down the tracks. He looked lost in a T-shirt his brother had outgrown.

Sean straightened and squared his skinny shoulders. "No slacking off, Gantt," he hollered. "Lazy bum."

Laura swatted a mosquito on her arm and tried to think of a smart comeback. She gave up and shrugged. Sean went back to work, laughing, but he couldn't fool her. She knew what he lived with.

Sweat trickled down her neck. She was sick of the heat, the scratches, the bug bites. There were snakes too. She tried not to think about the snakes.

Cassie stopped working to examine her fingers, stained purple with juice. "Ugh. I hate blackberries."

"I hate snakes worse," Laura said, thinking of Sean's father. The Halloran boys called him by his first name—Dale—to show their disrespect. Never to his face, though. They wouldn't dare.

Cassie moved closer between long-reaching canes that bristled with wicked little thorns. "Guess what?" she said quietly. "The Cheevers heard the Peeping Tom last night. He was pitching pebbles at their windows."

"Why do you act like it's good news? It's creepy."

"Yeah, but this town could use a little excitement. My dad says it's Slattery."

Laura shivered in spite of the heat. A sloppy, skinny man, Slattery lived in a run-down duplex just down the road. Nobody knew his first name.

"How would your dad know who it is?" she asked.

"He has a friend who's a deputy, remember? He tells us all kinds of stuff."

Laura dropped a handful of ripe berries into her bucket. "Your dad's friend should spend less time talking and more time catching bad guys."

"You're scared. Scared of a silly prowler."

"No, I'm not. My daddy has his guns."

"Bet you won't be so brave when the Peeping Tom's at your window. He—oh!" Cassie shrieked and giggled. "Mr. Gantt, you spooked me. Sneaking up like that."

Laura hadn't noticed her father either, but there he was. A curlicue of wood shavings clung to his shirt, and the humidity made his sandy-blond hair frizz where it escaped from under his baseball cap. He didn't seem to be in one of his moods, but she wasn't sure until he tipped his cap, his eyes twinkling.

"My apologies, Miss Cassie," he said. "I didn't aim to scare anybody. Looks like you've got that department covered, though." He wrapped his arm around Laura's shoulders. "Hey, sweetheart. Are you managing to comport yourself like a lady?"

"Always." Laura leaned into his sun-warmed shirt and that familiar smell of sawdust. "You don't have to keep checking on us. We're not babies."

"Even when you're a grown woman, you'll be my baby girl. No matter what."

Out of nowhere, a heavy sadness settled on her. Whether it was about his troubles or Sean's, it made her feel like a grown woman already. A grown woman who didn't mind being called her father's baby girl.

"And you'll always be my dad," she said. "No matter what."

He smiled and gave her ponytail a gentle tug. Then he nodded toward Cassie's sister. "Tigger's still a baby even if she doesn't think so," he said quietly. "Y'all keeping an eye on her?"

Laura and Cassie glanced at each other and swiveled their eyes back to him. "Yes sir," they said in unison.

He turned toward Sean. "Young Mr. Halloran. It's good to see you, son."

"It's good to see you too, sir." Sean spoke with so much respect that she half expected him to salute his hero. Her father, Elliott Gantt.

"I understand your brother enlisted," her dad said.

"Yes sir." Sean came closer to his idol but not too close. "He's in boot camp."

"You must be proud."

"Yes sir, I am."

"I hope he'll never have to go to war. If he does, though, he'll make you prouder still."

"Yes sir. I know he will."

Laura's dad stole a few berries from her pail. "Y'all behave, now." He studied Tigger, his expression softening. "You too, Tig. Be good for your big sister."

"I will," she chirped.

"You're always a good girl, aren't you?"

Tigger nodded and gave him an angelic smile, drawing a laugh from him and a subdued grumble from Cassie.

"I'll get back to work," he said. "That wood won't make itself into anything useful."

"Bye, Dad," Laura said. "See you at supper."

"Yep. And we'll have cobbler again, I hope. You and your mama make the best blackberry cobbler in Georgia." He swiped a few more berries, their color nearly matching the neat lettering on his muscular arm—"life everlasting." A memento of his army days, it was his only tattoo.

A bright yellow butterfly wove a wobbly path above his head as he waded through the brambles, finally disappearing in the tangle of green. He would come out on First Street, a block from his workshop in downtown Prospect.

"I wish he wouldn't keep checking on us," Laura said. "I mean, come on. We're twelve."

"Yeah, maybe he needs to loosen up a little." As Sean approached, Cassie lowered her voice. "Just be glad he's not like Sean's dad. What a creep."

Sean came closer, his pail bumping against the leg of his too-short jeans. He scowled at Cassie. "I heard that."

She scowled back. "Sorry, but it's true."

"That doesn't mean y'all have to go around yammering about it."

"You have to tell somebody," Laura said.

He squinted at her. "Tell somebody what?"

"Don't play dumb." She lifted his floppy sleeve so Cassie could see the new bruise on his sun-browned shoulder.

He yanked the sleeve down, moving so quickly that berries spilled from his bucket. "Mind your own business."

"You are my business," Laura said. "You're my friend."

He walked off without answering, his head high and his shoulders stiff.

Cassie wrinkled her nose. "What's wrong with him lately?"

"Everything's worse since Keith enlisted." Laura's eyes watered. "Now Sean's got nobody to watch his back."

"His brother must've been sick of looking after him. Like I'm sick of looking after Tigger."

"Don't say that. You're lucky to have a sister."

"Yeah, I'm real lucky. I'm always stuck watching her so she won't wander off. Some-times I wish she would."

"Cassie!"

"You know I don't mean it. I'm just so tired of having her tag along. Tigger the Tagger." Cassie stared into the distance, her eyes rimmed with smudges of the mascara she'd borrowed from her mom's bathroom. "Someday I'll get out of here. Out of Georgia. All the way to Hollywood, maybe." She brightened. "Mom bought some new nail polish. Sunset Boulevard Red. Let's go paint our nails."

"My dad doesn't want me to paint my nails until I'm older."

"You're older than you were yesterday, so you're older. Come on. He won't even notice, and your mom won't care. She's cool. Hey, maybe we can talk my mom into renting a movie." Cassie popped a berry into her mouth and walked away.

Laura studied her purple fingertips. Berry stains were allowed—and so was a tattoo, at least for her dad—but nail polish wasn't. It didn't make sense.

She continued tugging ripe fruits from their stems, aware that Sean was slowly working his way back. At last he stopped beside her.

He reached for a cane loaded with berries that hung like black jewels in the bright green leaves. "Sorry I got mad. I just don't like it when you tell me what to do."

"I can't make you do what I say, but you sure can't keep me from saying what I think."

He gave her a quick glance and went back to picking. "You're all right, Gantt. Sometimes. For a girl."

Cassie popped up from behind a bush. "Sean and Laura, sittin' in a tree," she chanted. "K-I-S-S—"

"Knock it off," Sean said. "We're just friends."

"We're all friends," Laura said. "All three of us." She looked over her shoulder. Tigger was singing softly, paying no attention to the rest of them.

Laura placed her bucket on a patch of relatively clear and level ground. "Put down your berries for a minute."

Sean and Cassie cooperated, but they looked hot and tired and skeptical.

"What's this about?" Sean asked. "Ordering me around again?"

"Yes. Listen up, y'all. Hands together, right now. We have a promise to make."

Three pairs of hands layered themselves together, stained and sticky with juice, marked with dirt and scratches and bug bites. The girls' hands were pale and small compared to Sean's bigger, darker hands. A bruise Laura hadn't noticed before circled his left wrist like a wide purple bracelet.

"Me too," Tigger said, bouncing toward them on her skinny legs. Her glittery pink hair clip was about to fall out of her silky hair.

Cassie pushed her sister away. "This isn't little-girl stuff."

"I'm not little! I'm almost eight."

"Let her stay." Laura drew Tig's hands in with the bigger ones. "We're just going to promise we'll always be there for each other." A glance at Sean made her heart hurt. "We'll look out for each other. Always." That wasn't half of what she wanted to say, but her throat had clogged up.

The others only stared at her.

"Say it," she ordered in a whisper. "Promise."

"I promise," Sean and Cassie said, and Tigger piped up with another "Me too."

Sean glared at each one in turn, his shaggy hair half-veiling his fierce blue eyes and hiding most of the tiny scars on his forehead. "But y'all have to promise you won't do anything stupid either." He looked straight at Laura. "Promise you won't go blabbing things that shouldn't be blabbed."

"I promise," Cassie said. "No blabbing."

"No blabbing," Tigger parroted.

Laura's hands were roasting. She felt as trapped as the times she'd knelt at the altar until her legs ached, but she didn't dare move in the middle of a moment that might have been sacred. This wasn't church, though. It was pure foolishness, probably.

"Laura," Sean said. "Promise."

Maybe this was part of being there for him, part of being his friend: promising to do things his way. Because, after all, she didn't know what kind of trouble she'd stir up for him if she told her folks about his bully of a father.

She let out her breath. When she inhaled, her

lungs seemed to fill with a deep sadness that seeped into every cell of her body.

"I promise. No blabbing."

Sean nodded. His face relaxed a tad.

A honeybee drowsed over his shoulder, breaking the spell. Laura flexed her fingers but couldn't free herself from the sticky, sweltering pile of hands.

Tigger yanked loose, releasing the rest of them too. "Sean, lookit," she said, picking up her pail. "I got tons of berries."

"That's a lot," he said. "Good work, Tig."

She scampered away, her pale hair catching the light. The sun always seemed to find her, even in the shade.

Cassie held her juice-stained hand to her heart. "There. We made a solemn vow, signed in the blood of a thousand berries." Dropping the dramatic pose, she laughed and walked away.

Sean poured his berries into Laura's pail, filling it to the brim. "Give 'em to your mom."

"You don't want any?"

"You think I bake pies and things? Nah. I'm gonna go drown some worms behind the Bennetts' place."

"Now? The fish won't be biting."

"That'll still be better than hanging around with a bunch of girls."

She gave his wiry shoulder a gentle shove. "Get out of here, then."

"Get out of my way and I will."

"Stop by later," she said. "I might be at Cassie's house for a while, though."

"Don't start slapping on the makeup like she does. I like you the way you are."

Laura blinked.

"And don't bat your eyelashes at me," he added.

"I wasn't—"

"Sure, you were." Sean gave her a quick grin and sauntered away.

He would follow the tracks north for a while. Then he would cut to the left on the dirt road that led to the Bennetts' little lake. He never had qualms about fishing on private property. But he hadn't brought a fishing line, and his house was in the other direction. He only wanted a place to hide out while his dad was home.

Sean didn't have a mom to stick up for him. Or to bake cobblers with. He would be all right, though. He was smart and strong and good. He would run away if he had to, and then Dale Halloran wouldn't have anybody left to kick around but the dog.

"Man, it's hot," Cassie said, slapping a mosquito on her neck. "Let's go."

"Yeah, I'm done too. Sean gave me his berries."

"Come on, Tigger," Cassie said. "Time to bounce along home."

Tigger pouted. "I have to fill my bucket first."

"Oh, all right, but come straight home. Stay away from the tracks. You hear?"

"Uh-huh."

"Tanya Jean Bright, say 'Yes ma'am.' " Cassie sounded just like her mother.

"Yes ma'am." Tigger's quick fingers went back to finding berries.

"Take some of mine," Laura told her. "Then your mom will have plenty and you can come home with us."

"No! I want to fill up my own bucket by my own self."

Laura pulled Cassie aside. "We can't leave her by herself. We just told my dad—"

"She'll be fine," Cassie said. "We can look out the bedroom window and see her. Shoot, she'll be home in five minutes. Even if she stays longer, she's smart about trains and stuff. C'mon, let's go paint our nails. My mom has tons of new makeup samples too."

Laura imagined herself drinking something cold and sweet inside the Brights' cool, dark house. Cassie's dad was at work, and her mom never interfered with girls who wanted to primp and giggle. Mrs. Bright was like an aunt to Laura. The fun kind of aunt.

She fell in behind Cassie. By the time they'd made their way up the bank to the shoulder of the road, Tigger had started singing again.

Her tiny voice floated behind them, growing fainter as they walked away.

Laura and Cassie were at the house in two minutes, their berries sitting on the coolness of the kitchen counter. Mrs. Bright was in her bedroom, fussing over a sewing project, but Cassie stuck her head in long enough to tell her they were back. Then she brought her mom's nail polish and makeup samples to the kitchen table where the lighting was good.

"Wash up and gimme your hand," Cassie said.

After a moment's hesitation, Laura obeyed. She wondered if the fruit in the Garden of Eden was the same lovely, warm shade of coral-red. Sunset Boulevard Red.

Half an hour later, her nails felt weighted and conspicuous. Her skin felt coated, her pores choked with something called Sunlight Bisque Foundation. Her eyes stung from their first exposure to mascara and liner. Staring at herself in a hand mirror, she decided she'd better scrub her face before her dad got a look at her. He'd say she was too young for makeup. He'd say she was just a little girl, not much older than Tigger—

Laura lowered the mirror. "Cassie? Tig still isn't back."

"Oops. We'd better go get her." Cassie was halfway to the door already. "I'm in deep doo-doo if my mom finds out."

They stepped outside, careful not to make noise and alert her mother to their exit. Once they'd reached the shoulder of the road, they ran, their sneakers making the gravel fly.

"There she is." Cassie pointed but didn't slow down.

They closed the gap quickly as Tigger trudged toward them. Her face was filthy, and she'd either spilled most of her berries or eaten them.

"What took you so long?" Cassie asked.

Ignoring Cassie, Tigger fixed her tearful blue eyes on Laura. "Your dad scolded me and told me to go home. And he told the creepy man to go—"

"What creepy man?"

With her free hand, Tigger pushed her hair out of her eyes, leaving a purple smear on her sweaty forehead. "The weirdo."

Cassie gave her a skeptical look. "Slattery? Yeah, right. Don't tell fibs."

"I don't. Laura's daddy yelled at him and"— Tig's fingers explored higher on her head, moving faster and faster. "Where's my new hair clip? It fell out!"

"Don't start bawling. I'll buy you another one." Cassie started finger-combing Tig's hair. "You're lucky we promised we won't blab. We won't tattle on you for staying by yourself at the berry patch. Right, Laura?"

Laura nodded, awed by Cassie's slick shifting of the blame.

"As long as you don't tell Mom, you're not in trouble," Cassie said, wiping Tigger's wet cheeks. "Hey, you want to try nail polish?"

Tigger's eyes widened. "Yeah!"

Her cheerfulness restored, she scurried toward the house. Laura and Cassie followed at a slower pace.

"Close call," Cassie said in a low voice.

"We're still in trouble. My dad will tell your dad."

"Uh-oh, you're right." Cassie made a face. "Well, if my folks decide I'm a bad baby-sitter, maybe they'll stop making me baby-sit."

The three girls trooped up the steps to the back door and into the kitchen. Tigger climbed into a chair and spread out her grubby hands for her first-ever fingernail polish.

Grateful that Tig had come safely home, Laura leaned against the counter and stared out the window at the bright blue sky. A train whistle moaned in the hills. Sean must have heard it too, up at the Bennetts' little lake where he hid out whenever he was afraid to go home.

Shivery sadness filled her again, as lonesome as the whistle of the far-off train.

Two

Eighteen years later

The preacher was stretching out the altar call as long and thin as he could manage. If, as he'd ordered, every eye was closed and every head was bowed, Laura could sneak out from her back-row seat before she got trapped in small talk with the old ladies in the pew ahead of hers. Their stale perfumes smelled as dusty as the hymnals.

She sneaked a peek at the red book in the wooden rack in front of her knees. A month ago, mid-April, she'd stood in the front row with a hymnal shaking in her hands as she tried to ignore the flower-covered casket a few feet away. Two days later she'd flown back to Denver, unable to come to grips with her loss. Instead, she'd worried about the cat shut up alone in the empty house. For a month, poor old Mikey had no company but Ardelle Bright, who'd offered to stop by every day to feed him. It wasn't ideal, but he'd survived.

The elderly women were busy murmuring to God and wouldn't even notice if she left. Laura dug behind her for her raincoat and pulled it on, then rose from the hard wooden pew and ducked into the aisle. Pausing beside the rain-sprinkled window, she faced the graveyard. The finality of it hit her harder now than it had when Gary Bright had called with the bad news, his voice hushed and strange. Instantly, she'd known someone had died—but her mother? Impossible.

Laura's eyes heated with tears. She turned away from the window and tiptoed toward the swinging door that opened on the tiny foyer. She pushed the door slowly so it wouldn't creak.

And there stood Sean Halloran, looking cramped among the coat racks and the lost-and-found box and a jumble of umbrellas along the wall. His straight, shaggy hair looked wind-blown even in the motionless air. Although he was only hiding in the back, he'd dignified his faded jeans with a white dress shirt and a necktie. His mouth still had the sarcastic little tilt that she'd loved since third grade or so.

She hadn't seen him since the graveyard service. Even then, at her own mother's funeral, he'd made those old longings flutter inside her like angels' wings. He was a charmer, after all, and the first boy she'd ever kissed.

She shut the door as quietly as she'd opened it. "What a nice surprise," she said, just above a whisper.

"Blame it on my weakness for older women."

The old joke about their three-day age difference made her smile but also brought a pang of regret. "This old woman is still on Colorado time and tired from the drive, so be nice."

"I'll think about it," he answered just as softly. His smile brought out pleasant crow's-feet at the corners of his eyes. "What time did you get in?"

"About two in the morning."

"I called the house awhile ago and you didn't answer, so I figured you were here. Have you talked to anybody yet?"

"No, I walked in late and sat in the last row."

She waited for him to tease her about being late for church when she only had to cross the road. But Sean looked away, one hand fidgeting with his necktie.

The preacher had worked his way up to a thunderous finish. The organist pounded out the first notes of a hymn. The service was officially over.

"I'd like to walk you home," Sean said, not smiling anymore. "We need to talk."

"About what?"

"You'll find out."

The door swung open. One of the elderly women exited in a cloying cloud of cheap scent. Recognition flashed in her eyes, and her red-lipsticked mouth moved in a babble of sympathy that Laura had heard all too often back in April.

Everybody started by saying they were so sorry and ended with something like "It must have been her time" or "I'll be praying for you." Nobody ever said anything original or entirely honest. Because Jess Gantt had drifted into some unorthodox beliefs, half the town thought she was new fuel on the fires of hell, but they were afraid to say it.

"Are you back to stay, sugar?" the woman asked at the end of her sermonette.

"No, I'm here to sort out my mom's things."

"And you're still teaching history in . . . where is it?"

"Colorado."

"That's nice, being a teacher. You'll have your whole summer free." The woman's claw-like fingers clutched the sleeve of Laura's raincoat. "It's a mercy the heart trouble took your mama quick before somethin' terrible like cancer could take her slow. Your poor daddy too, gone so sudden. Who knows what the good Lord spared him, unless it's like they say and—"

"Thank you, Mrs. Moore," Sean said, breaking the woman's grip. "May the good Lord spare you a slow death, too." He took Laura's hand and pulled her toward the exit. "Soon," he added under his breath.

She smiled a little inside. He'd always had a gift for soft-spoken, thinly veiled jabs.

"You're a blessing to have home, baby," the woman called. "I'll be praying for you."

"Thanks," Laura said, but Prospect wasn't

home anymore, and she couldn't bear one more person spouting the only things that were left to say when death blew holes in sweet beliefs about a God who answered prayer.

It wasn't heart trouble anyway. It was a cerebral aneurysm, out of the blue. God hadn't given her mom any last-minute chances.

Sean's hand released hers and settled on the small of her back. He ushered her outside, under the overhang and then down the steps and into the rain. He produced a black umbrella from somewhere and swung it over her. A gust of wind batted it off center, but he fought back and conquered.

"Let's get a move on," he said, glancing behind them.

"What's the rush? Scared of little old ladies?"

She'd given him a perfect setup for another wisecrack, but he didn't answer. Unnerved by his strange urgency, she walked faster.

On the hillside across the parking lot lay the graveyard where flowers had blanketed a white casket in April. If there was no life after death, her mother was only a dead body in a box. Her father was only bones that had rested at the bottom of Hamlin Lake for years now. End of story. No heaven, no hell. No Judgment Day.

Gram and Poppa Flynn, buried a few feet from their daughter's new grave, would have called that heresy.

The wet wind slapped Laura's face like a rebuke. Running out of walkway, she stepped onto the grass and turned toward home with Sean by her side. Her heels sank into the saturated ground, its wetness seeping through the seams of the shoe leather. If her dad were alive, he would have told her to wear sensible shoes.

Sunday mornings when she was a child, he'd always buffed her patent-leather shoes and polished his black wingtips. Then he'd walked her across the road to Sunday school, holding her hand. Back then, she'd thought her parents would be around forever.

Maybe that was why she'd dragged herself out of bed for church. She'd unconsciously hoped the familiar setting would let her pretend for a while that her parents were with her. That they hadn't vanished into the sweet by-and-by, wherever it was.

She picked up her pace. Just walk. Don't think. Just walk. Don't think. The mindless words beat in tandem with her footsteps and wrapped her in a stillness that nearly could have passed for peace. Deep inside, though, she was raw. The shock that had acted as anesthesia had worn off.

Sean slid his hand to her shoulder, slowed her down, reined her in. "Get back under the umbrella."

"You know I don't like umbrellas."

"I don't like you catching pneumonia. I was going to bring my truck over—"

"But the house is closer than the parking lot. I know. I'm fine, Sean."

She didn't want to be moved by his blunt kindness. And she certainly didn't want to be moved by his touch, but she was grateful for the warmth of his hand. She was cold. Colder than she'd ever felt in Colorado's snowy winters. Even in the mountains, Georgia shouldn't have been so cold in the middle of May. But maybe the chill came from the inside.

They reached the grassy bank above the road and stopped where crumbling cement steps led down to the pavement. A chain of vehicles threaded through the sharp curve, held back by a slow-moving dump truck with a blue tarp billowing over its load. The truck lumbered past, splashing the bank with muddy rainwater, then disappeared around the bend with its impatient entourage of smaller vehicles.

Laura glanced behind her. Umbrellas sprouted like flowers in the parking lot as people ran for their vehicles beside the little brick church. She was glad she'd escaped the small talk, but whatever Sean had to say might prove harder to handle.

She looked up at him against the black backdrop of his umbrella. Lines of weariness had joined the laugh lines around his eyes. She hardly knew this grown-up Sean, this somber stranger. Seeing him in a necktie took her all the way back to her dad's memorial service. That was the first time she'd ever seen Sean wear a tie. It was the first time she'd seen him cry, too. Raised hard by a hard man, he'd usually managed to hide his sorrows behind his blue-eyed devilment.

With one finger, he pushed a strand of hair off her cheek. "You need some sleep."

She shook her head. "I have too much to do. I can't sleep."

"Me either." His gaze darted beyond her and sharpened, wary and watchful. But there was nothing to watch in that direction. Nothing but a stand of pine trees that the kudzu would swallow before summer's end.

A chill hit her. The ghosts she didn't believe in were breathing down her neck again.

The latest rumor had Sean seeing things. Hearing things. The snap of a branch in the woods, a flash of brown in the green. It must have been a deer, foraging.

But Laura hadn't heard anything yet. He could break it to her gently.

She pulled away and shivered, her red hair frizzy from the damp. He tightened his arm around her shoulders.

"Let's get you home," he said.

Her big tomboy feet in fancy shoes started

29

moving down the steps, avoiding the rough spots. Her black raincoat flapped in the wind. Like all the tongues that were flapping. God help her if she heard the old biddies' tall tales with no warning.

Sean eased her to the left to avoid a long, green drape of kudzu at the roadside. Hanging from a sycamore and swinging in the wind, the vines were trying to grab a nearby dogwood and start devouring it, too.

Years ago, Laura's father had shown Sean how a dogwood leaf broken in two would still have thin, stretchy filaments connecting the halves. Like strands of memory and fact that held past and present together, Elliott had said. They would hold for a while, but not forever. He'd been a bit of a philosopher, Laura's dad, but he hadn't always made sense.

The man's lean figure drifted into Sean's imagination, slipped across the road in the rain, and vanished among the trees. He missed the man and his music and his stories. Wanted him back —alive—but wishful thinking couldn't raise the dead.

A fresh gust of rain pecked at the umbrella. Sean hurried Laura across the pavement, onto the circle drive, and up to the little brown bungalow that sat on a small peninsula of land created by the sharp curve of the road. They clomped up the steps to the wraparound porch where the wooden swing had hung until Elliott busted it up. A couple of his Adirondack chairs sat there now, but nobody ever used them.

Rain danced a jig on the tin roof of the porch as they walked around to the back door. Laura dug through her handbag, giving Sean a closeup view of those long fingers. The delicate bones of her wrists.

He didn't like this business of keeping his distance. Respecting her wishes. Being the ex-boyfriend instead of the love of her life. He'd had enough of it.

She drew a shaky breath that made him want to tuck her into a comfy chair with a hot toddy and a quilt. "Please don't tell me I've locked myself out," she said, still digging. "Sorry, I can't find the key."

He reached into his pocket. "I've got it."

She looked up. Her skin was pale, with shadows under the deep-set, dark brown eyes that were so much like her mother's. "You still have a key?"

"Sure I do. Half the county has a key."

Laura nearly smiled. "My mom was funny about that, wasn't she?"

"She was." Jess had been in the habit of locking herself out, so she'd had extra keys made and handed them out to her friends like candy. Her personal lockout-assistance service.

Sean unlocked the door, pushed it open. Leaving the umbrella dripping on the weathered

31

planks of the porch, he followed Laura in. The kitchen smelled like a florist's shop, the counters and table still crowded with potted plants from the funeral.

"You have enough plants to stock a nursery," he said.

"Tell me about it." Laura slung her raincoat over the back of a chair and bent to slip off her shoes. "I'll let you keep the key, in case I lock myself out again."

Just like her mom. "Good idea." Hiding a smile, he nodded toward a massive, foil-covered dish almost hidden by the greenery on the counter. "At least you won't starve. I'll bet Ardelle left that."

"She did. It's enough coffeecake to feed the whole neighborhood. Why don't you take some home?"

"Thanks, maybe I will. Lord knows I'm not much of a cook myself."

Laura smoothed the skirt of her dress although it clearly didn't need smoothing. "How's everything going for you?"

"It's crazy right now, getting ready for the festival. Once that's over, I'll get back to rehabbing the house."

"Funny," she said, leaning against the counter. "We're both back in the houses where we grew up—at least for a while."

"That reminds me. I heard Cassie's in town too."

A smile lit Laura's face. "She is? I'd love to see her. I guess Drew came too?"

"Nope. Seems to be a solo trip."

"Cass didn't tell me she'd be in town. Not that we're as close as we used to be, but we do stay in touch. I hope everything's all right."

"Everything's fine, most likely."

"Anything new with Dale?"

"He stops by a lot more often than I'd like. Every time I hear that rattletrap truck pull into the drive, I look for an excuse to say I was just leaving."

"How are Keith and Annie?"

"They're doing well," he said, remembering the message from his sister-in-law. "Annie said to tell you 'hey.' She would love to see you if you want to stop by."

Laura nodded but didn't commit herself to it.

The scent of the lilies on the counter reminded him of a long-ago Easter morning when Laura, wearing a new dress, stood hand in hand with her dad to sing "I Know That My Redeemer Lives." Elliott was perfectly on key while Laura wasn't even close.

She frowned. "What's that funny little smile for?"

He angled his head toward the lilies. "They make me think of Easter and your dad's favorite songs."

She studied the flowers for a moment, then met his eyes but said nothing.

He loosened his tie, tugged it off, and wound it around his hand like a bandage. "You must be freezing. You want to change into dry clothes before we get into this? Because what I have to say, Laura . . . it'll take some time."

She lowered her gaze to the necktie wrapped around his hand. "Okay. I'll be right back." She turned and walked into the living room. Mikey, stretched out on the couch, batted a languid paw at the hem of her dress swinging against her muscular calves, but he missed. Ignoring the cat, she headed down the hall.

Except for the plants all over, Jess's kitchen looked the same as it always had when Sean had stopped by for a cup of coffee and a chat. A little neater than it used to be, maybe. Her favorite mug, the pale blue one with rainbows and angels on it, hung from the mug rack beside the coffee maker. It was odd to see her possessions all around, outliving their owner. Elliott's too, years after he'd drowned. Dulcimers, mandolins, and guitars still lay around the house as if he'd set them down just days before.

The storm attacked the windows with fresh energy, the rain gusting sideways in belts and waves. Leaves bent backward, showing pale undersides. No birds calling. Only rain, wind, and the faint tinkling of Jess's miniature wind chimes in the backyard.

The storm had draped gray swags of mist over

everything, but once the weather cleared, Laura would have a good view of the family plot in the cemetery across the road. But Jess's grave was still too new to have a headstone, and Elliott had no grave. Only a bronze plaque that bore his name, a line about having served his country, and the dates of his birth and death.

Sean shook his head. That was a rough summer. A strange summer. He and Laura had turned eighteen that August, but their birthdays had been lost in the turmoil and ruined by his own naiveté.

Trying to shut out the memories, he turned around, only to face another reminder of the past. He'd sat at the Gantts' kitchen table many a time after Elliott rescued him. That wasn't too strong a word, either. Nobody else would have waded into Dale's fists to save a scrawny kid from another beating. Elliott took him home that day, patched him up, and turned him over to Jess for a decent meal while Laura looked on with wide eyes. Then Social Services got involved, and everything was topsy-turvy until Dale landed behind bars some-where and Sean's grandma moved to town and took him in.

He closed his eyes. How old had he been? Fourteen? And hungry for a father figure. Elliott had never been exactly stable, though. Or even quite sane. If the stories were true—the new stories that were spreading like a virus and the nightmares Sean had spun in his own head . . .

But they couldn't be true.

"God," he whispered. A one-word prayer. He figured the Lord already knew the rest of it.

Three

Laura stopped in the doorway to the kitchen. Sean, seated at the table, seemed not to notice her. While she'd been changing into jeans, he'd cleared a space by moving some of the plants to the floor and the wide windowsills. Drumming his fingers on the golden oak, he stared into space and frowned. Like he used to frown over her tangled geometry proofs.

Once, on the porch swing, she'd complained about all those aggravating angles and lines and curves in the textbook. He'd said the whole world was angles and lines and curves. Then he picked up a fallen sweet-gum leaf to illustrate his point, brushed the leaf across her cheek, and kissed her for the first time.

Contacts out, glasses on, she felt like that gawky, nearsighted teenager again. Sean, though, had lost everything awkward or gangly from his teenage years. He carried himself with understated confidence. With authority. He wore his thirty years well.

He looked up, eyes as blue as the sky but troubled as a storm. His fingers stilled. "Feel better?"

"Warmer, anyway."

"I can make you some coffee. There's always a bag of good Costa Rican stuff in the cupboard."

She smiled at his familiarity with her mother's kitchen. "No, thanks, but you go ahead if you want some."

He shook his head, and his hair fell into his eyes. If he didn't get a haircut soon, he would look like a wild man.

He ran a finger back and forth on the table. "The furniture your dad made, and his mandolins and dulcimers and all," he said, circling a knot in the wood grain. "They make me remember him like it was yesterday. He did beautiful work."

She sat across from him. "So do you."

"I learned from the best." But his pleasant words didn't match his worried expression.

"What's going on, Sean? What's bothering you?"

Sean, who'd never been afraid to speak his mind, hesitated. "There have been some crazy rumors floating around. I don't believe them, but I don't want you to hear them without warning."

"Rumors about what?"

He reached across the table and covered her

hands with his. A woodworker's hands, like her dad's, they bore a few small scars.

The quiet ticking of the clock on the wall filled the long stillness before he spoke. "Have you ever heard of a man walking away from his life? Just leaving?"

"Everybody wants to walk away sometimes. How many times did we hear Cassie say that? And she finally did, with Drew."

"I don't mean moving away like they did—like you did. What I mean is . . . vanishing. On purpose."

"Sure, it happens."

His grip tightened. "Half the town is saying we might know somebody who did just that."

"Who?"

"Do you remember Eric Rudolph?"

The bomber. The white supremacist. When Laura was a teenager, the papers had been full of him and his crimes, but she failed to see a connection between him and the sleepy little town of Prospect. She nodded though. "I remember reading about him."

"He hid out for years. Not far from here, in North Carolina. In the same kind of terrain. The mountains are like a big food locker for a man who knows how to hunt and fish and forage." He stopped, his gaze holding hers, then went on, slowly.

"Some folks are saying a man can stash

what he'll need to survive," Sean said. "Food. Clothing. Tools. Hunting and fishing gear. He makes his plans. He sets up a secret camp or two, somewhere in the wild. He gets everything ready. And then one day, a hot summer day . . . well, some folks say a man could fake his own drowning."

The words sank like heavy stones thrown into deep, dark water. The room swirled. The mingled smells of potting soil and lilies weighed on her. Choked her. Sean receded into a black distance.

"Laura, do you understand what I'm saying?" His features swam back toward her through a dark fog.

"Yes." She hadn't noticed pulling her hands away, but they were in her lap, twisting around and around, shaky and cold. Her head buzzed with her old theories, the wild ones her mother had scoffed at. This was different though. It was all wrong.

"I'm sorry," Sean said. "I had to tell you before you heard it with no warning. I don't know how to say it except straight out. A few people say they've seen him alive. Not just traces of where a man's been—though they claim they've seen those too—but actually . . . him. Your dad. Elliott Gantt. Older, thinner, crippled up. With long hair and a beard."

It couldn't be true. Nearly twelve years had gone by since her father had vanished in the deep waters of Hamlin Lake. Eleven years, nine months, and fifteen days. She'd worked it out on the long drive from Denver.

"I can't . . . that's . . . even if it's true, even if . . . No, after almost twelve years? He couldn't still be alive. Except"—the thought rolled in her heart like thunder—"he fought in Vietnam. He was trained to survive. To live off the land. Do you think there's any chance it could be true?"

Sean shook his head. "I don't, Laura. I really don't. It's absurd. But this morning I heard another rumor and decided I'd better tell you before somebody else did."

"What's the new rumor?"

The frown lines furrowed deeper into his forehead. "Remember Preston from high school?"

She nodded. Their biology teacher, "Presto" Preston had a penchant for bad puns and worse neckties, but he'd been a stickler for empirical evidence. He was so rational and logical that everybody said formaldehyde ran in his veins.

"I saw him this morning at the Shell station," Sean said. "He claimed to have seen your dad crossing the road by the old church camp on the lake, just before dawn. Preston said—"

"Wait. This morning? Preston saw him? Only hours ago?"

"Claimed to, anyway. He said he'd know your dad anywhere, the way he moved like a cat. Light on his feet. But lots of people move that way.

And it wouldn't make sense for him to hide out at the camp. There'd be too many people around."

"How long have these . . . sightings been going on?"

"The stories started a few weeks ago, after you'd been home for the funeral."

"Why didn't you call me?"

"I didn't want to bother you with a load of foolishness. People see things all the time. Me, I've seen Elvis. Up in Gatlinburg."

She tried to laugh, but it rang hollow. "So have I."

"I'm glad you're sensible, Laura. I was afraid you'd start scouring the mountains for him. That'd be crazy."

"But so was he—nearly. What if it's all true? I've believed crazier things. Just after it happened, I shared some wild theories with my mom. I thought maybe he nearly drowned but someone rescued him and took him off somewhere. If he was injured or had amnesia, he wouldn't have been able to reach us."

"What did she say to that?"

Laura stared at the table and relived her mother's brusque dismissal. "She said I needed to stop living in a little-girl fantasy and get off to college."

That week, in the strange new silence that had fallen upon their house, she'd decided to go to school in Colorado, not Georgia. She'd been accepted at both schools. The last-minute scramble to change her arrangements had allowed her to escape everything. Until now.

"The rumors can't be true," Sean said gently. "I've talked to the sheriff, and he says they're bogus. Nobody has a shred of hard evidence. Some people are taking it seriously, though. Doing their own investigations."

The way he said *some people* made her skin crawl. "You're talking about Dale, aren't you?"

After a moment's silence, Sean nodded. "Yeah. He's got a bee in his bonnet."

"What's he doing?"

Sean shrugged, as if he were trying to make light of it. "I don't know exactly what he's up to, but the other day he said the best way to catch a prowler is to go on the prowl yourself."

Of course Sean's father would want to find her dad, if he really was out there. Just for the sick pleasure of hauling him in, displaying him like a trophy of war.

Laura's throat was so dry she couldn't speak. Couldn't swallow.

She lowered her head to the table and closed her eyes. The tears wouldn't come, but a horde of unwelcome thoughts did. She shoved them to the back of her mind so she couldn't hear them screaming at her.

Chair legs scraped the floor. Sean walked around the table, stood behind her, and kneaded her shoulders while rain ticked at the windows and the bones of the house creaked. The oak table was cool and hard beneath her cheek. Her dad had built the table with his own hands—the hands that used to smooth her bangs from her forehead so he could plant a kiss there. And where were those hands now? Not at the bottom of the lake, after all?

She straightened, her chest an aching lump of lead. "I don't know what to do."

"Don't do anything. There's no need."

Wobbly and feeling detached from reality, Laura pushed her chair back, making Sean release her shoulders. She rose and faced him.

His fingers cool as water, he brushed her hair out of her eyes as tenderly as her father used to do. "What a way to come home. Buried your mama a month ago, and now folks would have you believe you're about to resurrect your daddy. But it's not true, Laura. It can't be true."

If it was true—

A sob tried to surface. She stifled it, tucking her chin down and pressing her lips together. Sean pulled her toward him, her bowed head barely touching his chest and keeping a space between them. A space between their hearts.

"You want me to stay awhile?" he asked.

"No." She shook her forehead against his warmth, her glasses bumping against him. His shirt was damp with rain. She pulled away and plucked at his rain-speckled collar. "Thanks, but I'll be fine. Go home, get into some dry clothes yourself. I need some time alone. To process everything."

"Are you sure?"

"I'm sure." She made herself smile.

His frown eased away. He returned the smile, giving her a glimpse of the younger, softer Sean who'd carved their initials into an old picnic table under the pavilion across the road. "Remember, it's a woman's prerogative to change her mind about absolutely anything." The twinkle in his eyes told her exactly what he was talking about.

Aching for the freedom to change her mind, to change their lives, she could only look away and hope he would understand someday.

"Call me anytime, day or night." He bent toward her as if he wanted to brush her temple with his lips, but then he only gave her shoulder an awkward pat and walked toward the door.

"Thanks for telling me what's going on," she said, following at a safe distance.

"Don't take any of it too seriously, now. You hear me?"

"I hear you."

"All right, then. I'll see you soon."

Sean made his long-legged way off the porch and down the steps, then across the road and up the bank to the church parking lot and a red pickup. She brought a hand to the hollow of her throat. It was the same '69 Ford he'd bought in high school with the wages her dad had paid him. She and Sean had shared a thousand kisses in that truck.

But he'd sold it. When had he bought it back? When she was in town for the funeral, he'd been driving a newer model. One that didn't barrage her with memories of high school and her dad's drowning.

A drowning that hadn't happened? She didn't want to grasp what it might mean.

She leaned in the open doorway, inhaling the wet air, her ears filled with the pounding of the rain on the tin roof. She didn't let herself look at the graveyard on the hill.

Sean climbed in, starting the engine even before he'd slammed the door. Headlights knifed across the gray afternoon, and the truck crunched away over wet gravel. One of his brake lights was out.

He'd forgotten to take his umbrella. He'd forgotten to take some of the coffeecake too. Maybe, like her, he'd been thrown off balance, rattled by this strange new world where her father might yet live.

She pulled the neck of her sweater higher. Closing her eyes, she listened to the storm pelting the world with rain and remembered a wet day in April when her mother's mortal remains had awaited burial under a green canopy. Green, the color of life.

She closed the door and paced, her thoughts shifting like a dark kaleidoscope. Her father—thinner than ever. Lonely, growing old, maybe half-crazy—but alive?

Who in town believed it? She imagined folks going home from church to eat Sunday dinner and spin yarns about a Vietnam vet flipping out and hiding in the mountains. Yarns that might be true.

He had always loved Hamlin Lake. It had the best fishing in the county. It was a beautiful spot, too. Bright blue water ringed by tall pines. A convenient boat ramp. And a blacktop parking lot where he'd left his truck and trailer the day his little boat drifted to shore at sunset, empty.

Laura dug her phone out of her purse. She scrolled through her contacts, overshot Marsh, B., and landed on Mom. Blinking back tears, Laura stared at the familiar number. She couldn't imagine deleting it.

Hardly able to read the screen, she selected Doc Marsh's number. He might have some answers.

Seated at a massive antique desk in his home office, Doc Marsh resembled a younger, thinner Colonel Sanders in jeans and a flannel shirt. Once the banjo picker of her dad's little band, he hadn't changed much in the twelve years since Laura had left home for college.

He smiled, his brown eyes magnified behind

thick lenses. "It's wonderful to see you, Laura."

"I'm glad to see you too. Especially in your home, where I know there won't be any medical procedures."

He chuckled. "Likewise."

The phone rang in the kitchen. His wife answered it and laughed. Muffled by a closed door, her cheerful, normal voice made Laura want to cry for some old, ordinary life that she'd never actually had.

"I hope you'll stay in town long enough to enjoy the bluegrass festival," Doc said. "It's not often that I drag out my banjo and play with anybody these days, but I never miss the festival."

"I must have a month's worth of work at my mom's house, so I'll be there."

He put his elbows on the desk and rested his goateed chin in his hands. "So will Sean. He's quite the up-and-coming luthier."

"Yes, he is."

"Y'all haven't been an item for quite some time, have you?"

"Not since we were eighteen."

"I'm sorry it didn't work out. He's a fine young man."

"He is, but put yourself in my shoes. Can you imagine Dale as your children's grandfather?"

Doc shuddered as if she'd made him drink one of those nasty liquid antibiotics he'd prescribed for her when she was small. "I'd rather not imagine." He cleared his throat. "Have you stayed in touch with Gary and Ardelle's girls?"

"With Cassie at least, and she always tells me Tigger's news. Did you know Tig and her husband are expecting their second baby?"

"My, my. And she still goes by that nickname?"

"Yes, but only the family still calls Cassie 'Eeyore.' Sometimes she still deserves it."

Doc laughed heartily, then sobered. "You didn't come here for chitchat about your childhood friends, did you?"

"No." Laura was suddenly afraid to ask the big questions. Rain dripped outside, but its steady rhythm did nothing to soothe her.

"Out with it," Doc said gently.

"Okay. Have you heard the rumors?"

"About your daddy?"

She nodded with a sad smile, remembering a college roommate who'd told her an educated adult shouldn't refer to her father as her daddy. The roommate had never had a southern friend before.

Doc took off his black-framed glasses and rubbed the bridge of his nose with his fingertips. "Everybody's heard the rumors."

"Do you believe them?"

"I don't know."

"Do you know if my mother believed them?"

He put his glasses on again. "I thought this

whole thing didn't start until after she'd passed away."

"But how do we know the sightings didn't start earlier? If she knew, she might have talked it over with someone. She might have written—" Laura frowned. She hadn't noticed her mom's journals anywhere. Making a mental note to look for them later, she went on. "But I'd really like to hear your thoughts about my dad. His problems."

Doc nodded soberly. "I thought the world of him. Some Vietnam vets get together, ride their Harleys, swap war stories, but he kept to himself. At least he never took to drinking like some folks do. PTSD plus alcohol can be a lethal combination."

"You'd call it PTSD, then?"

"I'm no shrink. I'm just a small-town family physician. But as long as you don't quote me . . . yes, I'd guess his struggles stemmed from combat-related PTSD. Of course he steadfastly refused to be anybody's patient, ever, so he never had an official diagnosis. In my opinion, though, he suffered mental injuries that should have been treated as seriously and as respectfully as a shrapnel wound. Mental injuries that shouldn't have had a stigma attached to them."

"But they did, and everything might have been even harder on him because he wasn't cut out to be a soldier."

"And your mom wasn't cut out to be a soldier's

wife. She'd married a troubadour, a musician, not a GI. Of course this happened long before you were born, but she nearly flipped her lid when he was drafted."

"I can imagine. When I was little, she was still pretty vocal about her antiwar beliefs."

"She was even more vocal before you came along. As his moods got worse, though, she learned not to throw fuel on the fire. She went from being a pacifist to being a true peacemaker, always ready with a calming word. I respected her for that."

Laura nodded, remembering her mom's ability to read her husband's moods. So many times, seeing him begin to react to a trigger, she'd stepped in with a soft word. He would always take a deep breath. He'd swallow. Sometimes he'd close his eyes as if gathering strength to battle the blackness. If she'd caught him in time, he'd say, "Don't worry about me. I'll be all right." Or he'd give her the little wink that meant the same thing.

Once, though, instead of soothing him, she'd blasted him with her old antiwar rhetoric when he was already on the verge of a major episode. She'd said it with such venom that Laura, eavesdropping from around the corner, had recoiled.

As she tried to shrug off the rest of the ugly memory, she had to face an equally ugly fear.

"Are there connections between PTSD and other problems?" she asked. "Alzheimer's, for instance?"

Doc's sad eyes answered her question even before he spoke. "We have more questions than answers. Maybe combat PTSD increases the risk for late-life dementia, or maybe PTSD is sometimes an early symptom of dementia."

"And if there's some family history of dementia?"

He frowned. "Is there?"

"I've wondered if my Grandpa Gantt might have been in the early stages of it when he died. He seemed to be . . . slipping. He wasn't very old, though. Sixtyish. A little younger than my dad would be now."

"Early onset," Doc murmured. "Could be. But with your dad, we obviously don't have enough data to go on. We don't even seem to have a patient."

"But if by some chance he comes back, what do you think his prognosis might be?"

"This isn't my area of expertise, so my opinion isn't worth much." Doc hesitated, fiddling with a paper clip. "Let's hope for the best."

"That's what people say when they expect the worst."

"You've always been a perceptive young lady." Doc swiveled his chair, chose a thick book from a shelf behind him, and slid it across the desk.

"This book has an extensive section on PTSD and related issues. Take it home with you. It might help you get a handle on things."

She took the book and stood. "Thanks. I'll do that."

"Keep the faith, Laura. Anything's possible. And no matter how this turns out, you can be proud to be his daughter." Doc's eyes were moist. "Go home, put on one of those old CDs, and remember him at his best."

Unable to reply at first, she clasped his hand in silence. "Thank you," she managed after a moment.

The rain had let up. Walking across Doc's wet lawn to her car, she looked up at the mountains that formed a backdrop to the town. If her dad was up there somewhere, his fate might remain a mystery like the dead ends she'd reached when she traced her genealogy. But in the long view of history, twelve years were nothing. Her dad's disappearance was so recent that she might still find clues. She might even bring him home.

Tears made the mountains a blue-green blur. "Please, God," she whispered. "Please."

❧ Four ❧

Sitting on the couch while the day-long storm ran its course and ushered the dusk into full night, Sean didn't turn on a light. He preferred to sit in the shadows while he brooded over recent events.

The town was no stranger to strange doings. Back in the late eighteen-twenties, Prospect had been home to miners with gold fever. North Georgia's gold rush brought both craziness and prosperity. Less than a century later, Prohibition brought a different brand of insanity, and an earlier generation of Hallorans added to their already sizable fortune by selling bootleg booze to thirsty citizens, far and wide. The Halloran Building still stood on Main Street, a monument to their illegal profits and a constant humiliation to Dale, who'd inherited the place and then lost it to foreclosure. Gary Bright, always quick to spot a bargain, had snatched it up.

Tourism brought the money to Prospect now. Senior citizens loved the spring wildflowers and the fall colors. Bikers loved the twisty mountain roads. Families tubed the Chattahoochee River, and hordes of musicians and fans came for the three-day bluegrass fest over Memorial Day weekend. Locals always griped about the out-siders clogging the roads but never missed a chance to make a buck. But if the money-grubbers started selling "Where's Elliott?" T-shirts, Laura would be devastated.

She'd loved her dad. Crackpot veteran or not, he was her father. When other kids had made fun of him, she'd stuck up for him every time. Sean had helped her finish a few of those school-yard scraps.

She'd mellowed, though. She'd conquered the hair-trigger temper she'd had as a kid, maybe because she didn't want to be like her dad, but sometimes Sean missed the girl who'd shown her raw emotions without filters. Without apologies.

He checked his phone for the time. He should have been holed up in his workshop, but he just couldn't get motivated. He had a few new instru-ments lying around the house too, so he could break them in, but for once in his life, his fingers didn't itch to play. It all seemed so unimportant.

A night creature rustled in last year's fallen leaves by the side of the house. Probably one of those raccoons living in the big oak. One of the young ones was an albino. With pink eyes and a white-ringed tail, it made an eerie sight, especially on moonlit nights. A ghost raccoon.

The animal outside moved closer. And coughed.

Sean sat up straight. That was no raccoon.

Maybe it was Dale, wanting to wheedle more

money out of him. But why so quiet and sneaky this time? Why on foot?

Because the house was dark. He thought nobody was home. Thought he'd play burglar, maybe.

Sean waited, holding his breath. The skin on the back of his neck prickled.

Feet padded up the back steps, and his senses snapped to full alert.

The doorknob rattled. The hinges creaked. The kitchen light came on. A knock finally came, an afterthought, not on the door but on the wall. He smiled, knowing who his visitor was.

"Sean? You home?"

He rose to his feet. "Hey, Laura. Come on in."

When she walked into the room, her glasses were so wet he didn't know how she could see through them. In a shabby, rain-sprinkled sweater, she looked like a lost little girl. She'd twisted her thick hair in a damp, red mess on top of her head.

Reluctantly, he vetoed the idea of pulling her into his arms. Right now she needed a friend, not a pursuer.

"Out for a walk in the rain?" he asked.

"Well, it had let up for a while, wasn't raining when I started. It turned loose again when I was passing Gary and Ardelle's house—their old house, I mean. I was about to run to the door when I remembered they haven't lived there in a long time. I came here instead." She spun in a circle. "You've done a lot of work. It doesn't look like the same place."

She was talking too fast, too brightly, in a scattered and disjointed way. It wasn't like her.

"Sit," he said, waving her toward the couch, hoping she'd relax. "And tell me again why you're walking around town in the rain."

She didn't sit. "I just needed time to think about the . . . the situation."

"Sure, I can understand that. You have a lot to process."

"This news about my dad . . . It changes everything." Her voice shook.

"Not news. Rumors. Somebody saw a man who looked a little like him, and that somebody told other people, and the story has grown out of proportion."

Her eyes burned like sweet brown embers. "But what if it's really him? Have you thought about the implications?"

"Implications," Sean repeated slowly, trying to imagine where she was headed with it. "Well, I can imagine your dad—if he's alive—would need medical care and counseling, at the very least."

"That's part of it. Oh, Sean. If it wasn't an accidental drowning, if it was deliberate, it knocks my feet out from under me. I have to question everything."

Sean studied her, trying to decipher her words,

her expression. He'd been so focused on hard facts that he hadn't given enough thought to the questions that would spring up for anyone who chose to believe the rumors. If Laura was hurt and confused, he didn't want to make matters worse with careless words.

"Those are big ifs, though." A lame response but the best he could come up with.

"I know they are." She pushed up the ratty sleeve of her sweater to check a watch that wasn't there. "I'd better get going," she said in that too-cheerful way.

"You just got here."

She smiled at him. "I'm tired, Sean. I didn't get to bed until three in the morning, and then I couldn't sleep. Every time I closed my eyes, I saw the road in front of me. You know what I mean?"

His heart melted as he pictured her driving fourteen hundred miles of interstate highways alone, facing the sad task of tying up the loose ends of her mother's life. "I'll give you a ride, then. Don't argue. It's still raining, and it's dark out."

"Well. All right. Thanks." Laura wiped moisture off her cheeks. She turned and hurried into the kitchen, her shoes squeaking on the hardwood floor.

Sean followed, wondering if she'd wiped away tears or rain.

• • •

Laura was intensely thankful for the ride home. It would have been a dark and spooky walk past the stretch of road where they used to pick black-berries.

She looked behind her when Sean turned on a floodlight that transformed the drizzle to a thousand tiny falling diamonds. He strode toward her, the wind ruffling his hair and his shadow looming large as he pulled on a flannel barn jacket.

He used his remote to start the door cranking upward on the little garage that stood apart from the house. "Same old truck," he said with a smile.

"I noticed. But didn't you sell it to the Browns years ago?"

"I did, but he's had to give up driving. I offered him a good price, and he took it."

"You have a brake light out. I noticed this morning."

"Yeah? Thanks for telling me. One more thing on my to-do list."

His garage smelled like motor oil, lumber, and paint. Laura walked past his lawn mower and a neat array of tools on pegboard. It felt wrong to go to the passenger side of the truck. Back in the day, she'd climbed in through the driver's door. They'd sat so close, she'd had to crane her neck to look up at him.

They climbed in simultaneously, shut their

doors simultaneously. Sean turned the key. The engine roared to life, and the radio came on. No bluegrass purist, he had it tuned to raucous country-rock.

Putting his arm across the back of the wide seat, he looked over his shoulder and reversed the truck into the brightly lit driveway.

"You still listen to that stuff?" she asked.

He smiled. "Sure. Especially when you're here to complain about it."

He lowered the volume, started the wipers, and hit the remote again. The garage door rattled shut. The truck rumbled backward down the drive, escaping the reach of the floodlight and leaving them in darkness except for the dim glow from the dash. The gas-guzzling engine sounded strong, and someone had installed a new windshield to replace the old one with its cobweb of cracks.

"The truck sounds good, Sean."

"Because it is good."

"You've always been Mr. Fix-it."

"Had to be," he said with a laugh.

True. The Hallorans had rarely had the money to buy anything new, or if they'd had it, Dale had spent it on liquor. Sean had always been so steady, though. So strong.

She wanted to scoot over and lean into his solid warmth, but she kept hugging the door. He kept both hands on the wheel. Now it was too dark to see him. Too dark for him to see her, and Laura was glad. He didn't need to know what a mess she was.

Neither of them spoke as he drove out of his own neighborhood and past the Brights' old house, its lights glowing behind overgrown shrubs. Then, in a flash, they'd passed the old berry patch.

Sean barely slowed the truck to cross the tracks at the bend of the road where town met country. In the old days, she would have sat close to him, laughing as the truck rocked over the rails and jounced her against him. Now she clung to the edge of the seat and held herself upright.

He pulled the truck around the corner, more or less ignoring the stop sign. The church steeple, softly lit from below, came into view above the trees. Sean swung into the circle drive and parked in front of the house. The truck idled, deep-throated and smooth.

"I'll walk you to the door," Sean said.

"No need. Thanks, though."

"Got a key?"

"In my pocket." She pulled on the door handle. Tugged harder. Nothing happened.

"Sticks sometimes," he said. "Gotta fix that."

He reached for the door, his flannel-clad arm brushing against her, his face nearly touching hers. She closed her eyes and leaned hard against the headrest.

Muttering a word best left unspoken, he man-handled the latch. The door clunked open, letting in a rush of chilly air, and the dome light burned brightly against her eyelids.

His breath warmed her. That meant he'd turned toward her. If she tipped her head forward the least bit, her lips would touch his. But she couldn't let it start.

"It's good to have you home where you belong, Red."

The nickname from high school jolted her eyes open. He was so close that she couldn't focus. Couldn't think.

Next thing she knew, he'd be calling her "honey" again, and "sweetheart," and finally "darlin'," and then he'd start stealing kisses and telling her he loved her. But it could never work.

He drew away by a hair's breadth. "I've missed you, Laura." His low voice went rough and ragged.

"I've missed you too." She wanted to hug him, but then she'd start crying and never stop. "Good night. Thanks for the ride." She gently pushed him away, swung her legs out, and climbed down.

"Wait." He leaned toward her, the strong planes of his face emphasized by the glow of the dome light. "There was something you'd started to tell me. The implications, you called it. You said 'that's part of it,' but what's the rest?"

"I don't want to say it."

"You can tell me. It won't go any further."

"I know. I know you'll keep it to yourself." She hesitated, afraid she'd say too much but desperate for help in carrying the burden. "You remember what it was like, Sean, the night they started the search. You remember how we walked back and forth on the shore, praying and crying." She couldn't go on, but she didn't need to. The grief in his eyes mirrored the grief in her heart.

"Of course I remember."

She took a moment to regain control, then sped through the rest of it. "Was my dad out there, watching? Was he in a hideaway on the other side of the lake, maybe? Spying on us? Hoping we believed he'd really drowned?"

"No," Sean said softly. "Laura, he really did drown."

She knew he hoped to console her, but the strange situation had put her beyond consolation. "I don't know, Sean. On one hand, I hope he's alive. I would love to have him back. I want to see his face and hear his voice and bring him home. But if he's alive, why did he do it? Why did he make Mom think she was a widow? I hate to say something so terrible, but was it some kind of cruel joke?"

"No," Sean said again. "He had his issues, but he was never cruel."

"No? I'd almost rather believe he drowned." The words tasted like poison on her tongue. "If he drowned, I can keep believing he really loved us."

"He did. He loved you and your mom, both."

"I wish I could know that for sure." Shutting the door before Sean could argue, she turned for the house and ran. She didn't know what to believe.

Stepping inside, she studied the kitchen clock. A sleek, modern model, it replaced the antique her dad had shattered with a well-aimed cast-iron trivet.

The argument between her parents still rang in her head like discordant bells. Her mother's voice had been brittle and angry beneath a false calm. *"You have blood on your hands."* She hadn't spoken such inflammatory antiwar rhetoric in years. Maybe he'd hit her hot button, so she'd hit his, forgetting to handle him with kid gloves.

"Don't try to hold that over my head," he'd answered. *"You've been unfaithful. Don't deny it. Don't lie to me."*

Laura, standing in the darkness just around the corner, had held her breath and waited for her mother to offer a sensible, soothing response to his irrational accusation. But he'd hurled the trivet, smashing the heirloom clock into a hundred pieces of glass and wood. Laura had let out a squeak of terror that went unheard and tiptoed away.

She'd never told anyone about her dad's accusation. Not even Sean. She hadn't believed a word of it at the time. She still didn't, but her father must have. He'd disappeared a month later.

Laura sat up, wide awake in the night. A pie tin was rolling down the road, clanging and clattering.

No, it was only the wind chimes jangling in the backyard as the storm troubled the branch they hung from. She'd been dreaming about pies, coffeecake, and casseroles. About Ardelle and all the other hometown folks who'd brought meals after the funeral, thinking good food and a hug could fix just about anything.

But one wild thread of the dream included a blurry glimpse of her dad trotting down a woodland trail with his hound dog, Geezer, at his heels.

She turned toward the neon-green glow of the digital alarm clock, a fuzzy rectangle of light, and squinted. Ten minutes past three. Lowering her head to the pillow, she curled into a ball and tucked her flannel nightgown around her icy feet.

Between snatches of sleep, she'd spent the night plagued with vivid memories of her dad and his buddy, Gary Bright. With their blue eyes, narrow faces, and sandy-blond hair, they'd always looked like brothers. They'd been as close as brothers too, since their days together at Prospect Elementary.

Gary was like family, still. If anybody could help her sort out the truth, Cassie's dad could. He might be as skeptical as Sean, though.

Something knocked softly in the night. Knuckles rapping on the back door? A silly notion, but she lifted her head from the pillow and listened, her skin prickling.

Nothing but wind. Branches bumping each other. One storm had passed, and another one was moving in. That was all.

She tugged the blanket more snugly around her neck.

A soft thud met her ears—and then a faint meow. That thud, at least, was only Mikey, probably jumping down from the table he knew was forbidden territory. The poor old kitty slept most of the day and roamed the house at night, wanting to escape to the great outdoors. He must have been going stir-crazy all month, cooped up by himself except for Ardelle's daily visits.

With a vague thought of fixing a hot drink to settle her nerves, Laura threw back the covers and swung her feet to the cold hardwood floor. The furniture hadn't been rearranged in years. Every time she came home, she prided herself in finding her way through the house in the dark. She could even brew tea without turning on a light.

By moonlight, Laura found her glasses and thick socks, then made her way into the living room to fetch the small quilt that lay folded across the back of the couch. Wrapping the quilt around her shoulders, she headed for the kitchen. She still didn't want to turn on a light. Just in case somebody was out there.

Silly, maybe, but she'd learned caution when she was a young girl and a prowler had roamed the town, tossing pebbles at window screens. Time to lock and load, her dad had said. They'd all breathed easier when the Peeping Tom turned out to be Slattery. An oddball, but harmless. Still, Laura had felt safer once he'd skipped town.

Now was her dad a prowler? *An oddball, but harmless.* That's what everybody would say. It hurt to think of people putting him in Slattery's category—sick, dirty, twisted—when her dad had always been upright and honorable.

The kitchen smelled like potting soil and flowers, earthy and flowery at the same time. Like she'd always imagined Eden. Recalling what Sean had said about the lilies, she closed her eyes, going back to long-ago Easters with her parents and both sets of grandparents. Her mom always put fresh flowers on the table, and she gave Laura the job of scattering candy-coated Jordan almonds across the white tablecloth like pastel confetti.

Every year, her dad began their feast by reading

a few Bible verses aloud. She'd loved to inhale the heavenly aromas—roasted lamb, scalloped potatoes, homemade rolls—while he read the amazing story. An angel. An empty tomb. The grave clothes, abandoned. Then the best part: *He is not here; He has risen!* It was the best twist ever, the happiest, craziest surprise ending. It always made her want to stand up and cheer, but she'd only wiggled on her chair and tried mightily not to sneak any more of the candy-coated almonds.

After dinner, it was time to hunt for Easter eggs and candy. All the loot was hers because she was the only child, the only grandchild. While the grownups sat and talked, she listened quietly and enjoyed her haul. The day seemed to be wrapped up in a big, loud *Alleluia* because her dad kept singing under his breath: *"Christ the Lord is risen today, alleluia! Sons of men and angels say . . ."*

Laura opened her eyes and faced the present. Her whole family was gone. She was the only one left.

Leaning against the counter while Mikey butted his scruffy head against her ankle, she looked out the window above the sink. It had no blinds to cover it, its only dressing a lacy white valance.

A fast-moving cloud drifted onto the half moon like a blanket that a child held up to his face to play peekaboo. Within moments, the cloud scudded past.

Her dad might be somewhere out there, under that cold sky. Homeless by choice. With no blanket, no bed, no roof, he'd be freezing. And crippled? Sean had said something about that. Crippled, freezing—and maybe not quite right in the head—but alive. Laura's breath came faster at the thought.

She shifted her gaze from the bare-faced moon to the moon-silvered road. Her heart crashed against her ribs.

A spot of blackness in the night, a swift-moving figure swept out of the yard, across the road, and up the hill to disappear in the shadows of the graveyard. She strained her eyes, but it—he?—had vanished.

Her dad? No, that was crazy. If it was her dad, and he wanted to see her, surely he would knock on the door and call her name. He wouldn't creep around in the night like a criminal.

Laura dropped the quilt. Nearly tripping on the startled cat, she ran to the back door and checked to be sure it was locked. She wedged a chair under the doorknob, then felt her way through the darkness to the front door to do the same thing there.

Making the rounds of the house, she locked the windows, even the small, high one in the bathroom, and drew the drapes and blinds tightly shut. Last, she opened the door on the colder air of her parents' room. Moonlight shone on the massive, hand-carved headboard that the young Elliott Gantt had made for his bride.

Laura dealt with the bedroom window and returned to the kitchen, trying to decide what to do. She didn't want to sic the sheriff's department on her prowler, in case he was her dad, and she didn't want to call Sean the skeptic, especially at three in the morning. She only wanted to communicate with her long-lost father.

She crossed her arms, rubbed her hands up and down on her shoulders, and closed her eyes. Then, holding her hands still, she pretended her dad's hands were gently resting on hers. She imagined him giving them a squeeze and asking her a teasing question.

"So, Laura girl, you think you deserve some answers?"

"I sure do," she whispered. "Where are you? What happened, really?"

In this very room, the night before his last fishing trip, she'd told him, "Good night, good luck, I love you." He'd kissed her forehead and said, "Good night. I love you too. Always."

Always. It wasn't something he usually tacked onto his "I love you." Once his boat turned up empty, she'd attached special significance to that word. She'd wondered if he'd had a premonition of his death. Now it seemed possible that he'd known he was saying good-bye for the rest of his life.

Energized by the idea that it was at least possible that he was her prowler, she turned on the kitchen light. She found a blank sheet of paper and a wide-tipped marker so she could write a note in large letters, legible from a distance.

Pacing the floor while Mikey watched from his refuge under the hutch, she pondered one message after another.

Dad, I still love you, no matter what.

I know why you stopped loving Mom, but did you stop loving me too?

Or simply: *Daddy, why?*

If she didn't know what to believe about him, she certainly didn't know what to write. And maybe he was long dead, and her prowler wasn't anybody she'd want to welcome.

Laura abandoned the blank paper on the table. Leaving the porch light on, she walked back through the shadowed rooms and climbed into bed. With the covers pulled up to her chin, she lay there, remembering so much she'd never told anyone. Not even Sean.

Especially not Sean. He'd loved her parents so much. Telling him what she'd overheard would only break his heart. She'd done too much of that already.

Five

Cassie slogged into the gorgeous, unfamiliar kitchen and avoided looking at the clock. The sunshine pouring through the windows told her all she needed to know.

Her mom never used to sleep late.

It was still too early to call Drew. The three-hour time difference made it hard to find time to talk, just when Cassie had so much to say. She should probably save most of it until she got home, though. She'd have to look him in the eye when she said it.

In the dining room, her dad adjusted his tie, using the glass doors of a huge, brand-new china cabinet as his mirror. Gary Bright, hotshot investor and the best dad in the world, had gained weight but only enough to make him look well-fed and prosperous. A fat cat is a happy cat, he liked to say. But she'd seldom seen him look so worried.

He noticed her and gave her his typical goofy grin. "Mornin', glory."

"Mornin', Dad. You're still here?"

"Yes, but I've been working since the crack of dawn. Now I'm off to an appointment in town."

He tucked his crisp white shirt more snugly into his khakis.

"Mom's still in bed?"

He nodded, and the worry returned to his eyes.

Cassie spoke softly even though she knew her mom was on the opposite end of the sprawling house. "Maybe you're worried about nothing. Maybe she just needs more sleep for some reason. And she's always been a neat freak. Shoot, she used to make me and Tig make our beds at five in the morning when we were leaving on vacation. Remember?"

He laughed. "I sure do. Well, keep an eye on her and let me know. Oh, Tig called an hour ago. They'll come over after Trevor gets out of school."

"Great." Cassie slumped into a chair at the table. She loved her kid sister's perfect family, but sometimes Tom, Tigger, and Trevor were just too cute, right down to their matchy-matchy initials. With another baby on the way, they were already hunting through the *T* section of the baby-names book. Baby Number Two was a girl, of course. Exactly what they'd prayed for.

Her dad eyed her. "Got up on the wrong side of the bed, Eeyore?"

"Always." Cassie yawned. "Does Tigger have to come over every single day I'm in town?"

"Yes. She has missed you since the day you ran off with Drew."

"We didn't run off. We thoughtfully spared you

the expense of a fancy wedding so you'd have more money to blow on Tig's."

He chuckled. "That was so kind of you."

"It was, wasn't it? By the way, I've missed her too. I'm not a cold-hearted monster."

"No," he said in a dry tone. "You're a warm-hearted monster."

"That's me." She squinted across the room at the coffee maker. The newfangled type, it made one cup at a time. "You feel like making me some coffee?"

"Sure." Frowning again, he stuck a coffee pack into the machine and pulled a brand-new mug out of the cupboard.

Everything in the house was new. Even the table. Cassie missed the old, scratched one she'd grown up with. She preferred their old house down in town too. This custom-built ranch on a hill looked like a model home, decorated by strangers. Sterile. Soulless.

"Do you ever miss the old house?" she asked.

"The one where I had to hack at the kudzu with a machete every year to keep it from swallowing the backyard? The one where you had to put your conversation on hold every time a train came by because you couldn't hear yourself think?"

"Yeah, that one."

"No, I don't miss it. Not one bit."

Cassie sighed. It was silly to prefer the old,

cramped kitchen to this new marvel of granite countertops and the latest appliances. It was silly to prefer the old view—of basically nothing—to a stunning expanse of smoky-green mountains. And it was ridiculous to miss the old house, where passing trains rattled the windows. Where friends might knock on the door and walk right in.

She'd been in town for three days, and except for Drew's parents, not one soul had dropped by. Not her friends. Not her parents' friends. If the UPS driver hadn't brought a package, nobody but family would have driven up and down that long driveway in days. Maybe her dad's new prosperity had scared everybody away.

He moved behind her and started massaging her shoulders. "It's great to have you home, baby. Thanks for making the trip."

"Thanks for paying for it, but I still think you're exaggerating the problem." Cassie let her head droop forward.

"I still think I'm not." He moved the massage upward. "Your neck muscles are tight as a drum. See, you needed to get away."

"To play shrink for Mom? It's hardly relaxing."

"I'm not asking you to play shrink. I'm only asking you to pay attention. And see if you can get her to open up. But that doesn't mean you can't get out and visit your friends."

Cassie perked up. "Laura just got into town, right?"

74

"That's what I heard."

"I'll call her. She might need some help sorting through her mom's things."

"No doubt. Jess lived in that house for thirty-some years and never threw anything out."

"Yes, but at least her house looked like *her*."

The dig went unnoticed. Or maybe not, because he stopped the massage abruptly and walked over to the window, hands in his pockets. He started whistling, so she couldn't have hurt his feelings too badly.

Cassie sat up straight and idly picked up the month-old newspaper that lay on the table, neatly folded to reveal the obituary. Her dad had mentioned it when he'd called to ask her to fly home for a while. It worried him, the way her mom had left the paper there, day after day. Cassie had to admit that was a bit strange, but the suddenness of Jess's death must have made a hard blow even harder.

Silently, Cassie read the obituary one more time. "Jessamyn Flynn Gantt is survived by her daughter, Laura Gantt of Denver, and was preceded in death by her husband, Elliott Gantt; by her parents, Hollis and Laura Flynn; by a brother, Robert Flynn . . ."

Some people would have argued that Elliott hadn't preceded Jess, but Cassie didn't want to believe it.

"Why didn't you call me when the rumors

about Elliott first started?" she asked her dad.

He turned from the window. "Same reason I didn't call Laura. It's all hogwash."

"That's what I think too."

"Rumors are like tumors. They'll spread in a hurry if you don't take care of them." He shook his head. "Poor old Elliott. He hated himself for those black fits that made Jess and Laura so miserable. If he'd lived longer, he might have done worse. God rest his soul."

"Yeah, it was hard on everybody. Especially Laura."

He brought the coffee to the table. "I just hope she won't hear the jokes. People say he'll be Prospect's new tourist attraction. You know, like some towns brag about sightings of Sasquatch or aliens? They say Elliott's our claim to fame."

"That's horrible. People can be so cruel. He can't be alive, though. He must have had a heart attack or something while he was fishing. And if that's what happened, at least his last day on earth was a reasonably happy one."

"I'd almost rather believe that than imagine my buddy hiding in the hills, half-starved, while people stuff their faces at the diner and gossip about him."

"Me too." Still, Cassie wished she could believe Elliott was back, for Laura's sake. But he wasn't.

Elliott and his little band had been a crowd favorite from the earliest years of the festival, their toes tapping as they played and sang. He'd often switch instruments between songs, going from fiddle to mandolin, or from mandolin to guitar. He could play—and build—all those instruments. Laura had been so proud of him. So loyal in spite of his problems. So crushed when he drowned. She'd be crushed all over again if she let herself start believing the rumors.

Cassie rested her head on the table, her eyelids as heavy as her heart, and wished she were home with Drew. With no worries but the bills. The bills came in faster than the money, though. At this rate they'd never be able to start a family. Not in California, anyway.

Somebody should have warned her that marriage wouldn't be all moonlight and roses. Some days, as much as she loved Drew, marriage was the hardest job she'd ever had. But Laura probably envied her just for being married.

Laura's life hadn't turned out as planned either. When they were sixteen or so, she'd thought she would go to UGA and come right back to Prospect to teach school. And marry Sean, of course. That was a given. That was the foundation of her other dreams and his too, until she went and broke his heart. But even if they'd married, they would have learned soon enough that the starry-eyed phase couldn't last.

"I'd better get out of here." Her dad was juggling two briefcases and a travel mug. "Get the door for me, Cass? Say, one of my third-floor apartments will be vacant in a few days. I'll give you the nickel tour before the new tenant moves in."

Not especially interested in the apartments in the renovated Halloran Building, she took a careful slurp of hot coffee before she spoke. "I've seen them before. Years ago."

"Yeah, but I like to show 'em off whenever I can," he said with a grin.

She opened the door for him and socked his shoulder. "You're worse than Trevor with a new toy. Okay, fine. Let me know when."

Moments after he'd walked out, her phone rang. She braced herself for a too-cheery conversation with Tigger, who'd be calling to announce her ETA, but caller ID showed Laura's number.

"Hey, girl," Cassie said. "Can you believe we're both in town at the same time? We have to get together."

"Absolutely." But Laura sounded rushed and abrupt. "I'm going out to the old cabin this afternoon. Will you come with me? I want company while I poke around."

"Sure. Tig's coming over, but she can visit with my mom until I get back. Poking around won't take all day, will it?"

"It probably won't." Laura still didn't sound

quite like herself. "Wear jeans and boots, okay? There might be snakes. I'll pick you up in a little while. Can't wait to see you."

"Same here," Cassie said. "We're in the new house now. Just outside of town, remember?"

"I remember. See you soon, Cass."

Cassie walked to the living room window that looked out on Prospect far below. Beyond the neat grid of downtown streets, beyond the new houses in the hills outside the city limits, lay the remains of the Gantt homestead. Laura hadn't mentioned the purpose of her trip to the old ruin, but Cassie knew.

Sean locked up the workshop and led Gary across the back lawn, past budding azaleas and a few late daffodils that the previous owners must have planted. "I'll tackle the yard work as soon as I can," Sean said. "Seems like spring barely got here, but summer's already knockin' at the door."

"The yard'll look great in no time," Gary said, slapping Sean's shoulder. "All those perennials and flowering bushes will appeal to gardeners. Azaleas, rhododendrons, hydrangeas—you have everything, don't you?"

"I guess so." But if they weren't in bloom, Sean couldn't tell one bush from another.

"It's a dandy little workshop too. Elliott would have been green with envy, boy."

Boy. Dale always used the word with contempt. For Gary, it was just part of his genial, I-love-everybody attitude.

Sean shot him a quick look, realizing he'd spoken of Elliott the way a sane person would— as if he was a dead man. "Still think the rumors are bunk, Gary?"

"Absolutely. Do you know if Laura's heard them yet?"

"I told her, just yesterday. She didn't know what to think."

"It's a tough time for her." Gary shook his head. "So . . . Ardelle's timing is lousy, but she wants to invite both of you to our grandson's birthday party. Trevor turns five next week, and she's throwing a party on Saturday night."

"Party hats and pin the tail on the donkey? That kind of party?"

"No, thank God. Tigger's throwing a kids' party on a different day. This is the one where the grandparents pick the menu and overindulge the kid in stuff he doesn't need. Cassie's in town, and I'm sure she'd love to see both of you."

"Drew didn't come?"

"No, just Cass. She's laid off, actually, and she . . . she wanted some time with the family." Gary looked away for a moment, frowning into the sun, then smiled at Sean. "You know you want to come."

"Sure I do."

"You and Laura don't mind hanging out together?"

"I don't, anyway."

"All right, then. You can expect an official invitation soon, probably via her."

"Great."

But the sympathy on Gary's face made Sean wonder if the whole world could see his heart on his sleeve. He supposed they all knew why he hated birthdays.

Shrugging it off, he opened the back door and waved Gary into the kitchen. "Sorry I didn't clean up the mess. I didn't know you'd be available so soon."

"This isn't a mess. It's progress." Nodding with satisfaction, Gary looked around the half-painted kitchen, cluttered with tools, masking tape, and cartons of tile to go on the floor later. He chuckled at the crayon scribbles on the walls— "The last owners really left their mark, didn't they?"—and cast a critical eye at the cupboard door that had sagged since Sean was a kid.

"Gotta fix that," Sean said.

"All in good time. You can't fix everything at once." Gary wandered into the living room, where light streamed in through bare windows.

Heavy drapes had covered the windows sixteen years before, when social workers stopped by unannounced. When Dale moved to the state pen for a few years, he'd probably been exposed to more sunshine than he'd ever allowed in his own home.

Sean ran his fingers over the smoothness of the newly painted wall. When he was eight or nine, his mom wanted to get rid of the ugly, outdated wallpaper. She'd pulled off only one narrow strip before Dale stopped her. It stayed that way for years, a jagged ribbon of off-white in a room where everything else was dark: wallpaper, carpet, furniture, drapes. The house had its first breath of fresh air when the bank foreclosed on it and sold it to the Clawsons, who sold it to the family of wall-scribblers. Sean bought it in February, with Gary acting as broker. They used the same bank that had foreclosed on Dale's loan.

Elliott had been a surrogate father, but Gary was like an uncle. He'd offered plenty of practical help through the years, including cash, but he never let Dale get wind of it. Gary had said he didn't want to be paid back. Pass it on to someone else, he always said. Pay it forward.

Gary continued his walk-through, checking out the bedrooms and the bathrooms too, and returned to the kitchen. "It's a pretty little house, and it's solid. Seems premature to sell, though. Except for the workshop, you've barely started the renovations."

"The workshop had to come first."

"Now you get to the rest of the house and you . . . what? Decide it isn't worth the trouble?"

"When I was a kid, I dreamed about kicking Dale out and making the house the way my mom wanted it. I thought it could somehow . . . undo the damage. As if fixing up a house could fix the past. It doesn't work that way." Mad at himself for being motivated by emotions instead of common sense, he shook his head. "I just want out."

"But you've set up the perfect little shop out back. Why let it go? Most places, the zoning rules won't even let you run a business from your home."

"I know."

"And you'll get a far better price if you finish the renovations."

"I know."

"But you still want out in a hurry? Why?"

As Sean looked around the room, he realized he'd hunched his shoulders and balled his hands into fists. His old defensive stance.

He straightened his posture and flexed his fingers. "No matter what I do to the place, I won't be able to get rid of Dale's stench. I don't mean that literally, but you know what I mean."

"I do, but you're the king of the castle now. You make the rules. You create the atmosphere. But if you can't stand to keep the place, you could put just a little more work into it and turn a nice profit. I'll list it right now if you want me to, but I've never known you to quit in the middle of a project."

"I've never tackled a project as tough as this one," Sean said. "I remember you tried to talk me out of buying it. I should have listened. You've never steered me wrong."

"Oh, I doubt that."

"No, you've never let me down. I wouldn't have survived without you and Ardelle. Elliott and Jess. Keith. My grandma."

Gary laughed out loud. "Not to mention social services, a couple of churches, and probably the PTA."

Sean laughed too, but he felt like a charity case. "I can't argue with that."

"What's this?" Gary moved over to the couch where that pretty little F-style mandolin lay, its carved top of Sitka spruce gleaming like gold against the rich blue lining of the case. He pulled it out, his big hands dwarfing the slender neck. "How much for this little beauty?"

"Brace yourself. It's my best piece yet."

Gary plucked a string, the sound a tiny, unpracticed sample of the mandolin's potential in the hands of a good picker. "How much?"

Sean couldn't keep the smile off his lips. "About three grand."

"Yowee." As gently as if it were a newborn babe, Gary tucked the mandolin back in its case. "You sell many at that price?"

"No, most of 'em are built and priced for casual musicians. This one's a custom job for a pro in Nashville. He's picking it up later this week."

"Gibby Sprague?"

"Not this time. This one's for a session musician. Gibby buys from me now and then, though."

"Will he be in town for the festival?"

"He hasn't missed one yet."

"Think he knows Jess passed away?"

"Laura must have told him. He and Elliott were pretty tight for a while."

Gary ran a finger over the smooth wood of the mandolin. "Elliott would have been proud of you. The apprentice has surpassed the master."

Sean shook his head. "I'm just starting to learn what I need to learn."

"You're too modest." Gary walked to the door. "About the house, you want me to go ahead and run the comps so we can talk about price?"

"No, I hate to waste your time with it."

"It wouldn't be a waste, but I hope you'll finish overhauling the place first. Why don't you sleep on it and let me know."

"Will do. Thanks for doing the walk-through."

"My pleasure." Gary stepped outside, scaring a mourning dove out of the bushes in a flurry of whistling wings.

As Gary's gleaming black Cadillac disappeared around the corner, Sean remained in the doorway, thinking. If he told Laura he'd heard about the party, she would feel obligated to include him in the invitation. If he kept quiet, she'd be free to decline the invitation or accept it. With or without mentioning it to him.

Funny, how a kindergartner's birthday party could be fraught with such significance.

Back in the living room, he picked up the mandolin and tweaked the tuning to perfection. Elliott had taught him that, along with a million other things.

A good man, Elliott Gantt. He'd had his moods, but he'd loved his family and friends. Loved them with his whole heart. Sean had envied Jess and Laura, except when Elliott's temper got loose. But the man had never laid a hand on anybody but Dale, who'd richly deserved it. And Gary, Sean corrected himself. Just once. Gary hadn't deserved it. He'd never been anything but a loyal and supportive friend to Elliott.

Sean closed his eyes, turning his fingers loose on the sweet-sounding strings. A little one-man jam session. Before he knew it, he was playing one of the tunes Elliott taught him.

Elliott had loved old songs and poems and stories. He'd often used archaic words just for the fun of it. After a while, the quaint speech had become his unconscious habit even in everyday conversation.

As Sean started humming along, the lyrics came to him.

Many a one for him makes moan,
But none shall ken where he is gone.
O'er his white bones, when they are bare,
The wind shall blow forever mair.

Sean couldn't help but wonder how many skeletons lay at the bottom of how many deep lakes across the county, across the state, across the country.

He returned the mandolin to its case. All the music had just gone out of the morning.

Six

Laura and Cassie exited the convenience store, Laura with peach iced tea and Cassie with her old favorite, an orangesicle slushie. With her first sip, Laura recalled her hankering for a hot drink in the middle of the night—and the tall, lean figure sweeping across the yard in the moonlight.

"Thanks," Cassie said. "Next time it's on me."

"You're welcome." Laura climbed behind the wheel and carefully fitted her plastic cup into the cup holder. "It's great to see your face again. How long has it been since we were both home at the same time?"

"Three or four years, probably. I don't remember. It's funny. Every time I come home, I remember why I was so desperate to leave. But I also remember how much I love the place."

"Me too." Laura backed the car out of its space, headed for the road, and glanced over at Cassie. Her hair was lighter than it used to be. Whether it was bottle-bleached or bleached by the California sun, it would be a different shade and style in a few months. Cassie had always had fun with her hair.

"That nail polish is a pretty color," Laura said. "Reminds me of Sunset Boulevard Red."

The name didn't seem to jog Cassie's memory. "I don't know what the shade's called," she said, examining her nails. "I borrowed it from my mom's bathroom."

"Like old times. Remember the day we left Tigger by the tracks and ran off to play with nail polish and makeup?"

"Yeah, not ten minutes after we told your dad we'd keep an eye on her. I guess he never snitched on us, because my folks didn't come crashing down on my head."

"My dad threw a fit, though. Not because we left Tig—he never mentioned that part—but because I came home wearing nail polish."

"Parents never make sense." Cassie fiddled with the air conditioning. "Do you mind if I crank up the air?"

"Go ahead. I can't believe how hot and humid it is. Yesterday was so cold and rainy."

"That's north Georgia for ya." Cassie turned the fan on, full blast, then took a slurp of her slushie.

Once Laura was on the main road heading out of town, she stole another glance at Cassie. She looked as cheerful as could be expected for a girl who had once deserved to be called Eeyore. Maybe Sean was right and everything was fine between her and Drew, but it wouldn't hurt to ask. Cassie could handle frank questions.

"Everything okay out in California?"

Cassie let out a little snort. "Yeah, except I got laid off. We love living there, but we can barely afford it even on two incomes."

"I'm sorry about your job. That stinks."

"Something will turn up."

Laura nodded, remembering Cassie's old dream of being a stylist to the stars. Instead, she'd bounced from one job to another because she had an uncanny talent for finding work with businesses that were about to go under. Hairstylist—but not to the stars. Waitress. Admin. Day-care worker. Meanwhile, Drew's techie start-up company wasn't bringing in much money yet. He probably couldn't take any time off, while Cassie had all the time in the world.

"I hope you'll have a nice visit with your folks," Laura said.

"It's not exactly a pleasure trip," Cassie said. "My dad asked me to come. He says there's something wrong with my mom."

Laura's heart plummeted as dire possibilities ran through her mind. Some debilitating disease like Parkinson's or MS. Cancer. Alzheimer's. "What do you mean?"

"I wish I knew. She's always been a neat freak, but Dad's afraid she's going all OCD on us. Or maybe she's depressed. He can't get anything out of her. So I'm here for a couple of weeks to help him figure out what's going on. Without letting Mom know that's why I'm here." Cassie made a face. "It's loads of fun."

"I'm sorry, Cass. When did your dad start noticing a change?"

"Around the time of your mom's funeral. Makes sense. They were best friends."

Only in Ardelle's mind. Laura couldn't say it out loud, but her mom had never seen Ardelle as a bosom buddy. Their longstanding friendship had been lopsided.

"Do you see the same things that are worrying your dad?"

Cassie shrugged. "So far, I don't see much of a problem except the uber-neatness, but she's always been that way. You know, wiping down the counters all the time and making sure the corners of the napkins match up exactly when she folds them. That's nothing new. On the other hand, she's all . . . fidgety, and she has this new habit of repeating herself."

"Like she can't remember what she said already?"

"No, she remembers. It's more like she'll start talking about something and then she just can't leave it alone. She'll come back to it over and over, using the same words. It's like . . . like picking at a scab."

"I wonder if this is related," Laura said slowly. "I noticed she went to extremes when she was watching the house for me. I only asked her to take care of the basics like the mail and the cat and the houseplants, but she vacuumed and dusted and straightened. All over the house. In rooms she didn't need to go into."

"But is that OCD behavior, or is it just a bored grandma with too much time on her hands?" Cassie said, apparently asking herself as much as Laura. "Anyway, I'll find a way to bring it up. Delicately."

"No, don't. Now that I'm in town, it doesn't matter anyway. She won't need to pop in anymore."

"You're right." Cassie squirmed around in her seat to face Laura. "Okey-doke. My tough subject's out of the way. Time for yours. Do you think your dad is at the cabin?"

Hearing it spoken aloud made Laura's heart lurch. "I can always count on you to be blunt."

She sighed. "I don't know, but I have a few reasons to think there might be some truth to the rumors."

"Like what?"

"For one thing, I've started wondering why my mom hung on to my grandparents' property and paid taxes on it all these years. She should have sold it."

"You think she kept it so your dad would have a place to go?"

"Maybe. Or she thought she'd get a better price if she waited. I don't know." Laura swung the car wide to give room to an old woman picking her way through the roadside weeds. Frail as a spider, the woman held a faded blue parasol upright above her head. "Granny Colfax," Laura said, glad for the distraction.

"I can't believe she's still alive and kicking."

"Me either."

Nobody's granny, everybody's granny, Ruby Pearl Colfax knew everybody and their business and didn't hesitate to express her opinions. Laura had always tried to give her a wide berth, but her parents had loved Granny, so it hadn't been easy to avoid her.

"Does she still live in that teeny-tiny house on the west side?" Cassie asked.

"Your guess is as good as mine. I haven't been around much either. No idea what she's doing out here."

Last in line at a red light down the road, Laura checked the mirror for the gray-blue of the parasol, but the shoulder lay empty, edged with green brush and trees.

Such an old woman to be walking alone in the boonies, although it wouldn't be the boonies for long. Prospect was sprawling in all directions, with new homes going up as fast as the builders could tuck them into hollows and scatter them across hilltops. Many of the For Sale signs bore Gary Bright's picture and his corny slogan: "The Bright team, prospecting for a bright future in Prospect, Georgia."

Good old Gary. He was rolling in dough. He'd earned it.

The light turned green, and half a dozen vehicles crawled forward with Laura's in the rear. When she'd left for college, the road hadn't had any traffic lights. It wasn't even paved, and there'd been more cows than houses.

Just in time, she spotted the wrought-iron post, minus its mailbox for years now. She braked sharply. Cassie shrieked and steadied both drinks as Laura swung the car into the driveway of the old Gantt home place.

The tires crushed masses of kudzu that blanketed the gravel. Long stretches of vacant land on either side of the property separated the cabin from its nearest neighbors, and a newly plowed field lay across the road.

Vines engulfed the tiny log home where her dad grew up. The roof sagged. The windows were black voids with no glass in them, curtained with big, heart-shaped leaves. If the barn and the shed still stood behind the house, they'd been buried too.

"Wow," Cassie breathed. "It just hit me. This is all yours now. You're rich, girl. Well, not exactly rich, but you do own some property."

"It's just starting to sink in," Laura said, careful to keep her voice on an even keel.

She'd inherited everything, of course. Her mom's personal effects. Her SUV. Her bank accounts. Her house and this property that had belonged to Grandma and Grandpa Gantt. But the cluttered bungalow was desolate and empty without her mom there, and this tumble-down cabin was a sad reminder that time had claimed her dad and his parents too.

Sure, she was rich in terms of real estate, but in terms of family, she was flat broke. She had nobody.

Battling a wave of loneliness, she climbed out of the car and faced midday heat that made yesterday's cold rain seem like a bad dream. She didn't know what she hoped—or feared—she would find under that ruined roof or in the outbuildings, if they still stood. Everything, even her grandma's red roses, had disappeared under those greedy vines.

"There's nothing left to do but bring in a bulldozer," Cassie said. "Nobody's been inside lately, that's for sure. You can't even see the porch steps."

"I have an old photo of this place when it was new, with Grandpa and Grandma Gantt standing on the steps, a little black dog sitting beside them. They must have been in their early twenties or so."

"That's cool."

"Yes, Mom gave me all the old pictures from the Gantt side of the family a few years ago. Once I find the Flynn pictures, I'll put everything together in an album."

"Just don't get obsessed with it like my mom's obsessed with her scrapbooks."

"Settling things up here before school starts . . . I don't have time to get obsessed. Later, maybe. I do love digging into family history. Part of being a history teacher, I guess."

"History geek, you mean," Cassie said with a smile.

Laura smiled too and started walking. "Let's poke around a little. That's why we came."

"Yeah, terrific."

Laura led the way to the side of the cabin. Wishing she had a long, strong stick, she gingerly parted the curtain of leaves to peer through a window that long ago lost its glass. The interior was smothered in greenery too.

"Nobody in his right mind would hide out here," Cassie said.

"But my dad isn't necessarily in his right mind."

"He wasn't stupid, though. He's not here, Laura."

"He might have been, not long ago. Kudzu grows incredibly fast. It could have covered up any signs that somebody has been here."

"You're dreaming. This spot isn't very secluded anymore. People drive past all the time, especially with my dad putting in a new subdivision just around the bend." Cassie held up a finger. "Listen." Beyond the bees droning nearby, heavy equipment growled from farther down the road. Metal clanked on metal. Men shouted at each other, their voices softened by distance.

"Your dad's doing quite well, isn't he?"

"He sure is." Cassie made a face. "I wish it'd rub off on me."

"Maybe he'll want to buy this acreage too. I'll sell it, sooner or later."

"Just don't sell your mom's house. It's too cute. The perfect size for starting a family too," Cassie said.

Laura laughed. "You and Drew want to buy it? I'll give you a great deal."

"I wish. No, you'd better hang on to it. You never know when you might need it."

Laura ignored the comment.

They tromped around to the front of the cabin. Cassie groaned and pointed toward the road. "Watch out. Here comes the old busybody."

Moving with eerie grace, Granny Colfax held her parasol as level as water. Like a neighbor who'd been invited for tea, she turned into the driveway, never slowing her pace. The parasol was sun-faded and threadbare. It must have been fifty years old—nobody used parasols anymore—and Granny must have been ninety. She was thin as a witch.

She came closer, her feet moving relentlessly in red sneakers with the toes cut out. A pale echo of the blue sky, her parasol never wavered.

"Hey there," Laura called. "You picked a warm day for a walk."

"Y'all ought to be ashamed," Granny scolded. "Traipsing on other folks' land. Snooping in other folks' houses."

"This was my grandparents' place," Laura said. "I know you. You're Granny Colfax."

Granny's deep-set blue eyes drilled into Laura. "Can't a body be decent and let a house die in peace?"

Was she deaf? "My grandparents lived here years ago," Laura said, raising her voice.

"You don't own this land, missy."

"Yes, I do." She was nearly shouting. "It belonged to my grandparents. The Gantts. I'm Laura Gantt."

"What's that you say? Gantt?" Granny's eyes softened. "Oh, that red hair. Lord, have mercy. Would you be Jessamyn's girl?"

A lump rose in Laura's throat. "Yes, and this is Cassie Cutler. Gary and Ardelle Bright's daughter."

Granny paid no attention to Cassie. "Land sakes, I'm sorry about your mother, child. And I still miss your old granny too. She was a fine lady. A strong one. Strong as an ox and stubborn too. You find a lifelong friend like that, honey, you hang onto her."

Laura gestured toward Cassie. "I've found one."

"Ha! You ain't lived enough years to know what *lifelong* means." Granny came closer, smelling like soap. Honest, clean—and astringent.

Laura licked her lips, tasting sweat and dust, and felt unreasonable anger rising up against the old woman who was, after all, a trespasser herself.

"What are you doing here?" Laura asked.

"Oh, I do like to forage. There's something in every season. Greens and nuts and berries. The old berry patch near the railroad tracks, that was the best one. Remember? Y'all used to pick there."

Cassie finally chimed in. "Yes, we did."

Granny faced her. "What's the name of your little sister, girl?"

"Tanya. But everybody calls her Tigger. She married Tom McTavish."

"Well, ain't that nice. And you skedaddled for the West Coast, didn't you? But you're back. Nobody ever stays away if they have any sense. This is the best place on earth."

Cassie's eyes narrowed. "Easy to say if it's the only place you've ever seen."

Granny hooted. "You think you're so smart. Smart and pretty too. Believe me or not, I had my pretty day. I had my day like yours. And y'all will have your day like mine."

A ghost's fingertip traced Laura's spine. She imagined herself with a shriveled body, an unused womb. Past being useful, past being pretty. Wearing sneakers with the toes cut out.

Granny eyed Cassie. "I bet your daddy wants to buy this place so he can put in big, fancy houses and make a truckload of money."

Cassie shrugged. "Maybe."

Granny chuckled. "Ain't no maybe about it. He loves to build big ol' houses where country folks kept goats and bees. It don't seem right. City folks don't know the first thing about making scuppernong wine or killing copperheads. They just like their pretty lawns and their air conditioning."

Laura stayed silent, remembering Grandpa Gantt. He'd never had central air. Never wanted it. He'd said it liked to give a body pneumonia.

The last time she saw him, he'd been whittling on the porch in the summertime heat. They'd both been whittlers, her grandpa and her dad.

What would her grandparents have said if they'd known their only son might stage his own drowning someday? They'd been so proud of him. Their soldier boy, they'd called him, but Laura had only known him as a craftsman and a musician. A father who was kind and gentle— most of the time.

Granny planted herself directly in front of Laura and cupped her chin in a wrinkled hand. "You fretting about those rumors?"

"Do you think they're true?"

"What I think don't have a thing to do with it, honey. Is that why you're here? Looking for your dad?"

"I thought, maybe, since he grew up here—"

"It's the first place you come to, ain't it?"

Laura nodded, her captive chin moving against Granny's callused fingers.

"Well, then." Granny took her hand away. "Why would he stay right where folks would look first? He's smarter than that."

"You're probably right."

"He went to war a boy, come home a grown man who'd seen too much. But he didn't get no hero's welcome like the boys who fought in the world wars. It ain't right." Granny patted Laura's shoulder. "But be done cryin', girl. Tears can't put the spilt milk back in the jug. You remember that."

"I'm not crying. I'm just—"

"What's done is done, and if a man did the best he knew to do, that's that. There'll come a day when we'll answer to God, every one of us, yes, and He'll answer us. He won't answer *to* us, you understand, because He's God, but He'll answer. Lord, how He'll answer."

"I want answers now," Laura said. "Not in the sweet by-and-by."

"No, you'd best leave things alone. Leave it be." Granny turned to go, then looked over her shoulder. "Might be snakes, so don't go prowlin' around too much. Don't tempt God no more. You hear me?"

"Yes ma'am, I hear you." Laura bit back a comment on Granny's unwise choice of footwear for foraging—on land that wasn't hers. The old hypocrite.

"Good-bye, then," Granny said crisply. She set her blue gaze on the road and picked her way back down the driveway, holding the parasol like a mace.

A mockingbird flew up from a bush smothered with vines. The bird swooped behind the house where kudzu-draped pines formed giant sculptures, strange and beautiful and looming like time. In a hundred years—or two hundred, what did it matter?—the lush growth would cover other abandoned houses, along with their pools and tennis courts. Mockingbirds would still fly. Old women would still lecture young women and envy and pity them.

"You about ready to go?" Cassie asked.

"First I want to know if the outbuildings survived."

Cassie folded her arms across her chest. "Go right ahead. I'm staying here."

Laura waded across a relatively shallow stretch of kudzu, trying not to think about snakes, and stopped near the corner of the cabin. Shielding her eyes against the glare of the sun, she searched the piles and mounds and mountains of green where the shed and barn used to be, might still be. Even if they'd collapsed, they might provide a corner of shelter.

"Dad," she called. "Are you there?" Her voice sounded faint and far away, as if it were drowning in the vines too. She tried again, louder. "Dad! Elliott Gantt! Do you hear me?"

There was no answer, of course, but two crows flew over, cawing.

The old woman's voice whispered in Laura's imagination: *"He's smarter than that."* Granny Colfax had spoken of him in the present tense. Maybe she'd misspoken, or maybe—a crazy thought—it had been a deliberate hint.

Laura turned and tramped back to the car, making a mental list of possible clues. Granny's slip of the tongue—if that's what it was. The prowler in the yard. Preston's story. Even the way her dad hadn't seemed like himself in the weeks between his big blowup and his disappearance. She didn't believe for a minute that his accusation of infidelity was true, but if *he'd* believed it . . .

Cassie was already opening her door. "Let's go. He's not here."

"Why are you so sure? Give him a chance!"

Tears filled Cassie's eyes. "You're just torturing yourself. We need to face it, Laura. He's . . . he's dead."

The words swept Laura back to the first time she'd heard someone say her father was dead. The finality of the statement still made her heart ache. Now she couldn't let anyone trample her newborn scrap of hope that it hadn't been final after all.

"He's alive." Her voice shook. "I saw him."

Cassie's fair skin paled further. She dived into the passenger seat, leaving the door open, and stared up at Laura. "Here? Now?"

"No, last night. At the house. Walking through the yard in the wee hours."

"And you really believe it was your dad?"

Laura hesitated. "I didn't get a good look at him," she admitted.

"Did you call the cops?

"No. I'm not calling the law down on my dad's head."

"But what if it wasn't him? What if it was some random pervert?"

"That's an awfully strong conclusion to jump to."

"Yeah, but you know how those creeps show up sometimes. What if this guy comes back? What if he breaks in?"

Laura walked around to her own door and climbed in. "I know where my dad's guns are, and I know how to use them."

"If you won't report it, I will." Cassie dug her phone out of her jeans.

"Don't you dare. Look, if it happens again, I'll call 911—or—or somebody."

"Promise?"

"I promise."

Cassie squinted at her. "I'll hold you to it." She put her phone away.

Thinking she'd better go solo on her future investigations, Laura started the engine. As she turned onto the road, she caught a glimpse of Granny's faded parasol disappearing around the bend, heading farther out of town. Then a black pickup truck approached from the other direction.

"Ugh," Cassie said as the truck rattled closer. "That's Dale Halloran."

Laura tried to catch a glimpse of the driver, but the truck was already past them. She hit the brakes, wanting to keep it in sight. "Are you sure?"

"Positive. He's driven the same nasty old truck for years, and I'd know his ugly mug anywhere too, beard or no beard. Man, how on earth did Sean and Keith turn out so good-lookin' and sweet?"

"I don't know." Laura frowned into the rear-view mirror. The truck's brake lights lit up.

"Ha! I got you to admit Sean's good-lookin' and sweet."

"Oh, stop it."

As Cassie prattled on, Laura watched in the mirror. The truck slowed to a crawl and made the turn into the Gantt driveway.

Slightly comforted to know Dale would find the cabin empty, she decided to buy a few No Trespassing signs and post them as soon as possible.

Seven

Dale had become a regular visitor at the boxy little house he'd once owned. When Sean got home from a run to an ATM, Dale waited in his beat-up truck in the driveway, pulling on a bottle of Jim Beam. He followed Sean inside, parked his raw-boned frame on the couch, and started rambling about his truck's brakes, the price of gas, and how his best buddy had landed in jail over a little misunderstanding about a woman.

It wasn't a social call. Dale wanted something. He always wanted something.

In recent weeks, he'd grown a scruffy beard. If he was cultivating the outlaw look, it wasn't far from the truth. People kept hiring him for odd jobs, though, knowing he did decent work when he was sober. He got by.

Bottle in hand, he heaved himself off the couch, ambled into the kitchen, and opened the refrigerator. "Pretty near empty. You got nothin' to feed your old man?"

Sean sat on his hearth and picked up the mandolin that lay in its case beside him. He tried a little riff he'd been working on but messed it up.

"No time to shop," he said. "You know. The upcoming festivities."

"You got no time for nothin' but your lutherie." Dale gave the word a ridiculous, pseudo-French pronunciation. "You're a pansy, boy. When I die, I'll leave you the pansy gun."

"Gee, thanks. Can't wait."

"It's all that's left."

Sean focused on the notes again and got them right. They reminded him of "Turkey in the Straw." He segued into the happy, fast-moving tune, hoping it might dispel the gloom that entered the house whenever Dale did.

Dale came back and leaned against the mantel, his eyes bleary slits. "So, the Gantt girl's back in town. I bet she's still a good girl." He winked. "You could fix that."

"Keep your filthy thoughts to yourself."

Dale raised his hand. Sean flinched, a reflex he thought he'd conquered.

"What's wrong?" Dale leaned closer, giving off the familiar smells of booze and onions. "Ol' crazy man Gantt isn't around to protect your sorry butt? Or is he?"

"I don't know, Dale. You tell me."

"I hope he's alive and well. At least as well as a psycho can be. Keepin' an eye on our fair city from afar."

That last phrase sounded like Elliott's old-fashioned speech. Coming from Dale, it was cruel mockery.

Sean returned the mandolin to its case, latched it, and tucked it safely away behind him. "If Elliott is around, you'd better not try to beat me like you used to. He could kill you with his bare hands."

"Like he nearly killed Gary Bright?"

"Don't exaggerate. It was a little scuffle between friends."

"You always stick up for your hero, don't you? We'll see what kind of hero he is now, after living like an animal for years." Dale reached under his shirt and scratched his belly. "What kind of man runs out on his wife and lets her think he's dead? At least I didn't do that."

No, but his cruelty would have run her off if she hadn't died first. Sean held his tongue.

"You believe he's back, boy?"

"No."

"You should. Somebody saw him on Sunday at the old church camp out by the lake. Somebody else saw him on Redberry Road last night about dusk."

"Somebody *thought* they saw him," Sean said.

"They saw him, all right. And I can find him."

"Oh, you'll just lie in wait somewhere and outsmart him? Not likely."

"It's plenty likely. When I find him, I'll truss him up like a deer and drop him off at the nearest funny farm. You got any clues about where he might be?"

"Sorry. I'm not going to waste my time on wild gossip."

"Well, excuse me, Mr. Luthier. I'd better let you get back to your hard, hard work." Dale pulled his keys out of his pocket and jingled them. "I'll be on my way."

Sean checked the time and stood up. He could play chauffeur and still make it back in time to meet his customer. "I'll drive you home."

"No, you won't."

"One of these days, you'll kill somebody. It

might be you, but we can't count on it." He reached out to seize Dale's keys.

"Back off, sonny, or you'll be sorry." Dale's voice was like a rasp on wood.

Bone-deep memories of pain seized Sean as if they'd been imprinted on his body as well as on his brain. A boot in his knee, a fist on his jaw. Even with youth and sobriety on his side, he wouldn't win. He could match Dale's strength but not his mean streak.

"Fine. Drive yourself home."

"Hey, gimme a little cash first. Just to tide me over. I'll pay you back."

"You never pay me back. Tell you what. Sell me the pansy gun. I'll give you a fair price."

"Nope. I'm not selling."

"And I'm not lending unless you want to leave the gun as collateral. If you don't pay me back, I keep the gun."

"No deal." With the too-careful movements of mild inebriation, Dale headed for the door. He slapped the half-painted wall. "Good luck with this ol' shack. You know, I never would've lost it if Gantt hadn't called the cops on me."

"He didn't call the cops."

"Sure he did, and then he lied about it."

"Elliott wasn't the one who was lying about things."

"You calling me a liar, boy? It figures. Gantt had you fooled. You needed every whack I ever gave you, but those idiots wouldn't even let me raise my own boy the way I saw fit. That's how I lost everything. They stacked the deck against me."

Sean shook his head. Always the innocent victim. That was Dale.

Leaving the door open, Dale walked across the lawn toward his truck. He was listing slightly to the left, but he made it into the truck without mishap. Backing out of the driveway, he rolled to the other side of the street and nearly hit Mrs. Gibson's mailbox and the container of garish silk flowers at its base.

Sean dialed the sheriff's department. The dispatcher assured him she'd take care of it. Within minutes, a cruiser would be on Stringer Road, hunting a DUI in a beat-up, black GMC pickup. He nearly suggested that they search Dale's tacky little studio apartment so they could bust him for being a felon in possession of a firearm, but the pansy gun really was all he had left.

Long after Dale's truck had rattled away, Sean stood looking out the window. He had a lot to think about, and he wished he could talk things over with Jess.

Sometimes it hit him all over again as if he'd just heard the news. Jess was gone. His mentor's widow, his girlfriend's mom.

Ex-girlfriend. Even after Laura dumped him and moved away, though, Jess had always been happy to start a pot of coffee and talk about books or music or politics. Except, somehow, every conversation was ultimately about her. She was kind and easygoing but also quite self-absorbed.

He pulled out the mandolin again, started playing and humming "Shady Grove."

Peaches in the summertime, apples in the fall.
If I can't get the girl I love, won't have none at all.

He abandoned the instrument and looked out the window. A movement in the trees caught his attention. He braced himself to see a man in camo, but it was only a wind-tossed branch against the sunset.

He had to watch himself. Laura nearly had him believing those incredible rumors. Like he'd nearly talked himself into believing some other loony notions, years ago. The long-ago memories plagued him still, so weird that they might have been hallucinations.

He tried to summon the details of a day late in the summer he'd turned twelve. He'd been sweating in the brush above old man Bennett's private lake, hiding there because he'd heard a car coming, down below, and he'd been run off twice before for trespassing. He didn't want to make it three times and wind up in the backseat of a cop car. Dale would have whipped him half to death.

But as it turned out, it wasn't Bennett driving up to the lake.

Sean gave his head a hard shake. He'd never told a soul what he'd seen, least of all the authorities. A trespassing Halloran—even if he was only a kid—wouldn't have found a friendly audience in the sheriff's department back then. Now the memory seemed so odd that he hardly trusted his own recollection.

His cell phone rang. He pounced on it. Laura's number. Maybe she wanted to tell him about the birthday party.

He put the phone to his ear, enjoying the notion that her voice didn't have to travel from a faraway state. She was back where she belonged.

"Hey there," he said.

"Hey, Sean. Do me a favor?"

"Sure. Anything."

"Come pick a lock for me."

Sean sat on the floor of Jess's den with his back against the wall and studied the cedar chest. Small, flat-topped, rectangular, the wheeled chest was set on short but graceful legs and stood low enough to serve as a coffee table. He'd installed its brass keyhole straight and true, with his mentor watching over his shoulder to make sure. For a beginner's work, it was a nice piece, but only because Elliott wouldn't settle for less. Now Laura couldn't find a key.

A few water rings marred the top—he'd have to rub them out—but the dark red wood was still beautiful, its warm color accented with lighter streaks. Like Laura's sun-streaked hair in the summertime.

He smiled, remembering the green-plum wars they'd fought in the alley behind his house. She'd played like a boy, loud and fierce but fair. Well, mostly fair. Once, she and Cassie climbed to the roof of a shed and ambushed him with a bucketful of rock-hard green plums. The girls had hugged each other and screamed for joy. Laura's scream could scare a banshee.

Looking at the chest again, he wondered if a few wiggles with the skinniest screwdriver on his Leatherman might do the trick. But maybe he wouldn't need it. Sometimes Jess had hidden spare keys in brilliantly obvious places.

On a hunch, he slid his hand across the smooth underside of the chest. There it was. A small, hard bump. Tipping the chest up, he spotted a square of gray duct tape. Typical. Jess had used duct tape for everything.

He turned the key in the lock, raised the lid, and jumped. Dark brown eyes stared up at him.

His heart thudding, he let out a shaky laugh. It was only a red-haired, life-sized baby doll. Laura's favorite. It had only one leg due to an accident. Laura had hauled it all over town on the handlebars of her bike during those years when she couldn't decide if she was a girly girl or a tomboy. Maybe she still hadn't decided.

The grimy doll and her grimier white dress lay in a clutter of sentimental stuff that included Laura's baby book, a tiny pink dress that must have been hers as a newborn, and some crayon drawings she might have made in kindergarten or so. That was only the top layer.

He flicked the doll's stiff-lashed eyes closed. They popped open again, keeping their plastic gaze on him. The right arm hung crookedly from its socket.

"I got it, Laura," he called.

She ran in from the kitchen, drying her hands on a dishtowel. Her eyes were as wide as the doll's. "Thanks, Sean. You're the fastest lock picker in town."

"No, just the smartest. I found a key taped on the underside."

She slung the towel onto a chair and smiled at the doll. "Well, would you look at that. I remember her. Katie."

"Katie needs a little medical attention." Sean manipulated the dislocated arm until it snapped back into the socket. "There. That's fixed, any-way, and a little WD-40 might fix the eyelids."

"Thanks, but don't bother. I wouldn't get fifty cents for her if I had a yard sale."

"You don't want to keep her?"

"Well . . . maybe." Laura knelt beside the chest and sorted through the clutter, making a pile on the floor. The baby book, the pink dress, some snapshots. An old-fashioned red-and-white gingham apron.

"Gram Flynn made that for Mom, but she never wore it," she said with a half smile. "She didn't want to spill on it."

"Isn't that what aprons are for? Catching spills?"

Laura nodded. She put the apron on the floor and gave it a pat before she resumed pulling items out of the chest.

Sean set down the doll, picked up the photos and thumbed through them. One was a nice shot of Elliott, Jess, and Gibby Sprague, standing in front of a blooming dogwood tree with their arms around each other. Whenever Gibby came through town, he'd visited the Gantts. They'd had fantastic jam sessions with Doc Marsh and Noodle Hammond. Sometimes Jess had sung along in a smooth alto that contrasted beautifully with Gibby's low, gravelly voice.

"I always wonder if Gibby's trying to be another Johnny Cash," Sean said. "He always wears black. Always lets his hair grow too long—"

"Like somebody else I know." Laura gave Sean's hair a stern look.

"And like somebody else you know, Gibby always wows the ladies."

Ignoring the bait, she leaned closer to study the photo. "I took that picture. I think it was the year he was between his second and third wives. He's probably on his sixth by now."

"Probably. I can't help but like the guy, though. And admit it, Laura. You and Cassie had major crushes on him—a middle-aged man—when you were thirteen or fourteen."

He wasn't trying to make her mad, but an angry blush hit her cheeks. Her pale skin made a beautiful canvas for it.

"I'm too nice to tease you about your crush on Shania Twain," she said.

"I did not have a—"

"Oh yes, you did."

"Okay, I did. I'm over Shania, but there's someone else I'll never get over."

Once again acting as if she hadn't heard, she pointed out a photo of orange lilies. "Mom's hems."

"Say what?"

"Daylilies. *Hemerocallis* is the botanical name. Some daylily lovers call them hems." She reached into the chest again and brought out a slender book. "Oh, I hope—no, it's just a book of poems."

Her obvious disappointment piqued his curiosity. "What kind of book were you hoping for?"

"I'd like to find her journals. I haven't really started looking yet, though."

"Don't you feel at all funny about wanting to read your mom's private journals?"

"Yes, but I'm so curious, especially considering the rumors." She opened the book and bent over it, her hair hiding her face. "Anyway, remember how she'd fill the last page of a journal and just toss it on a shelf somewhere? She was always so casual about it that I figure she never wrote any-thing too personal." She paused, turning a page. "But once Dad disappeared and I moved to Denver, she was living alone. She might have felt more freedom to write anything."

"About your dad, you mean?"

Laura nodded. "I'd love to read what she wrote just after he disappeared." She raised her head but wouldn't quite look him in the eye. "I don't want to say this," she said softly. "I don't even like to think it."

He leaned closer so he could catch every hushed word. "Whatever it is, it will stay between us."

Finally, she met his gaze, her eyes shining with tears. "I think she might have suspected that he didn't really drown."

"No way. Wouldn't she have said something to you?"

"Probably not. She wouldn't even listen to me when I came up with my theory about an accident and amnesia or something. Then everything got kind of strained between us, and I left for college." Laura shut the book and stared down at it.

"I don't know," he said cautiously. "The whole premise that he staged it doesn't feel solid. If he took such great pains to disappear, why would he come back at all? And why now, after twelve years?"

Laura nibbled on a fingernail and shook her head. "Maybe . . . maybe he heard about her death somehow, and it was a jolt to his mind. Or maybe he guessed I'd be back for the funeral and he wanted to see me, at least from a distance."

Sean fought the impulse to reach for her hand. "I hope that's not just wishful thinking."

"Consider the big picture, though." She looked up. "If the timing of the sightings is related to my mom's death, it points to my dad because nobody else would be more affected by it. Think about his background too. His survival skills. And his problems. Disappearing for years isn't rational behavior, but he wasn't always completely rational." She motioned toward a book lying on the floor beside the recliner. "PTSD, maybe. Doc Marsh let me borrow a book, and I've been reading up on it."

"A little research can't hurt, I guess."

She reached into the chest again. She brought

out a pile of newspaper clippings, more photos, and a chain that held Elliott's dog tag and a silver cross.

"He wasn't wearing those, that day on the lake?" Sean asked. "I thought he wore them all the time."

"Sometimes he would leave them hanging up somewhere for days. I never knew why. Never asked. I didn't want to set him off." She leaned back against the couch beside him and fingered the cross and dog tag. "I'd love to give them back to him," she said. "To welcome him home."

Sean kept his mouth shut. He didn't want to burst her bubble.

She lowered the lid on the empty chest and handed him the key. "I want you to take it."

"Excuse me?"

"I want you to have the chest. It was the first project you ever did with my dad. I thought it might mean something to you, and I have all these other things." She made a sweeping motion that took in the whole room, filled with furniture and instruments that Elliott had crafted.

Sean would have preferred one of the instruments, but Laura hadn't offered that option. He studied the key for a moment, then put it in his pocket and met her eyes. "Thanks, Laura. I'd like that very much."

She scrambled to her feet, leaving the mementos on the floor. "I'll help you carry it outside," she said briskly, bending to lift one end of the chest.

He took the other end, and they hauled the empty chest out to his truck. He padded it with an old tarp, shut the tailgate, and sighed. Laura would use him as her free locksmith, and she'd even give him a piece of furniture she treasured, but she wouldn't breathe a word about that silly birthday party. Apparently she'd rather go alone.

"Thank you," he said. "The chest does mean a lot to me."

She stuck her hands in her pockets and looked up at him. "Did my dad mean a lot to you?"

"What kind of question is that? He rescued me from Dale. Saved my life, probably, or at least my sanity. He meant the world to me."

"Then will you stop assuming he's dead? I don't understand why you refuse to see it any other way."

He shook his head, unwilling to admit to himself, let alone to Laura, why Elliott's return might be disastrous. "Let's not argue. Listen, I need to get home. I have a customer coming at eight."

"Okay," she said in a tight, locked-up voice.

He wanted to wrap his arms around her and tell her to cry on his shoulder, but she might have slugged him for it. So he settled for telling her good night and driving away.

He didn't let himself look in the rearview mirror for the quick, on-off-on flicker of the porch light that had once been her way of saying "Good night. I love you." It wouldn't happen. She'd dropped that habit on his eighteenth birthday.

Eight

Still in her pajamas at half past eight the next morning, Laura backed out of her mom's crowded closet and shut the door. No journals there. Just too many reminders of her missing parents. Both of them.

She headed down the hall to try the deep but narrow closet in the guest room. The low-wattage bulb didn't do a lot of good. Wishing she'd brought a flashlight, she pushed her way past electric fans, space heaters, and cardboard file boxes. Spotting a small carton labeled "For Laura," she opened it and found the old photos from the Flynn side of the family. It would have been a more exciting find if she'd had family to share it with. Her only Flynn relatives were distant cousins in distant places.

Setting the box of photos aside for later, she pushed farther into the closet. At the very back sat three large boxes. Someone had helpfully labeled them with a thick black marker: "Journals." But that wasn't her mother's graceful penmanship.

"Ardelle," Laura whispered. "Of all the nerve."

She tugged the first box into the light and went back for the other two. None of them were taped shut. Each one held an assortment of journals, ranging from cheap spiral-bound notebooks to expensive hardcovers. A quick check of their dates showed that Ardelle had packed them in chronological order. Had she read them too?

In no time, Laura found the journals that covered the year she turned eighteen. Cross-legged on the floor, she opened a thick hardcover notebook that started about a month before her dad's disappearance. Skimming carefully but quickly through the July entries, she found no mention of his worsening moods or even a hint of marital discord.

Her mouth dry, Laura flipped the pages to August and the very day he'd disappeared: If E. has any luck, we'll have fish for supper—with veggies, of course. The usual overabundance of tomatoes, cukes, and zukes. Why did I plant so much zucchini??

She turned the page slowly, delaying the moment, then made herself read the entry for the following morning: E. is gone. L. walks around like a ghost. I can't bear to write. I can't bear it.

The facing page held only a short entry written weeks later: Seems strange that L. is so far away. College should have been an adventure. Not like this. Now S. is the one who walks around like a ghost.

The remaining pages of the book were blank.

Not wanting to revisit her abrupt departure from Sean's life, Laura opened the next volume. It started near the end of September. The morning glories are at their finest. I hope we won't have an early frost this year. I always hate to lose them before their time.

More slowly now, Laura reviewed the months preceding and following her dad's disappearance. She saw no clue that her mom believed he'd staged it.

There was no mention of handsome and flirtatious Gibby Sprague, either. No indication that her mom had been unfaithful in thought or deed. That wasn't surprising, given the way she'd so carelessly left her journals lying around, but it reinforced Laura's belief that her dad's accusation had no basis in reality.

She sampled older journals too. An entry on a February day: E. built a bluebird house for me. On another page: E. took me to that new Italian place for my birthday. Nice atmosphere, decent marinara.

In one of the other boxes, Laura found the journal from the summer before she entered seventh grade. The summer her dad's problems intensified. There wasn't a word about his growing depression, though. Not a word about the blowups, always sparked by some trivial thing and followed by heartfelt apologies. Not a word about a father-daughter clash over nail polish, either. Looking back now, from an adult's perspective, Laura knew the nail polish was only a trigger.

She browsed through more of the journals. In beautiful penmanship, using a variety of colored inks, her mother had written about gardening, weather, birds. Books and movies. She'd written about a retirement party for a cousin in North Carolina and a fender bender in downtown Prospect. She'd even described the three cats curled up on the bed like furry throw pillows. Except for an occasional mention of Laura, almost everything was about *her*. Jessamyn Gantt. Her plans, her hobbies, and her superficial pet peeves. In more recent years, she'd even tried her hand at analyzing her dreams.

No wonder she'd never bothered to hide the chronicles of her life. She'd portrayed a lovely, unreal world, all sweetness and light. Maybe she'd used her daily scribblings, as she'd called them, to create the life she wished she'd had.

If Ardelle had snooped, she couldn't have found anything interesting, Laura thought with some satisfaction.

She toyed with the idea of confronting Ardelle about her prying ways, but they probably stemmed from her OCD tendencies. Better let it go. Anyway, after a month of feeding the cat, watering the plants, and bringing in the mail, she deserved sincere thanks, not a rebuke.

Standing up to stretch, Laura decided to put together a gift basket. She had to go out anyway to pick up the signs to post at the cabin. It would be fun to shop in downtown Prospect again, especially if she called Cassie to ask for some ideas first.

Sudden tears took Laura by surprise. She didn't have a mom to shop for anymore.

Gift basket in hand, Laura stood on the Brights' driveway and lifted her eyes to the distant peaks and ridges fading into the late-morning haze. Now that she'd grown accustomed to the Rockies, the southern Appalachians looked like mere foothills. And now that she'd become familiar with Colorado's mountain chickadees, the Carolina chickadees of the South looked and sounded different. Not wrong, just different, like the southern accents that had become alien to her ears. Even the common endearments of the South—*honey, sugar, darlin'*—sounded strange now.

And they never came from Sean anymore. She swallowed hard and turned toward the house.

The dirt was too orange. The sweet tea was too sweet. The pines were too skinny.

She rapped the shiny brass door knocker on the elegant door and waited.

"Coming," Gary hollered from somewhere inside. He opened the door a minute later and grinned. "Well, if it ain't my favorite schoolteacher. Come on in, sweetie, but Cassie's not here. She's having lunch with her mother-in-law."

"I know. We just talked this morning. I'm actually here to see Ardelle. Is she home?"

"She sure is. Ardie, come out of your cave! Laura's here."

"There's no rush," Laura said, stepping inside. "I could stand here all day and enjoy the view."

He smiled toward the back of the house and the windows that looked over an in-ground pool and miles and miles of hazy mountains. "It's nice, isn't it?"

"Breathtaking."

"Enjoy it for me." He opened a briefcase on a table by the door and chucked some papers into it. "I'm off to work. Glad I didn't miss seeing you, though."

Tall, big-boned Ardelle came around the corner wearing a hideous red-and-black running suit sprinkled with white cat hair. The source of the cat hair, fat and fluffy Arabella, trotted along behind her. "Why, Laura! What a nice surprise."

"This is to thank you for taking care of Mikey

and everything." Laura handed her the basket. "I don't know what I would have done without you."

"Oh, it was a pleasure, Laura. He's the funniest old thing. But look at all this loot!" She rummaged in the basket. "Coffee and tea and chocolates. Special scrapbook papers. Stickers and ribbons and stamps." She looked up, smiling. "How did you know I've taken up scrapping?"

"Cassie told me you're really into your scrapbooks. She thought you might like to adopt my houseplants too. Would you?"

Ardelle's eyes widened. "The plants from the funeral? Oh, honey, you should keep them. They were given in memory of your sweet mother."

"But I can't haul them back to Colorado. I'd love to give you as many as you'd like. After all, you're the one who took care of them for me."

"I don't have a green thumb like your mother did, but . . . well, I could sure enough try." Ardelle seemed to be trying for a solemn expression but couldn't quite keep the eagerness out of her voice. "If you don't mind."

"Of course I don't mind. They're already in the car. Every last one of them."

"All of them? Oh, how nice! Gary, would you help Laura bring them in? And I'll clear a space for them somewhere. Maybe by the fireplace? It's already empty and swept for the summer . . ."

Gary followed Laura out to her car, and they

began hauling plants inside: ferns, lilies, philodendrons, a small weeping fig, and others that Laura couldn't identify. As she and Gary brought in more plants, Ardelle arranged and rearranged them in front of the empty fireplace.

"There's nothing left but a couple of African violets," Laura said. "I'll get those last two, Gary. I know you need to get to work."

"Okay, I'll be on my way. Bye, Ardelle." He picked up his briefcase and blew her a kiss, then followed Laura outside and shut the door. "That was very kind of you."

"It's nothing. Ardelle was very kind to look after things for me."

"She enjoyed it, I think. She always likes to be helpful."

She certainly did.

A small flock of crows flew over, drawing Laura's attention to the sky where a trio of buzzards spiraled on an updraft, so high above the mountains that they must have been able to see every mountaintop and valley for miles around.

"I wonder if my dad's out there somewhere watching those buzzards," she blurted.

"Aw, Laura, honey. It's not likely."

"So you're on that side of the fence, huh? You think he's gone?"

"I'm just trying to be realistic," Gary said gently.

She sighed. "I know. Thank you for being honest. And thank you for being loyal and kind to my dad. He must have blown up at you a hundred times, but you always forgave him and went on being his friend."

"That's what friends do. He was a loyal friend to me too. Like a brother. Lord, I miss him. And your mom. Everybody does." His face somber, Gary gestured vaguely toward the house. "Just look at all those plants from the funeral. Everybody loved her. I still can't believe she's gone."

"Me either." Laura gave him a hug. For half a second, she pretended she was hugging her dad—but her dad would have smelled like sawdust or campfires, not aftershave. Her dad wouldn't be well fed and well dressed. If he was up in the mountains, he was all alone. Out of his mind, maybe, or at least nursing a broken heart.

She wanted to let the tears come. She wanted Gary to pat her back and tell her everything would be fine. To say that she wasn't alone, even if her parents were both gone. But she swallowed hard and stepped away.

"I'd better let you go before I blubber all over you."

He made a big show of examining his shirt. "Now how am I supposed to go to work if you smeared snot on me?"

She smacked his arm in mock offense. "Smear it off again."

"When did you start taking smart-mouth lessons from Cassie, young lady?"

They both started laughing. It was a blessed relief after too many moments of barely controlled grief.

Gary started walking toward the garage. "If there's ever anything we can do for you, just call."

"Okay. Thanks, Gary."

He hit his remote. The garage door slid up smoothly, revealing his black Cadillac. Ardelle's sassy little yellow convertible was missing, so Cassie must have taken it. For a moment Laura envied the Brights, for her dad's sake, yet she liked to believe her dad would be happy for his old friends too. Gary and Ardelle had always been kind and generous, and it was wonderful to see them prosper.

She pulled the two African violets out of the car and took them inside. As she shut the door, her breath caught in her throat. Back in her mom's kitchen, the helter-skelter placement of the plants hadn't affected her this way. Here, the carefully arranged greenery on the white marble hearth took her back to her mother's memorial service and the plants and flowers massed around the white casket in front of the altar.

Ardelle finished fluffing the fronds of a Boston fern. "Is that it?"

"Yes, these are the last two."

"They're gorgeous," Ardelle said. "They'll be perfect, right in front." She placed the white violets on the left and the purple ones on the right, then switched them. "There, that's better." She turned around. "Can you stay and visit for a while? This big ol' house gets lonesome."

"I wish I could, but I'm meeting someone in a few minutes."

Ardelle's face brightened. "Sean?"

"No, not Sean." Laura started for the door with Ardelle right behind her. "I'll see you soon, Ardelle."

"Did Cassie invite you and Sean to Trevor's birthday party?"

Laura made a face and kept moving. "Um . . . no."

"I asked her to, but she must have forgotten. We're having a little family party on Saturday night, about six, and we'd love it if y'all could join us. Think you can?"

Laura couldn't think of an excuse not to. Slowly, she turned to face Ardelle's eager smile. "Well . . . it might work. Maybe. Thanks for the invitation."

"Wonderful! We'll have so much fun. And it'll be good to see Sean. We hardly ever see him anymore. Oh, and I intend to drop off some supper for you sometime soon. We can't let you starve."

"I'm not starving. I promise." Laura gave

Ardelle a quick hug and then fled in earnest.

"Shoot," she whispered, running for her car. Maybe she'd find a way out. Maybe she wouldn't even need to mention it to Sean. The poor guy. He would hate every minute of it.

Next stop, the cabin. She'd bought four glaringly orange No Trespassing signs to post around the property. Sean would notice them, sooner or later, and he would probably ask why she thought they were necessary.

She still didn't want to tell him about seeing Dale's truck stopping there. Sean would blast Dale, stirring up more hard feelings on his part.

About to climb into her car, she looked up. The buzzards were still there, so high above the endless mountains that they were only specks circling in the blue. Maybe her dad really was watching them too.

Did he remember watching her and her mom on the lake shore the day he walked away? Did he feel guilty? Did he know how it felt to suddenly learn you weren't loved, after all? Maybe he did, or at least he thought he did, but two wrongs didn't make a right.

Neither did three.

"Come home," Laura whispered. "I'll be watching for you."

Cassie stepped out of the thrift shop with her purchase, a beautiful shirt for almost nothing.

Drew would say she'd done well, but she still felt guilty for buying something that wasn't strictly necessary. He was probably rolling quarters for gas money. Eating beans and rice while she ate well.

She'd enjoyed lunch at her in-laws' house though, and it would be even more fun to tool around town in an expensive little car. She needed some time alone too. She was beginning to understand the burdens that Laura and Jess must have carried. The tensions. The worries. The constant watching and wondering. Elliott's problems had been much worse than a touch of OCD too. Much more draining.

She glanced at the vehicles crawling through the roundabout by the old courthouse. Half tourist trap and half hick town, Prospect had several one-way streets and roundabouts that made navigation a headache even for natives who knew where they were going. On weekends, with tourists clogging the streets, everything backed up.

Shading her eyes against the sun, she studied the three-story building across the street. Her dad owned it now, but the Halloran name was carved into a decorative slab near the top of the third floor. The letters stood out in stark relief in the sun. Below the name, roman numerals gave the year it was built—1925—and a carving above the entrance portrayed ears of corn, sheaves of grain, grapes, and hops. Those long-ago Hallorans hadn't been shy about the source of their wealth.

The beautiful old landmark had fallen into disrepair, but her dad had transformed it. Trendy shops and a café flourished on the ground floor. The second floor held high-class office space, and the third floor had become luxury apartments. One of the apartment dwellers had risked planting red geraniums in a window box. Not a smart move when a late frost might still hit, but as her dad liked to say, risk takers got ahead.

Cassie brought her hand to her temple in a quick salute. "Way to go, fat cat," she said, not caring who might hear her.

But all the money in the world wouldn't make him happy if they couldn't figure out what was going on with her mom.

Frowning, Cassie looked across the street at the old diner, still a popular spot in spite of the competition from the new café. She'd tried to talk her mom into going out for breakfast, but she wasn't interested. Her mom wasn't even interested in clothes and makeup anymore. She was a neat freak about everything else, but she slopped around her picture-perfect house in ugly, baggy clothes.

Cassie started hoofing it toward her mom's car, its vivid paint conspicuous among the other vehicles parked at the curb. Her dad called it

"Bright yellow" as if it were a trademarked shade like a designer paint.

"Cassie, is that really you?" someone called from halfway down the block.

Cassie turned around and spotted slow-talking, slow-walking Kim Milton strolling along the sidewalk. A sheriff's deputy now but out of uniform, she was even prettier than she'd been in high school, thanks to softer makeup and gently highlighted hair.

"Hey, Kim. It's good to see you."

"It's been awhile. Are you doing all right? Still living in California?"

"Yes, and it's wonderful." Cassie decided to keep the not-so-wonderful parts to herself.

"I hear Laura's in town too."

"Yes, she is." Cassie's mind went straight to Laura's prowler. "You're still with the sheriff's department, right?"

"Yes ma'am." Kim seemed to swell with pride.

"What's the sheriff's take on the wild stories about her dad?"

"He says we're already overworked and understaffed, and until we have solid evidence that Mr. Gantt is alive, we'll assume he's dead. That's only the sheriff's opinion, though."

"You think he's alive?"

"I'm open to the idea," Kim said. "Stranger things have happened."

Cassie hesitated. It was tempting to tell Kim

about the prowler—after all, she was in law enforcement—but Laura would be livid.

Kim's eyes focused on something behind Cassie. She looked over her shoulder. Sean was walking up behind her, carrying a paper bag from the old-time hardware store on the corner.

Cassie grinned. "Sean! Boy, am I glad to see you."

"Good afternoon, ladies." He pulled Cassie into an old-friends kind of hug. "Mrs. Cutler. Long time no see."

"Way too long," Cassie said. "How are ya?"

"Not bad."

He released Cassie and gave Kim one of those gorgeous smiles that he should have been saving for Laura. Cassie wanted to smack him.

"How's everything, Kim?"

"Great, thanks." She gave his arm a friendly little clout. "I just heard about what you're doing. It's great."

He gave her a blank look. "Doing?"

"The music lessons for low-income kids."

"Oh. That. It's nothing."

Kim shook her head. "I know what music teachers can charge per hour."

He studied the sidewalk. "It's just something I've wanted to do for a long time."

Cassie's eyes watered. Bless him. He was doing what Elliott had done for him, years ago. Laura couldn't let such a good guy slip through her fingers.

"Well, I'd better run," Kim said. "See y'all later."

They all said their good-byes. Kim walked down the sidewalk, her shiny hair swinging, and Sean eyed the vehicles along the curb as if he were trying to remember where he'd parked.

"Don't run off," Cassie said. "Do you have time to go someplace where we can talk in private? It's about Laura's safety."

Sean's face clouded with gratifying concern, and he pointed toward the old café. "You bet I have time. Let me buy you a coffee, and let's talk."

Nine

Except for the rickety wooden arch marking the entrance, the old church camp on the northern side of Hamlin Lake was a lovely place. Wild daylily plants filled the roadside ditches, their pale green buds nearly ready to burst into orange. A mix of pines and hardwoods on both sides of the road offered shade against the afternoon sun.

The holy roller camp, half the town called it, but those Pentecostals were good people. Laura's grandparents on both sides had connections there. She and "Presto" Preston had parked their vehicles in the gravel parking lot, then walked back to the road together so he could show her the very spot where he thought he'd seen her father.

Except for having lost most of his hair, Preston hadn't changed much since Laura had taken biology from him in high school. Although she was a fellow teacher now, she knew she would never call him by his nickname or his first name. He was still Mr. Preston to her.

"Teaching history, eh?" he said. "You should come home and teach in Prospect. The pay's probably about the same anywhere."

She laughed. "You're right. It's not especially good anywhere. Now, tell me what you saw. And when."

"It was early Sunday morning, still dark but not too dark," he said, striding away from her. "I'll show you where I was when I first spotted him." He crossed to the other side of the road, turned, and looked in both directions. "Yeah, I was about here, and your dad"—he pointed to a thick tree trunk to Laura's left—"was about there, passing in front of that big oak. Moving fast, like he always did."

"Could you see his face, though?"

"Not clearly." With one finger, Preston pushed his wonky glasses higher on his nose. "It was more the total package that convinced me. His height, his build. The way he moved. And the way he obviously didn't want to be seen."

"But he must have heard your vehicle, must have seen your headlights, so why didn't he get off the road in time?"

"I was on foot too. Didn't Sean mention that? I was out for my morning walk, so I wasn't making any more noise than your dad was. But once he spotted me, he slipped into the underbrush and made himself scarce."

"Did you call out to him?"

"Several times. I called his name and yelled 'Come back' a couple of times, and I tried to follow him. But he'd vanished." Preston gestured toward the camp property. "There are lots of places to hide over there. He could have run from one building to another, from one stand of trees to another."

"But why would he hide out here, especially this time of year? There are too many people. Campers, staff, parents."

"Correct. I don't think he was hiding out here. Just passing through, maybe, before everybody was up and about. Like he was returning to the scene of the crime."

Laura didn't answer. It wasn't a crime for a man to go on a long wilderness trek without notifying his wife and daughter first. It was perfectly legal even if it broke their hearts.

"You look skeptical," Preston said. "Did Sean get to you? I know he's a skeptic, but that doesn't mean you have to be one too."

"I have mixed feelings. I'm trying to see it from all angles."

"Good. You know I always want solid evidence, and we don't have any yet." Preston squinted toward the mountains. "But the Nantahala Wilderness is the perfect refuge for a man who doesn't want to be found. He could live off the land for years too. When I was scoutmaster, twenty years ago, he did some demonstrations for my scout troop. He knew how to make his own fishhooks and rabbit snares. How to build a solid shelter from practically nothing—and camouflage it. How to doctor himself with wild plants. He'd mastered every survival trick in the book."

She tried to smile. "I remember." Still, she felt sick as she pictured her dad in the wild with no medical care. He was in his midsixties, the same age Grandpa Gantt was when he started showing signs of mental deterioration.

"So," Preston continued, "I wonder what happened. Did he drown or did he walk? If he walked . . . why did he walk? That's the important question."

She only nodded. Those were some of her questions too, but she didn't trust her voice not to crack from the utter confusion of her conflicted emotions.

Together, they headed back to the parking lot. Preston reached his vehicle first. After a few minutes of small talk, he said good-bye and drove away.

Laura stood beside her own car, taking in the sights and smells and sounds. Church vans and buses crowded the lot, but there wasn't a soul in sight. Young campers were gathered in the chapel, singing with shrill, happy voices. The clatter of pots and pans came from the mess hall as the staff cleaned up after lunch. A leftover lunchtime aroma wafted through the air. Spaghetti, maybe, or sloppy joes.

Those turkey sandwiches, the night her dad disappeared, must have come from that very building. The mess hall.

Some of the camp staff had driven around to the southern side of the lake that night, bringing coffee and sandwiches for the dive team and everyone else who'd gathered there. Not that anyone had felt like eating. The staffers had prayed with her mom—or they'd prayed *for* her, anyway. Looking dazed, she hadn't done much talking. If she suspected that they should be hunting for her husband's footprints instead of diving for his body, she didn't mention it.

Laura never went back to Hamlin Lake after that night. It was time to face it, and it might be easier from this side. The northern shore.

Half expecting a camp employee to stop her and ask if she had a visitor's pass, Laura set off across the parking lot. She walked across a weedy lawn, then continued to the coarse sand of the shore and the weathered planks of a fishing dock. The water lapped softly against the dock, and the wind tugged her hair.

Except for the spring flowers in the woods, everything probably looked much as it had on a hot summer day years before. In August, the kudzu's purple blossoms would have been giving off their sweet, musky scent, and the leaves would have been wilting and aging in the summer heat. Today, though, the vines hadn't bloomed yet. Their leaves were fresh and young.

Across the blue water lay the ramp where her dad had launched his boat one last time, and the shore where the sheriff had gathered his dive crew.

Laura had hung back from the commotion that night. In shock, trying not to think too hard, she kept looking at the camp's buildings on the other side of the lake, their windows spilling light across the dark water. She hadn't wanted to look at the lake itself. Every time she did, she imagined her dad's lifeless body in it.

Now she could imagine him alive and well. Not drowning, but swimming to shore—to this shore. He might have come out of the water on the rough, reddish sand and run lightly into the pines, abandoning everything. Not just his boat, truck, and trailer, but his business. His friends. His wife and daughter.

Laura squeezed her eyes shut against the hurt that threatened to overwhelm her. She needed to focus, instead, on learning what had really happened when her dad took his boat out for the last time.

The sun beat down on her head as she returned to her car. Its Colorado license plate reminded her she wasn't a resident of Georgia anymore. Little more than a month before, she'd been busy winding down the school year in Denver. She'd had one living parent and one dead parent. Now, maybe, they'd traded places.

The sun had barely set, but after hours of boxing up her mother's books, Laura was ready for the day to be over. Contacts out and teeth brushed, wearing warm pajamas and her mom's white terry-cloth robe, she'd made a comfy nest for herself on the couch. She had ten or twelve journals, a quilt tucked around her feet, and a cat sleeping in her lap. She was enjoying Mikey's company although he wasn't entirely conscious of hers.

Wanting to read for fun tonight, not for clues, she'd chosen early journals that ranged from before her birth to her toddler years. She opened one at random.

My honey redhead, my redhead honey. Poor little carrot-top baby, you look more like your mama than your daddy. Laura browsed for a while, but her mother's obvious enjoyment of motherhood only stirred up grief and remorse.

The mother-daughter bond could have been so much stronger. No doubt they'd used up most of their emotional energy on her dad's issues, but surely they could have talked more often and more openly. It might have helped them stay close even through the tough times. But they'd drifted apart just when they needed each other most.

Laura closed her eyes, recalling the heated remark her mom had made while they were still awash in shock and grief. *"Stop living in a little-girl fantasy and get off to college."* Then and there, a wall had gone up between them. It had never become a real estrangement, fortunately. They loved each other. They talked on the phone often. Their conversations were often strained, though, with mysterious undercurrents flowing below the surface of their chitchat.

Regret couldn't change a thing. Trying to steer herself out of a weepy mood, Laura focused on a droll description of one of her toddler tantrums. Apparently they'd been frequent and ferocious.

She jumped when she became aware of a familiar rumble outside. Sean's truck.

"Shoot," she whispered, slapping the journal closed and fluffing her hair in a hurry. "Move, Mikey."

The cat flexed one paw, dug a claw into the

robe, and made himself a dead weight on her lap.

The truck's door slammed.

"Move, tuna breath!" She finally nudged Mikey away. He departed in a huff, but Sean's feet were already pounding up the back steps.

"Laura," he called, knocking on the door. "It's me."

She sighed, resigned to being caught in her pajamas. "Come on in." She heard the opening and closing of the door and then his footsteps crossing the kitchen.

He loomed in the doorway to the living room, frowning. "Why wasn't the door locked?"

"Old habits are hard to break. Why didn't you call first?"

He smiled. "Sorry. Old habits." He inclined his head toward the kitchen. "It looks bare in there. Where'd all the plants go?"

"I gave 'em to Ardelle."

"Good idea." He noticed the journals. "Hey, you found them."

"Yes, but they're not terribly riveting so far. It's mostly stuff like this. Listen." Unwilling to give him a glimpse of herself as a bratty toddler, she chose an earlier volume and picked a page at random, near the end. "How soon the brightest blossoms can fade and wilt and fall, and then they rot on the ground." She shook her head. "That's not typical, though."

"She must have been in a bad mood that

day. But are they all like that? Philosophical rambling?"

"No, it's mostly trivia. Cheerful trivia. She wrote a million words about practically nothing. The garden and the weather and what she planned to buy herself for her birthday."

Laura flipped back to the book's first page and frowned at its opening sentence. How quickly things can blossom overnight . . . It was followed by a line about splurging on freesia-scented hand lotion. She shut the journal without reading the lines aloud.

"Actually, most of it's superficial," she said. "Shallow. Was my mom shallow?"

He didn't answer right away. "I don't know if that's the right word. From the times we talked religion and politics, I'd say she was a deep thinker. And you know she was a saint, the way she devoted herself to helping your dad deal with his moods."

"Still, she was sort of . . . self-centered. The journals are all about her."

Sean gave her a sidelong look. "Isn't that what a diary is for? To vent about your own life? Anyway, I'm not surprised. Every conversation somehow ended up being about her too."

"True. Well, at least that's one thing we can agree on."

"Two things. One, she had her faults. Two, we loved her."

Laura laughed so she wouldn't cry. "We can't even agree on how many things we agree on?"

Sean tilted his head and examined her. "You okay?"

"Yeah. Are you? What's on your mind?"

She must have fooled him into believing she was okay, because he settled back against the couch cushions.

"I ran into Cassie this afternoon," he said. "She told me about your prowler."

"Oh boy. This is why I can't tell her anything. She's a blabbermouth."

"You told Cassie the blabbermouth but you didn't tell me?"

"I knew you would overreact."

"I'm not. I'd just like to change your locks."

"Why?"

"Because, as we've discussed before, half the county has a key."

"That's an exaggeration and you know it. Mom only gave keys to people she trusted."

"Please, Laura. Let me change your locks."

"And then you'll tell me I need bars on the windows and an alarm system and a loaded gun by my bed. And a watchdog. No, thank you. I appreciate your concern, but I'm fine."

"I know why you think you're fine," he said. "You've talked yourself into believing your visitor was your dad."

"Just about. And why not? I met Preston at the

church camp today so he could show me exactly where he thought he saw my dad, and his story is pretty darned believable."

"Let's discuss what I call prowler logic," Sean said. The familiar cynical smile lifted one corner of his mouth. "If there's a prowler at your house *and* miles away—at the church camp on the lake, for instance—it's probably not Elliott. Therefore you should be on your guard."

"You think it's some random pervert, as Cassie put it?"

"That's a good possibility, anyway."

"What if it's my dad, crossing town to get where he's going? Isn't that possible?"

"Possible but not probable. Look, the whole town's on edge like it was years ago when Slattery was our prowler. Now, seems there's a new one around, and people are jumping to crazy conclusions. I can come up with a few other explanations too, including the fact that it just might be Dale. No matter who it is, I'd sleep a lot better if you had new deadbolts on your doors. And if you *used* them."

"Oh, Sean. You're such a worrywart."

"Only because you worry me. By the way, I drove past your grandparents' old place today and noticed somebody has posted No Trespassing signs."

She raised her right hand. "That was me."

"Why?"

She sighed. "Because I thought I saw Dale's truck pulling in there. I'm not absolutely sure because I didn't see his face. Whoever it was, he was trespassing. I didn't like it, so I put up the signs."

"I'll find out if it was Dale." Tension stretched over Sean's features.

"No, let it go. Don't worry about it. Focus on your business. On whatever it is you need to do to get ready for the festival. Are you making any progress?"

"Yes ma'am, so I've earned the right to badger you about changing the locks."

Maybe she could still make him drop the subject. "What did you accomplish today?"

"I picked up my new business cards, wrote up a brochure, and updated my fancy-pants website."

"You have a website?"

"I've had one for years. You think I live in the Dark Ages?" He dug out his wallet, pulled out a card, and handed it to her.

"Sean Halloran, Luthier." The printing blurred in front of her eyes before she could read the details. She'd never forgotten the dreams he'd shyly shared with her when they were fourteen and he'd just started music lessons with her dad.

"Do you still dream of playing Nashville?" she asked.

The half smile came back. "No, I'm a little

more in touch with reality now. I'll never be that good."

"But your instruments are good enough to be onstage, in the hands of big-name artists. It'll happen someday."

"You know what I'd rather see? My instruments in children's hands."

"Children can't afford your instruments."

"There'll be a few who can," he said. "One way or another. I'll see to it."

"I bet you will. You'd be a good teacher." She tried to hand the card back.

"Keep it," he said so tersely that she wondered if he meant the card or the sentiment. "When can I change your locks?"

"When I say so."

Sean muttered something. He got to his feet and walked toward the door, where he faced her again. "I'll lock up on my way out. Is the other door locked?"

"Yes."

"Good." He studied the journals piled around her, then met her eyes. "It's hard to lose your mother. I remember. For me, it came in waves. I'd think I was past it, and then it would hit me again, and I'd be back where I started, crying like a baby."

"You were only ten. You practically *were* a baby. And believe me, I've done my share of crying too."

"But never when I'm around. What's with that? Scared I'll give you a hug?"

She had to smile. "Something like that."

"Yeah, something like that. One of these days." He winked and slipped out the door before she could answer. Not that she'd had an answer handy.

Laura took another look at his business card. Her dad would have been so proud of his protégé.

If only they could be reunited, the master and the apprentice. For just one day.

Outside, the truck's engine started. The headlights came on, and Sean flashed them—off, on, off, on.

"Stop it, you brat," she said under her breath.

When they were in high school, he'd told her the flashing lights meant "Good night. I love you." It had taken her a couple of weeks to work up her courage and flick the porch light in response. Then she'd made a regular habit of it, but she'd never said "I love you" out loud. She'd never written it either.

They must have written a million notes to each other in high school. They'd left notes under windshield wipers, in jackets, in schoolbooks. He'd closed each one with *Love, Sean* or *I love you,* but she'd always been afraid to use that dangerous word.

Back when Sean's sister-in-law was almost a big sister to Laura, they'd had some heart-to-heart talks. As much as Annie had tried to play matchmaker, she'd been honest about what she called "the Dale problem." He was a horrible father-in-law, although he'd never hated Annie and her family like he hated the Gantts.

Maybe love could conquer hatred. Or maybe not. Laura was still afraid to put it to the test.

Ten

Surrounded by the flowery scents of detergent and fabric softener, Cassie was folding the last of her laundry when she heard her mom calling from halfway across the house.

"Good morning, Cassie! I hear you rattling around, but where are you?"

"See, I told you this place is way too big," Cassie bawled back. "Laundry room."

Back in L.A., she had to round up a pile of quarters, lug everything down to the basement, and hope the washer and dryer were available. Here, doing the laundry was almost fun now that she'd figured out the controls. Her mom's expensive new appliances offered too many options.

Cassie pulled her thrift-store find out of the dryer and shook out the wrinkles. A soft blue, the beautiful, hand-embroidered peasant shirt might pass for vintage. And vintage was cool.

Her mom walked in, wearing a dark, shapeless sack of a bathrobe. She unwrapped one of those low-calorie breakfast bars that always seemed to leave her starving. "Look at you. So industrious so early in the morning."

"It's not early. I did your jeans load and some of my stuff."

"Thanks, sweetheart. What a pretty shirt. Did you make it?"

Cassie laughed. "Me? Sew? Are you out of your mind?"

"I used to sew, but I don't have the patience for it anymore. That's why I started scrapping. It's my way of journaling, I guess. Everybody needs a good hobby." She took a bite of her breakfast bar. "What are your plans for today, hon?"

"Hanging out with you."

"Oh, good. You can help me plan the party. I'm so glad Laura and Sean are coming."

Cassie groaned. "I still can't believe you actually invited them. They'll find a way out of it."

"Why?"

"They hate birthdays. Remember? Elliott drowned just before their birthdays. The same week. Close, anyway. So don't be surprised if Laura suddenly has other plans for Saturday. Besides that, she and Sean haven't been a couple since high school. And anyway I doubt they'll care about a little boy's party, Mom."

"Sure they will."

Cassie refrained from rolling her eyes, but even she, the aunt, wasn't especially excited about Trevor's fifth birthday party.

It wasn't his fault. He was adorable. That was the problem, actually. Tigger's perfect little family was one hundred percent adorable, happy, and successful, and Tig could never shut up about any of it. She'd been a stay-at-home mom from the beginning too, without even cramping their budget. Sometimes it didn't seem fair.

"Sean's such a nice young man," Ardelle added. "I'm glad your father made that call."

Startled, Cassie started paying attention to her mom again. "Call? What call?"

"When he sicced the authorities on Dale."

"Huh?"

Ardelle gave her a look of big-eyed innocence. "Oh. Never mind."

About to ask questions, Cassie began to suspect that was exactly what her mother hoped for. It seemed like a ploy to open up a subject that might have been better left alone, so Cassie stayed obstinately quiet.

The silence wasn't broken until the cat sidled into the room, meowed piteously, and shook herself, releasing a long white hair to drift to the tiles. She meowed again.

"Arabella Antoinette, stop your begging," Ardelle said. "I already fed you."

"I still can't believe you named her that. Our other cats never had middle names. Or pedigrees."

"She knows she's in real trouble when I use all three names. Like you and Tig always knew. Watch this." She leaned over. "Arabella Antoinette Bright!"

Arabella laid back her ears and nipped out of the laundry room, her fluffy tail dragging the tiles.

"Cute," Cassie said. "You have a real way with animals."

"Don't I?" Ardelle peeled the wrapper of the breakfast bar down to the bottom and popped the last bite into her mouth. "I'll include Sean and Laura in the head count for the party."

"Plan on having leftovers, then," Cassie said, wishing she could ship them to Drew.

"They'll come. You wait and see." Ardelle dropped the wrapper into the wastebasket and yawned. "I didn't sleep well. Did you hear the thunderstorm about four in the morning? I lay awake for hours, thinking of poor Jess out there in the graveyard."

Obviously the weather didn't matter to Jess anymore, but Cassie reminded herself to be diplomatic. "Has it been hard on you?" she asked gently.

"Hard? To lose my very best friend in the world?" Her mother's voice trembled. "What do you think?"

"Mom, I only—"

"Don't you roll your eyes like a bratty teenager, Cassandra Jane, and don't be so cold-hearted."

Wanting to argue that she tried to keep her heart at an acceptable temperature, Cassie made herself think of a softer response. "I'm sorry. You know I loved her too."

"I know you did." Ardelle started rubbing her thumb and forefinger together, making a whispery sound. It was one of her annoying new habits. "Jess was such a sweet soul. I just wish she hadn't soured on church and all. She was starting to think she only believed in auras and angels and whatnot."

"I don't think she believed all that New-Agey stuff. She just liked to push people's buttons by talking about it."

"She believed it, all right. Once she told me she thought death might be some kind of recycling process and she'd be back, somehow, watching over us like a guardian angel."

Talk about recycling. It was the same little speech she'd made the night before, almost word for word.

"Mom, have you ever thought about talking things over with your pastor? Or a counselor?"

"Don't be ridiculous. I don't need counseling.

When we face losses, we just have to accept them and move on. Like the adults we are." Her chin quivered, but she straightened her shoulders and walked out of the room.

Cassie shook her head. Her mom acted normal most of the time, but like an orchestra with just one instrument out of tune, something wasn't quite right.

At least she wasn't keeping the obituary on the kitchen table anymore. That was an improvement.

Cassie pulled her threadbare pajamas out of the dryer and buried them under the other clothes in the laundry basket. Her dad knew she and Drew were barely scraping by, but they hadn't told her mom. She had enough troubles already.

Bluegrass rang from Laura's house as Sean climbed out of the truck. He ran up the back steps, rapped on the door and waited in the warm twilight.

She wasn't playing just any old bluegrass album. It was a CD Elliott and his band had made, back in the day when it was a big deal to produce a CD. Sean was only a kid then, and he wasn't accomplished enough to join in. How he'd envied them: Elliott, Doc, and Noodle, with an occasional assist from Gibby if he was in town.

Sean knocked again, to no avail, and finally tried the doorknob. Unlocked.

"Figures." He stuck his head into the familiar kitchen, and the music blasted him. "Laura," he called. "It's me."

Still no answer, so he walked in, shutting the door behind him. The song had just hit the bridge where Elliott went nuts on the fiddle, leading the rest of them on a merry chase.

Sean had planned to take fiddle lessons from Elliott sometime, but after he'd drowned it didn't seem to matter anymore. Sean had never even looked for a different teacher.

The music grew louder still as he followed it across the living room and down the hall. He stopped in the doorway to Jess's room. Laura sat cross-legged on the bed, surrounded by piles of clothes. She'd draped one of her mother's worn flannel shirts around her shoulders.

"Laura," he called.

Still deaf to his voice, she pulled the shirt's sleeves around her front. As if a shirt could be a stand-in for her mom's hug.

Laura let the sleeves fall. She folded a black-and-white bandanna into a triangle and tied it on her head. Unaware of her visitor, she studied her reflection in the mirror on the bureau. Her face reminded him of a picture of a saint in some old book. Solemn eyes, deep sadness, deeper calm. Like she had touched God, had survived with scars. It was like the Sunday school story about Jacob, who'd wrestled with an angel or maybe with God Himself. The man was marked for life. Crippled. Yet the crippling would make him think of God with every step, so even the injury was a gift.

Sean shook his head. He wasn't accustomed to thinking that way.

Tired of feeling like a stalker, he tried again. "Laura!" he shouted over the music.

Her head jerked up, her eyes wide. "Sean! You scared me."

"Sorry. The door was unlocked. I yelled but you didn't answer."

"You could have yelled again," she said tartly, pulling the flannel shirt off her shoulders and dropping it on the bed.

"I did. Mind if I turn down the volume a little?"

"Go ahead."

He found the stereo on Jess's dresser behind a clutter of toiletries and turned it down. "Music is best when it's good and loud, but there's a limit."

"The louder the better, my dad always said. What brings you by?"

"I wanted to make sure you were remembering to keep your doors locked."

Laura rolled her eyes. "Oh brother."

"Did I prove my point?"

"Yes. Happy now?"

"Not exactly."

The lively number ended. After a brief silence, a beautiful little guitar solo moved the band into a melancholy ballad with Elliott singing the lead. Doc and Noodle provided the unobtrusive harmony.

When water burns and granite turns as wat'ry
as the dew,
When horses run upon the sun, then shall my
love be true.

Elliott had written the song, trying to re-create the tone of an old Scottish ballad. Sean wasn't sure it worked on that level, but it captured the mood of heartbreak.

When cockle-shells turn siller bells, and
barley grows at sea,
When frost and snaw shall warm us a', then
shall my love love me.

Decrepit old Mikey, happy in his own selfish little universe, was curled up on a pillow against the dark red wood of the headboard. There used to be three cats. Mikey, Turbo, and Slinky had slept wherever they pleased. Sometimes there were two cats on a shelf, like bookends, or one cat snoozing on the mantel, squeezed between the knickknacks. Part of the décor. Now they were down to Mikey, the oldest, ugliest one. His fur was the same gray-brown as a possum, and he was about as useful as a possum.

Sean looked around the room. Laura had folded a lot of clothes already and placed them in bags and boxes. A brown purse lay flat and empty at the foot of the bed, its contents dumped beside it—an opened wallet, keys, papers, lipstick. A dozen other purses made a heap on the floor.

She started folding one of her mom's sweatshirts, a brown one with "Appalachian Trail" in green letters above a dogwood flower.

"Going through her clothes already?" he asked, just as Elliott was singing "then shall my love love me" again.

"Well, we know *she* isn't coming back," Laura said in a matter-of-fact tone that didn't fool Sean for one minute.

He sat on a corner of the bed while she folded the sweatshirt. She tucked it to her chest with her chin, exactly the way Jess did. The way Jess used to do.

The cherry-wood headboard shone red in the sunlight, a nice backdrop for Laura's hair. The headboard was one of Elliott's finest pieces, its focal point a distinctive knot design that he hadn't carved into anything else. A true-love knot, he'd called it. Its curves looped so gracefully around each other that they fooled the eye into thinking he'd tied the knot from a length of rope, then magically turned it to silky wood.

Laura's hair hung down, screening her face. Sean wanted to push her hair aside and give her a kiss with the old familiarity they'd lost. He wanted to tumble her down on the bed, right on the neat piles of clothes.

Needing something else to think about, he reached for Jess's wallet, turning it sideways to study her driver's license through its transparent window. The picture had been taken before her red hair had started to fade into gray. The wallet held a Red Cross blood donor card too.

"I didn't know your mom was a blood donor," he said.

"Oh yeah. So was Dad. Gary and Ardelle are too. Their civic-mindedness must have rubbed off on me, because I've started giving blood a couple times a year."

"Good for you. I should too, but who would want blood from a Halloran?"

She didn't answer except to purse her lips slightly. He couldn't decide if she had Jess's mouth or Elliott's, but she definitely had her mother's calm strength. Too much of it, maybe. And dark shadows under her eyes.

Sean closed the wallet. "I hope you're getting some rest," he said. "Stress can wear a body out."

"I'm not stressed. I'm just sorting through . . . stuff. And I mean that both literally and figuratively."

"Are you made of steel?"

Laura's mouth—the side he could see, in profile—twisted upward. "Stainless."

She tucked her hair behind her ear, giving him a better view, and picked up a flowery shirt. Her long fingers folded it quickly and neatly.

"Once the festival craziness is over, I can help you tie up the loose ends," he said.

"I remember doing some of that for Dad before I left for college. Canceling a dentist's appointment. Taking back his library books. They were overdue, but the librarian waived the fines."

"You'll need to cancel your mom's credit cards too. Turn in her driver's license. Do her taxes. Decide whether or not you're selling her SUV."

"I'll sell it. Guess I'd better start advertising."

"Slap some signs on it and drive it around town now and then too. It's not good for a vehicle to just sit."

She nodded. Still fussing with that shirt, she laid it on the bed in a neat rectangle and plucked the shoulders square. She'd always been a bit of a perfectionist in an imperfect world.

Finished with the shirt, she studied him for a long moment that was hushed and still. Even the stereo fell silent between songs.

"Can you humor me for a minute?" she asked.

"Sure," he said as the band launched into another of Elliott's originals, a mournful tune he'd called "Blue Mountains."

"Okay," Laura said. "Let me give you a tour of the closet."

"Excuse me?"

"You need to see Dad's side of the closet." She sat up straighter. "I think Mom thought he'd come back someday, because it's still full of his clothes."

"Your mom was a pack rat."

"Come on, Sean. Just let me show you what I've found."

"Laura, don't get caught up in these false hopes. I'm afraid they won't pan out and you'll be devastated."

No longer calm and saintly, she glared at him. "That's not what you're afraid of. You're afraid to face facts."

He dropped the wallet on the bed and stood up. "You don't seem to know the definition of the word *fact*. You need—"

"What I don't need is your advice. If you refuse to do something as simple as looking in the closet, you can just get lost, Halloran."

Locking eyes with her, he made his decision. He cranked up the stereo again and walked out. He was halfway down the steps by the time the three-man band started wailing about blue mountains and broken hearts under a lonesome moon. He climbed into his truck, slammed the door, and turned on the country-rock station as loud as he could stand it.

Laura would be afraid too, if she knew what he knew. A tour of the closet might have brought him to the brink of telling her.

Driving too fast, Sean headed back to town. Past the Brights' old house, past the library, past the old park. One quick glimpse of the picnic tables under the trees brought back the Fourth of July picnic when he and Laura were sixteen.

The smoke from grilling meats. Little kids shrieking and waving American flags. Firecrackers whining and popping in the dusk. The acrid smell of gunpowder. Then, when Elliott was already edgy from the crowds and the noise, Gary had smarted off about some fool thing.

Elliott had shoved him backward into a picnic table and nearly strangled him—and then wept and apologized and helped him pick the potato salad off his shirt.

He always apologized profusely and sincerely, but he'd proved himself capable of hurting anybody, over anything. Or over nothing at all. And that was exactly why Sean didn't want to tell Laura what he'd once seen at Bennett's lake.

Five minutes after Sean's truck barreled out of Laura's driveway, Ardelle's car pulled in with its top down. Gary was at the wheel. His straight, sandy hair was windblown, but Ardelle had a big scarf tied firmly around her head.

They charged up the steps, laughing about something. Wearing oven mitts, she carried a dish covered with aluminum foil. Gary was carrying a plastic bag that probably held food too.

"Go away," Laura said softly, watching through the screen door. "Go find Sean and smack him for me." She pasted on a smile and opened the door. "What a nice surprise. Come on in."

"Just long enough to unload these vittles," Ardelle said. "We're on our way to Wednesday night prayer. I wish Cassie would've come, but there's some silly show she always watches on Wednesday nights." She paused for a breath. "It's tuna casserole and lemon-poppy-seed muffins."

"Thank you so much." Still peeved with Sean, Laura was tempted to take it out on Ardelle by confronting her about the boxed-up journals and her other intrusions. But if she really couldn't help herself, accusations would only be cruel.

Ardelle placed the hot dish on an empty burner of the stove and tucked her oven mitts under one arm. "It's a lot for one person. You can invite Sean over. He'd like that."

Gary gave Laura an apologetic smile. "Or you could, you know, freeze some for later." He set the bag of muffins on the counter.

"Good idea," Laura said, grateful that he understood.

Ardelle moved the muffins to a different spot. "I'm sure enjoying those plants. And the goodies and the scrapping supplies. Next time you come over, I'll show you my latest scrapbook."

"That would be lovely."

"We'd better run. Come on, Gary. We don't want to be late for church."

Laura followed them onto the porch. Across the road, vehicles were pulling into the church parking lot, and the building's lights blazed in the twilight. "Looks like a good turnout for a weeknight."

"Oh, we love the new preacher." Ardelle trotted down the steps. "He preached a wonderful message for your mother's funeral, didn't he?"

"Yes." Actually, Laura hardly remembered the message. She recalled the music, though, because she'd chosen the hymns herself, wanting lyrics that would soothe her soul with peace.

Heav'n's morning breaks, and earth's vain
   shadows flee,
In life, in death, O Lord, abide with me.

Laura's vision went blurry and her throat ached. She hoped the Lord had still been abiding with a sinner who'd wandered far afield.

Gary leaned against the railing and gazed across the yard. "Look how those daylilies have multiplied. The whole slope will be full of flowers in a week or two, but Jess won't be here to enjoy them." He shook his head. "Sorry, Laura. That was insensitive."

She moved to stand beside him. "No. I think things like that all the time."

A wave of grief hit her again, as Sean had predicted. Her mom should have been there, chatting with her visitors or walking to the end of the drive for her mail. She should have been there, pulling weeds or picking wildflowers. She should have *been* there. Yet Laura was grateful that she'd had her mother for thirty years. Sean had had his mother for only ten.

She blinked hard and made herself focus on the present. Gary was still talking.

"The new daylilies are fancy, with ruffled petals or double blooms, but your mom loved the old-fashioned kind. That one is a golden oldie, you might call it, but it's more orange than golden."

Laura nodded, but they were just ordinary daylilies to her, no more special than the wild ones that grew in roadside ditches.

At the bottom of the steps, Ardelle turned around, working her hands together in a fidgety motion. "Come *on*, Gary. We can't be late."

"It's all right, Ardie," he said gently. "The world will go on turning if we're thirty seconds late for Wednesday night prayer." He moved away from the railing with tears in his eyes.

Ardelle's new agitation was so troubling. Laura's heart ached for both of them.

"Thanks so much for bringing supper," she said. "It means a lot that you're thinking of me."

"Always. I'm always thinking of you, Laura." Ardelle blew a kiss over her shoulder. "Don't forget the birthday party!"

They climbed into the car. Gary revved the engine and made the short hop across the road to the church. He put the top up and they hurried inside, holding hands.

Nearly in tears, Laura sat on the porch steps with her chin in her hands and stared at the churchyard across the road. Her mother's month-old grave had been covered with gravel to match its neighbors. The big floral tributes were long gone, but a few late daffodils bloomed near the family plot. They were delicate and soft compared to the garish artificial flowers on some of the graves.

Gram Flynn had always said believers' graves were seeds sown for the Resurrection, when dead saints would pop out of the ground like tulips in the spring. Every year, Laura remembered Gram when her favorite tulips bloomed, their white petals splashed with streaks of pink and red.

Gram had worshiped a wild and fearsome God who visited Holy Ghost revivals and tent meetings, who whispered to sinners on the mourners' bench and carried them home like lost lambs. She'd have been heartbroken if she'd known her daughter might one day drift away from the church and be accused of breaking her marriage vows.

"You've been unfaithful. Don't deny it. Don't lie to me."

Laura shook her head. It couldn't be true. Yet she couldn't forget the pain in her father's voice, nor could she forget the way Gibby had smiled down at her mom in the snapshot she'd tucked away in the cedar chest.

Even if something had happened between them, it was twelve years in the past. Most likely, nothing had happened. Nothing at all.

Going inside, she wrinkled her nose at the smell of the casserole. She wasn't a fan of tuna. Ardelle must have forgotten, but it was sweet of her to bring supper anyway.

Laura lifted the foil from the dish. "Here, kitty-kitty-kitty. Mikey, you want a special treat?"

Eleven

Halfway to his brother's place, Sean spotted old Granny Colfax hustling through the weeds by the side of the road. He'd be smart to steer clear of the old biddy, but on the other hand, she'd been around forever. Maybe she'd even give him a scrap of information about Elliott.

There he went again, half believing the man could be alive.

He slowed, passing her, and pulled over on the shoulder to wait. It didn't take long. For an old woman, she was in good shape.

He leaned across the cab and opened the passenger door. "Granny Colfax," he called. "Where are you headed?"

She stopped by the opened door and peered up at him. "My ears are bad, but there's nothin' wrong with my eyes. You're a Halloran."

"Yep." The less said about that, the better.

"Well, your smile makes you favor your mama, God rest her soul, and that's a good thing. Your hair flops into your eyes and onto your collar, and that's a bad thing. You look like a hippie, young man. Now, what did you ask? Speak up so I can hear you."

"Where are you headed?" he bellowed.

"To a friend's house."

"Whereabouts?"

"Oh . . . north of town."

"We are north of town."

"Like I said. North. Farther north. Where are *you* bound, young fella?"

"My brother's place. Climb in and tell me where to turn. Come on, it's getting too dark for you to be out on the road."

She gave him a shrewd, considering stare, then nodded. "Don't mind if I do. These achy ol' legs just ain't what they used to be."

She climbed in, settled a paper tote bag at her

171

feet, and pulled the heavy door closed but ignored the seat belt.

Sean checked the rearview mirror. While he waited for traffic to pass, he glanced down at Granny's paper bag. It was full of peaches. She must have bought them at the produce stand down the road.

"Don't you look funny at my old shoes," she said. "They're ugly, but they're broke-in and comfortable. Like me."

He hadn't even noticed her shoes. Sure enough, they were hideous. She'd cut off part of the tops, leaving her toes bare. They weren't any prettier than the shoes.

"Yes ma'am." He checked his mirror again.

"Seen Jessamyn's girl lately?" she asked.

He let out a short laugh. "I have."

"She's a sweet thing, in her way. I ran into her a few days ago, and she looked peaked, like she needed a hug. Back in the day, it was you she got her hugs from."

"Back in the day." Traffic had cleared, and he pulled the truck onto the road. "That was high school. Things change."

"Some things do, some things don't, but you and the Gantt girl always seemed to belong together."

He scowled at the road and didn't answer.

"I'm just glad to see you turning into a decent man, bein' as your daddy comes from a long line of scoundrels and liars—filthy rich though they were."

"Thank you so much."

"You're welcome," she said with a little laugh. "Now, here's the mystery. How did that nice Wilkins girl wind up married to Dale Halloran? A baby on the way, maybe? I don't remember the particulars of your big brother's birth, but I know a lot of babies seem to come early in this town. Eight-month babies at best, but most people pretend not to notice."

Sean sighed. His mother would have been better off as a single mom, but then he never would have been conceived. "Is that any of your business?"

"No, but why are you so down at the mouth? You got yourself some troubles? I never had no babies of my own, but that don't mean I can't mother folks who need mothering."

"I don't need mothering."

"All right, all right. I got no call to offer advice."

His phone rang. He pulled it from his pocket and checked caller ID. Mrs. Anderson, a customer with more money than manners. He hit "ignore" and put the phone on the seat beside him.

Granny eyed it with suspicion. "Folks are always talking, talking, talking on those silly things. All those calls, cluttering up the heavens.

Turning the whole sky into the tower of Babel. I wonder if anybody ever really listens to each other anymore."

"You might have something there."

"The other day, when I ran into Ardelle Bright down to the grocery store, that poor woman talked my ear off like nobody ever listens to her. She's the lonesomest woman."

Sean frowned. Over coffee, Cassie had told him about her mom's new issues. "She's a talker, all right."

"She comes from a hard place, but don't we all? Some of us wind up working for sin's wages. Some of us find grace in the eyes of the Lord. Not wages, but a gift." She reached across the broad seat to poke his shoulder with a bony finger. "Somebody had to pay for it, though. That's the way of it. Somebody had to pay."

"Yes ma'am." He waited for more sermonizing, but she must have spoken her fill.

The miles flew by, silent except for the truck's powerful engine. They passed the old Gantt cabin and then the road his brother lived on. A flock of starlings burst out of a tree and passed over them like a mob of miniature torpedoes with wings.

Granny's old eyes followed them too. She didn't miss a thing.

"Funny things, birds. Fun to watch, as long as they're flying free." She gave him a sly smile.

"That Granny Colfax, she's a strange old bird, ain't she?"

"I wouldn't say that."

"Sure you would. Everybody does. I'm young on the inside, though." She peered out the window and rapped on it with her knuckles. "Drop me at this next corner."

"I'll take you right to your friend's door."

"No, no. I'll walk that last little bit. I do like my exercise."

"If that's what you want."

"It's what I want. It's how I've lived this long. Exercise and right living."

He pulled to the side of the road at the next corner. "Ames Creek Road. Is this the right spot?"

"It is." She reached for the door handle. "Thank you for the lift."

"Hang on a second, Granny. I've got a question."

She squirmed toward the edge of the seat. "Don't take too long, son. My friend's waitin' on me."

Sean looked her right in the eye. She looked him right back.

"You have any opinions about Elliott Gantt?" he asked.

"Course I do. A fine man, if not quite right in the head sometimes. I always loved to hear him play. Loved to sing along too."

"I mean, do you have any opinions about the rumors?"

"That he's alive and well, walking around town at night?" She laughed. "Wandering around where he might get caught? No. Try the mountains."

"Needle in a haystack."

"Yes sir, and that'll keep you busy for a while."

"Even if the needle's there, it doesn't mean anybody's gonna find it," he said.

"Ain't that the truth. Now, I thank you for the ride." She grabbed the door handle. It didn't move.

Sean leaned over and opened it for her. "Be careful now, out there on the road."

"Don't you worry about me." She climbed out with her tote and gave him a smile as he reached over to close the door. "Thank you," she hollered over the engine's noise.

"You're welcome."

He made a U-turn in the intersection, gathered speed, and headed back toward Keith's place. Granny Colfax wasn't the most aggravating woman in the world—that honor belonged to Laura—but Granny ran a close second. Giving her a lift hadn't gleaned a bit of information.

Sean parked in Keith's driveway and waved at the sweaty, smiling boys bouncing on the trampoline in the side yard of the split-level house. Annie beckoned from the kitchen window.

Sean walked into the bright, tidy house, greeted her, and went straight to the fridge for a long-neck.

He twisted the top off and raised the bottle high. "Here's to all women everywhere. The good, the bad, and the impossible."

Keith came around the corner, slung his arm around Annie's shoulders, and gave Sean the once-over. "Which one is impossible? Laura?"

Sean returned the scrutiny. Keith was lucky. Except around the eyes, he resembled the Wilkins side of the family. His military bearing contrasted nicely with Annie's happy-go-lucky personality too. They were good for each other.

"Yeah," Sean said. "Laura. And Granny Colfax."

Annie arched her eyebrows. "Do tell. I'm listening."

He lifted the beer again. "And here's to nosy women. Cheers."

She snatched up a kitchen towel and snapped it at him. "You're lucky I love you like a brother, or I'd knock that chip right off your shoulder."

"You would, wouldn't you?" He sauntered out of the kitchen and onto the porch, the door banging shut behind him. He settled into a chair exactly like the ones on Laura's porch and his own. Half the population of Prospect owned at least one piece of Gantt furniture or a Gantt-built guitar or banjo.

He should have headed home. Instead, there he was, traipsing from Laura's house to Keith's and fuming about Elliott and that whole mess, whatever it was. Sometimes it seemed like an iceberg, with nine-tenths of the menace submerged but waiting.

A small plane droned across the sky like a bored insect. Its lights winked brighter as it neared the horizon where the sky had already darkened.

Sean's phone rang. Mrs. Anderson again. He turned off the phone and put it away, wanting to chuck it in the trash so nobody could track him down.

Keith had the right idea. He'd never bought a cell phone. He refused to, no matter how much Annie nagged him to join her in modern times. He'd probably get along just fine with Granny Colfax.

The door swung open. Keith came out with a Coke and sat in the other chair. He set the can on the wide wooden arm. When he popped the top, the hard surface amplified the sound, making Sean flinch. He hadn't been this jumpy in a long time.

"You might want to apologize to my wife," Keith said.

Sean walked to the door and stuck his head in. "Annie," he called. "I'm sorry I was rude."

A muffled but cheerful answer came from somewhere inside. Presumably her acceptance of his apology.

He returned to his chair. He wasn't feeling sociable, but he wasn't in the mood to be alone either. It was a comfort to have a brother a couple of feet away. An older brother who had his head screwed on straight.

"Windy tonight," Sean said, trying for a casual tone. "Another storm's coming."

"You didn't come over to talk about the weather."

"Nah. I came for a free beer. Thanks."

"You're welcome. Now talk. But I tell Annie everything, so keep that in mind before you start."

"Who says I'm talking?" Sean propped his feet up on the railing and tried to enjoy the tart refreshment of the beer sliding down his throat.

Keith sighed and settled more comfortably in his chair. "What's on your mind? Laura?"

"Laura. Jess. Elliott. Everything. I don't want to believe those stupid rumors, but I'm starting to wonder."

"Me too."

Sean looked across the long lawn, across the road, and up to the smoky-green foothills and the distant blue mountains, the colors softening as afternoon became evening.

The Smokies held endless places for a man to hide, except wealthy newcomers from the cities kept crowding into the backwoods. Hundreds of new homes perched high in the mountains now, so far away as to be invisible until the sun touched the windows and turned them to fire. Every new outpost of civilization made the wilderness that much smaller.

"Elliott was tough as nails," Keith said. "If anybody could survive, he could. Especially if he had help from a friend or two. And he had a lot of friends."

"Do you think it was the war that made him come unglued?"

Keith gave him a sharp look. "How would I know? And watch what you say. Not every combat veteran is a keg of dynamite looking for a match."

"I know."

They were silent for a while, Keith tapping his fingers on the arm of his chair and Sean nursing his beer. Nursing his thoughts. He didn't much like them.

Elliott was trained to survive. Trained to kill too, and he possessed a violent temper.

"What's bothering you, little brother?"

Sean shook his head. That childhood memory was crystallizing, getting clearer, like the moon seen through a good telescope. It was far away and always would be, but it was clear, its details distinct. The sun shining on glass and chrome and brown metal. And the water. That deep, dark water.

Maybe he'd imagined it, like Keith's boys imagined ghosts and haunted houses. Then they talked themselves into believing their own fantasies.

"No," Sean whispered. "I saw it."

Keith pointed at Sean's beer bottle. "How many of those did you polish off before you came over?"

"Zero. And I didn't drink when I was twelve. I know what I saw."

"I'm listening."

On the verge of retreating, Sean asked himself if he really wanted to keep the secret any longer. He'd worried over it for more than half his life. He'd tried to make sense of it but he couldn't. Maybe there was no sense. Keith might be able to help him see that, help him leave it behind. Or he too might imagine the worst.

Sean put the beer down. He wanted to start the story with virtually no alcohol in his system. Proof that he was in his right mind. Completely sober, anyway.

"Okay. First, all joking aside. Give me your word that you won't tell Annie. I love her, man; she's great, but this needs to stay between you and me."

Keith hesitated. "Just this once, I won't tell her."

"All right, then. When you went into the service, I started spending a lot of time in the woods, just roaming around. Staying away from Dale because you weren't around to watch my back."

"I wouldn't have enlisted if I'd—"

"No, you had your life to live. You didn't have to stay and baby-sit your kid brother. That's not what we need to talk about, anyway. This is what I saw. Listen up, because I won't want to repeat myself."

"Go ahead." Keith leaned forward, making his chair creak.

"I saw something very strange, once. At the lake."

"Hamlin Lake has seen its share of strange things."

"This wasn't at Hamlin. I'm talking about the little lake on old man Bennett's property. Remember him?"

"The grumpy old dude who made a fortune selling all those lake lots?"

"That's him." Sean closed his eyes. "I was up there, in the brush above his lake. All of a sudden, there was this little brown car, blasting its way out of the woods on one of those skinny dirt tracks that led to the lake. It was heading straight for the water."

He stopped, listening to the crickets and the peepers and the wind flexing its muscles in the trees. Keith stayed quiet.

"It slowed down some. The door popped open, and Elliott jumped out in the nick of time. The car flew out over the water and smacked into it —made this huge splash and a noise like a gun going off, almost—and then it rocked, back and forth, back and forth, sort of settling. And Elliott—he'd rolled a couple of times and stood up—he just watched it sink." Sean stopped. "You still with me?"

"Yeah. Go on."

"It didn't take long to sink, but the lake kept rippling for a long time. Elliott stayed there. Absolutely still. Watching and waiting. Like he wanted to make sure the car was really . . . drowned." Sean swallowed, remembering how he'd worried that the car would come boiling back out of the water, raised from the dead, because Elliott had seemed to expect just that.

"Is that all you saw?"

"Elliott hollered something. I couldn't make it out, though. Then he fell on his knees in the grass and cried. Rocked back and forth on his knees and cried like a baby."

"Weird."

"No kidding. A grown man, deliberately drowning a car and then crying his heart out. Like he'd changed his mind or something."

"What did he do then?"

"He walked back the way he'd driven in."

A noise behind Sean made him jump. The kitchen window was open. Annie wouldn't eavesdrop, would she? Keith didn't react though, so Sean decided he was imagining things.

"When was this?" Keith asked.

"I don't remember exactly. You know how it is when you're a kid. You don't look at the calendar. You don't keep track of the comings and goings of adults, either. So I'm not clear on the timing."

"But it was on Bennett's land? Whereabouts?"

"I don't remember." Sean picked up the beer again. "Even if I had a clue, I wouldn't recognize the spot now. It's been sold, subdivided, filled up with those fancy houses. No way could I show you where it happened."

"I was just wondering if we could find the car."

"It wouldn't be easy. They say that little lake is deep. Even deeper than Hamlin. But why would you want to find it?"

"Why didn't you call the cops?"

"Bennett had run me off a couple of times already. I was no-good Dale Halloran's kid. Why would I call the cops and admit I'd been trespassing? So Dale could pick me up at the station and beat the living daylights out of me?"

Keith didn't respond.

"Why would you want to find the car?" Sean repeated, dreading the answer.

"To see if there was anything—or anybody—in it."

Exactly. There it was again. Plain as day to Keith too.

The brothers sat in silence for a long time. The beer wasn't going to Sean's head. He felt clear, almost too clear, as if sharing the memory had ripped a veil from his mind. The new view was stark. Disturbing.

"Might be nothing," Keith said at last. "Might be nothing at all."

"I hope you're right." Sean polished off the beer and got to his feet. "I'd better head home. Thanks for listening."

"Hold on. You haven't told Laura about this?"

"No."

"Why not?"

"Well, first, because I haven't told *anybody* about it until right now. I didn't want to face it myself. But the thing is, if Elliott's dead anyway, why make Laura live the rest of her life believing he killed somebody?"

"What if he comes back?"

"Then we'll have a whole new set of problems."

"Think about telling her, though, Sean. Think hard. You might even try praying."

"I have. I've prayed about it for years. I've looked for an explanation that doesn't involve crime or insanity. Haven't found it yet."

"I'm not sure you ever will."

Dangerously close to losing it, Sean stood up. "You're probably right. Thanks for listening." Making his body language loose and relaxed, he strolled down the steps and climbed into his truck where he wouldn't have to pretend he wasn't crying.

Twelve

Nearly midnight. The wind chimes tinkled against a backdrop of coyotes yipping in the hills. Laura needed sleep, but she knew she would only lie awake and listen while a headache throbbed behind her eyelids.

The kitchen table looked naked now, bereft of the plants. One-legged Katie the doll lay there, literally naked while she waited for her dress to dry. Most of the stains had come out of the fabric, but the grime on her face was there to stay, the result of countless hours of outdoor play with Cassie.

Laura picked up the doll and wondered if she could create a new leg out of fabric and stuffing. Someday, maybe, if she hung on to the doll.

Restless, she put it down and moved into the den. There was a gap where the cedar chest had stood for years. She missed it already.

The past was slipping away in fragments. Even if Sean's descendants kept the chest long after he was gone, they could never know everything it represented.

Property, possessions, even memories would be gone someday. A family could record its history somehow, in journals or scrapbooks or even online, but nothing was safe forever. Websites and computers could crash, and even the most interesting family records could succumb to mildew or fire. Or some great-grandchild might throw precious old papers and photos in the trash, saying, "You can't hang on to everything."

In the long run, you couldn't hang on to *anything*.

The piano's rack still held one of her father's songbooks. Laura trailed her finger across the cover, a faded blue. He'd loved to sing the old ballads with Sean, their unschooled voices a perfect blend. Sometimes Sean had given her a subtle wink to accompany the corniest lines about true love.

She found one of the earliest journals and curled up in the double rocking chair her dad had built of sturdy oak and upholstered in a tapestry-like fabric. Wide enough to seat two, it had been a favorite spot for her and Sean when they were teenagers.

But she had to stop thinking about him.

She checked the date of the journal's first entry and realized it coincided with the approximate time of her conception. We stopped at the perennial farm in D'ville again, her mother had written. He bought me a daylily plant. He's so sweet.

Laura smiled sadly at the idea of the young lovebirds buying perennials in the late fall. The daylilies must have been in bloom by the following August when she was born.

Out there in the night, the daylilies still swelled with color and life. Her mother had loved them, not because they were anything special, but because they'd been a gift from her husband.

She'd never stopped loving the lilies. She'd never stopped loving her husband either. Still, Laura couldn't forget the body language in the snapshot she'd taken of her parents and Gibby in front of the dogwood. If someone had taken scissors to the picture, cutting her dad out of it, her mom and Gibby would have looked like a happy couple. Just the two of them.

The wronged husband might have cut himself out of the picture, so to speak, even if he'd only imagined that he'd been wronged.

"I hope that's all it was," she said softly.

Mikey seemed to think she was talking to him. He jumped up beside her, blinked, and curled up in a ball against her thigh.

Laura scratched the top of his head. "Do you remember my mom? Do you remember how much she loved you? She loved me and my dad too. I know she did."

A young cat twelve years ago, Mikey might have been snoozing on a kitchen chair when her folks launched into an ugly confrontation. While Laura fled to Cassie's house, Mikey might have dived under the hutch and heard the rest of it.

If only cats could talk.

❧ Thirteen ❧

The nickel tour of the Halloran Building started with the elevator ride to the third floor. Even the slow-moving elevator was posh, lined with dark, rich woods. Cassie leaned against the brass railing and smiled at her dad.

"Very nice," she said. "Nicer than I remembered."

"Most people will never see the third floor. Ground floor? Ordinary. Second floor? Very, very nice. Third floor?" He grinned. "Opulence, baby."

"Where do you find tenants who can afford opulence?"

"Oh, they're around. People who've moved here from other parts, mostly. I've already had a few nibbles on the vacancy."

"Is it true that Sean's great-greats built the place on their profits from bootleg liquor?"

"It's partly true," he said. "They had money before Prohibition. They were the bigwigs of Prospect. Civic leaders and all that. But they didn't mind sliding over to the wrong side of the law now and then to make a buck."

"However they made their money, it's sad that

Dale lost it all. Keith and Sean never got a cent."

"Don't worry about the Halloran boys. They've done all right, both of them."

The sluggish elevator came to a gentle halt. The door opened on a spacious corridor with plush carpeting and more of that luxurious wood. He led her to the first door on the right, unlocked it, and flung it open with a flourish. As if she'd never seen it before.

It was worth seeing again, though. An ornate ceiling soared high above her head. Simple but elegant woodwork trimmed the tall windows, and a massive fireplace stood empty, its mantel sleek and graceful.

"It's as awesome as I remember," she said, stepping inside.

"Check out the view, honey."

She walked to the window. The town lay before her, surprisingly large. Beyond it, the mountains rolled off to a smoky horizon. "What a beautiful little town."

"Think you and Drew might consider moving home someday? The cost of living is so much lower here. Why keep chasing that California dream if you can't quite afford it?"

Cassie kept quiet. She hadn't known the California dream would cost her the dream of starting a family. Now Drew was completely committed to living there. He'd invested his heart and soul, not to mention his savings, in his business. And she was the loyal and supportive wife who would stand by him as the years ticked away.

She put on a cheerful face. "There's nothing wrong with chasing dreams," she said. "Like you chased your dream of being a land baron."

He laughed. "Land baron? That's a stretch."

"I don't think so."

She moved away from the window and leaned against the wall, her hands behind her back, and pictured herself living there with Drew. Enjoying the fireplace, the compact kitchen, and the gorgeous views. Her dad would give them a bargain rate. She knew he would. And it would be good to be near both sets of parents again—especially if she and Drew started a family.

Her mom was having problems too. That was a separate issue, but it also pointed toward the wisdom of moving home.

"Have you made any progress with Mom?" she asked.

"About counseling? Nope. She won't even discuss it."

"Same here. I don't want to make her mad, so I keep backing off. But that doesn't accomplish anything."

"I don't see that she's getting worse, though. I've had some good talks with her about other things."

"I have too, a few times." Cassie frowned,

remembering a conversation that had puzzled her. "Can I ask you a question?"

"Sure." He came closer, cracking his knuckles the way her mom always begged him not to.

"Mom said something about a call you made to sic the authorities on Dale, but then she said 'Never mind' and clammed up. What was that all about?"

"Oh boy. She knows I don't want her talking about that. If I tell you, promise you'll keep your lips zipped?"

"Of course. What happened?"

"Remember the day Elliott stepped in to stop Dale from beating Sean? Elliott did the hard part. The brave part. I only made a phone call. Your mom insisted on it. She dialed the number and put the phone in my hand and stood there listening until I'd said everything there was to say. There's no such thing as a truly anonymous tip in a small town, but the authorities certainly understood it was especially important in this case. Dale already felt a bit unfriendly toward us."

She met her father's eyes. "Is that how you wound up owning this building? By turning Dale in?"

He shook his head emphatically. "No, it was just a windfall. You know the meaning of the word? It's like when the wind blows an apple out of the tree. Right into your hand."

192

"And you didn't give the branch a good shake?"

"Not intentionally."

Cassie studied her dad. "Making the call had nothing to do with wanting to buy Dale's building?"

He put his hand over his heart. "On my honor as a Boy Scout, I only wanted Dale behind bars for beating Sean. So did your mom. We didn't know Dale had borrowed money against the property, and it wasn't my fault that he ended up in prison and couldn't make the payments." He lifted his shoulders in a nonchalant shrug. "When the building came up at auction later, I put in the winning bid, but it was strictly business. Understand?"

Cassie nodded.

"Risky business too," he said. "I had to sink a ton of money into the old dump. It paid off, though. It paid off."

She nodded again. Most of his investments had paid off. A map on his office wall was studded with colored pins marking his properties. Rental homes, vacant land, commercial buildings. The Bright empire, ever expanding.

"It must stick in Dale's craw every time he drives by," he said with a chuckle. "Right downtown, for everybody to see. His name is on the building, but my name's on the rent checks."

"I hope you never gloat about it in front of him," Cassie said.

"I avoid him at all costs. I've got no use for him, and he's got no use for me. And that's that." He looked out the window again and smiled. "This view—and the view from the house—they almost make me forget the years I struggled to put food on the table."

"Did you really? I didn't know it was that bad."

"By the time you were old enough to notice, we were fine. We'd never been in danger of starving, but there were plenty of times when I couldn't quite cover the bills. I had to juggle them. I'd pay the light bill one month, the gas bill the next month."

"That gives me hope that Drew and I will survive too. Look at you now, the sole owner of the high-rent, first-class Halloran Building. Sweet revenge."

"Revenge? For what? What did Dale Halloran ever do to us?"

"Not to us. To Sean. Dale treated him like a punching bag. I'd love to return the favor someday."

"Ah, that ferocious loyalty. It's been there since y'all were in kindergarten. You three were an unlikely crew, you know. I guess you still are. There's Laura, the daughter of the whacked-out Vietnam vet—"

"Dad, that's not nice."

"But it's true. Then there's Sean, a nice guy

whose father is the meanest, drunkest drunk in town. And there's Cassie Bright Cutler, the beautiful daughter of the real estate agent who was too dumb to give up."

"I'm the daughter of the best dad in the world. I'm proud of you. You're pretty darned smart for a small-town guy."

"Nah. I'm a slow learner. Thank God, your mom puts up with me."

Cassie didn't like turning into a big blob of sentimental mush, but sometimes she couldn't help it. "She doesn't just put up with you, Dad. She adores you."

"You think so?" he asked with a wistful smile.

"It's mutual."

He crossed the room to the other window, the one that looked out on Fourth Street. Hands in his pockets, he started whistling. The fourth note in, Cassie knew the tune. "Michelle" by Lennon and McCartney.

After whistling a line or two, he switched to humming, then started singing it from the beginning. The same way he always had, slightly off-key and substituting *Ardelle* for *Michelle*.

"Ardelle, ma belle . . ."

In the good ol' days, he'd always made the family laugh by deliberately mangling the French lyrics. Now he sounded so sad that Cassie almost thought he was crying.

Nah. Her dad never cried.

• • •

Laura had always liked Sean's street, a neighborhood of small homes built in the thirties. The windows of his house were dark, but maybe he was out back in the workshop.

She parked directly across the street, then lugged the heavy tote bag across the pavement and entered the yard. She climbed the steps to the porch and rang the doorbell. As she'd expected, there was no answer.

She walked down the narrow driveway that led to the detached garage and the workshop. The windows of the workshop were dark too. The sign over the door swung in a light wind.

SEAN MICHAEL HALLORAN, LUTHIER.

Her eyes watered. Her dad would have been so proud of him.

Turning toward the house, she heard the knocking and grinding of a noisy vehicle, so close that it must have been pulling into the driveway. Dale's rattletrap truck?

Clutching the tote to her chest, she stepped behind prickly evergreen shrubs at the corner of the house and peered through their thin branches. A battered black pickup truck crawled into view.

The engine lagged into silence. A bearded and broad-shouldered man climbed out. Dale. Wearing a threadbare plaid shirt, dirty jeans, and greasy-looking boots, he walked around the front of the truck and headed toward the front door.

He might do exactly what she'd done. He might try the back door too, or the workshop. And there she'd be, trying to hide in the bushes.

Elliott Gantt's daughter, a coward?

Yes. A lily-livered coward. Dale frightened her on a level she didn't care to analyze.

She peeked around the bushes. Dale hadn't pulled far into the driveway. The truck's nose was even with the front of the house. Until he left the porch, the house would shield her from view. If she could sneak past his truck to the sidewalk while he waited at the front door, it would only be a short dash to her car. That was cowardly too, but she didn't want to be trapped in the backyard.

Now or never. She stepped out from the bushes. Moving as quietly as possible, she hurried down the driveway.

She was still yards from the truck when Dale walked around the plantings at the front of the house and onto the driveway. He didn't see her, though. He turned, facing the house, and squinted up at it as if he were inspecting the condition of the roof.

Keeping an eye on him, she kept moving. She hardly dared to breathe.

When she was a seven-year-old tomboy playing army with Sean and the other neighborhood kids, none of them would have marched straight past the enemy like this, out in the open. They would have dropped to the ground and crawled through any cover they could find, regardless of mud or thorns. But there was no cover here, and she was the girl whose father had humiliated Dale by putting an end to the last beating he'd ever given Sean.

Dale turned, his gaze lighting on her before she'd reached the truck. His eyes were bright blue like Sean's but cold.

A smile spread across his bearded face, and he started across the drive to block her path. "Hello there, Miss Gantt."

"Hello." She halted ten or twelve feet from him, leaving some room to maneuver.

"You here to see Sean too?"

"Yes, but he's not home." Too late, she wished she hadn't said it.

He came closer. "Chasin' my son again, are you?"

"Of course not."

"I see. You're too good for my boy now? Too good for everybody?" The smile curled into a sneer.

Her fear turned hot but so did her indignation. "Whatever, Dale. By the way, don't trespass on Gantt property again."

He feigned surprise, his eyebrows raised. "I wouldn't do that."

"Really? On Monday, I saw you pulling into the driveway of my grandparents' place."

"You calling me a liar?"

She moved forward, hoping to put the truck between them, but Dale's hand snaked out and gripped her elbow with shocking strength. A wave of pain rolled up and down her arm. The heavy tote bag slid from her shoulder. The strap caught on his hand and dangled, its weight adding to the pain.

"Let go!"

He loomed over her, a beer smell suddenly strong. "Answer me when I talk to you, girl. Are you calling me a liar?"

Glaring into his eyes, she tried to shake him off. His fingers cut harder into her flesh. Like they'd cut into Sean's when he was a scrawny, defenseless boy.

"Does it make you feel big and strong to pick on somebody smaller?" she asked.

"I'm just puttin' you in your place. Somebody's gotta do it."

"Take your hand off me, or I'll scream like you've never heard anybody scream before, and you'll be on your way to jail for assault and who knows what else."

"Don't forget trespassing. Big-shot property owners like you have to protect their precious real estate from the likes of me." He gave her elbow a sudden twist and let go. Pain scorched toward her shoulder.

Afraid she would drop the tote bag and its precious contents, she held onto it with her other hand and ran without a backward glance. She didn't care if she looked like a coward.

She reached the sanctuary of her car, dived in, and hit the locks. Her arm ached and her hands shook, but she found her key, started the engine, and drove away.

At the corner stop sign, she looked in the rearview mirror. The truck still stood in the driveway, but she didn't see Dale or anyone else. Either the neighbors hadn't noticed the confrontation, or they hadn't wanted to get involved—like they didn't get involved when he'd been beating Sean. They'd left it up to Elliott Gantt.

She reached over and slid her hand into the tote bag, needing to touch something her dad had touched. Something he had loved.

If Sean wanted the songbooks, he would have to come get them. She wouldn't go back to his house unless she was certain Dale wouldn't show up, and she couldn't be certain until he was behind bars again—or dead.

Fourteen

When Sean ran up her back steps hours later, Laura was grateful for the unexpected cold front that gave her an excuse to wear long sleeves. If he saw the bruises at her elbow, he would go ballistic. She'd already decided to offer a censored version of events, though, so he wouldn't be able to say she was keeping something from him.

It would be a very censored version.

Careful of her sore shoulder, she opened the door on a gust of cold air. "Come on in, Sean."

He remained in the doorway, hands in his pockets and eyes guarded. "I'm not sure I believe the message you left on my phone."

She frowned, trying to remember what she'd said. *"Stop by when you have time. There's something I want to give you."* "What do you mean?"

"After the way you kicked me out yesterday—"

"I didn't kick you out."

"No? 'Get lost, Halloran' didn't sound like an invitation to stay."

"I'm sorry, Sean. You just make me so mad sometimes."

"It's mutual, sometimes." He smiled.

She smiled too, and the tension dissolved. About *that,* anyway.

"Don't just stand there," she said. "Come on in before Mikey runs out."

He stepped inside, still smiling. Crowding her a little. His flirtatious pursuit bore no resemblance to Dale's rough violation of her personal space, but it was unsettling in its own way.

She led Sean to the kitchen table where she'd dumped the tote bag before she collapsed on the couch in tears. "These are for you." She put the bag in his hands.

He looked into it and shook his head. "You can't give me these. They're heirlooms."

"You know I can't carry a tune. What would I do with a bunch of old songbooks and sheet music? Don't worry. I kept a couple to remind me of Daddy."

"Thank you," Sean said softly. "I'll take good care of them."

"Don't be afraid to use them, okay? Enjoy them. Wear them out."

He nodded, returning the bag to the table, and then he closed the distance between them and hugged her. Blindsided, she could only hug him back. Carefully.

She would not cry. The Advil would kick in soon, and her shoulder would stop hurting, and she would not cry.

Sean had experienced far worse hurts. Remembering that, she let her hands absorb his warmth through his shirt. She wanted to make up for the brutality he'd endured as a boy. She wanted him to feel healed. Restored. Loved.

Enough of that. If she stayed in his arms any longer, he'd try to take it from hugging to kissing, and she'd be tempted to cooperate.

She pulled away and worked up a smile. "I

stopped by your house with the songbooks, but you weren't home. And Dale was there so I didn't hang around."

Worry filled his eyes. "Did you talk to him?"

"Briefly. Now, can you humor me about something, please?"

"That all depends."

"It's a small request, Sean. Just let me show you what's in the closet in my mom's room."

He balked, eyebrows lowered.

She tugged his arm. He didn't budge, so she took off without him.

Waiting for him to catch up, she surveyed the bedroom. When it came time to deal with the toiletries that crowded the top of the bureau, she'd probably throw everything out. The Jean Naté, though . . . her mom had worn that scent almost every day of her life. She'd said she started wearing it as a teenager and never grew tired of it.

Laura picked up the tiny bottle and unscrewed the cap. The light, lemony scent engulfed her, not with specific memories, but with the very air of her mother's presence. The fragrance was like the ghost of a ghost.

Hearing Sean's slow, reluctant footsteps approaching, Laura capped the bottle, took firm control of her emotions, and turned around. He stood just outside the room, regarding her with the stubborn expression she knew so well.

"I've found some pretty obvious clues," she said.

"About your dad, you mean? If he left any clues, the sheriff and his cohorts should have found them years ago."

"They weren't looking for clues. They never dreamed it was anything but an accidental drowning. Sean, look."

Laura opened the door to the small, deep closet and pulled the string dangling from a single bare bulb. She'd almost emptied her mother's side of the closet, but the rod and shelves on the right still sagged with the weight of her father's clothes. Years of dust covered the shoulders and collars of his shirts.

Sean propped himself up in the bedroom doorway, his expression skeptical. "Clothes in a closet. Some clue."

"Which shoes did my dad always wear when he went fishing?"

"His deck shoes."

Laura pointed at the neat but dusty lineup of men's shoes under the hanging clothes. "They're gone."

"Of course they're gone," Sean said softly. "They're at the bottom of Hamlin Lake."

The pity in his eyes made her want to scream. "But his hunting boots are gone too. When did he ever wear heavy hunting boots for a day of fishing?"

"Your mom might have given them away."

"She might have, and she might have given away his best hunting and camo gear. The things a man would need for a long camp out. They're gone."

"How do you know?"

"I know where he always kept everything." She made her way to the rear of the closet. "Come on, Sean, get in here."

He followed her in, grumbling, but he didn't take advantage of the tight quarters. Vaguely disappointed, then cross with herself for wanting him closer, she focused on the real issues.

Small puffs of dust rose from her father's hanging clothes when she ran a hand across them. For twelve years, she'd never given a thought to his comfort and safety. She'd assumed he had gone on to his eternal rest. Now, though, she worried that he didn't even have a roof over his head. One warm shirt or jacket might make a world of difference on a cold night.

She glanced back at Sean. "His church clothes are still here, and some of his work clothes. But his camo gear is gone."

Sean eyed the old wooden shelf above the closet rod. It held only neat piles of folded shirts and jeans. "This house has more than one closet. And bureaus. Have you checked them all?"

"Yes. Let me show you what's in his drawers."

Sean stepped aside, letting her exit the closet

before him. As she passed him, the faint scent of sawdust reminded her of her dad's workshop. Of him and Sean bending over a project together, working together like father and son.

Steeling herself against grief for Sean's losses as well as her own, she crossed the room and opened the top drawer of her dad's bureau. He'd built it himself. The drawers glided as smooth as silk, as strong as the oak tree they'd come from.

"Socks," she said. "Underwear."

"What's so significant about socks and skivvies?"

"Think about what's missing. His wool socks. The ones he liked for hunting trips." She shut the top drawer and opened the second one. "This is where he kept his long johns. I know because I always helped Mom put the laundry away."

He gave the contents of the drawer a cursory look. "I see some long johns. What's your point?"

"There's nothing left but some of the everyday kind. Where are his special long johns? The expensive ones he got by mail order? He wouldn't have worn them for a fishing trip in August."

"That doesn't prove a thing. Laura, please. Be sensible. Don't live in a fantasy about having your dad back."

"Now you sound like my mother." She slammed the drawer shut. "It's not a little-girl fantasy. It's a theory." She pointed to the tall gun safe in the corner, topped with a stack of books. "Let's open that thing."

He folded his arms across his chest. "I'll bet you don't remember the combination."

"Bet you're wrong."

Now that she'd practiced the combination a few times, she was fast. She had it open again in seconds.

She swung the heavy steel door open and stepped back. "Voila. The old BB guns and the .22s we used for target practice—remember those?—and the antique revolver he never trusted. But what about his good deer rifle? Ammo? Knives? Bows and arrows? Where'd they go?"

"Your mom must have sold them."

"If she had, she would have given you first pick of everything. You know she would have. You were like a son to my folks."

"Maybe she just moved them somewhere. Like the garage."

"I checked the garage. And the attic, cobwebs and all."

"Oh."

"Everything that's missing is something he would have needed in the wild. Weapons. Ammo. Basic tools. His mess kit. His flint. The best down sleeping bag. He wasn't planning a morning at the lake."

"You and your mom would have noticed him taking everything out of the house."

"Not if he took a little bit at a time. At the crack of dawn, before we were up. You know that's when he liked to set out. Remember what you told me on Sunday? A man could stash everything he'd need to survive. Clothes and food. Tools and hunting and fishing gear."

"I was only quoting what some other people have been saying."

"Maybe they're saying it because it's true."

He looked at the nearly empty gun safe as if wishful thinking could make the missing weapons reappear. "You're jumping to conclusions."

She moved closer, begging him with her eyes. "At least admit that he might be alive. Not that it's certain, not that it's even probable, but that it's at least possible."

Sean sank onto the edge of the bed with his hands on his knees, the same tense posture she remembered from the times they'd sat with Cassie on the bench outside the principal's office. "I don't know, Laura."

"What's your problem? Why do you only want to argue with me?"

"I only want to help you face reality. If you're not ready, I'd better head home." He stood up and walked out.

She chased him down the hall and into the kitchen, where she passed him and planted

208

herself in front of the door. "Tell me what's wrong, Sean. Tell me what you're keeping from me."

"What makes you think I'm keeping something from you?"

"The way you're acting."

"Baloney." He retreated two steps.

She followed, as close as a ballroom dancer. "Something's going on that you don't want me to know about. Will you at least admit that much?"

He was silent, not quite meeting her eyes.

"Thank you," she said.

"For what?"

"For admitting that something's wrong. By not saying anything."

"Sorry."

"Is that all you've got to say about it?"

"Yep." He grabbed the songbooks, sidestepped her, and made for the door.

She followed him onto the porch, into the cold evening air. He ran down the steps and climbed into his truck. With the door open, he looked up at her. No smile now.

"Did your folks ever own a little brown car?" he asked.

"Brown? Not that I remember. Why?"

"Just wondering. Good night." He shut the door.

"There you go again." She raised her voice, hoping he could hear her through the truck's window. "Acting weird."

The roar of the engine was his only answer. The truck jolted down the driveway and onto the road, where the taillights swerved and disappeared around the sharp curve with only a fleeting flare of the one operative brake light.

She hurried inside, bolting the door behind her, and tried to dismiss Sean's aggravating attitude from her mind. She had more important matters to deal with. Rubbing her arms to warm up, she recalled what her dad had always said about mountain weather. Just like a woman, it was beautiful but fickle, going from cold to hot and back again.

A fifty-degree night wasn't bad if you had a warm bed to sleep in, but a fifty-degree night without decent shelter would be miserably cold, especially for a man whose clothes must have worn thin by now.

Laura returned to the closet, hatching a plan.

Fifteen

Cassie had started seeing her parents with new eyes. Sure, they were middle-aged fuddy-duddies who could stand to lose a few pounds, but they were good people. They cared about other people. They'd once stuck their noses into Dale

Halloran's business for Sean's sake, even though there might have been serious repercussions.

And if her mom showed a few signs of obsessive-compulsive behavior . . . so what? Cassie was starting to think it wasn't a big deal. If a woman wanted to spend half her afternoon making a ridiculously organized grocery list, arranged aisle by aisle like a map of the store and color-coded for different kinds of coupons, that was her privilege.

Cassie propped her elbows on the granite counter and studied her mom's neatly written menu. "Steaks? For a little boy's birthday party?"

"Nothing's too good for my grandson," her dad bellowed from his home office.

"No fair," she yelled back. "You never bought steak for my birthdays when I was little."

"We couldn't afford steaks back then, Cass. Did it wound your tender little psyche?"

"Yes sir, it did. You need to make it up to me. Buy me a new car or something."

He laughed. "Don't hold your breath."

Her mom looked up. Seated at the table, she was searching through a shoe box full of coupons —as if she still needed to pinch pennies. "The steaks will be for the adults," she said. "Trevor will want a hot dog. He always does. Does Laura eat red meat? Or is she like Jess?"

Cassie sat beside her. "Except for tuna and sushi, Laura will eat just about anything. Like me."

"You? You've always been a fussy eater."

She smirked, thinking of Drew's running joke that they should write a cookbook with a thousand and one ways to cook beans. "Not anymore."

"I just hope she and Sean will come. He's such a dear."

"Ardie, sweetheart?" came a wistful voice from the office.

"Yes, Gary?"

"Will you pick up some good salsa from the deli, please?"

"Yes, darling, and I'll buy the really good tortilla chips."

"Thank you, my love."

"Ugh, I'm getting a sweetness headache," Cassie said.

Her mom ignored her. She added salsa and chips to her list, in exactly the right spots: Deli and Aisle 12.

"Wow, Mom. I just walk into the store and start throwing stuff in the cart."

"You could save money if you planned more carefully."

"Maybe there's a happy medium?"

Ardelle didn't answer.

Tigger breezed into the kitchen, her silky blond hair swinging. She proudly wore a maternity top although she was barely showing. Trevor tagged along behind her, explaining why he needed a magnifying glass for his birthday.

"And so I can see my insect collection better," he said.

Tigger smiled. "Oh, you and those bugs."

"They're insects, Mom. Only some of them are bugs."

Cassie wondered if anybody made a white lab coat to fit a kindergartner. Trevor had given off the mad scientist vibe since he was three or four and had to start wearing glasses. He'd started reading at four. He'd probably enter Harvard at fourteen on a full scholarship. Naturally, Tigger wouldn't just have a smart kid. She'd have a Boy Genius.

Ardelle stood up, having finished organizing her coupons and shopping list, and cupped one hand over Tig's belly. "Look at you, starting to show."

"You get to do that because you're my mom," Tig said with a tolerant smile. "When complete strangers try it, I threaten them with karate chops."

"Sure you do." Ardelle turned to Cassie. "I remember being pregnant with you and patting Jess's tummy and telling her she could borrow my maternity clothes once you were born. And she did."

"That's wrong," Trevor said, his eyes cheerful and big behind thick lenses. "A baby doesn't grow in a mommy's tummy. Tummies are for food. The baby grows in the mommy's loom."

"Womb," Tig corrected gently, keeping a straight face.

Cassie grinned, glad Trevor still didn't know everything.

Ardelle seemed to have missed the funny exchange. Her mind was probably on those cents-off coupons. "Tig and Trev, in case you're not here when I get home, give me my kisses now," she ordered.

They came forward obediently, bestowing and receiving kisses, and Ardelle left through the garage to do her shopping.

"We'd better go too," Tig said. "Trev, go get your backpack and say good-bye to Grandpa." She met Cassie's eyes and frowned. "What's wrong? You look unusually, um, sweet."

"I'm thinking you lead a charmed life, right down to having a great husband and an adorable and brilliant child."

Tigger's flawless face lit up with happiness. "I do lead a charmed life, don't I?" She rubbed her fingers lightly over her belly, like a prenatal love pat to go with those expensive prenatal vitamins she'd taken for months before they tried for Baby Number Two.

"Tigger the Tagger." Wary of karate chops, Cassie steered clear of the pregnant tummy and mussed her sister's shiny hair instead. Like old times. "Even though it irritates me to pieces, I'm really and truly glad you're happy."

"And I'm glad you are. But leave my hair alone, Eeyore."

"Yes ma'am."

Walking past the table to see Tig and Trevor out the door, Cassie stopped short. After all that work, her mom had left her list and coupons on the table.

Green, green, green everywhere. Kudzu would conquer the world someday, at least where the winters weren't cold enough to kill it.

Treading carefully through the vines, watching for snakes, Laura slogged toward the cabin, glad that her shoulder had improved overnight. The big black trash bag she'd slung over her back made her feel like Santa Claus, but there was no chimney left for Santa. Except for a corner in the rear, the roof had caved in.

The No Trespassing sign she'd nailed to the wall looked gaudy against the rough gray wood. It didn't belong there. But neither did Dale. The signs probably wouldn't discourage him anyway, but at least she'd put him on notice that she knew he'd been there.

With her dad's old work gloves tucked securely under her arm, she made her way around to the back. She couldn't imagine anyone using the cabin as a refuge, with its roof collapsed and its plank floor rotting into the dirt, but she couldn't think of a more likely home base for her dad.

Even if he never spent a night there, he might find the loot and haul it away to wherever he'd been staying. If it brought him any comfort at all, it was worth the trouble.

The back door hung at a crazy angle, its top hinge rusted away. She gave the weathered wood a cautious push and peered into the green gloom inside.

Nothing but kudzu.

She placed the black bag in the corner that still had a roof. Triple-bagged, the clothes and supplies should be safe against the weather for a while. She hadn't wanted to give him a heavy load to haul, so she'd brought just one of each article of clothing she thought he'd need. No duplicates except socks and underwear. She'd packed lip balm too. Toothpaste and a tooth-brush. Soap. A can opener and some canned goods. Since leaving the house, she'd already thought of a dozen more items.

From the back pocket of her jeans, she pulled out a tiny notepad and a pen. For hours, she'd contemplated what to write. She'd finally decided.

"Dad, please let me know you're okay. I love you." She signed her name and clipped the pen to the notepad.

Studying those old suede gloves, a peculiar shade of green, she wondered if he would recognize them. He might even recall that when she was little, she'd loved to put them on when they were still warm from his hands.

She tucked the notepad and pen inside one of the gloves and left them on top of the trash bag. She had more bags in the car, to drop off at the homeless shelter, but this bag was meant for one particular homeless veteran. He might never find it, though. She might have donated the clothing and supplies to some unknown trespasser—or to Dale.

She left through the broken doorway and waded through the kudzu. Back to her car, back to normal life. Except it could never be normal until she learned what had happened to her father.

Laura headed up the back steps with the mail in her hand but stopped short. Mikey was sound asleep in a puddle of sun on the porch. She'd left him inside, sleeping on the couch, and she remembered locking the door.

Walking past the cat, she tried the door. Unlocked.

The driveway showed no obvious signs that another vehicle had come and gone while she was out, but that didn't prove anything. The ground was too dry to show tire tracks.

Or footprints. Maybe someone had come on foot, in broad daylight.

Her heart pounding, she opened the door partway and stuck her head in. "Who's there? Dad?"

Silence. Of course.

She'd given her word that she would call 911 if she saw another prowler. But she hadn't actually seen one.

The sleeping cat was easy to capture. Holding him firmly, she took him inside, shut the door with her hip, and deposited him on the kitchen floor.

"What's going on, Mikey? Who was here? I wish you could talk."

He wobbled sleepily over to his food dish and started eating.

Laura sucked in a breath. She'd fed the cat early, and he'd wolfed it all down. He'd emptied his dish within minutes.

"Ardelle," Laura said. Ardelle had let herself in. She'd given Mikey a second breakfast and let him escape.

Trying to squelch her irritation, Laura looked around the kitchen. The mug she'd left beside the coffee maker was in the sink, and the bag of oranges she'd left on the counter was missing.

Ardelle always liked to refrigerate her fruit. Laura opened the fridge.

The oranges were in the produce drawer.

The tuna casserole sat on the second shelf. If Ardelle had lifted the foil, she would have known it was still untouched except for the spoonful the cat had enjoyed. Maybe that would hurt her feelings, but she had no right to snoop in the fridge or anywhere else.

Laura walked into the den. It smelled like lemon Pledge. Some of her dad's instruments had been moved, ever so slightly.

Nothing was out of place in any of the bedrooms, but the carpet was freshly vacuumed. The bathroom's surfaces gleamed.

She returned to the kitchen, shaking her head. Half the county had a key, but only Ardelle would have the nerve to walk in and act like she lived there. It was too much. The cleaning, the straightening, the journals packed away in a closet. Apparently the cabin wasn't the only place that needed No Trespassing signs.

There was no harm done, though, and she probably just couldn't help herself.

Laura filled her lungs, held her breath as long as she could, and exhaled slowly, trying to blow the anger right out of her system. She had to let it go.

But then she noticed the calendar that hung beside the fridge. She'd deliberately left it open to April, the last month that held neat notes about dentist appointments and garden club meetings. Now it was open to the blank squares of May.

A month ago, she'd begun to grieve the loss of her mother. The future held a thousand smaller losses. No more notes on the calendar. No more coming home for Christmas and filling each other's stockings with little treasures. No more swapping goofy birthday cards. Her mom had always loved the funny ones. Bonus points for finding her a funny one with a cat on it.

Mikey sidled over to the door and yowled.

"I should," she said. "I should let you out, you ugly old possum-cat. I should feed you to the coyotes."

But she remembered him as an orphaned, half-starved kitten, taking milk from a medicine dropper held in her dad's big, scarred hands.

"I didn't mean it, Mikey." She scooped him up and held him close. He must have been rolling in her mother's herb garden because his fur smelled like rosemary.

Laura closed her eyes and rested her chin on the cat's head. If she'd had more time with her mother, they might have mended their relationship. Or they might have gone on as before, never daring to talk about the mysteries that drove a wedge between them.

On Saturday morning, Laura pushed a shopping cart through Kroger's produce section and stopped beside the white peaches. The first of the season. Her dad had loved peaches.

The abundance of food brought tears to her eyes. She wanted to walk him up and down the aisles and buy him anything he wanted. Anything at all, even if it wasn't good for him. She wouldn't lecture him about pesticides or processed foods or cholesterol.

All this food was so *easy*. Ready to eat. She couldn't imagine twelve years of foraging for greens and berries. Shooting a rabbit or a squirrel and cooking it over an open fire. Retiring to some rough shelter for the night, all alone.

Sean's sister-in-law pushed her cart around the corner, jolting Laura back to the present. In T-shirt and faded jeans, her short hair tousled and her face bare of makeup, Annie Halloran still resembled a happy teenager more than a married mother of three. Completely focused on her shop-ping list, she didn't look up.

After Laura went off to college, she and Annie hadn't stayed in touch. Annie had come to the funeral, though. She'd given Laura a long, silent hug that had meant more than a hundred trite condolences.

She looked up and smiled. "Hey, Laura."

"Hi, Annie. You don't have the boys with you today?"

"No, they're home with Keith. Running him ragged, no doubt."

"I can only imagine." A twinge of envy stabbed Laura. If she'd married Sean, those three little boys with blazing blue eyes would have been her nephews, and her children would have had cousins. With Dale as their grandfather.

"How in the world do you handle having Dale as your father-in-law?" Laura blurted.

Annie's eyes widened. "That's an interesting question."

"Don't read anything into it," Laura added hastily, her cheeks heating.

"Oh, of course not." She leaned on her shopping cart. "Well, we avoid him as much as we can. Keith has ordered him to stay off our property."

"I wonder why Sean doesn't lay down some rules like that."

"I asked him once, and he said something about being merciful. He's too tender-hearted for his own good." Annie paused. "I think Sean still manages to love Dale just a little, in spite of everything."

Laura nodded. Stalling until she had control of herself, she picked up a tomato. Not ripe. Not even close. She put it back. "I hate store-bought tomatoes."

"Wait a couple of months, and I can bring you plenty from our garden. If you'll still be in town."

"I'm not sure I'll be here that long, but thanks."

"Sean will be sorry to see you go. He stopped by a few nights ago. Didn't stay long, but your name came up." Annie smiled. "Matter of fact, he said you're impossible."

Laura winced, wondering which tiff he'd meant. "I probably deserved it."

"No, I think he was using you as a scapegoat when he's really tied up in knots about the other thing."

"Other thing?"

"The . . . I don't know. I've always hoped y'all would get back together, and I thought that's what he and Keith were talking about, out on the porch, so I . . . listened in." Annie made a face.

"But that wasn't what they were talking about?"

"No. Sean was talking about a drowning he saw a long time ago. I only heard part of it, and Keith wouldn't tell me later. Sean never mentioned anything like that?"

"Never. He wasn't talking about my dad, was he? Sean wasn't anywhere near the lake that day —unless I'm remembering everything wrong."

Annie had become intensely interested in selecting a green pepper. "You should ask him." She dropped a pepper into a bag. "I shouldn't have said anything. I'm sorry."

"It's okay. Really."

"I'm still sorry. Well, I need to get home. Bye, Laura." Annie pushed her cart around the corner.

Before she could lose her nerve, Laura dug her phone out of her pocket and punched Sean's number.

He answered on the first ring. "Laura," he said in a cautious tone. "What's up?"

"Explain this business about seeing a drowning years ago. Please?"

He was silent for a moment. "Where did you get this information?"

He'd called it information. Not gossip.

"From Annie," she said.

He grumbled something unintelligible.

"What's it all about, Sean? Who drowned?"

"I don't know. Nobody, probably. It was sort of a figurative drowning. Don't worry about it. I have the neck of a mandolin half-glued. Gotta go. Bye."

"Wait. Don't hang up on me. I—I'm supposed to tell you about the party."

There was a long silence.

"Party," he said, finally. "What party?"

"Trevor's birthday party. His fifth. Tonight at six. Sorry it's so last minute. We're both invited. It'll be at Gary and Ardelle's house. I was supposed to ask you earlier, but—"

"But you didn't want to—until now, when you want another chance to interrogate me." Sean laughed softly. "I'm up to it. I'll pick you up a little before six."

And then he did hang up on her.

Waiting for Laura to come outside, Sean leaned against the porch pillar and looked across the road to the church's picnic pavilion where he'd carved their initials into a table on a winter evening. He'd kept coaxing her into deeper, longer kisses too. Make a cut, stop for a kiss. Make a cut, stop for three or four or five kisses. Night had fallen fast, the way it did in December, and the lights had come on in the little bungalow, reminding him of her dad's unpredictable temper.

He gave the pillar a pat. It was solid, like the whole house, and alive in a way that brick could never be alive. Wood could breathe. It had some give to it.

He especially liked a frame house with a wraparound porch. Or any house that had Laura in it—and that didn't hold echoes of Dale's rages.

The doorknob rattled. Laura stepped outside in a blue shirt and jeans. Holding a large, square package wrapped in garish dinosaur paper and topped with multicolored ribbons, she looked as fragile as the wrappings.

"I'm sorry I hung up on you," he said. "You're beautiful," he added unwisely.

Fragile or not, she glared at him in a way that made him think he was staring straight into a double-barreled shotgun. Loaded, cocked, and aimed. That was the Laura he remembered.

Fighting a smile, he lifted his hands in surrender. "I take it back. You're downright homely. Feel better now?"

She placed the gift in his upraised hands. "Hold this, please." She locked up, dumped her keys in her purse, and frowned toward the road. "Mikey escaped again. He's out there some-where."

Laura was like Jess. Whenever brakes squealed on the road, Jess had dropped whatever she was doing to count feline noses.

"He'll be fine," Sean said. "He always is. How much do I owe you on the gift?"

"Don't worry about it." Laura hurried down the steps.

"No, I'm splitting it with you." He chased her onto the driveway. "What is it?"

She went for the passenger door, opened it before he could, and climbed in. "A big remote-control truck. A red one."

"I'm glad you like red trucks." He closed the glossy red door and went around to his side. "You sure about going to the party?" he asked, setting the gift between them on the seat. "It's not too late to call and cancel."

"Out of the question. But I should give you fair warning. Don't be surprised if you see some OCD behavior from Ardelle."

"I know. Cassie told me. You think there's any truth to it?"

"Probably." She nailed him with that look again. "Now, back to this drowning that you're so determined not to talk about. Does it have any-thing to do with my dad?"

"It wasn't even the same year as your dad's

drowning." Maybe that would satisfy her curiosity.

He fired up the truck and tried to kill his thoughts in the noise of the engine, but he only heard that ugly *drowning* word reverberating in his brain. Stalling for time, he pulled the truck onto the road and hit the gas.

A gray blur flashed onto the road—a cat? Mikey—

He pulled the truck hard to the left, brakes screaming. He checked his mirror, afraid he'd see Mikey, but a squirrel scampered into the roadside weeds.

"Whew," he said. "It was only a squirrel. And I missed it."

Laura twisted her whole body to peer through the rear window. "Are you sure it wasn't Mikey?"

"I'm sure. I saw it."

She settled into her seat again. "I don't know if I could stand to lose Mikey too." Her voice faltered.

But the cat was old. Even if she kept him out of harm's way, he couldn't have more than a few years left. Not wanting to say it, Sean took her hand. She didn't resist.

Neither of them spoke in the ten minutes it took to reach the Brights' new place, high on a hill outside town. It was quite the spread, a sprawling, cedar-sided ranch-style home with an in-ground pool behind a privacy fence. They had a spectacular view of Prospect spread out below.

When Sean opened Laura's door—with difficulty, because the latch decided to stick again—she handed him the gift. She wouldn't meet his eyes.

He'd known her since kindergarten. He recognized the signs that she needed to cry. And between losing her mom and hearing the rumors about her dad—and half believing he hadn't loved her—she had plenty to cry about.

He placed the gift on the roof of the truck. "Come here, Laura."

She shook her head.

"Don't be that way," he said. "I'm a friend. Friends give friends hugs."

"It's awkward."

"So? Deal with it."

He opened his arms, fully expecting her to walk right past him, but she stepped close and leaned against him. Shielded from the Brights' windows by a row of shrubs, he held her and stroked her hair. She still wasn't crying. Not around him.

"Let's skip the party," he said. "They'll understand."

She shook her head against his chest. "Trevor wouldn't."

"He's only turning five. He'll hardly notice who shows up and who doesn't."

"Trevor? Ha! He notices everything. I remember that from my last trip home. Anyway, we're here. We're going in."

He tried to nudge her back into the truck. "No. I'll call and explain. You aren't up to it."

"I'm up to it. I want to see Trevor's face when he sees that big ol' truck. He'll be so happy."

Laura had always wanted everybody safe and happy.

"I love you," Sean mouthed silently into her hair. He kissed the top of her head so lightly that she couldn't have felt it.

Or maybe he hadn't made it quite light enough, because her head jerked up, smacking his chin. She escaped his arms, grabbed the gift, and hustled around the bed of the truck and through the front yard. Sean followed. Gary welcomed them at the front door. Always the genial host, he gave Laura a fatherly hug, then gave Sean a cross between a hug and a bout of back-slapping.

"Any more thoughts about the house?" Gary asked after Laura had disappeared in the direction of the kitchen.

Sean nodded. "Once we're on the other side of Memorial weekend, I'll hurry up and finish the renovations." Except then he'd have more orders for instruments. Less time for the house.

"Good decision. I'm glad to hear it." Gary lowered his voice. "How's Laura doing?"

"Pretty well, considering she lost her mom recently."

"Why do people have to die?" Gary asked under his breath.

Because the world would get a little crowded if they didn't. Sean bit back the wisecrack in the nick of time.

He walked into the kitchen in time to see Trevor accost Laura. "Hey, Aunt Laura," he said, his eyes gleaming behind his glasses. "Did you bring me something?"

Her face lit with a big grin. "I sure did, sweetie. Your mom can tell you when it's time to open it, okay? It's from Uncle Sean too." She set the birthday present on the table and knelt for a hug. It was complicated a bit by the way Trevor tried to see around her to check out the gift.

Sean smiled, pleased with his unofficial title. Neither of them was related to the Brights, but it did feel like family. Him and Laura. Gary and Ardelle. Cassie. Tom and Tig and Trevor.

He made the rounds to shake hands or hug people, as appropriate. Even the cat, that prissy, expensive parasite, welcomed him by jumping into his lap the moment he took a seat at the kitchen table. Arabella smelled like herbal shampoo, but she purred and shed fur like any ordinary cat.

Somebody had put bluegrass on the stereo—not Elliott's CD, but one of Gibby's. The ritzy home buzzed with music and laughter. Gary and Ardelle might have moved up in the world, but they hadn't forgotten how to let their hair down and have fun. Sean's heart wasn't in it, though.

When everybody else went out to the patio to harass Gary about how to cook the steaks, Sean retreated to the living room. The cat followed and claimed his lap again.

He closed his eyes. He heard Cassie coming in, shouting something to somebody. Her flip-flops slapped their way across the kitchen. The sound softened as they hit the carpet, and finally stopped in front of him.

He opened his eyes. She stood there, squinting at him.

"What's your problem?" she asked.

"Is it obvious?"

"Yes." She knelt beside his chair and roughed up the cat's fur. Arabella twitched but went on purring.

"I hate birthdays," Sean said.

"Oh, I know. Elliott picked a bad week to drown."

"Yeah, that's part of it. And there's the other."

Cassie frowned at him. "Other?"

"You know. Laura and me. She must have told you."

"Told me what? Darn it, Halloran, this sounds juicy. Out with it."

Knowing she wouldn't give up until he'd confessed, he let out a sigh and checked to make sure nobody was within earshot. "Okay. The day I turned eighteen, I thought I was all grown up. An adult. And Laura looked so lost—it was less

231

than a week since Elliott drowned—" Sean stopped, remembering the blank look in her eyes, as if she'd just peered over the edge of the world into the abyss. Marriage had seemed like powerful magic to shield her from more heartache.

"Go on," Cassie said.

"I asked her to marry me."

Cassie's eyes widened. "You did?"

"She never told you? Her best friend?"

Cassie shook her head, obviously enthralled. "Well, what happened?"

"She said we were too young to be thinking about marriage. Next thing I knew, she'd changed her college plans. Instead of going to UGA, she went to Colorado. Like she wanted to put some distance between us."

"The rat. I can't believe she never told me."

"I guess she wanted to spare me the humiliation." He smiled a little. "But I never knew I wasn't being talked about, so I felt humiliated for no good reason."

"See, she's the kind of woman who won't talk about an ex-boyfriend."

"I shouldn't talk about her either."

"This is a different kind of talking. The constructive kind. Wow, Sean, I hope she'll stay long enough to give us some time to work on her. Maybe she'll even move home, unless Mikey kicks the bucket."

"Why would Mikey have anything to do with it?"

"Don't you remember? She's crazy about the cat because Elliott rescued him from a Dumpster or something. But she can't have pets in her apartment, and nobody would want to adopt such an old cat."

"What are you getting at?"

"As long as Mikey's alive, there's a chance she'll keep the house and move home. You'd better work fast though. Go for broke." Cassie stood up, rubbed Arabella the wrong way again, and headed for the kitchen.

Sean shook his head, remembering how Laura turned him down. The moment he'd realized she was saying no, her words had turned to muddy fuzz in his brain. He only knew she'd been kind. Now, to find out she'd never told her best friend about his stupid, misguided proposal . . . well, it only made him love her more. Even if she refused to love him—or refused to admit she did. There was a big difference.

Voices wafted toward him from the patio. Gary's jovial banter and Ardelle's breathless chatter. Laura's low voice, carrying a hint of the West now. Cassie's big laugh and Tigger's giggle. Tig still sounded like a kid sometimes.

Both Bright girls were almost like sisters to Sean. Sometimes he wished they were his real sisters. Other times, he just envied them for having two reasonably normal parents who loved them. Gary and Ardelle were good to him too, but being a charity project wasn't the same as being a son.

Absently smoothing the cat's silky pelt and half listening to the bluegrass on the stereo, Sean closed his eyes and remembered after-school afternoons at Elliott's shop, soaking up the man's music and his kindness. Sometimes Sean had imagined being his son, a fantasy that lasted only until he realized that would make Laura his sister. That would never do.

Exhausted from an evening of feigned cheerfulness and too many Gibby Sprague CDs, Laura kept her eyes on the center line as Sean drove her home. She tried to concentrate on the way the headlights ran ahead through the curves, but it didn't help.

All night, she'd been reliving long-ago birthday parties with her parents and the Brights. They'd always had so much fun together. As if they were really and truly all one big happy family.

She made a sharp intake of breath, nearly a sob, before she could stop herself.

Sean squeezed her hand. "Everything's finally hitting you," he said. "Right on top of losing your mom, you have the rumors about your dad. It's too much."

Afraid her voice wouldn't work, she only shook her head.

"What are your plans for tomorrow?" he asked after a long silence.

Maybe she could get a couple of words out. "More sorting."

"Why don't you get some help from somebody? Cassie, maybe? Two birds, one stone. Visit with her and make some progress on the sorting."

"Good idea."

He parked in front of the house and shut off the engine. "Sit tight. I'll get your door. It tends to stick."

Like she didn't know that? But she waited as he walked around the truck.

The dome light came on, making her feel exposed. She climbed out. Sean followed, hovering just behind her as she unlocked the back door.

"Thanks for the ride," she said, keeping her left shoulder to him so she wouldn't have to look him in the eye.

"Thanks for inviting me. Hey, look who decided to come home. Mikey."

She turned around, her heart instantly lighter. Mikey sashayed up the steps and wound himself around her ankles. She scooped him up, caught Sean's smile, and remembered her earlier terror that Mikey had been hit.

"Oh, I forgot I'd been interrogating you," she said. "You still haven't explained what Annie said about a drowning. Aren't you going to explain?"

"What she overheard was a figure of speech."

"It wasn't a literal drowning?"

He hesitated a little too long. "I don't believe I've ever witnessed a literal, human drowning in my life, and I hope I never will."

"You have a way of not quite lying but not quite telling the truth, either."

"It's a gift." He walked across the porch and down the steps, then looked up at her. "Next time we go out, it won't involve six other people."

"That was not a date, Sean. We were not technically going out."

"But we will. Just you wait. Lock up, now."

He climbed into his truck, but he didn't start the engine until she'd had time to carry the cat inside, close the door and dead-bolt it. Then he flashed his headlights.

The old signal was as blatant as saying it out loud. *"Good night. I love you."*

She jammed her hands into the pockets of her jeans so her fingers wouldn't be tempted to flash the porch light in answer. The truck roared out of the driveway and around the bend.

Laura checked the clock. It was early. Not even ten. And as tired as she was, she knew she couldn't sleep. She might as well make a pot of decaf and try to accomplish something. Maybe she'd tackle those dresser drawers. She didn't look forward to invading her mother's private space, but it had to be done.

There was usually a bag of decaf in the freezer.

Laura opened it and started poking around. Lots of frozen veggies and fruit. Not much meat. No red meat whatsoever, no convenience foods, and if there was any decaf it was well hidden.

Reaching to the rear of the top shelf, she found a store-bought bag of peas and then a clear bag full of blackberries. Her mom had always placed the berries on a small pan, leaving space between them so they wouldn't stick together as they froze. Once they were solid, she'd tumbled them into plastic bags and returned them to the freezer, perfect little morsels of summer's sweetness for blackberry cobblers in midwinter.

Laura tossed the peas back in and clutched the bag of berries with both hands. Her mom must have picked them last year—by herself, because her young helpers had grown up. Lost in bitter-sweet nostalgia for the days of berry picking in the lush growth near the tracks, Laura closed her eyes. She and her friends must have brought home thousands and thousands of berries over the years.

Her fingers were freezing. Gently, she placed the bag on the shelf and shut the freezer. Her mom would have chided her for leaving the door open so long.

The wind was stronger now, the sound of the wind chimes clearer. She'd always loved their cheerful noise, but now it set her nerves on edge. She couldn't stand it.

Halfway to the back door, she recalled the shadowy figure sweeping across the yard. Onto the moonlit road. Into the cemetery.

No. She didn't want to go out there alone and thrash her way through the bushes to take down the chimes. They hung from a branch of the star magnolia, surrounded by a tangle of shrubs. It would be hard enough to find them in broad daylight but nearly impossible in the dark.

Far away, coyotes yipped, chilling her blood. Their eerie voices overlapped the random music of the chimes, like two radio stations coming in at the same time, competing with each other.

The shadow of the overhead fan batted incessantly at the wall, the blades making their swift circle. The coyotes went silent all at once. There was no sound but the wind in the trees and the chimes. Then the wind stilled. Everything was hushed, as if the whole world waited for something to happen.

Seventeen

Across the road, a small crowd of churchgoers milled around the doors in the usual preservice socialization time. Not wanting them to think she was spying on them, Laura settled into a chair on the porch where she'd be somewhat hidden by the lower branches of a pine.

Late last night, she'd found confirmation of one of her worst fears. This morning, in a fit of spite, she'd deleted her mom's number from her cell phone contacts. She'd used up the last of those frozen berries too. She wasn't sentimental about them anymore. Not after lying awake half the night, fuming over the note she'd found in her mother's lingerie drawer.

A whiff of baking cobbler escaped through the kitchen window.

Her dad had always loved blackberry cobbler. With vanilla ice cream if they had it. Or whipped cream. Real whipped cream. And he'd never put on a pound.

"Oh, Daddy," she whispered. His crazy accusation must have been true, after all.

She looked up at a cloud made of bands of white and gray, chevroned. The wind had run through them like a knife through marble-cake batter.

Across the road, the organist pumped out some unrecognizable hymn. Most of the churchgoers had disappeared inside the building, but stragglers were still arriving. She recognized a few vehicles, a few faces.

There was Gary's car. He swerved into a space, climbed out, and ran around to open Ardelle's door, then the rear door. Cassie climbed out of the backseat in jeans and a hot-pink sweater. The three of them walked toward the church entrance, pausing to speak with two young women in flowery dresses. Gary put his arm around Ardelle and threw his head back, laughing at something. The young women laughed too, the wind rippling their skirts. They clutched Bibles like anchors to hold them to earth in the strong wind.

Cassie looked over her shoulder toward the house. Laura leaned out from behind the pine and waved. Cassie waved back and made some kind of hand signal.

"Whatever," Laura said, watching all of them file into the church.

Minutes later, Cassie sprinted across the road, across the yard, and up the steps. Breathless and laughing, she plopped herself into the chair beside Laura's. "My folks probably think I'm sitting in the back."

"My dad always said you were a corrupting influence," Laura said.

"Well, I can be in church pretty much any Sunday, but how often do I get to sit and visit with my oldest friend? But if you want to go, let's go."

"Can't. I have blackberry cobbler in the oven."

"Mmm, that settles it. I'm not going to church."

"It's pretty obvious you didn't plan to anyway. How's your mom doing?"

"Pretty much the same. She has good days

and bad days. She won't talk about anything important, and she gets mad if we suggest counseling."

Laura nodded. Her dad had resisted counseling too. Not that her mom had ever pressed hard for it. Maybe she hadn't really cared.

Mikey hopped onto a windowsill and meowed at them through the glass.

"Poor baby," Cassie said. "Can't he even come onto the porch?"

"No, he'd be gone in a flash, and there's so much traffic now."

"Maybe he wouldn't last long outside, but he'd die free and happy."

"Happy? Under somebody's tires?"

"But he might be smarter than you're giving him credit for."

"I doubt it. He always heads straight to the road." Laura sighed. "I've been trying to decide whether or not to mention this, but I think you should know. Mikey escaped a couple of days ago because your mom let him out."

"My mom?"

"Remember I told you she was overstepping her bounds? It was sweet of her to take care of things for me, but it was supposed to stop when I got into town. On Friday, she let herself in when I wasn't home. She tidied up again, and she fed Mikey and let him out." On the verge of mentioning the boxed-up journals, Laura stopped, troubled by the worry in Cassie's eyes.

"I'm so sorry, Laura. I'll say something to her."

"Don't. I just thought you should know. It might be part of the big picture of whatever's going on with her."

"Maybe. Anyway, I didn't come here to talk about weird parents. I came to talk about marriage proposals. I cannot believe you never told me Sean asked you to marry him. And you turned him down?"

"He told you?"

"He certainly did, and if we hadn't been in the middle of Trevor's party I would have dragged you off somewhere and smacked some sense into you."

"His timing was terrible, Cassie. It was right in the middle of losing my dad. And we were so young. Then I took off for college in Colorado, and Sean and I sort of grew apart."

"Grow back together then. Duh."

"It's not that simple." Laura hesitated, running a finger back and forth on the arm of her chair while she sought the right words. "Even when we were sixteen, seventeen, I knew I didn't want to be the daughter-in-law of a mean drunk."

"Oh, come on. Do you ever hear Sean calling Dale his father? No. Sean doesn't see him as his father, so you wouldn't have to see Dale as your father-in-law."

"Cassie—"

"Wait, I've got it." Cassie clapped her hands. "Ask Sean to move to Denver. He'd start packing. You know he would. And you'd never see Dale again."

Laura didn't answer, but if there was any chance that her dad would come home, she couldn't stay in Denver. She'd have to return to Prospect—where Dale lived.

Cassie scowled at her. "What are you so scared of? Marriage in general? Or marriage to Sean?"

Laura shook her head. "Can you at least understand why I couldn't even think about marriage the week we turned eighteen? The same week my dad disappeared?"

"You're right, Sean's timing was terrible, but that was then. This is now."

"Now wouldn't be great timing either. With all that's going on, I'm a mess."

"Yeah." Cassie slumped back in her chair. "You are."

"I was worse then, though. You wouldn't believe what a mess I was."

"Well, sure. You'd just lost your dad."

"It was more than that." Laura stopped, weighing her words. "Now that you've had a taste of what it's like to live with a parent who has some issues—even though your mom's issues are minor compared to my dad's—maybe you can understand better. He'd become so hard to live with. You have no idea. Then, when we thought he'd drowned, I felt a huge sense of relief and freedom. I was glad he was gone. Cassie, I was *glad*. And I hated myself for it."

Cassie didn't answer right away, but she didn't seem shocked. Finally she shrugged. "That sounds pretty normal, really. And now you think you want him back?"

The muffled, faraway sound of the organ floated across the road toward them as the organist murdered "Amazing Grace." Laura had sung that song with her dad so many times. She'd give anything for a chance to sing it with him again. She'd give anything to tell him that although she'd hated his unpredictable mood swings, his volatility, she'd never hated *him*. She'd loved him then and she loved him now. No matter what.

"Yes, I want him back," she said. "Even if it takes a miracle."

"You'll need more than one miracle."

"Then I'll ask God for two. Or ten or twenty. Whatever it takes."

Laura closed her eyes, and once again she inhaled the sweet aroma of blackberry cobbler. She'd never eat another blackberry her mom had picked. Never again.

Sean crouched on his back deck to watch the little albino raccoon feasting on the corn and table scraps laid out for him in the far corner.

Silvery-white in the moonlight, the baby coon looked up, more curious than wary.

Nobody needed another ordinary trash-can raider, but this white one was a novelty. Casper the ghost coon.

Sean knew he shouldn't feed it. Hunters didn't feed coons, much less name them. Keith would never let him live it down if he found out about it.

He wouldn't, though. Nobody would.

Casper wouldn't last long. He was too easy to spot. Easy prey.

Sean straightened. Casper scampered away, claws skittering on the smooth wood of the deck. Three seconds, and he was in the oak. He was easy to track through the branches, a pale blur in the night.

The flash of white high in the tree took Sean back to the kite he'd lost to the same tree when he was ten, not long after his mother passed away. Night after night, it had beat itself to death against the branches while he watched from his bedroom window.

Dale had come home one day with an unexpected gift: a white and yellow kite. Sean's first kite ever. Sensing that it was an apology for especially harsh treatment the night before, he'd dared to hope that things were changing.

"Do your chores, boy," Dale had said. "Then I'll help you put it together." But he was too drunk to help by the time Sean finished his chores.

Keith was at work, bagging groceries, so Sean assembled the kite himself. Afraid he'd be in hot water if he went as far as the park, he tried to fly it in the yard. Within minutes, it took a nosedive into the tree. Once Dale noticed, he wasn't too drunk to administer another beating.

That was the last day Sean ever called him Dad. Following Keith's example, Sean started calling him Dale behind his back.

A train was coming through from the south, its mournful, two-tone whistle piping a lonesome tune while the wheels beat a steady rhythm. Sean cocked his head, listening. He'd never minded living near the tracks. A train in the night was evidence that he wasn't the only soul awake.

Was Laura awake, brooding over everything? He hadn't heard from her since he'd dropped her off the night before. He hoped he hadn't scared her off by flashing his headlights.

He went inside. The thunder of a coming storm mixed with his worries to keep him awake long after he'd crawled into bed. He was wrestling with that vague memory of the car in the lake when his phone rang. He grabbed it from the bedside table and checked caller ID.

It was Laura—and it was too late to be a happy call.

He sat up straight. "Hello."

She didn't answer. Outside, a vehicle rushed past on the wet street, going too fast for a rainy night.

"Hello," he said again, hearing a faint noise on the other end. "Laura? You okay?"

"Sean!" There she was, her voice high-pitched and shaky. "He's back."

"Who?" Sean's feet hit the floor. He switched on the lamp and grabbed his jeans from the chair.

"At the window. He—" The phone started cutting out.

Words and fragments of words flitted in and out of his ear. Something about a beard.

"Was it your dad?" He struggled to pull on his jeans with one hand, clamping the phone to his ear with his other hand.

"I don't—" The reception cut out again.

Cursing the lousy connection, he fought one-handed with his zipper. "Laura? You still there?"

Silence.

The phone slipped out of his hand, hit the floor, and slid under the bed. He ran down the hall for his gun.

❧ Eighteen ❧

Nobody in his right mind would be out in this weather.

The truck slued around the corner and fishtailed on the rain-swept road. Sean maneuvered around a downed tree branch, swerved back to his own lane, and tromped on the accelerator. Between the swipes of the wipers, he could hardly see through the streaming glass.

In less than a minute, he outran the neat layout of city blocks and crossed the railroad tracks at the edge of town where a criminal would have plenty of places to hide—if he didn't mind lurking under tall trees in a thunderstorm.

Kim would have advised calling the professionals. He couldn't, now that he'd dropped his phone, but a loaded gun had to be worth a couple of phones.

The truck fishtailed again as he hauled it around the bend by the church, tires sliding on wet pave-ment. The house was dark. He pulled into the drive and killed the engine but left the headlights shining while he put his hands on his gun.

He didn't see anybody, but that didn't mean

somebody wasn't out there. Elliott? Dale? Or a stranger. A stranger might be easier to deal with.

He shut off the headlights. The church's security lights still reached toward him from across the road. They'd make his bare skin as visible as the albino coon's white fur. He should have grabbed a shirt. A black one.

Gun in hand, he opened the door and slid out. With cold rain pelting his back, he crouched beside the truck. But he didn't know which side of the truck the intruder was on.

He held still, letting his eyes adjust to the dark. No noise but wind and rain . . . and a strange absence, like a hole in the night. Spooky.

No time to figure it out.

He straightened, closed the door, and started for the house at a fast walk. Didn't want to run; didn't want to show his fear. He was soaked before his feet hit the steps.

The rain pounded the porch's tin roof like artillery, masking his knock, but Laura cracked the door open immediately. She opened it wider, beckoned him in and pushed him to the side. He heard the bolt sliding home, the scrape of chair legs on the floor and a metallic sound. She was shoving a chair under the knob.

"Where was he?" Sean whispered, his heart pounding, his nose dripping rain.

"Looking in the kitchen window. I screamed. Dropped a mug in the sink—smashed it—and he ran." That clipped, staccato speech wasn't her usual style.

"Did you get a good look?"

"No. It happened so fast. He was there—he was gone. And you know how nearsighted I am without my contacts or glasses."

His eyes were growing accustomed to the black room. Laura was wearing Jess's white bathrobe.

In the silence, his breath coming fast, he tried again to identify why the wind and the rain sounded so different tonight. Something was missing.

Goose bumps stirred the hairs on his wet skin. "You've seen somebody twice, just since you've been back in town."

"Yes," she whispered.

He could only think of the flash of brown in the green, the first day Laura was back in town, when he'd walked her home from church. It might have been a man in camo, and that made three times.

"Tonight, it was my dad," she said. "I know it was."

"How can you know, if you couldn't really see his face? And if it was your dad, why did he run?"

She pulled in a sharp breath. "Because I screamed. I screamed at the top of my lungs. I didn't mean to. I didn't want to scare him away."

The scream that would scare a banshee.

"Let's go in the den," Sean said. "That's where you always felt safe when Slattery was prowling around, remember? Maybe we've got ourselves another Slattery."

He led her there, holding her hand. The den was pitch-black, its heavy drapes drawn tight. He placed the gun on the floor, switched on a lamp, and tugged her down beside him on the double rocking chair. He was freezing, his shoulders still wet.

She'd found her glasses. She studied him with those solemn brown eyes framed by brown plastic, but she didn't speak.

"We need security lights everywhere," he said. "We'll light up the place like Vegas. You need new locks too. And an alarm system."

She only shrugged.

He put his arm around her but resisted the notion to kiss the top of her head. He started the loveseat rocking. It should have been a comforting motion, but it only created a breeze on his damp skin, chilling him.

A gust of wind and rain battered the house. Laura tensed. Not wanting to scare her off, he resisted the impulse to pull her closer. As long as she was in his arms, she was safe from whoever had been at her window. Except one man's body wasn't much of a shield. He couldn't be with her twenty-four hours a day, either.

"There are guns in your dad's gun safe," he said. "You have the right to defend yourself if anybody breaks in. And you have a phone. I'm glad you called me, but you need to call 911 too, if it happens again."

"I'm not calling 911," she said. "You told me the sheriff thinks the rumors are bogus. He won't even care."

"He'll care about a man who's walking around town, looking in windows. If you won't call the sheriff, you're staying somewhere else. My house, the Brights' house, I don't care. Or I'm staying here."

"Then you're staying here," she said.

She sat stiffly in the dark, breathing fast and trembling like a hummingbird's wings.

At a quarter to four, rain still hammered the windows. The house was an ark tossed about on a stormy ocean, with only two souls aboard. Three, if she counted the cat. But someone else had been out there in the night.

Trying to remain calm and act normal, Laura walked into the kitchen and caught Sean scratching Mikey's chin and crooning some kind of nonsense to him.

"Since when have you been so nice to Mikey?" she asked.

He looked up, wearing a blue shirt that brought out the intense color of his eyes. He must have borrowed it from her dad's closet. "How about some coffee?"

"Why not? We'll never get back to sleep anyway."

"Coming right up." He went straight to the cupboard that held the good Costa Rican stuff. He knew where the coffee filters were too, and he knew how to coax the beat-up coffee grinder into operating.

Laura opened a different cupboard to pull out a couple of mugs. There was her dad's favorite, right where it belonged. She rested her fingers on the handle. Black, plain, the mug had a hairline crack and a white chip on the rim. Mom had nagged him to throw it out but he wouldn't. She could have thrown it out once he was gone, but maybe she'd turned sentimental about it. Maybe she'd even come to regret the affair.

Or she was just a pack rat.

Laura pulled the mug from the cupboard. So many times, she'd seen her dad warming his big hands around that chipped mug. Sometimes he'd curved a hand tenderly around her mother's cheek too, in a kind of benediction.

"Laura." Sean's voice was nearly in her ear.

"What?"

"You okay? I don't think you heard a word I said."

He'd been talking?

"I'm fine." Ignoring Sean just behind her, she

put the black mug on the counter, chose one for herself, and rummaged in the cupboard for the sugar bowl.

Sean poured coffee for both of them. "Still take yours like a man?"

"Yes, thanks." She took her black coffee to the table and wrapped her hands around the heat of the crockery. "Now, what were you talking about?"

"Nothing important." His spoon clinked softly as he stirred in his usual boatload of sugar.

She tried her coffee. He was right. The Costa Rican stuff was good. Good and strong.

"Is that cobbler?" he asked.

"Yep. Help yourself."

"You don't want any?"

"No, thank you."

She closed her eyes, seeing those purple berries piled up in a bucket in the late-summer sun. Seeing her mom's long, slender fingers brushing the frozen berries into a plastic bag. Tucking them away for later.

"The perfect breakfast," Sean said. "Coffee and cobbler."

She kept her eyes closed and didn't answer, just listened to the sounds as he clattered around, dishing up a serving of the cobbler and then settling into the chair across from hers.

His fork clinked against the plate. "Delicious. Your mom's recipe?"

"No. It's one I found online."

She hadn't wanted to open her mom's recipe file. It would have unleashed memories of baking together. Making her dad's favorite suppers. Being a happy family, most of the time. But she couldn't forget that last big blowup either.

Laura shuddered and opened her eyes.

Sean had his last bite of cobbler halfway to his mouth. "What's wrong?"

"Nothing."

"No. Tell me what's wrong."

"The cobbler," she blurted. "It's the last . . . the last . . ." She couldn't say it.

Looking bewildered, he pointed the fork toward the dish on the counter. "No, there's plenty more. You want some?"

"No. I don't mean . . . It's not the last of the cobbler." She steeled herself, making her voice hard and clear. "I made the cobbler with the last of the berries my mom ever picked."

"Aw, Laura." Abandoning his last bite, he came around the table and crouched beside her. He took her hand in his. "You'll be missing her for a long, long time."

"But that's not it. It's . . . it's about something I've kept from you too long. Oh Sean, I don't want to tell you, but you'll need to know—especially if my dad comes back."

"All right." Sean sat in the chair beside hers. He didn't let go of her hand.

"This will sound stupid. You'll think there's no connection between blackberries and this . . . other topic. But bear with me."

"Okay."

"When we were teenagers, I heard my folks arguing." Wanting to stop right there, she made herself keep going. "Dad accused her of being unfaithful."

Sean flinched almost as if she'd slapped him. "Did they know you were listening?"

"No. They were right here in the kitchen, and I was around the corner. I'd left to spend the night at Cassie's house, but I came back for my toothbrush. I only listened for a minute."

"When was this?"

"About a month before he disappeared. She had an affair, Sean. He found out. He made his plans, and he walked away."

"If you thought it was related, why didn't you mention it when he went missing?"

"We thought he'd died, remember? And I . . . I didn't want to believe it was anything more than his paranoia. I thought it was best to give her the benefit of the doubt."

"Did she acknowledge that there was any truth to it?"

"I don't know. I didn't eavesdrop long enough to find out."

He shook his head. "Maybe it wasn't true."

"But since then, I've wondered about things I

256

saw over the years. Clues that she was a little too friendly with a certain someone." She stopped, hating to say it. "Last night, I found a . . . a naughty note in her dresser. A note in masculine writing. There's no signature, but it's not my dad's writing."

"Does anybody else know about this?"

"Nope." Then Laura managed a half smile. "I expect the other man knows."

"Do you know who it was?"

"Think for a minute, Sean. *You* know. It'll come to you." She started a silent count to ten.

At six, Sean's eyes widened. "Gibby."

"That's my theory. By the time we were in high school, my dad was practically impossible to live with. Maybe she'd started looking for someone new, and there was Gibby. Always so charming and available. And he came through town every few months."

"He still does. He'll be here for the weekend."

"I could ask him if it's true, but part of me would rather not know. I'd rather just forgive both of them, as if I know it's true, and let it go."

"That's probably a good way to handle it. But remember, you don't know the timing of the note. It might have been written long after your dad was gone."

"Maybe, but the simplest explanation is that the argument I overheard was about her and Gibby. And Dad walked away a month later." Seeing the sadness in Sean's eyes, Laura squeezed his hand. "I didn't want to tell you, Sean. I'm sorry."

"I'm sorry too, but I'm glad you told me. It does put a different spin on things." He tilted his head, studying her. "You think this proves that your dad walked away instead of drowning, don't you?"

"I'm about ninety-nine percent convinced."

"That's a mighty big leap."

"I know, but it all fits. I only hope that if he's alive, he won't pick next weekend to come back. When Gibby's in town. That could be a real problem."

Frowning, Sean reached across the table to retrieve his coffee. It must have cooled, but he drank it anyway, staring into space. He made no move to finish eating his cobbler.

"Now it's your turn," Laura said. "I told you a whopper of a secret. When will you explain that figurative drowning?"

He looked up, startled, then smiled. "Compared to what you just told me, it's nothing. Years ago, I saw somebody sending a car into the little lake on old man Bennett's land."

She pondered it for a moment. "You mean . . . like somebody stole a car and had to get rid of it?"

"That would make sense, wouldn't it?"

"It's just funny that Annie made such a big deal of it."

He picked up his fork and worked at straightening a crooked tine. "I guess she didn't hear every-thing so she had to fill in the blanks from her imagination."

"I guess."

Thunder boomed, making both of them jump.

"Here comes another round," Sean said. "Nobody will be out in this."

Laura was sure he'd meant to make her feel safe from intruders, but she could only think about her father, cold and wet and miserable. Somewhere.

❧ Nineteen ❧

Laura woke, her feet cold and her cheek itching against the rough fabric of the couch cushion. Instantly, she remembered the bearded man at the window.

She and Sean had sat in silence for a long time after they'd moved back to the living room. They hadn't turned on any lights, though an occasional flash of lightning had shown her his troubled expression.

She sat up and examined her elbow. In a few days, the bruise wouldn't be visible anymore. Sean still hadn't noticed it.

The heavy old quilt lay across her. Sean must have tucked her in after she nodded off. With his gun by his side, he lay on the hooked rug on the hardwood floor, his angular features softened by the shadows of morning. No pillow, no quilt. His hair was tousled and messy. His stubborn mouth was relaxed in sleep.

She had her work cut out for her, but she had to convince him that her visitor wasn't a criminal, wasn't a ghost. It was Elliott Gantt in the flesh, wandering around in a terrible storm and frightened away by his own daughter's scream. She could hardly bear the thought.

She swung her feet to the floor, then arranged the warm quilt over Sean's long frame, pleased with the idea of transferring her body heat to him. He didn't stir, even when she pulled the quilt up to his whiskery chin and touched his cheek with one finger.

"Some bodyguard you are," she said.

He still didn't wake.

He should have been in his own bed, getting a good night's sleep. No, he should have been hard at work already, making all those mysterious little tweaks to the nearly finished instruments that he wanted to sell at his festival booth. He should have been proofreading his brochures so the printer could have them ready by Friday morning at the latest.

To get Sean back where he belonged, working

toward his dream, she'd have to convince him she wasn't in danger. After last night, it wouldn't be easy.

She tiptoed around him and went into the kitchen, where Mikey swatted her leg in a silent demand for food. She gave him a can of chicken and liver, his favorite. When she opened the trash to throw the can away, she saw shards of angels and rainbows—the remains of the angel mug that she'd dropped in the sink when she saw the man at the window. Sean had cleaned up the wreckage.

The window framed a sky of the brightest blue. Small tree limbs and scattered leaves lay across the yard, varying shades of brown and green on the lawn. Sunlight glistened in still puddles. No branches moved. The wind had worn itself out in the night.

She recalled those deep-set eyes meeting hers for a fraction of a second. She'd screamed, and the man had ducked out of sight.

It could've been Dale. He had a beard too. But his eyes weren't that deep set, were they? She was almost certain it was her dad, but after all that time in the wild, his appearance would have changed. His mind and his heart might have changed too.

He might have left signs of his visit.

After Laura dressed, she put her phone in her pocket. Blocking Mikey's escape, she stepped onto the leaf-strewn porch. It was cold and damp beneath her bare feet.

Beyond the borders of the yard, green billows of kudzu were taking over. A whole regiment of men could hide in the luxuriant growth.

The world was holding its breath. No wind blew, not even enough breeze to move the chimes. She couldn't see them, hidden as they were by shrubs, but she imagined the silvery cylinders hanging motionless among the drenched leaves.

There would be no footprints. The storm would have washed them away. Just as time had washed away the evidence of her mother's guilt or innocence. Then the aneurysm had taken her life.

Her voice had been so calm, last Christmas, when she casually mentioned that she'd already made her funeral arrangements, wanting to get them off her mind for good. Less than six months later, she was gone. Maybe she'd had a premonition.

She opened her phone and checked the time. It wasn't too early for a call.

Cassie answered on the second ring, sounding groggy. "Good morning, but next time remember I'm still on California time."

"Good morning, Eeyore."

"Yeah. What's up?"

"I have a favor to ask." Laura made her voice

bright and cheerful. "Sean is so paranoid about prowlers, it's ridiculous. He's sticking to me like glue. Playing bodyguard."

"Lucky girl. He's one cute bodyguard."

"He's one busy luthier. He needs to be in his shop, doing prep work for the weekend."

"What's to do? He only needs to show up at his booth and flash that adorable smile at the ladies, and he'll sell instruments like hotcakes."

"There's a little more to it than that. And would you please stop trying to make him sound so—so—"

"Gorgeous and sweet and sexy?"

"Cassie. Stop it."

Cassie laughed. "Okay, okay. What's the favor?"

"If I'm here, he'll insist on being here too. Can I hang out at your house today? And spend the night? Or is that a problem, given your mom's situation?"

"Not a problem. She's pretty darned normal most of the time. Come on over, anytime."

"Thanks. Maybe I'll bring some of my mom's papers to sort through."

"Good idea. Bring enough busywork so my mom won't draft you to help with her eternal scrapping." Cassie yawned. "We'll have a sleepover tonight. I'll see ya when you show up."

"I'll be there soon." Laura closed her phone, pleased with herself for having told the truth but not the whole truth. Cassie didn't need to know about the man at the window. Not yet.

Throwing off the remnants of sleep, Sean raised his head and frowned at the quilt on his chest. He couldn't comprehend how it got there.

Something poked his side. "Rise and shine, bodyguard. You've been sleeping on the job."

He blinked. Laura came into focus, sitting on the couch with her big toe prodding his ribs. She'd changed to jeans and a sleeveless white shirt. The outfit reminded him of long, hot days, fishing on Hamlin Lake before it had become the scene of a tragedy. Before she'd moved to Denver, where she turned pale in the wintertime. He wanted her to move back, to go fishing with him and get her fisherman's tan back—except she'd insist on sunscreen for both of them.

He seized her foot. "Sorry, but that's the kind of service a client gets when she doesn't pay her bodyguard one red cent."

Her foot escaped his grasp. "The coffee's free, though. You want some?"

"Yeah. I'll make it."

"Why do you always insist on making it?"

"You make it too strong."

"Wimp," she said.

Her smile wasn't quite genuine. And no wonder, after the bomb she'd dropped on him in the middle of the night. But if she didn't want to talk anymore about her mom and Gibby, neither did Sean. He'd rather not even think about it.

He rose, dropped the quilt on the couch, then picked up his gun and placed it on top of Jess's tall, thirty-year-old television cabinet that hadn't held a TV in years. In the kitchen, he pulled the coffee out of the cupboard. He filled the lid of the coffee grinder with beans and dumped them into the hopper. But the grinder was obstinate.

He picked it up and shook it. "This thing has a short in it somewhere." He pressed the button again, and it decided to work.

He faced Laura, his mind swimming with ideas about security lights, alarms, peepholes in the doors. "We need a plan."

"I've got one. Part of one, anyway. I'll spend the day at the Brights' house. The night too. Then you won't feel like you have to baby-sit me."

The knot of tension inside him began to unwind. "Good idea."

"I'm already packed, and Cassie's expecting me. She says we'll have a sleepover. I guess she'll want to watch movies and eat junk food."

"Excellent," he said, already starting to tune out the rest.

As the coffee brewed, he made his plans. With Laura safe and sound at the Brights' place, he'd be free to take care of business.

She poured coffee for both of them, putting hers in a travel mug, and regarded him with a solemn expression. "While I'm gone," she said softly, "if anybody shows up, whether it's my dad or someone else, I don't want any guns. Understand?"

Sean hesitated, picturing himself face to face with an intruder. Keith had learned in the service that if somebody's aiming at you, you don't mess around. *"It ain't Hollywood,"* Keith said. *"Aim to kill—or be killed."*

"The guy at the window probably wasn't your dad, Laura. Understand?"

"You have no way of knowing that. But here's the bottom line. My dad's safety is my top concern. Don't be trigger-happy, just in case it's him. Do *you* understand?"

Sean was silent. As far as he knew, Elliott had never hurt anybody except the time he blew up at Gary and the time he decked Dale. Maybe the fact that Gibby lived in Nashville had saved him.

Laura took a step closer. "Sean, I know you're safety conscious, but accidents happen. You don't want to accidentally shoot Dale either, do you?"

He chuckled. "Now that you mention it . . ."

"That's not funny. Promise me. No guns."

"No guns while you're gone," he said with a sigh.

"You mean it?"

"I mean it." But when she came back, that was a different story.

"And don't go around telling people what

happened last night. Remember, I don't want the sheriff's department to get involved. I can't tell law enforcement 'no guns.' "

Sean considered her request. He was willing to get the law involved if Laura's safety was at stake, but not just to track down rumors. She'd be perfectly safe at the Brights' house. And he would find a way to make her stay longer than over-night.

"You're right," he said. "I won't tell anybody."

"Okay, then. I'm off. And don't you dare baby-sit the house all day." She tapped his chest with her forefinger. "Sean Michael Halloran, up-and-coming luthier, doesn't have time to moonlight as a house-sitter. The festival starts on Friday."

"Friday's just the warmup, remember? I won't open my booth until Saturday morning."

"And Saturday will be here before you know it. Go home and get to work."

He was already making a mental list of the tools he'd pick up. His phone too. He couldn't live without his phone.

"Yes ma'am," he said.

Finally, she smiled. "Good boy." She picked up Mikey and kissed the top of his head. "You be a good boy too. Don't run off."

Sean moved closer. "I should stick my head between you and the cat so you'll kiss me by accident. You might even like it. I promise I don't have fleas."

"Neither does Mikey—and he never bosses me around." She rubbed her face against Mikey's and set him on the floor.

"But I'm a better kisser than Mikey," Sean said. "I have real lips. I'm sure you remember them. Like I remember yours."

Her cheeks turned pink, but she didn't answer. She slung the handles of a small overnight bag over her shoulder and crouched to pick up a cardboard file box that looked a little too heavy for her.

"Let me get it, whatever it is."

"It's Mom's papers to sort through," she said in a matter-of-fact tone that belied the blush on her face. "It'll give me something to do while I listen to Ardelle's chitchat."

"Good luck with that." He nudged her out of the way and took charge of the box.

She headed toward her mom's SUV instead of her own car. She'd already put For Sale signs in the windows. He followed, hobbling barefoot across the sharp gravel.

While Laura climbed behind the wheel, he put the box in the back of the SUV and shut the door. The vehicle had been kept in the garage since shortly after Jess died, and old, dried marks from the wiper blade still made a gray peacock's fan on the dirty glass of the rear window. The last time she drove to town, it must have been a rainy day. Her last day to run errands.

"Bye," Laura called, using that matter-of-fact tone again.

"Bye. Be good."

"You too." She started the engine and then leaned her head out the window. "Thanks for staying with me."

"I'm glad you called."

Picking his way back over the gravel, Sean remembered finding that secondhand SUV for Jess. She'd wanted something reliable to last ten years or so. He'd kidded her about ditching her old minivan because she was tired of the soccer mom image that came with it. She'd joked about wanting to be a soccer grandma one day.

He pictured three or four redheads playing soccer. Riding their bikes. Bouncing on a trampoline, screaming, having a ball. Maybe one of them would be a little girl dragging a doll along everywhere she went.

Lord willing, someday he'd be the kind of father who would teach a kid how to fly a kite or swing a hammer or play a guitar. The kind of father who gave hugs. The kind of father who couldn't make a kid cower in a corner just by looking at him.

On the steps, he brushed gravel from the soles of his feet and looked up in time to see the SUV disappear around the bend. He blew out a long sigh of relief. Laura was safe.

He wondered what he would do if their

trespasser had a gun. Especially if he proved to be Elliott after all.

Sean couldn't imagine firing at a broken-down wreck of a man, but he couldn't picture Elliott that way. He'd always been a lithe, strong outdoorsman with a quick smile. He'd had a simple tattoo on one muscular forearm, the lettering vaguely Celtic in style. The two words looked as if they'd been lifted from the middle of a sentence because they weren't capitalized: *life everlasting,* with the tail of the *g* curving into the purple vein on his wrist.

Elliott had never volunteered anything about the significance of the tattoo, and Sean had never asked.

Slowly, he walked inside. Life everlasting was all well and good, but he had to focus on the here and now. He'd start with a trip to the hardware store.

Twenty

Laura was about to lower the file box to the Brights' doorstep so she'd have a hand free to use the shiny brass door knocker, but the door swung open. Cassie stood there in a tank top and cutoffs, her hair turbaned in a pale yellow towel.

She took the box, leaving Laura with nothing to carry but her purse and the overnight bag.

"Come on in," Cassie said. "Let's go back to my room. Well, it's the guest room. I don't exactly have my own room here."

"Where's your mom?"

"On the phone with Tig."

Laura followed Cassie across travertine tiles to the living room, where the funeral plants were still clustered around the fireplace, then down the hall to the plush white carpet of a sunny bedroom. The walls were an even softer shade of the towel's yellow. The bed linens and the curtains were tastefully subdued but almost too well coordinated with each other.

"Very nice," Laura said, taking it in. "Just like the rest of the house. I feel like I've stepped into a decorating magazine."

"Yeah, it makes me feel like a peon. We live in the tiniest, ugliest apartment ever. You'll have to come see us sometime so you can feel superior. Aw, rats. Here comes my mom already."

Ardelle stuck her head in. "Is that Laura I hear? Hey, honey. It's so good to see you. Are you doing all right?"

"Most of the time."

"Oh, I know it's hard. Your mom was the sweetest soul. She and your dad loved each other so much." Ardelle came closer, twisting her hands together. "We'll never know what he went

271

through in the war, but she was so good to him even when he had his moods. She never even looked at another man after he drowned."

Laura only nodded, keeping her expression neutral, although her heart felt like a battlefield.

"It'd be such a shame if it's true that he's alive, now that it's too late because she's dead—"

"Mom," Cassie scolded. "Don't be insensitive. You're about to make Laura cry."

"But wouldn't it be wonderful if he's alive? Tig says old Mrs. Gustafson is spreading stories about seeing him on the road by their house."

Laura's heart thumped. "When?"

Ardelle waved the question away with her plump hand. "Oh, I didn't ask for details. You know I don't like to meddle in other folks' business."

"Mother dear," Cassie said firmly, "you are the biggest meddler and gossip I know."

"I am not."

"You let yourself into Laura's house a few days ago without permission, didn't you?"

Laura put her hand on Cassie's arm. "Stop, Cassie. Let it go."

But Cassie was on a roll. "And you let the cat get out, Mom. He could have been hit by a car."

Ardelle hung her head. "I was only trying to help."

"It's called breaking and entering," Cassie snapped.

"Jess gave me a key! I was her most trusted friend." Ardelle's eyes filled with tears. "Laura, you asked me to feed the cat and all, and now you're calling me a thief?"

"No," Laura said gently. "Nobody's calling you a thief. It's just that I don't need your help anymore, now that I'm in town."

"Well, I never! You *asked* for my help." Ardelle's chin quivered. "If you don't want me in your mother's home, I don't want you in mine." She flounced out of the room.

Laura stared at the empty doorway. What had happened to warm-hearted, fun-loving Ardelle?

"I don't believe it," Cassie said. "The drama mama is kicking you out." She flopped onto the bed, flinging one arm over her face in a fake swoon. "Let's ignore her awhile and see what happens."

"No. Not when she's this upset. I'd better not stay."

Cassie lifted her arm just enough so she could peer at Laura. "You're abandoning me?"

"Sorry, but you're the one who got her riled up, so you're the one who gets to calm her down. Don't be too hard on her, though. She might not want to behave the way she's behaving."

"I know," Cassie said mournfully. She sat up on the bed. "It was really weird, wasn't it? Really unlike her. I hate to worry Dad, but I'd better tell him."

"He absolutely needs to know. I'll call you later and see how she's doing."

Laura gathered the things she'd brought and headed out again. She'd stay away for a while. Ardelle's comments had hurt.

But there was no time for tears. Driving back to town, Laura tried to remember exactly where the Gustafsons lived. With a little luck, shy Mrs. Gustafson might be home alone and able to describe exactly what she saw, without any interference from her bossy husband.

Sean hit the brakes, approaching the long curve by Jess's house. Laura's house, now, but probably not for long. A dollar to a doughnut, she'd put it on the market and head back to Denver. He'd move there too, if he thought she might want his company.

It was nearly noon. That gave him time to finish by dark. He was still waiting for a call back from a security company, but he'd already picked up everything he could install himself. If he could talk Laura into staying with the Brights until everything blew over, maybe his pre-cautions weren't even necessary. But they couldn't hurt.

The house came into view—and Jess's SUV stood in the driveway, bold as brass. The vehicle Laura had driven away in.

There she was, at the edge of the road. In one

hand, she carried a big plastic pitcher like the kind his mom had always used for mixing up Kool-Aid. In the other hand, she carried a tall tin vase.

Either not noticing him or ignoring him, Laura hurried across the road, her hair somewhat tamed by the black-and-white bandanna she'd adopted as her own. Surefooted as a kid, she started up the steps set into the grassy bank.

Sean parked behind the SUV. Leaving his purchases in the truck and feeling like a paranoid fool, he followed her across the road. He didn't expect any trouble on a bright, sunny afternoon, with the pastor's car parked in the lot, but he wasn't letting her out of his sight. And he was glad to have his phone in his pocket again, just in case.

A mourning dove burst out of the dogwood by the Gantt family plot as Laura slowed and stopped there. She set both containers on the ground and twisted her hands behind her back, her head bowed.

Not wanting to intrude on her privacy, Sean waited at a distance and looked around the cemetery. Bushes and small trees had been planted beside other graves too.

Some of the headstones were tipping. Some had fallen. Some were covered with lichen and darkened with age. Jess's grave, though, was all too recent and still unmarked by a headstone, and the bronze plaque that bore Elliott's name still gleamed as if it were new.

He eyed the jungle of vines that backed the graveyard. A day at a time, an inch at a time, the mass of green crept forward, slashed back annually by a small army of men from the church and browned every winter by the first frost.

The church's weathered picnic pavilion stood on one side of the property, the cemetery lay on the other, and the church stood in the middle, dividing life from death. Keeping them at arm's length.

The life side—picnics, parties, supper on the grounds. The death side—funerals, headstones, bones. But all those crosses didn't mean a thing if death wasn't the doorway to eternal life.

He looked back at Laura. Her coppery hair spilled down her back from beneath the bandanna, bright as a new penny in the sun. She'd always stood out in a crowd like a redbird in a flock of sparrows.

She reached into the pitcher and pulled out clippers, then walked to a mass of pink azaleas that bordered the church property. Working quickly, she gathered an armload of long branches bursting with blooms. The hedge was so full, nobody would notice she'd cut some.

Tired of waiting, he moved a step closer. "Laura," he called in the no-nonsense tone he used on Keith's boys when they tried to pull a fast one.

She turned to face him. "Hey, Sean."

"I thought you were staying at the Brights' place."

She waved it away. "Long story. Anyway, I thought you were going to work. Why did you come back?"

"I'm installing some new locks and so on. But you won't be here overnight, will you?"

"Yes, I will. Ardelle got pretty upset with me. She thinks I accused her of being a thief."

"Did you?"

"Of course not. I was a little irritated with her because she'd let herself in one day when I wasn't home, but Cassie made a federal case of it and things escalated. Let's just say Ardelle isn't the same old fun-loving Ardelle I remember from years ago."

"Stay at my house, then."

"No, Sean. Thank you."

His jaw tightened as she returned to the family plot, where she filled the tin container with azalea branches and placed it at her mom's grave. She walked to the nearest faucet, filled the pitcher, and came back to pour water into the vase.

No flowers for Elliott, of course. She believed he was alive.

"There," she said, putting the clippers in the empty plastic pitcher. "Now it doesn't look so abandoned. So lonesome."

The almost imperceptible trembling of her

voice prompted Sean to take a closer look at her. "You okay?"

"Not really. I just . . . well, yesterday morning I was so upset about that stupid note in Mom's drawer that I deleted her number from my phone and I used up the last of the blackberries on purpose, and now I see how petty and mean-spirited that was and I want to tell her I'm sorry, but she's not here." She stopped to take a breath. "So I'm putting flowers on her grave, but it doesn't do any good."

"Sounds like you're having a rough day," he said cautiously.

She made a face. "I've crammed a lot of craziness into one morning. After I left Ardelle's I checked out a rumor about a prowler—"

"The Gustafsons? I heard that one too. Turned out to be their neighbor."

She nodded sadly. "So that was a wild-goose chase. Then I didn't know where to go. Ardelle doesn't want me there, and you don't want me here. So I went to the cabin."

Sean tensed, not liking the idea at all. "Why the cabin?"

She studied the ground. "You'll think this is stupid, but on Friday I left some food and clothes there for my dad. They're gone."

"Oh, Laura. Anybody could have taken them."

She raised her chin. "I know, but it didn't do any harm to leave them there."

Sean moved closer. "Don't go back alone, though. We don't know who might be hanging around. We still don't know who was at your window last night either, or what he was up to. If it's not a good time to stay at the Brights' house, you can stay at mine. Then your night-time visitor won't know where to find you."

"Don't you understand? I *want* him to find me."

"Not if it's a stranger, you don't. A criminal. Please, be reasonable."

"I'm being perfectly reasonable," she said sweetly. "You're the one who isn't." She looked both ways for traffic and ran back to the house with her plastic pitcher.

That was her idea of being reasonable? Thoroughly exasperated with her irrational decisions, he followed slowly. After she'd gone inside, he glanced over his shoulder, wondering if someone might have been watching them from the far side of the cemetery. In the noon-day sun, the azaleas were such a vivid pink that they didn't look real.

He stopped at his truck to retrieve his tools and the bags from the hardware store. He sorted out his purchases, found one of the new locksets, and sat down on the porch with the front door open so he could remove the old lock.

Laura walked up behind him. "If you have to sit there with the door wide open, I'd better lock Mikey in the bathroom."

"Thanks. I forgot about Mikey. But I wish you cared about your own safety as much as you care about his. He's just a cat. If it's his day to die, it's his day to die."

Laura cornered Mikey a few feet from the door and scooped up a writhing armful of resentful feline. "Today isn't that day."

She carted Mikey away. Sean heard the soft plop as she deposited the cat on the bathroom floor, and then the click of the latch as she shut him in.

She came back, her face solemn. "I do appreciate everything you're doing, Sean. Really, I do. Thank you. You need to let me know what I owe you for the locks and all. But as soon as you've finished, you need to hole up in your shop and finish those instruments. You want to see some of them on stage in Nashville someday, remember?"

Not as much as he wanted to see them in the hands of children. Children with his last name and Laura's red hair. But that would never happen if he couldn't keep her safe.

"In a little while, maybe I'll run home and bring back some projects to work on," he said. "You can come with me."

"Won't I be safe behind the new deadbolts? In broad daylight?"

He shrugged and went back to work.

"Oh no," she said. "You know what I just realized?"

"What?"

"The new locks will make it look like I *really* think Ardelle's a thief." She sighed. "I'd better call Cassie and see if her mom has calmed down at all."

She retreated into the depths of the house, leaving Sean alone with his worries.

❧ *Twenty-one* ❧

Her mother's morning freak-out had left Cassie drowning in guilt. It was her fault for coming down so hard on her.

The sharp knife hit the cutting board in a steady rhythm as Ardelle made exquisitely thin tomato slices—far more than she needed for only two sandwiches. They were going to be awesome sandwiches, though.

Cassie's folks didn't eat cheapo white bread anymore. Now they could afford whole-grain bread from the bakery and expensive, thin-sliced meats from the deli. Deli cheese too, and fancy mustard. The kind that cost four bucks for a four-ounce jar. That was sixteen dollars a pound.

Her mom had been fussing with the sandwiches for at least ten minutes, but finally she was satisfied. She sliced them on the diagonal, placed them on pretty plates, and started garnishing the plates with gourmet bread-and-butter pickle slices.

Cassie's cell phone rang. She'd expected a call back from Drew, but it wasn't his ring tone. It was Laura's. "Mom, I've got a call. Go ahead and start eating without me."

"All right, sweetie," her mom said. "Tell Drew hey for me."

Cassie walked to the far side of the sunroom and looked out over the glittering turquoise of the pool. " 'Sup?" she said softly.

"Hi," Laura said. "I just wanted to check in. Is your mom still upset?"

"Not really. Now she's being super sweet, like she feels terrible about overreacting. I feel terrible about it too, but it might've been good that it happened, you know? She might wake up and realize she needs some help."

"I hope so."

"Everything okay over at your place?"

"Pretty much, yes. Sean's changing the locks, but it has nothing to do with keeping your mom out. It was his idea, in case my prowler comes back."

"He's such a great guy. So's Keith. Their mom must have been a good influence on them before she died, because they're not a bit like Dale."

"Enough," Laura said firmly.

"Right." Cassie turned toward the kitchen. Now

her mom seemed to be rearranging the stacks of pickles on the plates. "You wouldn't believe how long it took my mom to make a couple of sandwiches just now," she said softly. "She's still fiddling with them. It's insane."

"Nobody is one hundred percent sane." Laura's voice wavered.

"Aw, Laura. You sound like you need a shoulder to cry on."

"If you try to point me toward Sean's shoulder, I will hang up on you."

"All right, all right. Are you okay, though? Really?"

"I'm sorry I snapped at you. I'm just so tired. Once everything calms down, I'll want to make sure everything's okay between your mom and me. Bye."

"Okay. I'll keep you posted."

But Laura had already ended the call. She never ended a call so abruptly. She must have been about to start crying.

She wasn't the only one. Cassie's insides were a muddle of worries. She wanted Drew to help her sort things out, but he was so tied down to his business that she couldn't keep him on the phone long enough for a meaningful conversation. He cared. Of course he cared. He was just too busy to talk to his wife.

Her dad had been too busy for his wife too, for years. If all entrepreneurs were that way, Sean would be too busy for Laura. They'd be better off without each other.

"Give up on the matchmaking," Cassie whispered. Marriage wasn't all it was cracked up to be.

Sniffling a little, she practiced a happy face for her mother's benefit and walked back inside.

It was only late afternoon but Laura was so short on sleep that she could have sworn it was midnight. She and Sean had eaten an early supper because they'd both forgotten to eat lunch. Finished with the cleanup, which meant throwing away paper plates and a pizza box, she peeked out the kitchen window.

Sean stood at the porch railing, looking up at the mountains. After a nearly windless day, a healthy breeze streamed through the gap, playing with his wild-man hair that lay straight and long on his collar. His shirt nearly matched the shade of his faded jeans.

He'd stood there a long time. Either he expected to see her dad stroll out of some little hollow, or he thought it was a good spot to play bodyguard.

He took the role seriously. Except for a quick trip to pick up the pizza and to grab a few things from his house, he'd stayed all day, obsessing over the locks and the security lights while she sorted her mom's belongings.

Blocking Mikey's escape route with her foot, Laura stepped onto the porch. She hoped the stiff wind would blow itself out before dark. She didn't want to spend another night with her imagination making footfalls out of every gust and her dad's voice out of every scraping branch.

Sean hummed some sad tune as he studied the mountains. She'd always loved to watch him when he was wrapped up in a song, his eyes dreamy. She could have stood there all night, listening.

He had always been there for her. He'd stuck up for her, from the playground in primary school to the halls of the high school. Sure, he tried to act like he was her boss—then and now —but that went both ways. In spite of their eternal power struggle, they would always be friends. Maybe they could be more than friends again, someday. Somewhere far from Dale.

She recognized the melody Sean was humming—an old Scots ballad about crows watching a man die in the wilderness. It had been funny in a macabre way when her dad sang it, years ago. Now? Not so much.

"That's a gruesome song," she said.

"Yeah. Sorry." He looked at her, looked at her hard. "Are you all right?"

"Yes. Go on home, Sean. Nothing has happened all day, and nothing's going to happen all night. I'll be fine, especially now with the new locks and the security lights."

"I'm staying. Deal with it."

Laura didn't argue. Deep inside, she didn't want to be alone.

She joined him at the railing. Scanning the hills, she imagined her dad home again. She could almost remember his voice. Almost.

"What's wrong?" Sean asked.

Drat him. He read her too easily.

"It has been kind of a tough day," she said. "And maybe it's just because I'm so tired, but I can't seem to get Dad's face out of my mind, but I can't quite remember him either. Not clearly. Not his face, not his voice. It's all muddy."

"I know what you mean."

"And it's like my heart is divided. One part hopes I can have him back. The other part is afraid I can't—or I'll have him back but he'll be too changed."

Sean only nodded, leaving her to sort out her fears in silence. Even if her dad was alive, even if he came back, he might be beyond mending. He might as well have died. Yet she still hoped.

Fear and hope. Like tectonic plates, those opposing forces shoved against each other, building pressure. Something had to give.

Let him go, said one voice in her head. *He's gone already.*

Another voice said: *Hang on. Keep the faith. Keep believing.*

It was like straddling a fault and waiting for an

earthquake to hit. On one side of the fault, her dad still lived and was, somehow, fixable. Could be restored to his old life. Could be loved and comforted, at least. On the other side lay a plane where she'd never have her dad back—at least not the way she'd known him. But she couldn't decide which side of the fault to stand on, and she couldn't arrange the outcome, anyway. She could only try to brace herself for the coming cataclysm.

"I know you must cry in private sometimes," Sean said matter-of-factly. "You can cry in front of me too, honey."

She let out a puny laugh. "You really want me to cry, don't you? You think it would be therapeutic."

"Yes ma'am. Would you just shut up and cry, please? Stop fighting it."

"I'm not fighting anything."

"You're fighting a normal reaction to all the stress you're under. You've lost your mom, you want to believe your dad is back, and now you're dealing with your mom's indiscretions. Alleged indiscretions, that is. Then there's your trespasser—"

"My dad isn't a trespasser, Sean. This is his house."

"Laura, at some point you might have to face the fact that he really isn't back, can't come back, ever."

Suddenly she'd decided where she stood.

"That's not a fact. It's an opinion. I believe he's alive, and I believe he's not beyond help."

Sean had no quick comeback this time. His expression had changed in some subtle way, as if he'd tuned her out.

"Listen," he said abruptly. "That's it. That's the hole in the night."

"What are you talking about?"

"When I drove over at three in the morning, I noticed but I didn't understand. Just listen. Then tell me what you hear."

A distant siren, miles away. Birds. The wind, rushing through millions of green leaves and brown branches.

Laura held her breath. Something was missing.

She didn't hear the random music that had always sung along with the wind. Something had stilled her mother's wind chimes—or someone had taken them.

Only one person on earth would want those wind chimes.

Giddy with fear and hope, she turned toward Sean. "He's back. He's really back."

Sean didn't answer, but she saw the doubt in his eyes.

He opened his arms and drew her close. They had chosen different sides. Different tectonic plates. She clung to him anyway, while the wind ran around the little house like water around a boulder in a stream.

● ● ●

Sean stood in the living room and studied the rope he'd taken down from the little magnolia tree. The rope was thin, brown, discolored by years in the weather. It ended in a fresh cut, delivered by a sharp instrument. The center of the rope was white and clean.

Who would have gone into the backyard to cut down Jess's wind chimes? If the house stood in town, close to other homes, a difficult neighbor might fuss about the noise and cut down the chimes out of spite. Out here, though, nearly in the country, with lots of room between houses? Nobody had ever cared. Elliott had given them to Jess one Valentine's Day, long before he disappeared.

Laura's theory was that Elliott had taken them. Sean wasn't inclined to agree with her, but whoever it was, he'd used a very sharp knife. He was probably the same man she'd seen at her window. That was the night the new silence had started, but Sean hadn't realized the chimes were gone until tonight.

He moved toward the couch, careful not to wake her. Even after their unsettling discovery, exhaustion had caught up with her.

At least she'd eaten a little. Not much, though. He wished Elliott's old hound dog was still around to eat the leftovers. Geezer was long gone, though. After a couple of weeks of moping for his vanished master, the dog had disappeared too.

Fighting off the image of Elliott at the edge of the woods, whistling softly for his dog, Sean crouched beside Laura. He brushed a lock of hair off her cheek. She didn't react.

He straightened. He had to talk things over with his brother—on the porch, so his voice wouldn't wake her. But the sensor had already kicked the security lights on, and he'd feel like he was on stage. An easy target.

At the back door, he hit the switch that killed those too-bright lights. Instantly, it was a normal twilight. He walked onto the porch and around the side where he could see across the road. In the fading light, the azaleas in the tall tin vase looked more purple than pink.

From this angle, looking across the hillside, the graveyard was like a little cityscape, the gravestones its skyscrapers and towers. The plots, divided by cement curbs, were city blocks. Even the flowers decorating the graves fit into the scene, looking like flowering shrubs beside the towers. A city of the dead. A city that awaited another new citizen.

Someone was going to die.

The notion settled on him like a blanket of ice. A premonition, he would have called it, if he'd believed in such things.

But everyone was going to die, someday. It

was only a matter of time. Tonight, though, or tomorrow or next week, it had better not be Laura. He wanted to see her live to play with their grandchildren. Their great-grandchildren too, if they didn't waste too much time.

He walked toward the far end of the porch. The side that looked out on mountains instead of graves. He settled into the chair, pulled out his phone, and tried to collect his thoughts. He had to swear Keith to secrecy and bring him up to date. He shouldn't get involved unless he knew the whole story and what a mess it was. Adultery . . . maybe . . . and lies . . . maybe. And maybe there'd even been some bloodshed early on, if that car in the lake meant anything.

The conversation proved to be even harder than he'd anticipated. Keith blasted him.

"All this is going on, and you haven't called the sheriff? Sean, that's flat-out irresponsible."

"Laura has her reasons for wanting to keep the law out of it."

"Does she have a better answer than the law?"

"We just want to find Elliott before somebody else does. If he's alive, that is."

"Stop saying 'if,' okay? We're going to play a little game of Let's Pretend. Pretend he's alive. He doesn't want to be found, obviously. Even if he's close to town, we could search for months and never find a trace of him—unless we get into his head."

291

Sean fell silent, trying to drop his skepticism and be a willing believer. Just for a while.

Where would Elliott hide? How close to town? Where would he feel at home?

At his boyhood home. The old cabin. Out of town, but not too far. It was a falling-down wreck, but Elliott could create a shelter out of nothing.

"I think the cabin makes sense," Sean said.

"I do too. It's within walking distance of town. A long walk, but doable."

"I should stake it out. Soon. You want to come?"

"I'll think about it," Keith said. In the background, there was a sudden crash, followed by the shrill wail of his youngest. "I'd better go rescue Annie. I'll talk to you later."

Sean put his phone away, resigned to doing his stakeout alone. Keith was a family man and a sensible guy who listened to his wife. Annie would tell him he didn't need to run around the countryside chasing a phantom.

Night had fallen fast. The mountains loomed black against the dark sky, seeming closer than they really were. If Sean blocked off the lights of the church with his hand, he could imagine himself in the midst of the Southern Nantahala Wilderness, miles from another living soul.

Night sounds gathered around him, took him in. Far away, a fox barked. Nearby, spring peepers and a whippoorwill made their racket against the backdrop of a constant wind.

A sudden yipping and yelping exploded in the hills. Coyotes. They sounded like a flock of demented birds. They usually saved their eerie ruckus for early morning, but something must have set them off. He was glad Mikey was safe inside.

Time to go in, before he started believing in ghosts and haunts. He went in and turned on the outside lights again. They threw the yard and the porch into stark, artificial daylight. He didn't blame Laura for hating them.

She lay still, her breathing easy and slow. For a moment he tormented himself with the idea of kissing her as she slept, but the kind of kiss he was imagining wouldn't go unnoticed. She'd wake up and claw his eyes out.

He gave her foot a firm squeeze instead. Still no reaction.

He was bone tired too. He never turned in so early, but maybe he'd at least lie down for a while. But where? Not in Laura's bed; a man just didn't fall into a woman's bed without her permission, even if she wasn't in it. And the guest bed was piled high with clothes she planned to donate somewhere.

Jess's room? No, he wasn't sleeping in a dead woman's bed. He was too spooked already, for a variety of reasons.

Once again, his truck would be in the drive-way overnight. He didn't care about the old hens and their gossip, but Elliott might be out there somewhere, watching. A classic case of the over-protective father. He might be upset that his baby girl had a man staying in the house.

"Keep your hands where they belong," Elliott had warned Sean years ago. *"Some men might not protect their daughters, but I'll always protect my little girl."* In the next breath, Elliott had made Sean promise to take care of her.

"I'm trying, man," Sean said quietly. "I'm trying."

He found a sleeping bag in the hall closet and spread it on the floor by the couch. It was better than the night before, when he'd slept on nothing but the hooked rug. He felt sorry for himself, a little, until he thought of Elliott in the wild.

Sean shook his head. The game of Let's Pretend had already contaminated his mind.

He went outside, pausing to look and listen for anything unusual, and retrieved his gun from the rack in the truck. Back inside, he slid the weapon under the couch. He would still obey Laura's no-guns rule if he could, but he wanted to be prepared for anything.

Lying on the sleeping bag, he listened to the new silence. He'd never realized how much the chimes had been a part of every storm.

A single night-light shone on the wall, casting a faint reflection off the gleaming wood of the grandfather clock as it ticked. Knowing he wouldn't be able to stay awake, he closed his eyes and hoped for a guardian angel or two. Not effeminate Hallmark-style angels, but the real McCoy with flaming swords in their hands and the power of God behind them.

Twenty-two

Laura woke to the aroma of fresh coffee. Everything was blurry without glasses or contacts, but she saw a sleeping bag rolled up and sitting on the floor. Sean's boots lay cattywampus by the front door.

Now the coffee made sense. Long before bedtime, she must have fallen asleep on the couch. She'd slept straight through, and he'd camped out on her floor again.

The old ladies would have a field day with that. Not that it mattered. Gossip wasn't important anymore, unless someone had a new rumor that held a grain of truth.

But the truth was simply that her dad had been lurking around his own house. Cutting down the wind chimes he'd given his wife. He wasn't hiding in the mountains. He was somewhere within walking distance. The thought made her pulse quicken with excitement.

She sat up, running a hand through her messy hair, and squinted at the white glare of the new lights outside. They ruined the sunrise.

Wearing jeans and a black shirt, Sean walked out of the kitchen carrying two identical green mugs, part of a set she'd given her mom for Christmas a few years ago. "You awake, sweetheart?"

"Just barely."

He'd already moved on to *sweetheart,* and she'd answered without even thinking. It was as if they'd time-traveled back to high school. Except everything had changed.

He set both mugs on the coffee table, then sat on the floor beside her and leaned against the couch. He picked up his coffee, took a sip, and yawned.

Out of his line of vision, she brought one finger close to his hair and imagined playing with it. Or cutting it. She'd have to talk him into a haircut. He needed a shave too.

She sat up straighter and wrapped both her hands around her coffee to keep them out of his hair. The security lights assaulted her eyes through the curtains.

"I hate those new lights."

"I knew you would, but relax. They'll go off as soon as there's enough natural light."

"Or as soon as I hit the switch."

"I see," he said in a weary voice. "I went to all

the trouble of installing them just so you can be your usual uncooperative self."

"I'm sorry, Sean. I really do appreciate your efforts to take care of me."

"It's only what I promised your dad."

She stared down at the top of his head. "You did what?"

"When we were seventeen, he gave me the 'keep your hands off my daughter' lecture, and then he made me promise to take good care of you."

Suddenly she was wide awake. "You mean . . . like he thought he wouldn't be around?"

"No. More like he thought we'd marry someday. Which is a fine idea."

"Sean, stop it." Once she'd conquered the lump in her throat, she dared to speak again. "You should spend the day in your workshop. If I need you, I'll call. You can be here in three minutes."

He was silent for a little while. "All right. I'm not too worried about what might happen in broad daylight. As long as you keep your doors locked, you can kick me out during the day, but I'm staying here again tonight. Like it or not."

"Ooh, the rumors will fly. People will say you've moved in."

"I don't care. I'm not leaving you here alone at night." He rose, leaving his coffee on the table, and looked down at her. "I'll be back."

"See you later, then." She gave him a little

wave, then closed her eyes, deliberately shutting him out. Afraid of what he might say or do next.

"Later," he echoed. "Behave yourself."

He crossed the floor, his boots making a heavy tread. His keys jingled. The door shut firmly, and the lock clicked.

Still keeping her eyes closed, she listened to the sounds of his departure. Once the sound of the truck's engine had faded into the distance, she opened her eyes. If he'd flashed his lights again, she'd missed it.

It was Sean's favorite time to be in the shop, when the slant of the late sunlight gave the room a dramatic glow. Dale had arrived just in time to spoil it.

He was getting cagier. He must have parked around the corner, and when Sean walked to the street for his mail, the old man slipped through the side yard and into the shop.

Sean was packed up and itchy to return to Laura's place before nightfall, but Dale never stayed long. He'd been roaming around for five minutes now, examining everything and fingering most of it, but even in his half-tanked state he had the sense not to open the door to the spray room and wood storage.

He swayed on his feet as he pointed vaguely toward the window. "Isn't your sign a little too, you know, fancy-schmancy?"

Sean shrugged. When he made the sign, he'd taken great pains to keep the style simple, but he should have left off his middle name. "Sean Michael Halloran, Luthier," sounded pretentious. The sign didn't even show from the street, though, so it didn't much matter.

"It's my name and my occupation," Sean said. "That's all."

"It's a pansy kind of occupation."

"I know, I know. That's why you'll leave me the pansy gun when you die. It's something to look forward to."

Dale slurred an ugly curse.

"Why, thank you," Sean said, earning himself another one.

Dale laughed. "Where'd you learn to be so polite, boy? I sure didn't teach you that."

"You sure didn't."

As Dale made a slow, unsteady circuit of the shop, he kept glancing back at Sean as if to gauge his mood. Sean knew what was coming next.

"You got any cash?"

"If you want to sell me the pansy gun, I do."

"I ain't a gun shop. I ain't selling."

"And I'm not a bank."

Dale rubbed his eyes. "They put out any reward money on Gantt?"

Sean almost laughed at the absurdity. "No. And they won't, so forget it."

"That's all right. Just findin' him will be enough

for me. He's back. I know he is. Once he has the guts to show his face, I'll get even."

"Get even for what?"

"That call."

"What call?"

"You know, idiot. The phone call. When you were a kid."

"The one that saved my life?"

Dale snarled another curse. "Why do you always exaggerate?"

"I don't. And Elliott couldn't have made the call. He was too busy patching me up. Don't try to get revenge for something he didn't do."

Dale cracked a smile. "I wouldn't hurt him. I'd just kick him around a little. Pay him back for stealing my son. It ain't right for a man to do that. Gary Bright too. He did the same."

"They never stole a thing from you, Dale. Sure, they helped me. They both did. You wouldn't believe all the ways Gary has helped me, and he never asks me to pay him back. Pay it forward, he says. You, though? You're always begging me for cash. And sympathy. Poor, poor Dale, always the innocent victim."

Sean ducked just in time. Dale's fist hit air and he reeled.

"Get out." Sean seized him before he could catch his balance and frog-marched him to the door. "Get off my property and stay off. Stay off Laura's property too." With one final shove,

Sean evicted him, then nipped back inside and drew the deadbolt.

Dale howled, probably not in pain but in rage, then stumbled and fell face first on the grass. He lay motionless in the same spot where Sean had assembled the kite so many years ago.

About the time Sean was getting worried, Dale picked himself up and limped toward the front yard. Leaning like a tree in a strong wind, he disappeared around the corner of the house he'd once owned.

So angry he could hardly form a coherent sentence, Sean called 911 to report the DUI in a black pickup truck. Once again, the dispatcher said they'd be on the lookout.

After he'd hung up, Sean nearly called back to report Dale's illegal ownership of a handgun. It wasn't hurting anyone in a closet in Dale's cramped apartment, though. It probably hadn't been fired in a generation or more. He was afraid to fire it, afraid to take it out of its case, even afraid to admit that he had it. The last remnant of the Halloran family's wealth, it was his only remaining treasure.

Sean moved around the shop, touching his fingertips to the instruments he loved. Dale hadn't harmed anything yet, although there was always the chance that he'd set the place on fire some night. Or show up with a sledgehammer and start swinging.

The workbenches and the pegboard walls held instruments in all stages of gestation. Some were held together with clamps and vises. Some awaited their final finishes. Some needed nothing more than price tags and new owners.

He inhaled the smells of varnish, glue, and wood and savored the satiny sheen of the instruments. The utilitarian beauty of the tools. The clutter of strings and picks and capos. Elliott had introduced him to all of it—the world of music—the day he'd handed him a broom and said, "Sweep. I can't pay much, but I'll teach you everything I know."

Sean had swept like crazy. He would have swept a path to the moon for Elliott. Or for Laura. Still would.

He'd better get over there. She might feel a little too secure with those new locks. There were ways around them, including a simple knock. She wouldn't open the door for just anybody, but she might open it for her dad. Or someone who claimed to be him.

Choosing only one mandolin and one guitar that still needed breaking in, Sean tucked them into their cases and locked up. As he backed the truck out of the driveway, he saw the albino raccoon inching his way down the trunk of the big oak. Sean hadn't seen him in a couple of days and was glad the little guy was still around.

He rolled down his window. "Casper! Get

back in that tree. Don't come out until dark."

Casper froze, hugging the trunk, but didn't retreat.

"Good luck to you, then." Sean rolled up his window and hit the gas. He must have gone nuts. He was giving survival advice to a baby raccoon.

By the time he reached Laura's house, a healthy sense of victory had crowded out the anger he'd felt toward Dale. Sean slowed at the curve, his eyes drawn to the graveyard. All over the cemetery, the wind had toppled real and artificial flowers. Laura's tall tin vase had fallen, spilling pink azaleas across the grave. He hoped she wouldn't notice. He didn't want her in the graveyard at nightfall.

Pulling into the driveway, he spotted her on the far side of the porch, facing the mountains at the rear of the house. He decided to use the front door for a change, to see if she was remembering to keep it locked.

He carted the instruments and his duffel bag up the front steps. The door was locked.

"Good girl," he said under his breath, juggling everything while he found his key.

Leaving his things in the living room, he walked through the kitchen and out the back door. Laura still leaned against the railing at the far end of the porch.

She'd pulled her hair into a neat, school-teacher-ish bun that wasn't half as sexy as the messy, curly ponytails of her tomboy days. Sexy enough, though. He wanted to sneak up behind her and kiss the nape of her neck, but Elliott had taught her some painfully effective ways to discourage unwanted attention, using nothing but her hands and feet.

Reluctantly ending his unobserved survey of her, he shut the door and stepped onto the porch. "I'm back." Then he felt like an idiot for stating the obvious. No doubt she'd heard his truck from a quarter mile away.

Looking over her shoulder, she gave him a wary smile. "Did you accomplish much today?"

"I did." He wanted to add *I kicked Dale out,* accompanied by some chest thumping, but it wasn't something to brag about.

"Did you bring any work with you?"

Careful not to crowd her too much, he joined her at the railing. "A little bit."

"Some guy from an alarm company stopped by with information. I told him I'm not interested. Got it?"

"Yes ma'am." It was her house. Her life. He couldn't make her decisions for her.

A blue jay sailed past, its feathers bright against the dusky sky, and lit in the feathery branches of a pine. Ten feet below the jay, a woodpecker rattled against the furrowed, moss-patched trunk. Two birds on one tree, when they had hundreds to choose from.

How many millions of pines were there? How many thousands of tree-covered ridges? When he'd gone online to search satellite images of Prospect and the surrounding mountains, it had been daunting to see so much wilderness so close to town.

The mountains were full of ruined cabins, hunting shacks, bat-haunted caves. Abandoned gold mines and logging camps too. Then there were the primitive campsites on federal and state land, or a man could create his own little spot. If Elliott could avoid the meth labs and weed operations that plagued public lands now, he could find a new hiding place every night. But what had he been trying to pull, making everybody think he was dead and gone if he was only . . . gone?

Laura shifted her position, placing her elbows on the railing. Resting her chin on her clasped hands, she studied the ground below as if it held something fascinating. "Sometimes I wish I could have a do-over for high school and—and everything."

Startled, he answered without thinking. "I'd like a do-over for that poorly timed marriage proposal."

She shook her head so hard that a bobby pin dropped from her hair, bounced off the railing, and hit the porch. Her bun began to slip from its moorings. "It wasn't even a real proposal."

"You think it was a phony one?"

"It was your kind and honorable attempt to take care of me when we thought my dad had died. But it was unrealistic."

"You're right. I had no business talking about marriage. We were just kids. I didn't even have a job because my boss had just disappeared. I didn't have any plans for my future except college, maybe, and having my own workshop someday."

She frowned up at him. "I'm glad you can see how impractical it was."

"We should have talked about it years ago. The elephant in the room."

"Bigger than that. A brontosaurus, maybe."

"Can we start over, then? Friends?"

"We've never *not* been friends."

"You know what I mean, though. Even friends have a hard time communicating when a brontosaurus keeps butting in."

"You know it'll never go away completely," she said.

"Maybe not," he admitted. "But maybe we can shoo it far enough away that we won't keep stepping in brontosaurus, uh, poop."

She laughed out loud, her eyes softening as she searched his face. He could practically see her heart softening too, as if talking about the awkwardness had begun to erase it.

Slowly, she extended her right hand, apparently

expecting him to shake hands. Instead, he captured her hand in his left hand and turned toward the mountains. Taking her cue from him, she faced the mountains too.

Standing side by side, holding hands, he felt more connected to her than if he'd had both arms around her. She held his hand tightly, like a child. It took him back to the days of skinned knees and scraped chins. The games they'd played on hot summer nights. Green-plum wars, kickball games, watermelon-seed spitting contests.

He stole a peek at her just as she stole a peek at him.

"Don't look at me that way," she whispered.

"Sorry. Can't help it."

"Yes, you can."

"Easy for you to say. You're not the one looking at you."

She smiled, barely, and returned to her study of the high ridges.

That brief smile was enough to keep his hopes on life support. The hand holding was a bonus. Anything else would have to wait until Laura was ready.

❧ Twenty-three ❧

Six-thirty in the morning and there they were again, having their coffee in the living room like some old married couple. Except she'd slept in her room and he'd slept on the couch—or he'd tried to, anyway. It was too short for his long legs.

"Why didn't you use the guest bed, Sean? I moved the clothes and things off."

He drained the rest of his coffee before he answered. "I want to be between you and the door."

"Oh, you're so paranoid."

"I don't mind if you call me paranoid, as long as I can call you safe." He glanced at the grandfather clock and set his empty cup on the coffee table. "Sorry to run off so early, but this is Wednesday. Trash day. I don't want to miss the truck."

"Go then, and stay as long as you need to."

He sat there, staring straight ahead. Maybe he was thinking what she was thinking: if they were an old married couple, he wouldn't walk out the door without a kiss.

But she hadn't kissed him since his eighteenth

birthday, moments before he'd made that goofy, tender, hopelessly ill-timed marriage proposal. The sheriff's dive team had still been dredging the lake. She'd been a wreck.

She still was. She was afraid of the baggage she brought with her. Afraid of Sean's baggage too. Afraid of Dale and his hatred.

If her dad was back, Dale would be cruel to him. No doubt about it.

She brought her mug closer. Staring into her coffee, she relived the moment, days ago, when she'd dropped the angel mug in the sink and stared into the eyes of the man at the window.

Her dad—or not? She'd never seen him with a beard and long hair. He'd always been clean-shaven, clean-cut, and in good physical condition. But he might be in terrible shape now—physically, mentally. He'd be no match for Dale.

Sean stood up. "I should go. Although I'd like to stay."

"Go. I'll be fine."

He sat beside her to put on his boots. Then he reached under the couch, pulled out his gun, and laid it across his lap.

"Please stop hauling that thing around with you, Sean. We said no guns, remember?"

"That's what we said on Monday. The day you'd planned to stay at the Brights' house. My exact words were 'no guns while you're gone.'

You came back." He stood up, pointing the barrel at the floor. "Don't worry, it's not loaded."

"But you could load it in no time. Would you actually start shooting if somebody showed up?"

"Only if that somebody proved to be a threat. And if it was a clear case of self-defense."

"What if it's my dad? And how could you tell the difference between him and a stranger? We don't know what he looks like now. Not really." She got to her feet and backed up, putting some distance between herself and the gun. "Get that thing out of here. And don't bring it back."

Sean let out a sigh of exasperation. "Yes ma'am. It's your house."

He walked toward the door, still keeping the barrel down. Always so safety conscious. But holding that big gun, he looked like a soldier going off to war.

Her stomach went queasy. If the unthinkable happened, she wouldn't be able to live with herself. She'd spend the rest of her life knowing that her fear of Dale had robbed her of her chance to love Sean.

She couldn't lose him. She couldn't. He had to come back, safe and sound.

"Come back," she whispered.

Sean must have heard. He leaned the gun against the wall, turned around, and started back.

She shook her head. "I didn't mean—"

It was too late to explain. He was there,

reaching for her. He cradled her face in his hands and kissed her like he had when they were teenagers in love, making her heart pound and her common sense fly out the window.

She hadn't expected everything to happen so fast, and she hadn't expected it to feel so right. So natural. Their lips fit together like they always had, like they'd been designed for a game of giving and taking pleasure.

He pulled away, studying her so somberly that the romantic moment shattered in her sudden recollection of his reasons for being there. His reasons for carrying a gun.

"I'd better go," he said. "Call if you need me. And keep your doors locked."

"I will."

"Whatever you do, don't forget the most important thing."

She held her breath, trying to guess what kind of warning he'd give her this time. Whatever he meant to say, he was taking forever to get it out of his mouth.

"What?" she asked, finally. "What's on your mind? Say it."

His eyes twinkled. "I knew you wanted me to say it again. I love you, Laura."

Oh, no. She wasn't ready for *that*.

"I know you do," she said gently. "Because we've been friends since we were little kids."

"Don't play like that, sweetheart. You know

what I mean. I *love* you love you." He curved his hand around her cheek and gave her one more kiss, then took the gun and walked outside, into the artificial light. He locked the door behind him.

With her knees about to buckle, she collapsed on the couch and dragged the quilt up to her chin. She tried to organize her chaotic thoughts into neat little categories, but everything was interconnected. Sean. Dad and Mom. Gibby. Dale's vicious grip on her arm. Bluegrass and kisses, wind chimes and guns. Over it all hung the fear that if her dad came home, something would go terribly wrong.

Sean parked in his driveway and sat there for a minute, trying to understand why he didn't feel more victorious. He should have been celebrating Laura's wholehearted participation in those kisses, but some unnamed worry kept getting in the way. He couldn't pin it down. Whatever it was, it had been bothering him ever since he'd left her.

His vague uneasiness might define itself as he whipped through part of his routine. He needed to put the trash out. Shower and shave. Then he'd spend some time in the shop, doing the bare minimum and picking up something to work on. He needed to proofread that brochure, too, and get it to the printer.

Laura wanted him to stay away all day, working. Maybe she was right, but he hardly cared if his competitors sewed up all the orders this year. There would be other years, other festivals.

Operating in a blurry fog of stress and exhaustion, he climbed out of the truck. He grabbed his trash can from its spot at the side of the house and rolled it out to the curb. Even if the world was falling apart, he couldn't miss trash day.

Sean looked up and down the block. He half expected to see a lean figure lurking in the early morning shadows, but friendly, overweight Wally Morse came around the corner with his yellow Lab tugging him along. Glad to see something so normal and right, Sean lifted his hand in greeting.

Wally waved back while the dog paused to sniff the fake flowers at the base of Mrs. Gibson's mailbox post. They'd blown over again. It happened with every storm.

Like the flowers in the cemetery—

Sean stiffened. That was what had been bothering him. Those pink azaleas. He couldn't process it, couldn't find a rational explanation, but he knew what he'd seen.

It might have been nothing, or it might have been the answer to Laura's prayers, but he couldn't share it with her yet. Maybe he'd never be able to tell her.

He wanted to drive hell-bent for leather back to her place, but he made himself lock up the truck, leaving the gun on the rack. Then he proceeded to the front door. He fumbled the key in the lock, walked in, and shut the door behind him. He stood there staring at the cedar chest, but in his mind's eye, he saw only pink azaleas.

All day, Laura's thoughts had kept straying back to the interesting developments at dawn. Sean had not only kissed her but also told her he loved her. Next thing she knew, he'd be talking about marriage again—and she'd worry about genetics again.

When they'd studied genetics in Preston's biology class, she'd wondered what the combination of Halloran and Gantt genes would produce. Their future children, should they have any, might be calm and kind and normal, like her mother. Like Sean and Keith. Or they might be walking disasters, cursed with a blend of her dad's volatility and Dale's drunken cruelty. But any marriage was a gamble. Having children was a gamble. Life itself was a series of gambles.

She blew out a long sigh and told herself to get to work.

Earlier, sorting through a pile of papers in the kitchen, she'd found a dozen unopened sympathy cards that Ardelle must have set aside for her. Laura gathered a box of thank-you notes, a pen, and stamps and took them to the backyard where a garden bench sat in the sun not far from the spot where the wind chimes had hung.

She was surrounded by reminders of her parents. Trees they'd planted together. The old metal garden markers poking up among their prized perennials. Their birdhouses and bird feeders. Even the garden bench where she sat. Her dad had built it, and her mom had painted it a soft green that blended in with the bushes.

The first envelope came from one of the elderly, unmarried Flynn cousins in North Carolina. Laura pulled out the card, its artwork a flowery swirl of pale pastels like an old woman's scarf. Inside, Annabel Flynn's shaky writing expressed regret that she hadn't been able to attend the funeral for dear cousin Jessamyn. The printed verse was soberly biblical in nature. Laura wrote a thank-you note and moved on to the next envelope.

A heavy, high-quality envelope in a soft shade of gray, it bore no return address, but the sender had written Laura's name and her mother's address in bold, masculine penmanship that matched that of the naughty note she'd found.

She checked the back of the envelope. No return address there either. She ripped the envelope open and pulled out a card. The same color as the envelope, its front was blank.

Slowly, she opened it.

Laura,

I was so sorry to hear of your mother's passing. She was a lovely woman. I'll never forget her. God bless.

Gibby

It was true, then. Her mother wouldn't have saved that naughty note unless it had meant something to her. They'd had more than a brief flirtation in a moment of weakness.

Tempted to call Sean, Laura shook her head. He would be back soon. She would have plenty of time to tell him later.

She wrote Gibby a short, kind reply. With every word, she reminded herself that she'd chosen to forgive him and her mother.

With every word, she thought she felt her father's heartache.

It was all too much, coming on the same day she and Sean had so suddenly resurrected their old relationship. She closed her eyes, listening to the wind in the trees and remembering the chimes that used to sing in every storm. To her father, their soft tinkling might have become as unpleasant as clanging cymbals.

She hated to argue with St. Paul, but love sometimes failed.

Twenty-four

Sean had come back earlier than Laura had expected, but as she'd expected, he'd greeted her with another round of lingering kisses. As much as she relished revisiting their teenage romance on a deeper level, sometimes panic threatened. Everything was happening too fast, adding to the tension that accompanied the mystery of her father's fate.

Something was bothering Sean too, but he refused to talk about it.

Sitting on the couch, he was frowning over the printer's proof of his brochure. He hadn't bothered to shave when he made his quick jaunt back to his house, so he looked more like a wild man than ever.

"Are you happy with the brochure?" she asked.

He gave her a blank look. "Excuse me?"

"Your brochure. That piece of paper you've been brooding over for ten minutes. What's wrong with you, Sean?"

"Nothing. It looks great."

She raised her eyebrows. "You'd better get the order going before it's too late, then. Just because it's a quick-print place doesn't mean you can procrastinate until the last minute."

"Yes ma'am." But instead of picking up his phone, he picked up a mandolin he'd brought with him to break in.

Leaving him inside, Laura moved to the porch with a few more notes to write. She hadn't yet told Sean about the card from Gibby.

She settled into one of the Adirondack chairs her dad had made and opened a sympathy card from one of her fellow teachers in Denver. As she wrote a brief thank-you, she tried to imagine explaining her dad's situation to her friends there. She wouldn't even know where to start.

Inside, Sean played a few notes, stopped to work on the tuning, and played a few more. Again and again, he started a song, interrupted it, and went back to it. Or started a different tune. Sometimes he'd nearly reach the end of a song, but he'd stop abruptly before the last line, leaving the song hanging. Unresolved.

"Sean, can't you at least finish a song once in a while?" she called.

The music stopped.

The door creaked open. He stuck his head out. "Excuse me?"

"I can't stand it when you never finish a song."

"Sorry. I'm not thinking about the songs. I'm thinking about the tuning. The sound."

The weariness around his eyes made her

wonder when he'd last had a good night's sleep. She smiled, softening.

"I'm sorry, Sean. I was just being difficult. Go on; get back to it."

Instead, he joined her on the porch and studied the dogwood tree that stretched a branch over the porch. Hands in his pockets, the wind ruffling his hair, he kept quiet.

Leaving her correspondence on the chair, she stood in front of him. She reached up to push his hair off his forehead, revealing the small scars from the time Dale shoved him through a window on a summer night. Dale wouldn't let him see a doctor, so Sean had cleaned the cuts, sprayed them with Bactine, and applied a butterfly bandage to the worst one. By the time school started in the fall, the cuts had healed. But he would always have the scars.

Hands still in his pockets, he gave her a quizzical frown. "Yeah, I know. I need a haircut."

"But that's not what I want to tell you." She stretched upward to give him a quick kiss. "Gibby sent a sympathy card."

"That was nice of him."

"The writing matches the note I found in my mom's drawer."

Sean sighed. "I'm sorry that your mom and Gibby had a fling, Laura. I really am."

"Me too. Especially for my dad's sake."

Sean took his hands from his pockets and

reached out to tug a dogwood leaf from its branch. "You know what your dad told me once about dogwood leaves?" He ripped the leaf, gently, so it was still held together by tiny threads. "See those? He told me they're like strands of memory and fact that hold past and present together. They'll hold for a little while, but not forever."

"What's that supposed to mean?"

"Facts don't change, but sometimes memories do." He tugged the two halves of the leaf completely apart, breaking the delicate filaments. "Even if we uncover some unfortunate facts, some ugly truths, hang on to your good memories."

"You mean you don't want me to forget all the good I ever knew of my mom, even if she cheated on my dad?"

He dropped the two halves of the leaf over the railing and watched them fall to the grass. "I was thinking of your dad too. He might have changed, but we need to remember the man he was. Honor the man he was."

"You sound almost like you're ready to admit he might be alive."

"I'm starting to believe it's possible. But be prepared for the worst. If he comes back, he might be in rough shape."

"You think I don't know that?"

Swallowing the urge to cry, Laura turned her back on Sean—and faced the cemetery and another dogwood tree growing green and healthy near the family plot. Every time she saw a dogwood now, she would remember the leaf Sean had ripped in half. The way the past pulled away from the present, one filament at a time. One hour at a time.

"He's bound to need . . . some help," she said, keeping her voice on track, no wavering or wobbling allowed.

"Then we'll get him some help."

"Imagine what it might be like to bring him home. To cook him a good meal. To let him sleep in his own bed and wear clean clothes."

"Lord willing, that's going to happen," Sean said. "But we just don't know."

Laura went to sit on the steps. "He had the heart of a poet. He's the sentimental one, not Mom." She stopped, realizing she'd mixed present tense and past tense. "He was the one who always cut fresh flowers for his parents' and grandparents' graves, and for Mom's side of the family too."

Sean sat beside her. "He did that?"

"On Mother's Day, Father's Day, Easter, and Memorial Day. Don't you remember?"

"Come to think of it, yeah. And it's almost Memorial Day."

"Those are all spring and summer holidays, though. When I was little, I always felt sorry for dead people because they didn't get fresh flowers all through the winter, and that's when I thought they would need them the most. To cheer them up."

Her dad had laughed softly when she'd shared that little-girl worry with him. He assured her it wasn't the dead people they needed to worry about.

"No, it's the living who need flowers on their loved ones' graves."

"Why, Daddy?"

"To make us stop and remember who they were and why we loved them."

That was all he'd said, and she hadn't pressed him for more. By kindergarten, she'd learned not to trigger his moods by asking too many questions.

"He even knew the language of flowers," she said. "You know, that silly Victorian thing. Grandma Gantt taught him when he was a boy. Irises for good news. Daisies for innocence. Pansies for loving thoughts."

Sean smirked. "Pansies for loving thoughts. I like that. My inheritance from Dale will help me think loving thoughts of him when he finally kicks the bucket."

"What are you talking about?"

"The pansy gun. He says he'll leave it to me when he dies."

"I've never seen it. Does it have pansies engraved on it or something?"

"No, he calls it the pansy gun because it's a

woman's gun, designed for a small hand." He measured with his fingers to show a gun no more than four inches long. "I haven't laid eyes on it in years. It belonged to his grandmother, and it's the only gun he has left. He's a convicted felon so he can't buy another one except on the black market. He shouldn't even have the pansy gun."

"Why don't you report him?"

"I don't have the heart to. He'd wind up behind bars again. Besides that, I would feel like I was taking away his last shred of dignity."

"You could at least blackmail him into handing it over now instead of making you wait for him to die."

Sean smiled faintly. "I could give it a try."

The wind was gathering strength, but it had no chimes to play on. A train's whistle blew in the distance, tone-on-tone, like two or three ribbons of sound that crossed each other and separated again.

If her dad was out there, not too far away, he heard the same train at the same moment. With every breath she took, he took one. With every beat of her heart, his heart beat. And the moments went by. Days went by. Life went by.

Almost twelve years had passed. Had he thought she wouldn't miss him?

Sean reached over and laid his hand over hers. She stretched her arm alongside his, matching their pulse points, wrist to wrist. They'd done that as kids, one cold night when their arms were covered with goose bumps. Ghost bumps, she'd thought they were called, but she'd been careful not to let herself believe in ghosts. Her dad had told her ghosts weren't real.

Now he'd become almost a ghost himself, in a sense. A phantom.

"Why did my dad have to run?" she asked. "Wouldn't divorce have made more sense than abandoning us?"

"Are you still afraid he stopped loving you?"

"I know parents sometimes abandon their children, Sean. It happens. But most parents wouldn't try to fool their children into believing they'd died."

"Maybe he thought that was the kindest way to handle it."

"Because of the affair, you mean? Or because of his issues?"

"A combination, maybe."

"Or he sensed that Mom didn't love him any-more—and that I was just so tired of his moods that I—I might have been glad if he disappeared. Oh, I hope he didn't think that." Even though, on some particularly difficult days, it might have been true.

Sean squeezed her hand, then lifted his head to study the sky. "I wonder if it'll storm tonight."

Her throat hurt from trying not to cry. She took

a deep breath, harnessing her emotions. "No, it'll blow over. That's what the weatherman says, anyway."

"You can take a storm and make music out of it," her dad had said with a smile on that long-gone Valentine's Day when he hung the miniature chimes from the star magnolia. A storm had been rolling over the shoulder of the mountains that day.

"I'm going to stake out the cemetery tonight," Sean said.

"Because I told you my dad used to put flowers on the family plot? But that was so long ago. And he wouldn't do it anymore if he doesn't want people to know he's hanging around."

"If he doesn't want people to know he's around, seems like he'd stop hanging around—if that's really him."

"Maybe he's conflicted," she said. "He halfway wants to be caught. Or maybe he has problems beyond PTSD by now, especially after living in the wild for years. He could even have Alzheimer's."

Sean only drummed his fingers on the step beside him.

She stilled his restless movement with a firm grip. "What's wrong? You're so edgy, you're practically vibrating."

"Are you sure you don't want to stay at my place tonight?"

"I'm sure. Especially if you'll be right across the road. If he shows up—it's just my dad, Sean."

"Your dad, the guy who flipped out on a regular basis. The guy who caught us snuggling on the porch swing and busted it up with a sledge-hammer. The guy who—"

"The daddy who sang lullabies to me even when I was too old for lullabies, just because I loved to hear him sing. The animal lover who fed a tiny starving kitten from a medicine dropper. He had the kindest, softest heart. He would never hurt me." She took a quick breath. "You just told me to keep remembering the good about him. Stop contradicting yourself. You're as conflicted as he must be. And I am too."

After a long silence, Sean nodded. "Okay. You stay here tonight. I'll have my phone. You can call me if you hear or see anything out of the ordinary. Call even if you're scared and you don't know why."

"No, you call me if *you're* scared," she said, trying to lighten the moment.

Sean didn't even smile.

A gust of wind scattered her thank-you notes that were stamped and ready to go in the mail. She jumped up and chased them down. "It's too windy," she said, gathering the rest of her things. "I'm going in."

"Me too." But he couldn't seem to keep his eyes off the churchyard.

•••

The night was dry but chilly, the wind wrestling with the trees. He would be half-frozen by morning.

Sean turned his cell phone to vibrate and returned it to his pocket. Armed with a flashlight and a thermos of strong coffee but no gun, he headed for the graveyard. Unless someone was watching from the woods or the kudzu jungle, nobody knew he was there. Nobody but Laura.

Directly across from the house, he stood in the shadows and took in the view from the graveyard. The interior lights were out, but the security lights illuminated the yard and the porch. Laura would still be awake, listening to every sound.

He'd scouted the lay of the land before nightfall, and he'd found the most logical place for a person to hide and spy on Laura. Then he'd found a place for himself, a place where he could watch for a watcher—a wooden bench, deep in the corner of the graveyard, behind an especially large gravestone. He could see the Gantt family plot, its cement curb barely visible by moonlight.

From this vantage point, he could see a portion of the road too. If he kept scanning, back and forth, he wouldn't miss a thing—unless someone crept up behind him.

He sat on the bench and settled in for a long wait, his eyes adjusting to the darkness. On his side of the road, the brightest thing around was the steeple, its white paint lit from below, like a beacon trying to point people toward heaven.

Not counting the time he'd hid out in the vestibule to spirit Laura away from the old ladies, the last time he'd been inside that church was for Jess's funeral. He'd slipped into the service a few minutes late. Standing in the rear, he'd found the back of Laura's head, in the front row. A lamp had hung on the wall in front of her, perfectly centered, its light making a nimbus of rays around her gold-red hair while her slightest movement had made the lamp's finial seem to bob like a golden tongue above her head. Like Pentecost and those tongues of fire, he'd thought, remembering her Pentecostal grandparents, the Flynns. They were buried right there in the same graveyard.

A gust of wind blew down the hill, chilling him. North Georgia could be plenty cold, even in late May. The night would be a long one.

His eyelids were already drooping. He'd never thought he could be sleepy in a graveyard at midnight.

To keep himself awake, he tried to imagine how many lives were represented by gravestones in this one little plot of ground. Each grave held the remains of somebody whose day-to-day doings had added up to a life. Kindergarten, grade school, high school. Cars and cats and ball games. College, jobs, weddings. Kids and grandkids and old-folks' homes, and finally the graveyard with all its crosses that preached silent sermons about the life to come.

Sean preferred that to Jess's notion that people died and then came back around again in some new form. He would rather live just one life that mattered. One life that ended with his hopes fixed on the resurrection of the dead.

He unscrewed the lid of his thermos and fortified himself with hot, sweet coffee. He couldn't doze off on his watch.

When Keith had called back, he'd said Dale had stopped him downtown to rant. He was sure Elliott was the rat who'd made that phone call years ago. Dale intended to find him, somehow. So Dale was roaming around, seeking his prey. Elliott was prowling around too, doing God knows what.

When Mrs. Gibson's fallen silk flowers had jogged Sean's memory in the early morning light, he knew who Laura's prowler was. He couldn't tell her, though. If he was wrong, it would break her heart.

Last night at dusk, her tall vase full of pink azaleas had toppled in the wind, like the other tall and top-heavy flowers all over the cemetery. But this morning when he'd stepped onto the porch at first light, Jess's flowers stood straight and tall again.

Someone had righted them between dusk and dawn. Someone who cared about Jess's flowers and hers alone.

Twenty-five

After a long night of fitful sleep, Laura rose before dawn and dressed. Two minutes into her morning, she could tell it was going to be one of those days.

Her favorite shirt had lost a button. She put on a lightweight sweater instead, and it had a snag in it. She'd run out of hand lotion. And when she went to make the coffee, the grinder finally died for good. She threw it in the trash and headed into her mom's room to take some lotion from her bureau.

Laura shook her head at the clutter there. She needed to deal with it soon. Reaching for a tube of hand cream, she realized the tiny bottle of Jean Naté cologne was missing. She—or Mikey—must have knocked it to the floor. If it wasn't tightly capped, it could leak and ruin the hard-wood.

On her knees, she felt under the bed. Her

fingers bumped into something but she couldn't get a grip on it. Flat on the floor, she peered under the bed. The Jean Naté wasn't there, but she pulled out a hardcover book with an illustration of pink columbines on the cover and a lavender grosgrain ribbon peeking out to serve as a bookmark.

Breathing fast, Laura sat on the bed. She opened to the first page and read the date. This was the final journal, starting near the end of March. It was the only one Ardelle hadn't found.

Her mom had always picked up her pen at first light. The UPS driver had found her on the porch at ten in the morning, so she'd probably written her final entry only a few hours before her death.

Laura started at the beginning. Like the journals she'd found earlier, it was daily trivia. Nothing about possible sightings of a supposedly dead husband.

She'd recorded her dreams, though, as she'd begun to do a few years before, and she'd tried to analyze them. She'd used different colors of ink, perhaps for different moods—light blue, lavender, green, bright red.

Twenty pages in, Laura reached the last entry, written in ordinary blue ink. It closed with Rain, rain, and more rain, but April showers will work wonders for my May flowers. It wasn't an especially significant sentence to close out a lifetime of journaling, but she lingered on it.

Jessamyn Gantt's last word: flowers. And that was the end of her thousands of journal entries. The end of her life—on earth, at least.

Laura ran a finger across the blank page that faced the last entry. She didn't want to think about what might have come next for a woman who'd been raised on Holy Ghost revivals and altar calls and the blood of Jesus but had drifted into vague beliefs about being at one with the Supreme Being and the universe. According to her mom's new, enlightened views, there was no such thing as sin. Just failings.

With a sigh, Laura took the journal into the living room and compared it to a cheap spiral notebook from the early years. Her mom had used plain blue or black ink then, and she hadn't analyzed her dreams. Her penmanship had changed gradually over the years, but her love of flowers had never altered.

In the early volume, Laura studied yet another line about gardening: Sometimes, a beautiful new plant springs up from the rot, from the dirt. A few short words followed, but they'd been scratched out, black ink over blue. Laura couldn't quite make them out.

She turned on a bright lamp and looked again. The last word was probably *me,* but she couldn't be sure.

Footsteps sounded on the porch. Sean, back from his night in the cemetery.

"Laura," he called. "It's me."

"Coming." She ran into the kitchen as he unlocked the back door and walked in, unshaven and bleary-eyed.

"Mornin', Red."

"Good morning. You look exhausted."

"I'm all right." He seemed to be gauging her mood as he closed the door.

"Did you see anything? Hear anything?"

"Nothing but birds and bugs. Anything happen here?"

"Nothing but wind, all night long. Where did you hide out?"

"On a bench, behind a big ol' tombstone. Nothing happened, nobody came. I guess that's good news."

"I guess," she echoed, studying him.

He acted too casual. Too relaxed. Yet she picked up new worries in the undercurrents of his voice, in the faraway look in his eye. But it became a hungry look when he crooked a finger at her.

"No," she said. "Absolutely not. Not until you've brushed your teeth."

He smiled. "Did you brush yours?"

"Yes."

Sean ambled down the hall to the bathroom. She heard the sound of running water, the toilet flushing, running water again. He came back, not looking any more civilized but smelling like peppermint toothpaste.

"Better?" he asked, pulling her close.

"Better," she said, and for a couple of minutes, she could nearly forget why he was there. Why he'd sat in a cemetery all night.

He pulled back and studied her. "That was a long, cold night. I'm glad to be in a warm house with bright lights—and you." He released her, walked over to the counter and pulled one of the lemon-poppy-seed muffins out of the bag. "Something tells me you didn't get a lot of sleep, either."

"Yeah, well, I have a few things on my mind."

"No kidding." He pulled off a piece of the muffin and sat at the table.

It was the same place where he'd sat on the day her dad had brought him home, so bruised from that last beating that he could hardly move. Sean had put on a show of being fine. Just fine. A little hungry, maybe. But when her dad ruffled his hair and called him son, she knew Sean had gone to a new level of hero-worship. He hadn't seen her dad as a wigged-out Vietnam vet. Sean had simply loved him.

He pinched a piece of muffin between forefinger and thumb and frowned at it. "Stale muffins aren't worth eating. Got coffee?"

"Sorry. No coffee. The grinder broke for good, and there's nothing in the house but whole beans."

"That settles it." He stood up. "We're going out for breakfast."

"No. I don't want to."

"Never argue with a man who's been awake all night in a graveyard." He opened the fridge and pulled out a Coke.

"Coke? For breakfast?"

"I need some caffeine for the road. The old diner opens early. Let's go there. Not that new froufrou place. I want real food."

"But I want to be home in case he comes back this morning."

"It won't take long to grab a bite to eat. He hasn't shown up in broad daylight yet, has he?"

"Are you actually admitting that he shows up sometimes in the night?"

Lounging against the counter, Sean studied her for a long moment before he answered. "I'm not admitting anything, darlin'."

He was weakening, though. He'd practically acknowledged that her dad was back. A thrill ran through her, nearly distracting her from the fact that Sean had progressed to calling her "darlin'."

The residents of Prospect were gearing up for their biggest event of the year, and in spite of the early hour, the party atmosphere was in full swing. It did nothing to calm Laura's nerves. The main stage had been erected in the town square, and several smaller stages stood at a distance. Bright banners flapped from streetlight poles, and US flags flew everywhere in honor of

Memorial Day. Posters adorned the windows of every business, including the diner.

As Sean held the diner's door open for her, Laura glanced at the newspaper rack beside it. The headline of the weekly paper, printed every Wednesday, read "Bluegrass festivities start Friday." The lead article featured a photo of Gibby, dressed in black as always but his hair a handsome silver now.

Sean paid no attention to the paper. Coke can in hand, he nudged her right past the "Please wait to be seated" sign toward an empty booth by the window, set with napkin-wrapped silverware and two white coffee mugs, upside down.

He settled down across from her and drained his Coke can. A teenage waitress scurried up to the table with laminated menus in one hand and a coffeepot in the other. Sean turned both mugs right side up. Unshaven and weary, he looked like a wild man who'd just crawled out of a cave.

"Please," he said before the waitress could speak.

"Good morning," she chirped as she filled Laura's mug. "How are y'all?"

"Fine and dandy, thanks," Sean said. "How are you?"

"Fine." She poured his coffee. "It's gonna be a beautiful day."

"Yep." He pulled the sugar packets toward him and doctored his coffee. "You want the special, honey?" he asked Laura. "The big breakfast? Yeah, you do. You need to eat. Two specials, please."

Laura decided not to argue this time. It wasn't important.

The waitress set the coffeepot on the table and whipped out her pad. Laura answered the questions without much thought. Over medium, whole wheat, hash browns, bacon, whatever. She would eat maybe ten percent of it.

"Same, please," Sean said. "Except grits." He slid the empty Coke can across the table. "And throw this away for me?"

The waitress nodded, scribbling.

He raised his coffee mug to his lips. Leaving it there, he closed his eyes.

"Anything else I can get y'all?" the girl asked.

"That should do it, thanks," Laura said, since Sean seemed to have gone into a trance.

"I'll get that right up." The waitress retrieved the coffeepot and walked away.

An older waitress walked past, the aroma of bacon and pancakes competing with her too-strong cologne. Laura sat up straighter, remembering.

"Sean, I forgot to tell you about the Jean Naté. My mom's cologne. This morning I noticed it's missing from her bedroom."

He opened his eyes. "Who could have been in the house after I changed the locks?"

"I think it was Ardelle, days ago. Before you changed the locks. She popped in at least once that I know of, when I wasn't home. She got defensive when Cassie brought it up, remember? Ardelle said she wasn't a thief. Maybe she was defensive because she *is* a thief."

"Cologne hardly seems worth stealing. She probably threw it out. Thought she was helping you de-clutter."

"Why would she stop with only one item, then? I hate to worry Gary with it, but I should talk to Cassie, at least. She can help me figure it out."

"Before you call her, take another look," Sean said. "In case you missed it."

"Good idea."

Silence fell between them, making Laura aware of the background music. Instead of the usual soft rock, it was bluegrass in honor of the festival.

Their food, when it came, was tasteless. Laura played with it, picked at it, pushed it around her plate.

"You've got to eat, sweetheart," Sean said. "Even if you don't feel like it."

"Don't worry about me. I'll be all right."

He lowered his fork and searched her face. "That's exactly what your dad always said when your mom was trying to keep him from flipping out. Or he'd give her that little wink. Remember?"

Laura nodded, fighting tears in earnest. Trying

to evade Sean's gaze, she looked across the crowded restaurant. Nearly filled to capacity, the room rang with laughter and chatter. She wondered if any of the conversations included her father's name.

The sheriff and a young but balding deputy had walked in, conspicuous in their khaki uniforms with their shiny badges and black holsters. The sheriff had aged since Laura had seen him last. His slicked-back hair was touched with gray now, but he'd kept his trim build.

Law-abiding public servants, the men stopped beside the "wait to be seated" sign. The hostess greeted them. Like a mama duck with two ducklings in tow, she led the men toward a table near Sean and Laura's booth.

Watching them approach, Laura decided the timing was a godsend. If her dad chose this weekend to come back, perhaps drawn by the music, the sheriff's department should be on the lookout. Even though they didn't believe the rumors, they might need a reminder that if he turned up, he might be in bad shape. In need of help and protection. She glanced at Sean. He was studying her, his expression weary yet alert.

"What are you thinking?" he asked quietly.

"I should have a word with the sheriff."

"Last I heard, you didn't want him to get involved."

She didn't have time to explain. The men had

arrived at their table, exchanging friendly banter with the hostess as they took their seats. She walked away, and the sheriff looked directly at Laura.

"Good morning, Miss Gantt. Sean."

They echoed his greeting, and then Laura addressed the sheriff.

"I'd like to ask you a question or two," she said.

"Sure," the sheriff said with a fatherly smile. "What's on your mind?"

She leaned toward him, not wanting to speak more loudly than necessary. "I understand you're skeptical of the rumors about my dad."

The sheriff's smile faded. "I'm sorry, but I haven't seen any evidence to back them up."

"We need to talk, then. I might have some evidence."

"If you have facts, ma'am, I'm interested. If it's just more speculation . . . well, I'm up to my eyebrows in speculation."

"It's more than speculation."

He sighed. "If you'd like to come by my office sometime, we can talk."

"How about now? As soon as we've all finished eating?"

He shook his head. "I'm sorry, but I've got my hands full with the festival."

Laura's temper began to stir. "A few minutes after breakfast is too time consuming?"

"When I get this weekend behind me, I'll have a lot less on my mind."

"But it's a three-day weekend."

He gave her a puzzled look. "And?"

"I don't want to wait until Tuesday. Tuesday might be too late."

"Miss Gantt, how long ago did your dad disappear? Ten or twelve years ago? After all that time, I don't believe a few more days will make much difference."

"What if it were your father out there?" she asked fiercely, not caring anymore who heard her.

"Honey, I don't believe it's *your* father either. Feel free to stop by the office on Tuesday morning, though. About nine would work for me."

His condescending tone nearly provoked her into a caustic reply, but Sean's boot came down on her shoe, gentle but firm. A secret signal. She looked at him, his disheveled hair hanging across his forehead, hiding those scars. One side of his mouth gave in to that sarcastic little upward tilt. His eyes shone like blue jewels.

After all the times she'd worried that he would overreact, now he was reminding her to keep her cool.

She winked, just enough for him to see it. *Don't worry about me. I'll be all right.*

He winked back.

"All right," she told the sheriff. "Tuesday morning at nine, I'll be in your office."

"See you then." He moved his attention to the waitress approaching his table, and the conversation was over.

"So much for that," Laura said under her breath.

"I love you, Laura Gantt," Sean said, loud and clear. Right in front of everybody. He pulled out his wallet, extracted some money, and dropped the bills on the table. "You're not arguing," he said with a smile. "That's progress."

"I can never talk any sense into your head anyway." She slid out of the booth.

Sean got up too and draped his arm around her shoulders. They went outside, into bright sunshine and a brisk wind that made the bluegrass banners tug hard against their tethers. Hammer strokes bounced off the planks of a temporary stage and reverberated across the square. A trash truck backed up, beeping. The air rang with the slap and thud of lumber being unloaded by the stage.

The vendors' booths were up, and the vendors themselves would appear soon to hawk their wares. Food and drink, CDs, songbooks, instruments. And Sean would be there bright and early on Saturday morning if she had to hogtie him and drag him there.

Unless her dad came back, and then nothing else would matter.

"You okay?" Sean asked. "Not too mad at the sheriff?"

"It's just frustrating. And all this"—she motioned toward a flurry of activity near the main stage. "It makes me imagine my dad showing up in broad daylight. Walking right down the street."

"If he does, some kind soul will recognize him and help him track you down."

"What if he's back to track Gibby down? And what if Dale's right in the middle of it too?"

"Stop imagining the worst possible scenarios, Laura. You'll live longer."

She shook her head, weary of arguing with him.

"You have any plans for tonight?" he asked as they approached his truck.

"Not really. You?"

"Please understand why I'm not inviting you to tag along, but I'd like to camp out at the cabin tonight. To see if anybody turns up."

She felt a chill. "You mean my dad?"

"Dale, more likely."

She realized she'd unconsciously placed her left hand over the fading bruise on her right elbow although her sleeve hid it.

"Why tonight, though?" she asked. "Has something changed?"

"Tomorrow night, I'd like to get some sleep so I'll be in decent shape to man my booth on Saturday. Tonight's my last chance to stake out the cabin before the weekend."

She stopped walking and faced him. "Hold it right there. I don't like the way you put that. A stakeout is for cops, looking for bad guys. My dad's one of the good guys."

"One of the best," Sean said. "Absolutely."

"No guns. Understand?"

He shot her a look of pure irritation. "No guns. But you're not staying alone at the house. Stay at my place."

"Sean, it's not necessary. I'll be fine."

"Would it hurt, though?"

She took a moment to consider her options. "I guess it wouldn't hurt," she said, carefully non-committal.

"Here's a key to my front door." He placed it in her hand.

"Thanks, Sean." Afraid he would read her mind if she looked him in the eye, she hurried to climb into his truck.

Twenty-six

Outside, chain saws buzzed like hornets as Cassie walked toward the kitchen to rustle up some breakfast. Her dad had hired a crew to take down some sickly pines before they died and fell on the house. The men had been hard at work since eight in the morning. That was only five,

California time. She was not in an especially good mood.

Hearing voices—or at least one voice—she peeked around the corner. Her mom stood at the counter beside the sink, dumping a handful of sliced potatoes into her slow cooker. She seemed to be moving in slow motion, and she was talking to herself.

Cassie crept closer, her bare feet noiseless on the smooth ceramic tiles, and listened.

"I can't do anything right," her mom said. "Can't measure up." She lifted one hand to her face as if to wipe away tears. "I can't even spell," she added in a stronger voice.

"Whoa," Cassie mouthed silently. She backed up a few steps and moved to one side for a better view.

"I can't be anybody else. I can't be anybody but me." Her mom picked up a potato and the peeler.

Cassie's phone rang in her pocket. Her mom whirled to face her.

"Darn, I wanted to talk to you and now somebody's calling me." Cassie pulled out her phone and decided not to mention it was Laura.

"Who is it?" Her mom set down the peeler and the potato. She wiped her wet hands on her black sweatpants, the potato starch making pale smudges on the fabric.

"It's, um, an old friend of mine." Cassie made a hasty exit through the sunroom to the pool deck and took a deep breath of fresh air filled with the sweet scent of the butchered pines. The chain saws were annoyingly loud, but they'd be a good cover for the phone call.

She opened the phone. "Hey, Laura."

"Hey, Cass. How's your mom doing?"

"Pretty much the same," Cassie said softly. "What's new with you?"

"Well . . . I need to tell you what your mom has been up to lately. Or at least I *think* she's the one who's responsible."

"Oh boy. What did she do now?" Cassie sat in one of the poolside chairs and waited for the bad news.

"It wasn't necessarily your mom who did this, but somebody went into my mom's room and took a little bottle of Jean Naté. Her favorite fragrance."

"You're sure it's missing?"

"Yes. I looked and looked, but it's really gone."

"What does it smell like?"

"Sort of fruity. Lemony. Spicy."

"I'll see what I can find out and let you know. Hey, I'm going to try to talk her into hitting the festival tomorrow. Will you be there?"

"Probably not. The live music won't start until tomorrow night, and Sean won't open his booth until Saturday morning. That's where I'll be, if only to make sure he's there instead of here."

"Okey-doke. I'll look for you at his booth on Saturday. See ya."

Cassie returned to the kitchen. Now her mom was chopping onions.

"Mom, you want to hit the music shindig sometime? We can check out the bands. Eat a funnel cake or two."

"Mm-hmm," her mom said in a vague tone.

Moving closer, Cassie inhaled deeply. She didn't smell anything lemony or fruity. Just onions, and they made her eyes water.

"Wow, those are strong onions."

"Mm-hmm. That's nice, honey."

Cassie blinked hard and fast. Now she was crying real tears, not onion tears. She couldn't deny it any longer. Something was wrong with her mother.

Sean climbed out of his truck at the QuikTrip, swiped his card, and started pumping gas. He should have showered and shaved first, to wake up his weary brain, but it would have made as much sense as a shower and a shave before a hunting trip.

Bad analogy. Elliott wasn't prey.

Just down the street, one of the banners for the festival snapped in the wind, its bold blue-and-green design the same one the town had used for years. It was finally getting some recognition.

By tomorrow night, the town would be packed

with musicians and fans. Rowdy drunks and noisy bikers. Affluent tourists and penny-pinching locals. The crowds were bigger every year, threatening to make it one of the biggest music events in the Southeast.

Of all the crazy times for Elliott to come back.

Sean was starting to hate that word—*crazy*—but as much as he wanted to believe Elliott would never hurt anybody, there was no telling what frame of mind he'd be in. Or what he might be charged with someday.

Sean rubbed the tight muscles in the back of his neck. He was glad Laura had agreed to spend the night at his house. She wasn't happy about it, obviously, but she hadn't argued much.

He bought a bag of ice and poured it over a six-pack of Coke in his cooler. Between him and Keith, they would have Coke, coffee, flashlights, plenty of bug spray, and at least one snake-bite kit. No guns. He'd given his word.

He put the lid on the cooler and checked the sky. He'd make it to the cabin before dark, and Keith would show up as soon as he got off work. Sean was still amazed that Annie had put her stamp of approval on the expedition.

Before he could get away, a white car pulled up next to him. Doc Marsh rolled down the window, his kind face burdened with worry. "How goes it, Sean?"

"Oh, it's interesting."

"It sure is." Doc kneaded his steering wheel with his pink hands. "Half an hour ago, I saw Dale's truck at the Gantts' old cabin outside of town. I thought I should let you know."

"Great, maybe it'll be a family reunion." Sean didn't try to hide his sarcasm. "Keith and I are planning to stay there all night tonight to see if Elliott turns up."

"If he does, he might need some serious help. You know where to find an old doctor who still knows his stuff."

"Thank you. I'll keep that in mind."

"All right, then. Treat him right—if you find him. And God be with you."

"Thanks." Sean climbed into his truck, threw it in reverse and glanced behind him, the empty gun rack snagging his attention. All his guns were locked up tight at home. Laura was safe and sound under his roof too. It should have given him a measure of peace.

Driving down the road, Sean remembered Elliott whittling on his porch one night, rambling about every subject under the sun. He'd said there was a difference between justice and revenge. And sometimes, he'd said, eyeing his knife, a sin wasn't a crime. Sometimes a crime wasn't a sin.

Obviously, he'd had his own ideas about justice.

Maybe they'd still have a happy ending, though. Sean could imagine finding Elliott lounging against a tree trunk somewhere. Whittling a piece of wood, maybe. He'd be old and grimy and skinny, and maybe he wouldn't be entirely rational, but he'd still be himself in the ways that mattered. He'd still be a good man with a kind heart.

"Hey, Sean," he'd say, setting down his knife. *"It's been a long time."*

"Yes sir," Sean would say. *"Welcome home."*

"Thank you, son. You about ready to start those fiddle lessons?"

"Maybe. You about ready to explain that car in the lake?"

If the cabin and the house were the two most likely places for her dad to show up, she couldn't spend the night at Sean's house. And what he didn't know couldn't hurt him. Laura knew she'd be fine, home alone behind the new deadbolts, and she had more than enough reading material to last through her vigil.

Sitting on the living room floor, surrounded by dozens of journals, she chose one at random and opened it to an entry from a January day: *The crocuses will be up soon.* In the middle of winter, her mom had longed for flowers. They'd been a recurring theme in her life.

Having recently browsed through the bulk of over thirty years' worth of journaling, Laura saw other themes too. It was like working on a thousand-piece jigsaw puzzle. She had gradually become familiar with colors and patterns. She'd started to see which pieces might fit together to make recognizable images. But she didn't have a puzzle box with the complete picture printed on it for reference.

If it were a puzzle, she'd start with the edge pieces that hemmed everything in. Then she'd look for pieces that held distinctive elements, like lettering on a sign or unusual colors.

But she couldn't distill the years of a family's life together into a single snapshot. If it could be an image at all, it would have to be a panoramic view that covered both space and time. A cross between a timeline and a map of her family's journey with their fellow travelers. It would include landscapes and weather too. She couldn't separate them; they existed in each other. Sunshine beating down on the streets of Prospect. Storms rolling through the mountains.

A sprawling picture began to take shape in her mind. Railroad tracks curved across one corner, bringing a train into town through the bright green of the kudzu. In sharp detail in the foreground, blackberries gleamed in the brambles. Flowers bloomed everywhere in every color, under a sky of a million shades of blue and gray.

On the far left, she saw young lovebirds as they'd been before their baby girl came along. A gentle musician turned combat-scarred veteran. His flower-child wife who'd never dreamed of being married to a soldier.

Farther along, there'd be a carrot-top mama with a carrot-top baby on her hip. Farther still, there'd be a red-headed toddler playing with blocks on a sunny kitchen floor or falling asleep to her dad's lullabies.

Then came school days with Cassie and Sean —and tow-headed Tig dogging their steps.

Darker colors came next. The veteran's moods worsened, but even the darkest days included the bright threads of his wife's soothing words and the loyalty of his friends. Not just Gary and Ardelle, but the musicians who'd drifted in and out of the house. Especially Doc, Noodle, and Gibby. She wished she could erase Gibby from the picture. Dale too, but he was part of it. His wife hid in the shadows, barely there.

In her mind, Laura moved toward the right side of the panorama. High school. A bright-red truck. Initials carved into an old picnic table. Sean's blue eyes and wry smile. The childhood scars he hid under his shaggy hair.

The argument she'd overheard as a teenager would be there too, in dark, muddy paints slashed with a violent red and venomous green. Betrayal, jealousy, rage.

Hamlin Lake haunted the background, its bright blue waters beautiful and dangerous. The mountains stood behind everything else, holding their secrets tightly.

Jessamyn Gantt had held her secrets tightly too, all the way to the grave, but her husband might come back from the dead and reveal at least some of them.

❧ *Twenty-seven* ❧

It was late, and Cassie wanted to go to bed. The three of them had been sitting together in the living room for a solid hour, and it was beginning to feel like an interrogation room. Her head hurt and her heart ached for her parents. Her mom seemed incapable of cooperating, and her dad's patience had worn thin.

"Come on, Mom," Cassie said in her most soothing tone. "Just admit it. It's not a big deal if you took a partially used bottle of cologne. Laura would have thrown it out anyway."

Her mom sniffled. "Stop fussing at me. I didn't do anything wrong."

"At least admit that you let yourself in sometimes when she wasn't home."

"Of course I went over there sometimes. I missed going over to feed Mikey. I liked walking into the house. Sometimes I could almost believe

Jess was still alive. I could pretend she'd walk in and start a pot of coffee and we'd have a nice, long talk."

"That's a little weird, Mom."

"Don't be rude, Cassandra Jane. Yes, I might have done more than Laura asked me to do, but stop accusing me of things."

"Ardie," Gary said softly. "I've smelled a new scent on you lately. Like the one Laura described to Cassie. The one that's missing."

"Stop it!" Ardelle stood up, her chest heaving. "I'll be scrapping. Leave me alone." She walked out of the room.

Cassie rubbed her eyes and peered at her dad. He looked like a guy who'd been on a bender. Bleary eyes, messy hair, his shirttails hanging out. It was so unlike him.

Moving like an old man, he heaved himself out of his chair. Then he stood motionless. The mover and shaker didn't know what to do next.

"Mom needs help," Cassie said. "She needs counseling."

"Of course she does. I'll ask Doc for some recommendations." He hung his head. "She'll be so embarrassed."

"She shouldn't be. She shouldn't be embarrassed if she needs meds either. We'll get through this. Together. All of us."

"I hope you're right."

Cassie had never seen him so sorrowful. So

lost. She crossed the room, kissed his cheek, and felt tears on his skin. "Oh, Dad. It'll be okay."

"I hope so. We'll just have to start looking for that perfume. Cologne. Whatever it is."

"Why is it so important to find it?"

"If we find it, she'll have to admit she took it. She'll have to admit she's been lying—about all of it, probably. That might be the first step."

Cassie didn't like his theory, but she didn't have anything better to offer. "This is a huge house, and it could be anywhere."

"Then let's get busy." Still moving like an old man, he left her there.

Shaken by the condition of her parents' marriage, Cassie was suddenly terrified for her own.

Late in Georgia was still a decent hour in California. She sank into the cushy chair again and pulled out her phone. Searching for cologne could wait until she'd tried one more time to snag Drew's undivided attention.

Voice mail. She groaned.

Waiting for the tone, she gave herself permission to be brutally honest. To say whatever came to her mind, no matter how bad it sounded.

The tone came.

"Drew Cutler, I love you," she said, good and loud. "But I'm tired of sharing you with your mistress. Your business. And I'm tired of being

355

broke and far away from my family and your family, and I want to have your babies before I'm too old and I want them to look just like you because I love you so much, but if you decide you'd rather be married to your business instead, then you can have little business-babies some-day with your business-mistress but I'm not sharing you anymore. Do you understand?"

She slapped at the tears wetting her cheeks. "If you love me, you'll call me back this instant, and we won't stop talking until we've worked things out, and the stupid cologne hunt can just wait. Call me back *now*."

Closing her phone, she started crying in earnest. He would think she'd gone crazy. Maybe she had.

In the middle of a horrible, ugly sob, she jumped out of her skin. That was Drew's ring-tone. Afraid to answer, afraid not to answer, she stared at the screen.

Sean and Keith had parked their trucks at a construction site down the road and walked to the cabin. Now they were hiding high on the hill above it. Dale's truck was gone before they got there, and if Elliott was near, he wasn't making himself obvious.

They'd caught no scent of wood smoke, no motion, no light except the stars and the moon-light and the occasional airplane cruising across the sky. Most of the long, uncomfortable night still stretched out before them. Hunkered down on a small tarp atop the springy leaves, Sean wondered how many snakes might be annoyed with the intruders and how many ticks and kudzu bugs might be impervious to bug spray. Best not to think about it.

Before night fell, he'd taken a good look around. The cabin, nestled in a shallow valley, was nearly covered with kudzu. One look at the fallen roof and vine-choked floor had told him no sane person would try to live there.

Therefore Elliott might.

Sean checked his phone to make sure it was on. Laura probably wouldn't call, but he wanted to be available if she needed him.

He leaned back on his folded jacket, watching the lights of a jet bound south for Atlanta. Even up in the mountains, miles into the wilderness, a man wouldn't be able to escape civilization completely. Every few minutes, another plane flew over.

He thought of a September morning when four planes screamed down from a blue sky and changed America forever. He wasn't a military man, but the video clip that had moved him the most had shown a mob of people racing down the sidewalks of DC. He'd thought they were running away, but then the camera had panned out, showing the truth. Those people were running *toward* the Pentagon. Bent on rescuing friends and strangers, they'd run straight into death and destruction.

Elliott, if he'd been there and in his right mind, would have been in the thick of it too. But he probably hadn't been in his right mind for years. Probably wouldn't be, ever again, unless God worked a major miracle. A miracle on a par with restoring lost limbs.

Sean had never seen even a minor miracle. Not one. And he lived in the Bible Belt.

The lights of another plane drifted into view, reminding him of those few, eerie days when no planes flew. The sky had been empty. Nothing came between the earth and heaven. Nothing came between humanity and the eyes of God.

The brothers stayed silent, watching lights glide across the black sky, watching the changeless darkness in the direction of the cabin. Sean fought to keep his eyes open.

The tarp rustled as Keith shifted his weight. "I still say it's past time to get a little help from law enforcement," he whispered.

Sean drew a slow breath. "Maybe. But the sheriff thinks the rumors are bogus, and he doesn't understand some of the underlying issues. I'd rather leave him out of it."

"Okay, but we should at least track down all the sightings and plot them on a map. Who saw him, and when and where. It might help narrow it down."

"We might not have time for a scientific approach."

A faint, metallic ping charged the air. Sean froze, electrified. Keith caught his breath and held it.

They sat in complete stillness, listening, but it didn't happen again. The sound, so brief and unexpected, could have been a small noise nearby or a loud noise made faint by distance. The hair rose in prickles on the back of Sean's neck like it did when he was hunting and a deer was nearby.

"Could've been Dale," Keith said, barely audible.

But Sean thought of the missing wind chimes. When he cocked his head, listening, he thought he heard a soft, faraway laugh.

Although it was nearly three in the morning, Laura hadn't even been tempted to nod off. The journals scattered across the floor would have kept her thinking even if she hadn't been watching for her dad's return.

If she didn't connect with him soon, she might miss her chance forever. And there had to be at least one person who would give Elliott Gantt a chance to prove he was harmless. She had to welcome him home with open arms.

She'd spent hours browsing her mother's writing. Most of it was shallow, self-absorbed nonsense, but the earliest journals had been different. They'd bubbled with life and love. Now Laura wasn't even sure where to find them. She'd made a mess of Ardelle's chronological order—on purpose, maybe.

Laura stood up and walked among the stacks and spills of the slender volumes. She found half a dozen of the cheap, spiral-bound notebooks from the early years. Taking them back to the couch, she curled up with the quilt.

She started with the one that opened with Jess Gantt as a young, pregnant wife. E. worries about Agent O., she'd written. Such a pessimist. I keep telling him the baby will be absolutely perfect.

Tears sprang to Laura's eyes. She'd never given much thought to it, but it made sense that he would have been exposed to Agent Orange. Of course he would have worried about birth defects, not to mention health issues for himself.

She opened three more notebooks, checking their dates, before she found the one that covered her birth. There was nothing for the day she was born, but on the next day her mother had written: No time to journal yesterday. Laura Lillian made her appearance at 4:48 p.m. My baby girl is perfect. E. said she looks just like me, and he added with a grin: "Thank God!" I am SO thankful.

Laura shook her head. Early in their marriage,

her parents must have been happy. They must have been in love.

A faint meow brought Laura back to the present. Two frail old souls were out there tonight: her dad and Mikey, who'd slipped between her feet hours before when she went out to get the mail. The cat had made himself scarce, but now he was yowling at the door.

Pathetic old thing. He wanted his independence, but he was too elderly, too frail to live in a world filled with fast cars and mean dogs and coyotes.

In warm sweats, Laura left the quilt on the couch and walked into the kitchen, dimly lit by reflections from the outdoor security lights. She breathed faster, remembering the bearded man who'd watched her from the window. She still wasn't absolutely certain it had been her father.

But it would only take a few seconds to let Mikey in and lock the door again. The chances of someone being out there at that particular moment were minuscule. She would be fine.

The cat meowed again. In the distance, a dog barked.

"Hang on a second, Mikey."

Aware that the glaring lights might make her visible too, she felt for the switch and shut them off. The instantaneous blackness provided a new sense of concealment. She unlocked the door and opened it a few inches, just wide enough to admit a skinny cat.

Mikey hurtled between her feet like a small, furry rocket.

Through the crack, she saw a dark figure approaching from the far corner of the porch. She screamed, slammed the door and slapped the deadbolt home, her fingers like ice. Footsteps whispered unevenly but swiftly across the planks and down the steps.

She leaned on the door, holding her breath. Listening. Her pulse hammered in her ears.

"Dad," she called with her mouth to the door. "Dad, is that you?"

A tree branch creaked.

"Daddy?"

There was no sound but the wind and the fierce pounding of her pulse.

She could almost believe she'd imagined seeing someone, but she knew she hadn't imagined the footsteps. Limping footsteps.

Dale didn't limp. Her dad had never limped before, but maybe he did now. Maybe he cut down wind chimes and prowled church camps and visited porches in the middle of the night. Maybe he didn't want a reunion with her.

What did he want, then?

"God, help me," she said softly. "I don't know what to do."

Chilled all over, she pushed a chair under the doorknob then retreated to the den, where she opened her phone. Trying to decide whether to call 911 or Sean, she hesitated.

If he knew someone had been on her porch, he would make the 911 call himself. The sheriff and his deputies would show up with their cars and searchlights, with guns and dogs. They would go after her dad like they'd go after a common criminal.

Laura shut her phone. She wasn't calling anybody. He deserved a chance. And if the man on the porch wasn't her dad . . . she still had his guns, and she knew how to use them.

Twenty-eight

Cassie glared at the bedside clock. Five? Seriously, she was awake at five? *Eastern?*

She'd stayed up half the night talking to Drew—wonderful, adorable Drew—but then she'd tossed and turned for hours, trying to imagine their unsettled future. Might as well get up and keep looking for that blasted Jean Naté, but she was starting to doubt Laura's crazy accusations.

Wrapped in a warm robe she'd snagged from her mom's closet earlier in the week, Cassie padded slowly down the hallway toward the bathroom and tried to decide which room to search next. She didn't want to make a lot of noise while her parents were sleeping.

Then she noticed a light under the door to the scrapping room.

Her mom wouldn't be up so early . . . would she?

Slowly, Cassie turned the doorknob. Slowly, she opened the door.

In her favorite flannel pajamas, her mother was sound asleep in her comfy swivel chair in front of the cabinet where she kept her supplies. Her mouth was open, and she was snoring ever so faintly.

Cassie tiptoed across the room to the worktable. A half-finished scrapbook lay open to pages devoted to photos of Trevor. They were artistically arranged, embellished with stickers and shiny confetti, and captioned neatly.

"Halloween—Trevor as Captian Jack," one of the captions read. The misspelled word was glaringly obvious.

Cassie looked back at her mother and was struck by the odd placement of her chair, smack-dab in front of the cabinet. As if she were guarding it.

Pondering her options, Cassie realized she couldn't open either of the cabinet doors without nudging her mom's legs aside and waking her up. But there'd be no better way to startle her into an unrehearsed reaction.

Cassie approached, quickly but quietly. She

bent over and opened the right-hand door until it bumped against her mother's leg.

"Oops," Cassie said cheerfully. "Sorry. 'Scuse me."

"Mmm?"

"Scootch over a little, please."

Still half-asleep, Ardelle obeyed. She even scooted her chair a little, making things easier. But when Cassie opened the door fully, Ardelle came fully awake.

"Get out of my cabinet!"

"Too late." Cassie reached for the tiny bottle of Jean Naté. "Oh, Mom. What else have you got?"

Sean ached with fatigue as he and his brother trudged back to the construction site, just past dawn. What a waste of time. They'd sat on the cold ground all night but hadn't seen or heard anything except that faint, metallic ping. And birds and bugs. And—maybe—someone laughing at them.

Long before dawn, birds had started calling. Mosquitoes woke up, hungry. A big, hazy peach of a sun came up. Hoping for a sign of life, they'd stayed a few more minutes. No dice.

Keith, facing a day of work on no sleep, drove away first. The taillights of his truck disappeared around the curve as Sean was still climbing into his own truck.

A quarter mile down Porter Road, he spotted Granny Colfax walking the other way. There wasn't much traffic yet, just a few people headed out to start their ordinary days. He couldn't remember the last time he'd had one of those.

He swung into Laura's driveway and rubbed his eyes. What was her car doing there? She was supposed to be at *his* house. But a few lights were on inside, and everything looked normal. Maybe she woke early and came home to feed the cat.

He climbed out and headed up the steps. The door swung open. She stood in the doorway, wearing her mom's black-and-white bandanna.

"Good morning," she said.

"Good morning." He stopped two feet away from her, noticing the circles under her eyes. "Sleep okay?"

"Um, no." A faint blush stole across her cheeks. "I was up all night. Mostly."

"You didn't stay at my house, did you?"

She shook her head.

"Why not? This is the second time you said you'd stay somewhere else and then reneged on it."

"I wanted to be here in case my dad came back. And maybe he did. At three in the morning." Her eyes flickered to his left. "I opened the door, and somebody was on the porch." She pointed. "Right there. Whoever it was, he ran right past me."

No wonder they'd had no luck by the cabin.

Elliott had been at the house? On the porch?

"You opened the door in the middle of the night?"

"I was letting Mikey back in, all right? And then my dad—or whoever it was—came from the corner of the porch. I screamed and slammed the door. He ran off the porch, limping. I yelled through the door because I thought it might be Dad." Her lips trembled. "But he didn't come back."

"Did you get a good look at him?"

"No, it was too dark—"

"Dark?" He looked up at the porch ceiling, where the high-intensity bulbs should have been blazing until full light. "What happened to the security lights?"

"I turned them off so if anyone was out there, they couldn't see me."

He shook his head, but he couldn't chide her. He'd done the same thing—but not at three in the morning.

She jerked in a short, sharp breath, her bravado dissolving. "I sl-slammed the door so fast. I—No! Mikey!"

The cat had darted outside again, past both of them. Now he was hightailing it toward the road. For an old cat, Mikey sure could move.

Laura ran down the steps, doing the "Here-kitty-kitty-kitty" routine that usually brought the cat on the double. Not this time. Mikey was gone in seconds, disappearing into the tall road-side weeds.

"We shouldn't have been standing there with the door open," she said, stomping up the steps. "He'd better not get hit."

Sean couldn't remember the last time he'd seen her so edgy. He couldn't blame her, but he wasn't in the mood to worry about a cat.

He held the door open for her and followed her into the warmth of the house. "What time did this happen?"

"About three."

"Three. That's right. You told me." Several hours after he and Keith had heard the noise near the cabin. So that could have been Elliott too.

Or Dale. Or a stranger. The man on the porch might have been a stranger too.

Or even Ardelle. Was it possible? Nothing had gone missing since he'd changed the locks, but that didn't mean she wouldn't try to get in. She didn't live within walking distance anymore, though.

It was already nearly full light. Afraid they were running out of time somehow, Sean paced the room, trying to think. Trying to focus.

"If it was your dad, why didn't he answer when you called out?"

"I don't know, Sean. Same possibilities we've talked about over and over again. Maybe he was more afraid of me than I was of him."

Sean shook his head, still trying to put everything together, and remembered the theory that had occurred to him in the middle of the night. If Laura was right about Gibby and Jess, it could explain not only Elliott's disappearance but also his reappearance. Maybe he'd wanted revenge on Gibby but hadn't wanted to hurt Jess by acting on the impulse while she was alive. But if Elliott had somehow learned that she'd passed away, he might have resurfaced . . . just when Gibby would be in town.

Far away, a faint clang reminded Sean that the weekend was on its way. The PA system would start the canned music soon. Tonight the live bands would play. Main Street would be blocked off and swarming with tourists and locals. Downtown would smell like funnel cakes and cotton candy and beer. It seemed like some faraway planet, some silly world he used to live in.

Laura's hand on his arm jolted him. "What's wrong, Sean?"

He tried to smile. "Just about everything." Reaching with his other hand to pat hers, he noticed a yellowing bruise at her elbow. "What happened there?"

"It's nothing, really. Just a bruise."

Her strange evasiveness piqued his curiosity. "How did it happen?"

"I . . . well. You know, sometimes bruises just happen and you hardly remember how, later."

But this one completely encircled her arm in a pattern all too familiar.

"The truth, Laura."

Her shoulders rose and fell with a deep breath, and she met his eyes. "Remember the day I gave you the songbooks? The day I ran into Dale in your driveway? He thought I was rude, so he grabbed my arm as I was walking away. That's all."

"That's *all?*" Sean took her arm gently and examined the bruise. "He's not getting away with this."

"It's no big deal," she said, but there were tears in her eyes.

"Why didn't you tell me?"

"I was afraid you would overreact." She gave him an impish smile. "So prove me wrong, okay? Don't overreact."

"Our definitions of that word probably aren't the same."

"I know, but let it go. Please. A little ol' bruise won't matter if this is the day my dad comes back." She dabbed the corners of her eyes with her fingertips. "Maybe he'll sleep under his own roof tonight."

She was pale. Exhausted. Shivering, probably not from cold but from nerves. Sean pulled her into his arms and leaned his head against hers, feeling her damp hair on his cheek and smelling her shampoo.

"Whatever happens, we'll go through it together." Closing his eyes, he flashed back to a hot August day. Laura, Cassie, and Tigger, their hands piled together with his, making a promise. "We'll always be there for each other. Remember?"

Laura nodded but didn't speak.

"When I say always, I mean always. The rest of our lives."

She stiffened. She seemed to stop breathing.

He held his breath too, waiting. She had to know he was talking about marriage.

She looked up, her eyes shining with tears. "I'm afraid."

"Afraid of what?"

She lowered her gaze to his chin. When she finally spoke, he could hardly hear her. "Your father."

"Don't call him that."

"Refusing to acknowledge that Dale is your father doesn't change facts. And even though I know you're nothing like him, I still . . . I worry. He must hate me like he hates my dad."

"Don't worry about it. Dale hates everybody."

"He hates my dad in particular. For rescuing you."

"Laura, we've been close since we were kids. I thought you'd always been able to get past how vile Dale is. But now—we don't have to stay here. If you want me to move to Denver—or anywhere else—I will."

She finally looked up, her eyes dark with sorrow. "What if my dad's back in Prospect? What then?"

"Then we'll figure something out. Together."

A long shriek of squealing tires twisted in the air.

"Mikey," Laura said with a catch in her voice. "Mikey's been hit."

"Or missed." Sean looked out the window. "I'll go see. Not just about the cat but about any signs that your visitor might have left behind."

"I'll go with you."

"No. Please. We still aren't sure who we're dealing with. Stay inside, doors locked. I don't care if the cat learns to speak English and comes back and says pretty please, don't open the door to anybody but me."

He stole a quick kiss and left her standing there. He ran to the road and looked in both directions but didn't see a cat carcass anywhere.

He'd be elected gravedigger if the cat had finally bought the farm. He was already Laura's locksmith, bodyguard, and detective. Who had time to run a business? Or talk a woman into marrying him?

Twenty-nine

From the window, Laura watched Sean cross the road, his hair rippling in the wind. He slowed on the grassy shoulder and climbed the steps to the churchyard. At the top, he checked the view in all directions. He descended the steps and started down the road, walking fast.

Somewhere on the north side of town, a slow-moving freight blew its mournful whistle. The train would roll through Prospect, past the streets that were blocked off for the weekend. Past the kudzu jungle that had overtaken the berry patch. The train would pick up speed and keep going, leaving the town far behind.

Wherever her dad was, he heard the whistle too. He was out there, somewhere. Listening.

Ardelle's yellow convertible swung into view and came to a stop behind Sean's truck. Cassie was at the wheel.

Forcing her face into some semblance of serenity, Laura opened the front door. Cassie hurried up the steps, holding a small cardboard box. One of those old, bronzy-green garden markers stuck out of it. Her face was pale; her hair unbrushed. No makeup, no jewelry, and her eyes were puffy. She might have just rolled out of bed, or maybe she'd been crying for hours.

"You okay?" Laura asked.

"I spent half the night having the most wonderful knock-down-drag-out argument with Drew," she said with a funny little smile. "I'll explain later."

"Come on in. What's in the box?"

"You're not going to believe it," she said, coming inside. "Mom can't keep denying that she took anything. She'd stashed all kinds of stuff in her scrapbook cupboard." Stepping carefully through dozens of journals on the floor, Cassie made her way to the couch and sat down, still holding the box. "You ready for some craziness?"

"I hope so." Laura sat beside her.

Cassie held up the bottle of Jean Naté. "It's a scent Laura wouldn't wear anyway," she said in a spot-on impression of Ardelle's voice. "Then there's this." She held up a tube of peachy-pink lipstick.

"That looks exactly like a lipstick that used to be on my mom's bathroom counter."

"Why am I not surprised?" Cassie reached into the box again. "She had these photos of your mom's flower beds—my mom says that's okay, they're duplicates and she's sure you wouldn't mind—and a copy of your mom's obituary, but that's not something she swiped. It's been sitting around our kitchen for weeks. And there's one of those garden markers. Let's leave it in the box. I don't want to get dirt on your couch."

Bewildered, Laura shook her head. "Is there more?"

"Oh yeah, and it gets weirder. She had the chain your dad used to wear." Cassie reached into the box again and handed Laura the chain with the silver cross and the dog tag still dangling from it.

"What? I'd put them away in a drawer! Why would she snoop like that? And take something that's not hers? A memento of my dad, of all things."

"She didn't even try to explain that one. Or these." Cassie fanned out three Red Cross blood-donor cards on the couch. Red and white plastic, like credit cards.

Laura spread them out further to read the names. "What on earth? She had my mom's card, your dad's, and *mine*? She took it out of my wallet? When? How?"

"I don't know." Cassie shook her head. "I'm sorry. I don't get it."

"Me either. If I wasn't home, I would have had my wallet with me. And if I *was* home—" Laura stopped. "When I was here for the funeral, she came over to help with housework. She was here for a couple of hours—so she could have taken my card and Mom's, right under my nose. But why?"

"That's what Dad was trying to get out of her when I left. He'll call me if he can make sense of it."

Laura took a closer look at the Red Cross cards and her dad's dog tag, and her brain seemed to shut down. Maybe she was in denial, but she couldn't accept the most logical explanation. It didn't jibe with what she already knew. Or thought she knew.

Why *Gary's* donor card?

"This is all wrong. Cassie . . . remember in high school . . . those boxes? What are they called? Punnett squares?"

Cassie frowned. "Don't ask me. I didn't do well in geometry."

"Not geometry. Genetics. Biology with Preston. Oh, I wish I'd told you everything a long time ago—but this doesn't fit anyway."

"Laura, what are you talking about?"

"I'm pretty sure my mom had an affair. With Gibby."

Cassie's mouth fell open. "Gibby?" With wide eyes, she stared at the Red Cross cards. "What are you saying? What does that have to do with . . ."

"I don't know. My brain's on strike." Laura's voice cracked. "I need to borrow someone else's. Who understands genetics?"

"Preston."

Of course. Preston.

Laura picked up her phone and called him. Afraid she'd lose her nerve, she jumped into it the moment he'd said hello. "Mr. Preston, this is Laura Gantt. I have a quick science question for you. About blood types. If the mom is AB and the father is A, can they possibly have a baby with Type O?"

"That scenario isn't bloody likely." Preston laughed at his pun, then launched into a rambling explanation that included alleles, genotypes, and phenotypes. Laura, focused intently on the dog tag marked with her dad's blood type, wasn't in the mood to grasp every last detail, but the gist of the matter was clear.

Unless either the US Army or the American Red Cross had made a serious clerical error, she wasn't Elliott Gantt's biological daughter.

"Thank you," Laura said. "That helps. I've got to run. Bye for now." She managed to get through it without letting her voice break.

"What did he say?" Cassie asked.

"I'm pretty sure they had their affair when I was a teenager, so it doesn't make sense that I'm—I'm the wrong blood type."

"What? Laura, I don't understand."

"I'm the wrong blood type to be my dad's biological child." The weight of the statement pressed heavy on her shoulders.

Cassie's eyes widened, then narrowed. "No way. Based on . . . you mean . . ." Her voice trailed off. "Wait a minute. Let's think this through. It could mean . . . either you're wrong about the timing of the affair, or your mom had more than one affair. Shoot, I can't imagine her having even *one*. But where did you get your idea about the timing?"

"I heard my folks arguing about it the summer after we graduated from high school."

"So you thought it had just happened?"

"Yes."

"But maybe that's only when the truth came out."

Laura nodded slowly. "Maybe."

Cassie stood. "I need coffee."

"There's no coffee. No grinder. There's tea."

As Cassie walked into the kitchen, muttering to herself, Laura reached for the last item, the garden marker from one of her mother's flower beds.

Hemerocallis Honey Redhead.

Hemerocallis. The botanical name for daylilies.

Laura took a sharp breath. She lifted her hand to her hair.

My honey redhead, my redhead honey. Poor little carrot-top baby, you look more like your mama than your daddy.

Somewhere in the back of her mind, she was aware of a vehicle roaring into the driveway. A door slamming.

"Whoa," Cassie called from the kitchen. "My

dad's here, and he looks upset. *Real* upset, like he might be crying. Laura, this is scary. He never cries."

"Yes he does," Laura said under her breath.

She'd seen Gary with tears in his eyes. The day they'd dropped off the tuna casserole. She'd thought he was worried about Ardelle's agitation, but he'd been talking about daylilies. Jess Gantt's ordinary daylilies. They'd had the power to make him cry?

He bought me a daylily plant. He's so sweet.

He, she'd written. Not *E.*

How quickly things can blossom overnight . . .

A month or two later, in a new journal, she'd added the gloomy line that made Sean say she must have been in a bad mood. Something about the brightest blossoms turning to rot. Laura had just read that entry but couldn't quite remember it.

Burying her face in her hands, she tried to recall the other sentence that included the word "rot," followed by three more words that had been scribbled over. A three-letter word, a four-letter word, and *me.*

Recalling their shape and size—and beginning to understand the context—Laura knew what her mother had written . . . and why. It wasn't merely that she'd been in a bad mood. She'd been in the depths of despair. She'd written about it in a sort of code except for the last three words.

A beautiful plant can spring from the rot, from the dirt. God help me.

An affair had blossomed quickly but went sour just as quickly? And then she'd learned she was pregnant.

Gary stepped inside, shutting the door with a clatter. His usually neat hair was a mess, and he was breathing hard. "Laura. Where's Sean?"

"Across the road, looking for my dad."

"He just might find him. The latest is that somebody saw him trotting alongside the road a few miles from here. Heading this way."

Laura shot to her feet. Maybe her dad was the man who'd been on her porch—but that made it even more urgent to discuss the rest of it with Gary. She had to know.

"Gary . . ." She couldn't believe she was about to say this. "There's something you and I need to clear up, right now." Ignoring Cassie's bewildered whispers behind her, Laura picked up the garden marker. "Did you give my mother an old-fashioned daylily called Honey Redhead? The one that has bloomed in her yard for thirty years or so?"

Gary swallowed, his eyes shifting from side to side. "Yes. Yes, I did."

"Did you know about the carrot-top baby, the honey redhead who looked more like her mama than her daddy? No, you've never read my mom's journals—but I think Ardelle has."

With watery eyes, he stared at the sad little prizes on the couch. "I didn't know. Not until now. She—Ardelle—just told me what all these things mean. She knew about Jess and me."

Cassie gasped. "Dad!"

His chest rose and fell in a big breath. "You have to understand." His voice broke. "I . . . with Jess . . . it just happened. It didn't last long." He wiped tears away. "I never dreamed . . . Jess never said a word about a baby." He met Laura's eyes. "I always thought you were Elliott's."

She was bewildered to the point of numbness, but she had no reason to doubt him. "I believe you."

He stared at her as if he'd never seen her before, and she stared back. Flesh of his flesh, bone of his bone, fruit of his sin—and her mother's.

That sandy blond hair, the same color as her dad's. Blue eyes. A similar build. Gary Bright and Elliott Gantt had sometimes been mistaken for brothers.

Gary started talking fast. "It wasn't long after he got out of the service. She fell apart when she was telling me about his new moods. His black moods. I gave her a hug, a friendly, brotherly hug, and . . . that's how it started. I never told Ardelle. I thought it would be better that way, but she knew. Or at least she suspected. All this time. It has been terrible for her."

"No kidding!" Cassie's sass began to come

back as she got in his face. "Admitting it's true is the first step. That's what you just told Mom about a bottle of cologne. You hypocrite!"

"I didn't . . . didn't mean to be a hypocrite," he said. "I only meant to leave it in the past. I've been faithful to your mother ever since. Cassie, I'm so sorry. So sorry."

Cassie started talking right over his endless apologies. Laura, hardly listening, tried to process these strange new truths, but she could hardly breathe. Couldn't think. And Gibby? He hardly seemed to matter now.

"I'm sorry," Gary said again.

"Not as sorry as you should be," Cassie said. "How can you claim you didn't know? Look at Laura! I see it now. Sure, she has her mom's eyes, but she looks like you too. Dad, I'm so ashamed of you."

Gary nodded, hanging his head, then turned to Laura. "Your dad knew?"

"I don't know. I heard him confronting my mom, years ago, but I thought he meant . . . someone else." Her own voice seemed to come from a great distance.

Gary's face turned pale. "What will he do to me if he comes back? I deserve it, but . . . oh God. He nearly strangled me once for making a stupid wisecrack. What will he do if he knows about me and your mother? And . . . and you? The baby."

Shaky and cold, Laura studied the cross and the dog tag on the silver chain. Emblems of Elliott Gantt's faith, his service to his country, and his blood type, but she hadn't a drop of Gantt blood in her.

Had he found out suddenly, a month before her eighteenth birthday? And staged his own drowning?

She stood. "I can't take any more of this. I can't sit here and hash things out while my dad—" Tripping on that word, she met Cassie's glistening eyes. "Looks like we're half sisters."

Cassie rushed her, enfolding her in a fierce hug. "There's nothing halfway about it. We're sisters. We've always been sisters."

"Elliott was a brother to me." Gary let out a gut-wrenching sob. "I didn't just betray my wife. I betrayed my brother."

With the silvery chain still dangling from her fingers, Laura hugged Cassie back, but she was frozen inside. Frozen and numb and very much afraid of what might happen next.

Feeling alone and naked without his gun, Sean had walked down the road a quarter mile in each direction. He'd found no clue about what those shrieking brakes had meant. No cat, no man, no vehicle.

Now, standing by Jess's grave, he heard the whine of a motorcycle's engine. No, two. Two high-powered bikes flashed into view, chasing the curves. Their riders crouched low in their bright leathers and whipped past, stirring the roadside weeds. The moment crystallized like a snapshot: the two bikers—life, noise, color, speed—flying past the mild-mannered sign in the church's parking lot: COME WORSHIP WITH US. PASTOR HORACE REESE. THIS IS THE DAY.

The day for what? They should have quoted the rest of the verse.

The sound of the bikes faded into the distance as Sean studied Jess's grave. He felt cheated. No clues here. No footprints, no gray hair snagged on a branch. None of the convenient evidence that always popped up in TV shows.

The azaleas had fallen over again. This time, nobody had righted them.

"Please, God," he whispered. "If it's some-body's day to die . . . make it the cat."

But even if he found Mikey alive, how could he corral a tough old critter that wanted to remain free?

Or if he found Elliott . . . what then?

The prospect of seeing him again gave Sean a rush of that desperate old need for a father. If Elliott came back, though, he'd be the needy one.

Sean thought he heard someone speak, some-where behind the church. He held still and listened.

Nothing but a cardinal's shrill, repetitive

whistle now, but he wanted to make sure.

He leaned around the corner of the church and surveyed the expanse of kudzu-covered trees and bushes. It went on for acres, interrupted by an occasional stand of pines that hadn't yet been conquered.

He walked farther into the wild vines. He was dwarfed by the green towers that had once been living trees. They made a weird, alien landscape where a man could hide, silent as a deer, and wait.

Downtown, bluegrass blared from the PA system, reminding him of Elliott and his upstart, part-time, ragtag band. Every year, they'd earned standing ovations. They were that good.

Bile rose in Sean's throat. His mentor, a talented man who'd crafted fine musical instruments and furniture, was living in the wild like an animal. He'd abandoned his family and friends, his business, his responsibilities. All because his wife might have cheated on him? Laura had paid the price too, although she wasn't to blame. She'd been paying the price for years.

Fury boiled up inside Sean. He'd had enough of Elliott's game.

"Elliott!" he yelled. "Where are you?"

The dense vegetation swallowed his voice. It produced no movement, no sign of life, no sound except a jay squawking as it flew over.

No planes marred the blue, blue sky overhead. Nothing came between him and the eyes of

God, who knew exactly where Elliott Gantt was. No, Sean would never have a father on earth, and if there was a Father in heaven, he wasn't talking.

He opened his mouth to scream at the Almighty but heard familiar laughter and whirled around.

Dale stood there, raising a clenched fist like a prizefighter who'd just won the big one. Beside him, in the grip of his other hand, stood a stoop-shouldered man with terror-stricken eyes in a gaunt, bearded face.

Thirty

Elliott Gantt, in the flesh. Emaciated flesh.

His filthy gray shirt reeked of wood smoke and sweat. He rolled the tattered hem of it between bony, contorted fingers that must have been pounded with a sledgehammer, the bones left to set any which way. His bedraggled beard ruffled in the wind, gray as his shirt but streaked with white.

"I nabbed him out by the old cabin," Dale said, grinning. "I was takin' him to town, but the old geezer jumped right out of the truck, just up the road. I had to slam on the brakes and chase him down."

"Laura's in trouble," Elliott said in a rusty voice. "We have to hurry."

"Yeah, we've got to find her." Dale winked at Sean. "Before it's too late."

Sean read the fear in Elliott's moist eyes and knew what Dale had done. "Laura's fine," Sean said. "I don't care what he told you, Elliott, but it's a lie. She's safe."

Confusion played across Elliott's features. "She's in danger." With a crippled finger, he pointed across his sunken chest toward Dale. "He told me so."

"Shut up," Dale mouthed silently to Sean.

"Dale lied," Sean said. "He just wanted to lure you out. Laura's fine, Elliott. I talked to her a few minutes ago."

Dale smiled, pretending innocence, and tugged Elliott's elbow. "Let's go downtown, then. Wouldn't you like to be onstage one more time? Waving to the crowds?"

So Dale wanted to make a spectacle of Elliott. Even in the opening hours of the festival, there'd be more people than he'd seen in more than a decade. He would freak out. And he'd get a free ride to a psych ward.

"There's no need to go into town," Sean said.

The old man's breath came in hard, fast rasps. "I don't care about the town. Where . . . where's Laura?"

He didn't look like he could harm anybody.

He seemed to slide in and out of the present, his eyes clear one moment and foggy with confusion the next, but always glistening with tears.

Sean hesitated, remembering that Laura had mentioned Alzheimer's. "Have you been trying to see her?"

"Yes, but she was so afraid. It made me sad. I want to see her, but I don't want to scare her." He let out a dry sob from deep inside his bony chest. "And I'm . . . so grubby."

"Come with me, then. I'm grubby too. I need a haircut and a shave." Sean patted his own whiskered mug. "Laura will want to clean us up, both of us."

"She won't run from me?"

"No sir. If she knows it's you, she won't run. She just wants to know you're okay."

Elliott's lips moved, but he said nothing, like a child trying to work out an adult-sized problem. Dale still gripped Elliott's elbow, and Sean took his other arm.

Dale let Sean win the tug-of-war. "Plan B," he said. "Don't lose 'im, boy." He moved a few feet away and pulled his phone from his pocket.

"Hey," Sean said. "Who are you calling and why?"

"It's my turn to call the cops. I want this freak hauled in."

"Elliott hasn't committed a crime."

"It was a crime all right, what he did." Dale turned and walked toward the church.

"Come on." Sean steered Elliott away from Dale. Toward home. "But there's something you need to know, if you don't know already. About Jess."

The faded blue eyes sparkled brighter. "I know, son. She's gone. It's grievous to my heart, as death ought to be."

"Yes. I'm sorry."

They moved a few feet closer to home, Elliott moving as lightly as a cat. A weak and wobbly cat.

"How did you hear about Jess?" Sean asked.

"Ruby Pearl kept me up on the news, especially these last weeks since I came down from the mountains."

"Ruby Pearl? Who's that?"

Elliott held a mangled fist upright, like a flag bearer holding an imaginary flagpole. "Old girl with the fee-faddle. The—the rain thing."

"Granny Colfax? With an umbrella? Parasol?"

"That's it. Ruby Pearl Colfax. She's a good one for keepin' secrets. Brings me news and necessities out to the home place when I stay there." He smiled. "Ruby Pearl was a killdeer to me. She lured folks away from my nest, a time or two."

So, Granny Colfax had toted more than news and necessities. She'd carried a big secret, all this time. No wonder she walked the country roads, rain or shine.

Elliott sighed. "Now, son, you want to know why I left my family. I can see you do. It's hard to explain."

"You don't have to explain a thing."

"I was afraid. I'd killed before, so I knew I could kill again."

Sad for the old soldier, Sean shook his head. "It was part of your job."

Elliott coughed, his shoulders shaking. "But I wanted Gary dead."

"Gary? Don't you mean—"

"When it was over, Jessamyn was carrying Gary's baby."

Sean's mind reeled. Gary? *Laura?* The timing was all wrong. "Are you sure?"

"I'm sure." Elliott drew a raspy breath. "I didn't know for years. When I found out, well, I entertained murderous thoughts toward him. Like a friend ought not to do."

"You don't act like you'd want to murder anybody."

Elliott laughed softly and raised his ruined hands. "I did that. Did it to myself."

"Why?"

"So I wouldn't be able to hold a gun. I couldn't trust myself not to harm a friend or . . . the woman I loved."

Sean's skin crawled, first at the thought of

Elliott firing at Jess, then at the thought of a man deliberately ruining his own flesh and then suffering alone in the wilderness. It wasn't normal. How could he even bait a fishhook with claws like that? There'd be no fiddle lessons now, that was certain.

"And I dropped my guns in the lake," Elliott said. "Lest I should use them for evil. Then I took myself far away, just to be sure. But when I found out Jess was gone, I knew Laura would come. I had to see her."

"I'm starting to understand," Sean said, looking ahead. One more curtain of kudzu to wade through, and they'd be back on the weedy grass within view of the house. "What matters now is you're back, and I'm glad."

"I thank you kindly, son."

Sean looked behind them. Still on his cell phone, Dale lurked at the corner of the church building. He flashed a phony smile.

Sean ignored him. "Elliott, are you ready to see Laura?"

Elliott's eyes widened as if he'd forgotten her existence. His chapped lips curved into a genuine smile. "Ready. Yes sir, I'm ready."

As they crossed the rough lawn, he stumbled on a tuft of grass that the mower had missed. Sean tightened his grip, holding him upright.

Elliott wore ancient brown moccasins, slick with wear. His big toes were poking out, the toenails black and ragged. And all those good shoes had been going to waste in his closet.

They were only a minute or two from Laura—who wasn't his child?

But there might still be some joy at the end of his strange journey. At least he could enjoy food and a bath and a clean, soft bed. Simple comforts. Elliott was a wreck of a man, though. Laura would go into shock if she were to see him with no warning.

"I'll give Laura a call," Sean told him. "You can't just walk in, unannounced. You'd give her a heart attack. Like you nearly did when you were on her porch. That was you, wasn't it?"

"It was. I had a late start. I had to sneak away slow-like in the wrong direction. I've had too many visitors, coming too close to my shed."

There was a shed at the cabin? It must have been buried in the kudzu. Sean shook his head. He'd have to tell Keith they'd been so close.

He pulled out his phone and called Laura's number. She answered after one ring, sounding sad and scared.

"Laura, honey, I have good news."

"What is it?"

Down on the road, nobody was driving by. Nobody was watching as Elliott Gantt's frail legs carried him home from the wilderness.

"Brace yourself," Sean told Laura, his eye on the house. "I want you to look out the window.

We'll be walking across the road. Coming home."

"Home?" Her voice quavered. "Who's coming home?"

"Your two favorite men in the whole, wide world."

A stunned silence. A long, slow inhalation of air, like she'd been starved for oxygen and she'd finally found some.

"Don't lie to me," she said, louder now. "Sean Halloran, don't you dare. Don't say it unless it's true."

"He's not like he used to be, but I'm walking your dad home."

He waited, expecting the wild, joyful scream of a girl who's beating a boy at a green-plum war. Any second now, she'd yell "I told you so!" at the top of her lungs.

A crash hit his ear. She'd dropped her phone. Fainted, maybe. And he'd thought he was doing such a good job of breaking it gently.

With a gentle tug to Elliott's arm, Sean encouraged him a bit closer to the road in case Laura's view was blocked somehow. "Over this way, partner," Sean said. "You okay?"

Elliott nodded, trembling. Sean was shaking too.

Across the road, the front door banged open. Laura, Cassie, and Gary spilled through the doorway, but only Laura ran to the edge of the porch. She stopped there at the top of the steps.

The sun glinted on something metallic dangling from her hands when she pressed them together as if in prayer, fingertips touching her lips. Then she raised her hands like an old-time Pentecostal grandma praising Jesus.

That metallic something flew into the air and landed somewhere with a faint tinkle. Laura hurtled down the steps. Barefoot, with her red hair flying behind that snug bandanna, she raced toward the road.

Sean patted Elliott's shoulder. "Here she comes. She's a sweetheart, isn't she?"

"There's my Laura." Elliott stretched his broken hands toward her. "She's my girl."

Glancing at Gary, who stood motionless on the porch, Sean could only wonder.

Thirty-one

Laura could hardly believe her eyes. They stood together, two tall, lean figures with wild-man hair. One was dark, with a barely started beard; one was gray, his feathery beard ruffling in the wind. He bore no resemblance to the strong, strapping man who'd once saved a skinny boy from a beating.

She stumbled through prickly weeds and

lunged across the road, the bank hiding the men from her view. Sharp stones and burrs cut her feet. Then the cement steps were underneath her. She scrambled up them. At the top, she gulped a breath and took a long, hard look at her dad.

Her dad, alive—but he was so thin! Tottery, stooped, long-haired. Ragged clothes hung on his bony frame. Still, she would have known that smile anywhere.

"Daddy, Daddy, Daddy!" She raced up the hill, crying.

"Laura." He opened his arms, an old, broken bird spreading crippled wings.

His hands were contorted. Twisted. The sight jolted her almost to a stop. Careful not to hurt him, she forced herself to a walk.

His feverish blue eyes faded from clarity to confusion and back again as she approached. "Excuse me if I stare," he said. "You're not the little girl I remember."

"But it's me," she said, stepping into his wiry, smelly embrace. She wanted to ask what had happened to his hands, but she didn't want to ruin his homecoming with tears.

"You're all right?" His voice was thin with fear.

"I'm fine, Dad. Just fine. But what about you?" She pulled back and took in his hollow cheeks and his watery eyes. "You okay?"

He reached out to brush her hair off her forehead. Like talons, his fingers couldn't uncurl enough to make solid contact. "The man said you were in danger," he said fretfully. "It's . . . Slattery, isn't it? Slattery's back."

She looked toward Sean again. He shrugged, apparently as mystified as she was.

"I'm fine, really. But Dad, Slattery's long gone."

"He's not after you, now? If he is, I'll—" He stopped, his forehead puckered. "No, you're right. He's gone. I made sure of it. The lake, you know."

"Aw, no." Sean's face paled. "No, Elliott. Don't."

"What?" Laura asked, lightheaded now. "What are y'all talking about?"

"Slattery." Sean wheeled around, strode a few paces away, and came back, pressing his fingers to his temples. "You didn't hear that, Laura. You didn't hear that." He looked behind him. "Is Dale close enough to—thank God, he isn't. Oh, Lord."

"Hear what?" she demanded. "What does it mean?"

Her dad rambled on. "He's gone, Slattery is. He's with his car in Bennett's lake. I remember now, mostly." He passed one hand over his forehead. "They couldn't keep him in prison, so I took care of it for 'em. He'll never stalk another little girl."

"Enough," Sean bit out. "We don't want the details."

Her dad kept going, his voice thin but clear. "After 'Nam, I vowed I would never kill again. And I vowed to protect the innocent, like I sometimes couldn't, over there. Then came a day when I had to break the one vow to keep the other." He blinked, and twin tears trickled down the sides of his nose. "God help me, but I had to do it. I don't quite recall how, but I did it."

Slattery hadn't skipped town, then. And Sean hadn't witnessed some unknown car thief hiding his crime. He'd seen her father.

The blood rushed from Laura's head. The sunny day wobbled around her, everything slanting off balance. When her mom had accused her husband of having blood on his hands, it wasn't antiwar rhetoric. She must have known.

"When?" Laura asked. "Where?"

"Summertime," her dad said. "Late summer, by the tracks. The little one . . . you know. The happy little one. Nobody was watching her. She didn't know Slattery was after more than her black-berries. I—I stopped him before he could take what he wanted."

"Tigger," Laura whispered. Her knees lost their strength. Sean grabbed her elbow, steadied her.

Late that summer, the year Slattery disappeared, they'd picked a bumper crop of berries. But one day, Tigger stayed to fill her bucket by herself. Laura's dad had returned to check on her, and he'd kept something terrible from happening.

He'd dealt with Slattery somehow. No wonder he'd been in such a black mood that night when Laura came home with painted nails like a grown woman.

His face clear now, no trace of trouble on it, he cocked his head toward distant music. "Listen. 'Foggy Mountain Breakdown.' There's a good tune." The wreckage of his fingers fidgeted as if he were coaxing notes from a fiddle. "There's not much music in the mountains. I've missed it." He patted his chest pocket, producing a metallic clinking. "This is my only music now. For Jess. My Valentine." When he lowered his hand, the silvery wind chimes peeked through a hole in his pocket.

Sean laid his hand on her father's narrow shoulder. "Looks like you've missed a few meals. What would you say to a bite to eat? Maybe a bath? Some clean clothes?"

"I would say thank you very much, sir." He inclined his head toward Laura in a familiar, courtly nod. "But first, together, let's pay our respects to your sweet mother."

Together, they walked toward the family plot. The head of the grave wasn't far from the bright pink bushes where Laura had cut azaleas days ago. The tin vase had fallen, and the flowers were limp and faded.

The wind picked up, sending an empty paper cup rolling down the slope. Distracted, her scarecrow of a dad laughed at it. Then he started singing an old ballad, but not the one the PA system was pumping out, downtown. The two songs clashed in key, in rhythm, in mood.

"Where did you stay last night, O Randall, my son," he crooned, out of tune.

He'd once had perfect pitch. Strong, skillful hands. His own business. A circle of friends who'd loved him. A wife and daughter—yes, she was his daughter! As much as if he'd adopted her from an orphanage and claimed her as his own.

Laura stole another look at his ruined hands. They had crafted sweet-voiced mandolins and cozy rocking chairs and doll furniture. Those hands had protected. And they'd killed.

The PA system kicked into another number, louder and faster, spinning into a toe-tapping reel. Her dad tilted his head, seeming to focus on the music, or maybe he was listening to a train. Another one was approaching town on the long curve from the north.

"Where did Dale sneak off to?" Sean asked abruptly, turning in a circle.

Laura spotted him first and pointed. Leaning against the brick wall of the church, Dale watched them.

She turned her back on him, and movement across the road caught her eye. Gary was walking down the porch steps. With his shirttails flapping, he started across the road, toward the steps that led up the bank to the graveyard. He kept to his deliberate pace as he climbed the steps and then the hillside.

Laura moved close to her dad, taking his arm and leaning her head against him. "Dad, I know you and Gary have—have clashed before, but this isn't the right time to fly into one of your moods. Sit tight. Keep yourself under control."

His dry laugh seemed to mock her worries. "Don't fret about me. I can handle my old compadre."

Gary slowed. He stopped, maybe at some inner Rubicon, then thinned his lips and started moving again.

He drew nearer, hiking up the gradual slope, and didn't stop again until he'd nearly reached them. "Elliott," he said. "Welcome home."

"Thank you kindly."

Gary hung his head. "Cassie just finished ordering me to face you like a man, but I guess you already know what I did."

"Yes, I do."

Laura's pulse quickened. Her dad knew everything, then? Knew about both affairs? Even knew she wasn't his baby?

"I'm very sorry." Gary extended his hand. "Will you forgive me?"

Blinking back tears, Laura wondered how

many times her dad had said those words to Gary. Now the tables were turned.

She lifted her hand from her dad's arm, and he stepped forward.

"I have already forgiven you," he said, extending his claw-like hand to Gary. "I've forgiven my good friend and my dear wife."

Gary's eyes were wet. "Thank you. I want to make amends. I want you to have whatever you need. All the best. The best care. The best doctors."

"I hate doctors. Hospitals." He released Gary's hand. "I . . . I . . . you won't do that to me. No sir, you will not."

"You don't hate Doc Marsh," Sean said. "He won't put you in a hospital."

Paying no attention to that, her dad turned and walked to the grave. Laura, Sean, and Gary turned in unison to watch as her dad righted the tin vase. Slowly and carefully, he began to straighten the azalea branches.

A stillness settled over her, an acceptance that was very much like peace. She couldn't change the past, nor could she know the future. She had this moment, though, with her dad only a few feet away. It was strange and wonderful to see a living man so close to his name on a memorial plaque. He was alive. Alive!

"Hurry up there, old man." Dale's raspy voice came from behind her. "You got places to go. People to see."

As Laura faced him, so did Sean and Gary. A rush of courage swept her. The three of them stood between Dale and her dad. Together, they could keep him safe.

She glanced behind her, meeting her dad's puzzled gaze. He held a small stem of azaleas in his mangled fingers.

"It's all right, Dad," she said. "We'll be home soon."

"Oh no you won't." Dale came closer. "Mr. Gantt has an appointment with the law."

Sean clenched his fists. "You really called the cops? Why?"

"He's a criminal," Dale said. "A prowler. So I turned him in. Like he turned me in. He made me lose my job, my house, my building."

"No, that was me," Gary said mildly, as if he didn't mind the accusation.

Dale's chest seemed to grow larger, puffing up. His eyes, usually so cold, burned with hatred. "You, Bright? *You* made that call?"

"I did. I don't regret it, either."

"That's how you got your filthy hands on my building?"

Gary shook his head. "Now, Halloran, you'd better get your facts straight."

"I got all the facts I need," Dale said. "That's how you can afford to be the big, generous rich man. You turned me in. You sent me to prison. You stole my building. You stole my son."

"You don't deserve your sons," Gary said, his eyes wet. "Either one of them."

"Shut up before I shut you up, Bright. You lying thief." Dale's face was flushed. Sweating.

"Gary never stole anything," Sean said. "He has given. And given."

Dale turned on Sean. "Yeah? You want me to pay it forward for you, Mr. Luthier? Here's how I pay you and your highfalutin pals." He pulled something small and shiny from his pocket—a toy gun.

"Give it to me," Sean said quietly. "You don't want to go there, Dale."

Laura took a sharp breath. Not a toy. Tiny but real. The pansy gun?

In the silence, she heard a faint stirring behind her. Felt a small breeze.

Her dad brushed past her. "I love you," he whispered with a wink that said *I'll be all right.* He stepped in front of Gary.

A huge blast ripped out of the tiny gun. Laura screamed. Her dad crumpled backward, his arms twisting around his head. He fell into Gary, knocking him over.

Laura hit her knees and crawled to her dad. Blood was already spreading across his threadbare shirt. Screaming again, she looked up—into the barrel of the tiny gun.

Sean, in a blur, rushed Dale. Another shot

exploded in the burning air. Sean roared and fell beside Laura.

Sandwiched between them, between the warmth of their bodies, she smelled smoke. Sweat. Blood. Spitting out grass and dirt, she tried to speak but lost her own voice in the confusion and shouting.

Afraid to look, she looked anyway. Gary was shoving Dale to the grass. Pinning him there.

Laura struggled to sit up, to see. Her daddy was gone, his eyes open but sightless. A baby doll's eyes. His chest, a ruin of blood. Feathery gray hair, streaked with white, lifted by the wind. Chimes, spilling from his pocket. In his hand, faded pink flowers splashed with red. On his skinny forearm, *life everlasting.*

Sean moaned. Laura twisted, bending over him. High on his chest, a red hole spurted blood on his shirt in time with his pulse.

Blue eyes wide, he stared at her. Blinked.

"Sean!" She scrambled up, gravel grinding into her knees.

Pressure points. Pressure points. What had she learned? Something about the clavicle. Collarbone. Arteries, pressure points. She couldn't think.

"No!" A distant scream—her own. "No!"

She'd lost her dad—again—and Sean's lifeblood was spurting out of him. Faster now. A regular rhythm, speeding fast, faster. Bright red blood. An artery.

She tore her bandanna off her head and pressed it hard against his chest. Scarlet blood pulsing into white-and-black cotton. Soaking it, so quickly.

Laura leaned closer. "Don't you dare die. I already lost Mom. I can't lose you and Daddy and Mikey all in the same day. I won't have it! Do you hear me?"

His eyes opened. "You'd rather . . . have . . . the cat," he said faintly, one corner of his mouth curling up. His eyes rolled up in his head. The lids fluttered and closed.

Desperate, she looked for help. A sheriff's cruiser swept into the church parking lot. An officer climbed out. A woman. It had to be Kim Milton. Speaking into a radio, so far away that her voice was inaudible, she headed up the slope at a slow jog, her revolver drawn.

"Kim!" Laura screamed. "Help! Hurry!"

Somewhere in town, a siren wailed. The train whistle blew, fading into the south.

Dale ranted unintelligible words but couldn't escape. Gary, straddling him, cursed and cried. Cassie flew at him too, shrieking. Kicking.

Sean's eyes opened, glassy and strangely calm. They closed again with no sign that he'd seen her. His skin was white.

Squeezing two fingers to the cold skin of his wrist, Laura sought his pulse. Still there. Fainter. Faster.

Her shoulders heaved with deep, rasping sobs. "Sean, stay with me!"

The wind blew her hair into her mouth. Did Kim even see that two men were down? One dead, one dying. The two men Laura loved most.

"I need help *now,* Kim! Help!"

Sirens wailed over the fiddles and banjos. The train's whistle faded, a ribbon of sound sliding away into the distance. Her hair covered her face, her eyes. She couldn't see Sean. She could hardly breathe.

His pulse fluttered faster now. Weaker. He was slipping away. He'd be gone even before the train.

Thirty-two

On Saturday afternoon, Laura walked Tigger and Cassie out to the lobby of the hospital. After giving them quick hugs, Laura stepped back and tried to smile.

"Tig, did Cassie ever buy you a new hair clip?"

"Hair clip?"

"To replace the glittery pink one you lost in the berry patch."

Tig shook her head. "I don't know what you're talking about."

It was a blessing that Tig didn't remember much about that day, and Cassie had never learned the worst of it. She never would.

"Never mind," Laura said. "Thanks for stopping by."

"We'll be back," Cassie said. "Keep your chin up, sis."

Almost in unison, she and Tigger waved and headed for the bright sunshine outdoors.

Cassie's phone rang just then and she whipped it out of her pocket. Laura couldn't hear the conversation, but she knew from the happiness in Cassie's voice that Drew had called. Again. They'd been on the phone almost constantly since the shooting.

Laura turned and began her trek back to Sean's bedside. She was glad Gary hadn't come today. She didn't have the emotional energy. It wouldn't be awkward forever, though.

Maybe he and Ardelle would be all right too.

Poor Ardelle. She'd admitted to Gary that she'd suspected his infidelity thirty years before. She'd found one smudge of peach lipstick on his collar, and she'd recognized the scent of Jean Naté on his shirts. Her suspicions had flared again, six weeks ago, when he cried at the funeral. Then she'd read between the lines in some of the journals she'd boxed up. But until she'd compared the dog tag and the Red Cross cards, she hadn't been sure Laura was his child.

Ardelle must have known the significance of the daylilies too, or she wouldn't have pulled the garden marker out of the dirt. She was a lot smarter than some people gave her credit for.

The plants from the funeral, massed around the fireplace . . . had she wanted to rub Gary's nose in the fact that Jess had died? Or maybe all of it was like picking at a scab, like Cassie had said.

A set of big automatic doors slid open, farther down the corridor. A tall man came through, walking slowly, keeping his eyes on the floor. Gibby Sprague was seventy if he was a day but still strikingly handsome. He was dressed all in black. Silver hair curled over his collar. A gold watch chain shone against his vest. He didn't notice Laura.

"I forgive you, Gibby," she whispered, mostly to remind herself she'd made that choice.

But she still wanted the truth. The closer he came, the more she wanted it.

He looked up and opened his arms. "Laura. I can't believe—any of it."

She stepped into his hug. "I can't either."

"How's Sean?"

"He's hanging in there. There's not much change."

"God love 'im," Gibby said. "You all right, honey?"

"I'm as all right as I can be."

He draped his arm around her shoulders and they continued walking. "Is there anything I can do for you? Anything at all?"

"Yes. You can answer one question. Did you and my mom . . . ?"

"Now, now. You know I love the ladies, but a gentleman never tells."

Laura's lofty notions about forgiveness evaporated in an instant. She stopped walking, pulling herself out of his reach. "How could you? My dad trusted you. He *loved* you, and you and my mom betrayed him. That's why he left, Gibby."

"What are you talking about?" Gibby's bewildered expression slowly changed to one of comprehension. "You've got a little knot in your timeline, baby. Whatever did or didn't happen between your mother and me, it wasn't until about two years ago. It wasn't for lack of trying on my part, but she wouldn't give me the time of day as long as she held out hope that your daddy might come back."

"What? She believed he was alive? And—and she told you?"

"She believed it, up to a point, but she finally decided to move on. Don't fault her for it."

"I . . . I . . . no, of course not. But I can't believe she told you. She never told me."

"She may have had her reasons," he said with a shrewd smile. "She was an original, God love her. And I think He did. Does." He pulled a gold watch from his vest pocket. "I had to stop by to ask how Sean's doing, but I'm playing on the main stage in half an hour."

"You'd better get going, then."

"Call me sometime, you hear? Let me know about Sean."

"I will."

"No hard feelings between us?"

"Of course not, Gibby. I'm sorry I thought . . ."

"It's all right." Always the gentleman, he bent over and kissed her hand. He turned and walked away.

Her heart should have been lighter as she continued walking toward the ICU.

If Sean made it, maybe he'd live to play with Gibby someday—and to teach some young Hallorans how to play guitar and mando and banjo.

If he didn't make it, she wouldn't care about anything, ever again.

Women, talking. One, young and angry. One, old and crotchety. Loud.

"Life hurts, honey," the old one said. "You don't get over life until you die."

Bright lights pounded his eyelids. Nasty smells. Irritating noises, like . . . like supermarket scanners.

Where was he?

He tried to open his eyes but the lids were too heavy.

A sharp memory flashed into his mind. Something about a gun. Half his chest had blown up.

Then he was walking across the church grounds. No, he was floating. Trying to stay on the right side, the side with picnics and weddings. Trying to stay away from graves and darkness.

He fought, finding his way back to an old house. A house that breathed. A swing on the porch, lilies in the yard. A red-haired girl hugging a skinny cat . . .

The pain grew and faded. Grew and faded.

Now, the light brightened. No, dimmed. The women kept talking.

Now he heard men. Keith. Gary. Grown men, crying. Gary, saying something about an auction.

"I didn't plan it that way," Gary choked out.

It's okay, Sean tried to say. He couldn't make his lips move.

Morning. Had to be. The light was different now, even on his closed eyelids. How many mornings had come and gone?

The old lady, talking. Talking too loud, like she was deaf and thought everybody else was too.

Then the sweet one. The angel. Laura?

He tried to hold on to her voice, but it faded. In and out. Coming and going. She said something about quenching a smoking wick.

411

"God said He wouldn't do that, but He did, and if He ever does it again, He'll hear about it."

That was Laura, all right. Mad at God. Trying to tell Him how to run the world. But God could handle her.

"What's that you say?" the old lady shouted. "Speak up, baby. God, you say? No, God didn't pull no trigger. That was Dale."

Another memory. A tiny, familiar handgun, aimed at . . .

No. Don't . . . don't . . .

The women ceased chattering for a moment, then resumed.

A light exploded in his head. Then he remembered. A shot. Another one. Incredible agony. The smell of something burning.

Screams. Sirens. Pain.

It was all coming back. He didn't want it to.

If the nurses and that mumble-mouthed doctor would leave him alone, he'd have time to think. Time to grasp what couldn't be grasped.

The official-sounding voices receded toward the door. Grew fainter. Faded away.

Peace. Quiet. Now he could think.

Behind closed eyelids, Sean pictured the train pounding past the berry patch where a happy little girl loved to pick berries. Two men saw her there alone. A good man and an evil one.

412

Now the evil one was dead. So was the good one.

Everybody would die one day.

I don't want to die.

Nobody answered.

Sean tried again. *Lord, I'm not finished yet. I have to take fiddle lessons. Sell a house. Marry Laura.*

A gasp from across the room. "Did he try to say something, Granny?"

He tried to nod his head. A lump of lead. Heavy.

"Sean?" A hand touched his. Clasped his. Squeezed.

He squeezed back.

A sharp intake of breath. "Sean? You in there?"

Where else would I be, woman?

The words refused to come out of his mouth.

With intense effort, he fought to open his eyes. There she was. A blurry slice of Laura, bending over him, her hair haloed by a light behind her. His angel. The sad angel he'd seen at the funeral. No tongue of fire on her head today.

He was hallucinating. Dying, maybe.

"Sean." She was crying. "Oh, Sean, you're back."

"Elliott," he whispered, finally managing to make a sound. "He's . . ."

Her smile dimmed. "He didn't make it, Sean. I'm so sorry. He's gone."

Gone? He just came home. And he'd said

something important. Something Laura needed to know, but it had faded away to the edges of Sean's memory. He might never remember.

"He took a bullet for Gary," she said. "Dad walked right into that bullet, and then you took the next one. For me. For all of us."

He remembered now.

Elliott, heading straight into trouble instead of running away from it. He'd rescued his buddy. Gary.

Like at the Pentagon. People had run into hell to rescue friends and strangers. They'd gone in after them. Elliott had been at the front of the pack—

No. Elliott hadn't been at the Pentagon . . . or the Twin Towers . . . but if he'd been there, he would have run in the right direction. A hero.

Sean closed his eyes. Fatherless. It hurt. He was still hungry, so hungry, for a father who wouldn't hurt him. Wouldn't betray him. Wouldn't disappear.

His angel's voice faded.

Then, another nurse. He hated nurses. Always prodding and poking and talking about vital signs.

He pretended not to hear her. She left.

He opened his eyes again. Laura leaned over him, deep grief written all over her face. Then she smiled, the corners of her mouth wobbling up and down, up and down, and her chin quivering.

He tried to breathe deeply. It hurt too much. "Gary okay?"

"He's fine. He and Ardelle have a tough row to hoe, though."

It took a moment for that to sink in. Jess and Gary. Incredible.

"Dale?"

"He's behind bars."

"Good." Sean fought to find the courage to speak the truth. The words came out rough and broken, the way he felt inside. "My . . . father murdered your father. With the pansy gun. I was stupid . . . to let him keep it. Laura, I'm so sorry."

"I don't think my dad's sorry that he walked right into God's arms. There really is a sweet by-and-by. Oh, I don't know what I'm talking about. I only know there's a kind of love that never fails."

"There is," Sean managed to whisper.

Her fingers ran lightly across his hand. "Remember how my dad always called you son? I'm sure he meant it. He still would."

Sean was silent for a moment. "I had something else to tell you. Can't remember."

"It's all right." She gave him that wobbly smile again. "Kim saved your life. The doctors said she got there just in time."

"Mikey?"

"He came back. That poor old cat. It wasn't his day to die."

The cat lived. Gary lived. But Elliott died.

For Gary, picnics and parties. For Elliott, the graveyard. The doorway to heaven.

"Elliott was a good man," Sean said.

"You're right about that." The old lady, there. Granny Colfax. She clicked her tongue. "He was a good soldier too. Sometimes soldiers give their lives for innocents. You know it's Memorial Day?"

Why wouldn't she just go away?

"There's a proverb in the Good Book," Granny continued. "Goes like this. 'The wicked shall be a ransom for the righteous.' But sometimes, it's the other way 'round. Sometimes, the righteous give themselves as ransom too." She sighed, long and loud. "Nobody took his life. He gave it. He gave it."

Laura, blessedly silent, bent over Sean, her hair falling like a curtain of flame. Her warm tears spilled onto his cheek, mixing with his. She smoothed his hair off his forehead and bent to kiss him.

Then it came to him. The message for Laura.

"He told me," Sean whispered. "Your dad told me why he ran. It wasn't . . . that he stopped loving you or your mom."

"I know he loved me. I saw it." But her eyes were sad. "Why did he run, then?"

The thin old voice came back to him. *"I couldn't trust myself not to harm a friend or . . . the woman I loved."*

416

"He didn't trust himself . . . not to harm Gary," Sean said.

She drew in a long breath, her face softening, her eyes filled with tears.

She didn't need to know the rest. It would be their secret, his and Elliott's.

Sean mustered his strength for a few more words. "And he still called you 'my girl' to the end."

With that off his chest, Sean fought to stay awake. To keep his angel's face before him. To hang on to the light.

Thirty-three

Weeks later

A blue jay flew into a pine grayed by the morning mist. Sean lifted his eyes, as blue as the bird's feathers, to follow its flight.

Laura settled back on the damp seat of Keith's rowboat and savored the view.

It was becoming a habit to slow down at random moments. To savor a little piece of life. To listen to the ripple of the water, to smell the pines.

To feast her eyes on Sean's living face.

She shook her head. So close. He'd come so close.

He regarded her with a mixture of amusement and suspicion. "What?"

"Just thinking." Just picturing a gravestone. Sean Michael Halloran, luthier, laid to rest among his moonshine-running ancestors. But he'd lived. Thank God, he'd lived.

She clamped her lips together to keep them from trembling.

"No crying," he ordered with a half smile.

"I thought you wanted me to cry. Make up your mind."

"It all depends on what you're crying about." He reached into the cooler for a Coke—for breakfast—and popped the top. "If you're still fretting about Slattery, stop it." He eyed her over his Coke can. "It's over. No blabbing. We don't need to share our information with the law."

"You're only saying that because you've never had a particularly friendly relationship with law enforcement."

"That doesn't mean I can't think straight. What good would it do to dredge up the car? To dredge up the past?"

"Slattery's family, whoever they are, might like to know what happened to him."

"He wasn't the kind of man a family could be proud of. Maybe it's best if they never know."

"Maybe you're right."

Let Slattery's sins die with him, then—whatever they were.

Let her dad's sins die too. And her mom's. And Gary's. And the sins of selfish girls who'd been too busy painting their nails to keep an eye on Tigger.

Every day, the bittersweet shock hit her all over again. Cassie and Tigger were her sisters. But Gary was . . . just Gary. He wasn't her father except in the biological sense, but he'd been her father's friend. Her dad had loved him to the end. Had forgiven everything.

Laura gazed into the deep blue water—the water she'd once thought had swallowed her dad's body.

When she was twelve, another lake, a small one, had taken a little brown car and the body of its owner. Someone might find the remains one day, but she hoped it would be beyond her time. A hundred years in the future. Two hundred years. It didn't matter now; it couldn't change Slattery's fate, but she still had questions.

It was June. Flowers bloomed everywhere. Soon, the purple kudzu blossoms would fill the air with their sweet, musty spice. Not long after that, the leaves would turn brown. The cold would kill the luxuriant vines and expose whatever ugliness they had been hiding.

You could cover up the truth, but you couldn't change it. That was one kind of covering. There was another kind too. Love that covered a multitude of sins.

"All right," Laura said. "Let's say nobody ever needs to know my dad engaged in some vigilante justice. Maybe even pre-emptive justice, if there's any such thing."

"Good." Sean tipped his Coke up for another swig. "Let's say that. We can't change what happened, so we'll let it lie. Like we'll let Slattery's bones lie at the bottom of Bennett's lake."

"But how could my dad be sure Slattery intended to harm Tigger?"

"I don't know. I wasn't there." Sean leaned forward. "I only know your dad will be remembered for giving his life. Not for taking a life." He pointed at her. "And don't feel guilty because we lived and he died. It was his choice. Like it was Dale's choice to pull a gun." He lowered his finger but kept his glistening eyes on hers.

She ached for him. She wasn't the only one who'd loved a father and lost him. In spite of everything, Sean had never shut Dale out of his life.

"It still hurts," she said slowly. "And I know it hurts you too."

"It'll hurt for a long time. All of it. But I hope you know how much he loved you. And I hope he knew how much you loved him even when you still weren't entirely sure he loved you back." He smiled. "I'll never forget the sight of you flying up that bank screaming 'Daddy' like a banshee."

"I guess he never forgot it either. He didn't have time to."

Sean was quiet for a while. "Sometimes, I don't like the way God handles the details. But when I look at the big picture, I know we're in good hands."

A woodworker's hands. Scarred, with blood on them. But beautiful. So beautiful.

Some hearts were broken by another person's sin. Some hearts were mended by another person's sacrifice. Sometimes life just didn't make sense.

Ardelle was in counseling. So was Gary. Cassie, home with Drew now, kept nagging Laura to start counseling too. She probably should.

Back in May, when she'd sat in church smelling stale perfume and dusty hymnals, she'd doubted God's ability to run the world. Now, breathing fresh air and the sweetness of summer flowers, she'd gone from death to life without quite knowing how. Sean had too. He'd never said much about it, but he'd changed during those days in the hospital.

He stifled a groan. He'd reached for the bait bucket too quickly.

"Don't move so fast," she said. "Are you due for another pain pill?"

"No," he said curtly.

She hid a smile. Sean could hardly stand to let anybody look after him. His hospital stay had been pure torture for him, but far worse for his nurses. Laura, though, rather enjoyed the challenge.

"Here, let me bait your hook for you," she offered.

He hesitated but handed over his pole. "I knew there had to be some advantages to dating a tomboy."

"You call this a date?"

"Yeah, and if I can make my girl fish for her own supper—and even row the boat for me—that's better still."

She reached into the bait bucket and proceeded with the job. "Why do I put up with you?"

"Because I love you and you know it."

On the verge of telling him she loved him too, she hesitated, collecting her thoughts.

When her dad came back, she hadn't told him she loved him. Everything had happened too fast. She'd had only a few minutes, and she'd missed her chance.

Her dad had said it, though. Those had been his last words, said with clear-eyed certainty just before he took a bullet for a friend. Then he was past hearing. Past seeing. Past pain. He was . . . mended.

Sean, too, had loved her with his very life, putting his flesh and blood between her and the pansy gun. The last remnant of the Halloran inheritance. But there was a new Halloran heritage now. Kindness, honor, courage.

"Here." She handed his fishing pole back.

"Thank you."

She rinsed her fingers in the lake and looked up. The sunlight made a bright path across the water, leading to the pines on the far shore where the camp's early-bird chapel service was in full swing. An old hymn floated across the water, jazzed up with guitars and drums. The "Doxology."

She'd sung that song with her dad, years ago, during those days when he'd walked her across the road to Sunday school. He'd taught her to fold her hands and pray. She'd copied him and mouthed the words of a creed she didn't quite understand.

"I believe in the Holy Spirit, the holy catholic church, the communion of saints, the forgiveness of sins, the resurrection of the body, and the life everlasting."

She would never understand any of it completely. Not this side of heaven.

Sean heard the music too. He cocked his head, listening, and sang along so softly that it was barely above a whisper. "Praise Him above, ye heav'nly host; praise Father, Son, and Holy Ghost."

She studied his lean, clean-shaven face and

pondered what had made him the man he was. Dale Halloran's son, like it or not. Elliott Gantt's protégé, nearly a son.

Laura Gantt's . . . boyfriend? Again? They had never exactly defined their relationship. Just enjoyed it. As May lazed along into June and she'd decided she belonged in Georgia, she and Sean had drifted into cozy companionship punctuated by occasional quarrels and frequent moments of sheer joy.

Yet she'd never told him she loved him. Not even when he was about to die. Why was it so hard to say?

Because it meant taking the next step too. It meant believing love was stronger than fear. Stronger than hatred. Longer than time. Worth every risk. It meant accepting the sorrows of the past and giving her heart to a brand-new family with its own share of sorrows.

Sean, very much alive, was looking across the water toward the camp. Hard times hadn't made him hard. They'd made him kind. They'd made him—

She blew out a puff of air, a surrender to the truth. The hard times of Sean's life had made him the man she loved.

Her heart soared on dreams for the future. *First comes love . . .*

"Sean?" Her voice sounded tiny, even to her own ears.

"Yeah?"

"Have I ever told you I love you?"

His head swiveled her way. "No ma'am, you've always been real careful to skirt around that issue."

She dabbled her fingers in the cool water. A fish splashed, close to the surface. A silver dart, full of life.

She glanced over at Sean. He leaned forward. Waited.

"Well?" he prompted, eyebrows lifting. That sarcastic tilt to his mouth, not quite a smile, was the same one she'd adored practically forever.

"Well." She clasped her hands in her lap, dribbling lake water on her jeans. "I love you."

He really smiled then, the crow's feet touching the corners of his eyes. "I know you do."

Her lips parted. "Is that all you've got to say about it?"

His laughter echoed across the water like a song. "Darlin', you know I love you too, and I'd give you a big ol' kiss, but we'd tip the boat over."

She felt a grin coming from somewhere deep inside her, from long-ago happy times with Sean, her best friend, the first boy she'd ever kissed. "We sure would."

"Just wait till we're on solid ground." He winked.

The wind picked up, a chilly note. Sun and

wind, mingled together. Love and loss, life and death, all mixed up together. All held in good hands.

She closed her eyes. The sunlight warmed her face, so much like a soft kiss that she almost thought Sean had somehow moved close without rocking the boat. No, it wasn't him. It was someone even closer. Someone who brushed her ears with old whisperings she'd only begun to understand.

Readers Guide

1. Laura, Cassie, and Sean were friends from an early age. To what extent do you think they remained true to their long-ago promise to "be there" for each other?

2. By age twelve, Laura was pondering the meaning of her father's tattoo ("life everlasting") and she knew "she'd always believed in things she couldn't see." How much do you think her spiritual sensitivity was related to growing up in Appalachia with its old-time religion?

3. Sean and Laura were high school sweethearts, but their fathers' issues created complications. Given the outcome of Dale Halloran's hatred for Laura's father, what might improve her chances of having a happy future with Sean?

4. Sean is a "fix-it man" when it comes to vehicles, houses, and even an old baby doll. How does this facet of his personality affect his campaign to make Laura admit that she loves him?

5. What kind of advice do you think Cassie might give Laura about the "starry-eyed" phase of love and marriage?

6. In spite of his troubles, Elliott became a father figure to Sean, teaching him the skills of luthiery and furniture making as well as many fine character qualities. How do you think Sean will pay it forward?

7. Some members of the armed forces survive their tours unscathed, while others come away with physical, mental, or psychological problems. How can we make life better for "wounded warriors"?

8. Elliott's long-ago choices hurt people, including his wife and daughter. How might the hurts have been any less if he had immediately faced the consequences of his crimes?

9. Every family has its secrets, and a secret keeper might wonder if it's right or wrong to share the truth with others. What are some of the issues to be considered before telling a secret?

10. Jess's journals eventually revealed her biggest secret. Why do you think she planted hints in the journals?

11. The lyrics of some of Elliott's songs refer to his heartbreak, yet the wind chimes endure as a symbol of his love for his wife. To what extent do you think Jess loved him back?

12. Laura gains new family relationships in an unusual way. If you were her friend, what advice would you give her about her future relationship with Gary and Ardelle and their daughters?

13. Elliott and Gary grew up as close as brothers. Do you think their closeness made it easier or harder for Elliott to forgive Gary? Why?

14. As Laura faces the future with some of her family's secrets revealed, what's her best tactic for surviving small-town gossip? Do you think public opinion even matters to her?

15. At first, Laura and Sean are somewhat cynical about faith and the church. By the end of the story, their cynicism has begun to dissolve. What events and epiphanies softened their hearts?

16. As the story ends, Tigger still doesn't know that she may owe her life to Elliott. Why do you think Laura and Sean decided to keep the whole truth from her?

Acknowledgments

Sometimes, writing a novel seems to take forever. I began this story so long ago that I'm in danger of forgetting its genesis as well as some of the helping hands along the way.

Years ago, I entered several writing contests that were judged by published novelists who were generous with their time and their honest feedback. I owe many thanks to Gayle Roper, Kathleen Y'Barbo Turner, and several judges who remained anonymous. Your encouragement helped me to hang onto my vision for this story.

I'm also grateful to my editors. Shannon Marchese, Jessica Barnes, and Nicci Jordan Hubert all had a hand in this story's trip to publication, as did the entire team at WaterBrook Multnomah and my excellent agent, Chip MacGregor.

I can't imagine the writing life without my wonderful writing buddies. Special thanks to my critique partner Deeanne Gist, who makes me dig deeper and work harder, as well as to Lindi Peterson, Missy Tippens, Maureen Hardegree, Sherrie Lord, Suzan Robertson, Sally Apokedak, and all my friends at ACFW North Georgia.

As always, my family members are supportive even when they lose me to the computer for long stretches of time. Thank you for putting up with my tunnel vision and for believing in me. Jon, you must be the most patient husband ever.

I appreciate my readers too. You don't know how much your e-mails mean to me!

Most of all, I'm grateful to the Lord of the universe for His unending love.

Meg

Center Point Large Print
600 Brooks Road / PO Box 1
Thorndike ME 04986-0001 USA

(207) 568-3717

US & Canada:
1 800 929-9108
www.centerpointlargeprint.com